# BARBARIAN OF THRACE

# REVOLTING SLAVES

Revolting Slaves: Barbarian of Thrace is published under Reverie, a sectionalized division under Di Angelo Publications, Inc.

Reverie is an imprint of Di Angelo Publications.
Copyright 2023.
All rights reserved.
Printed in the United States of America.

Di Angelo Publications
4265 San Felipe #1100
Houston, Texas 77027

Library of Congress
Revolting Slaves: Barbarian of Thrace
ISBN: 978-1-955690-21-8
Paperback

Words: David P. Morris
Cover Design: Savina Deianova
Cover Illustration: Olga Tereshenko
Interior Design: Kimberly James
Editors: Elizabeth Geeslin Zinn, Cody Wootton, Ashley Crantas

Downloadable via Kindle, NOOK, iBooks, and Google Play.

For educational, business, and bulk orders, contact sales@diangelopublications.com.

1. Fiction --- Historical --- Ancient
2. Fiction --- War & Military

BARBARIAN OF THRACE

# REVOLTING SLAVES

# DAVID P. MORRIS

*For my siblings—no longer shadow, no bigger shoes.*

# INTRODUCTION

Something deep in the soul of humanity yearns for the heroic, for persuasive illustrations of the battle between good and evil, liberation and oppression, masculine and feminine forces both in conflict and in complement with one another. Historical novels done well, like David Morris' *Revolting Slaves,* anchor history within the embrace of myth and the living specificity of a story with its universal patterns that do not age.

Such is this delightful and informative read. The author is well-versed in the early history of Rome and the more general geography of Italy. Within this cauldron is the famous epic hero, Spartacus and his equal in many respects, the lovely and courageous Helica. And, struggling to become who he is as a person of wholeness, is Publipor (Publius), the narrator on his own epic journey into maturity and free agency in a violent world.

As I read it, I recalled the fury of Achilles in Homer's Iliad, Odysseus' hunger for home and his family in the Odyssey, and even earlier, in the quest of Gilgamesh after losing his beloved Enkidu to find the source of death and destroy it. And further back in history is the warrior Arjuna struggling on the eve of battle to claim his land, in the *Bhagavad Gita,* part of the larger Indian masterpiece, the *Mahabharata* many centuries earlier. Each of these figures is called to a destiny, to a purpose and to a life of authentic wholeness. As we read each of them, we see more clearly Morris' fine addition to this rich tradition.

More importantly, each of these epics involve trafficking with the gods, the immortals, fates and destinies that govern all of our lives. Revolting Slaves settles neatly into this tradition.

But what is finally most critical in Morris' poetic creation is that he narrates an exciting story about the deep yearning in the soul of individuals to be free, whole, integrated within a life of meaning. Telling a memorable story is Morris' greatest achievement. I recommend his journey to everyone.

**Dennis Patrick Slattery, Ph.D.** is Distinguished Professor Emeritus of Mythological Studies at Pacifica Graduate Institute in Carpinteria, California. He is the author, most recently, of The Way of Myth: Stories' Subtle Wisdom and The Fictions in Our Convictions: Essays on the Cultural Imagination.

# PREFACE

The name Spartacus echoes across time as the ultimate insurgent and revolutionary. *Revolting Slaves* is a work of historical fiction that uses Professor Barry Strauss' *The Spartacus War* as its framework of whom, what, where, and when. Most deviation from Strauss' speculations are mostly of people, a few characters being completely fictional. Others have had their nationality altered with the explanation that 'Gaul' was used as a catch-all for every slave by the Roman. The hardest conveyance to a modern audience is the absolute brutality of the time and the complete disregard for human life. Slaves and their treatment are impossible for a civilized person to comprehend. When our washing machine wears out, we discard and replace it. Rome used people as we use appliances.

Spartacus was married; Professor Strauss describes a cunningly intelligent Thracian woman that history has forgotten, erasing even her name. Modern renditions make no mention of her and yet the woman's prophecy about a serpent coiled over Spartacus' face survives to this day. A woman with enough zeal to capture the attention of chauvinistic Roman historians deserves a name. In this version, our Thracian woman is named Helica, the spiritual leader and mastermind of the gladiator breakout. The worship of her cult will be outlawed after she is gone.

Anglicization of the "dead" language Latin expressed in

contemporary American English is difficult. Understand that modern slang would have had an ancient equivalent. Regional dialects and vocabulary inflections lost to time are expressed as Americanized tropes. Hard to pronounce names have been retained for authenticity. In this era, Latin is the universal language of commerce across all civilized nations. Greek, being the language of sophistication.

Reconning of time, a Roman would have marked their beginning at Rome's founding. The day Romulus committed frattricide, declaring his capitol 753 years prior to the birth of Jesus Christ. Our three-year saga begins seventy-three years before then. To a Roman, the year would have been 682 *auc, anno urbis conditae* (year since SPQR founding). Our "before common era" is really a countdown to the savior, a man born of woman who will change the world forever. Rome's "*auc*" would have been an accounting of their city's perpetuity. Rome's famous Colosseum will not be completed for another one hundred years. In the year AD 73: *Anno Domini,* the year of our Lord.

Myopic research on the slave revolt soon broadened, revealing a nearly thousand-year-old representative republic being torn to pieces by a handful of powerful elites for personal gain. The political parallels of then and now reminds us that some things never change. The story of Spartacus is one of many events happening throughout the world simultaneously. The longest surviving representative government of, for, and by the people is teetering on the precipice of empire and perpetual dictatorial oligarchy. This is also a time of gods, spirits, and ghosts.

**"...being a Thracian mercenary, had become a soldier, and from a soldier a deserter, then a highwayman, and finally, thanks to his strength, a gladiator."**

**—Florus,** ***Epitome***

Florus records ashamed that Spartacus served as a soldier for the legions. His single sentence records a concise resume of a warrior's lifetime. That *mercenary*, Spartacus, was a native of Thrace, modern-day Bulgaria, and belonged to a nomadic tribe infamous for horsemanship and cattle theft. It would not be a stretch to assume his *soldiering* would have been with the cavalry. In this telling, Spartacus' age at death is forty-five years. This places him ringside to the most monumental events of the late Republic during the prime of life. The transition, *"...soldier to deserter,"* would have spanned a career that may have gone as such.

In 95 BC, Sulla invades Greece. Spartacus, aged twenty-one, is conscripted. By 91 BC, at age twenty-five, Spartacus swears allegiance to Sulla, having crossed the sea to put down rebellion in Italy. At twenty-seven, Spartacus would marvel at an unnamed comet streaking across the Italian sky of 89 BC. In 88, a year later, he would hear the herald, bear witness to a purge, and sack Athens. The second war with Mithradates in 85 concludes with a hasty treaty. Together, Sulla and Spartacus race back to Italy and attack Rome in a bid to save the city from itself. There, the story nearly ends at the battle of the Colline Gate, where Spartacus' thirty-four-year-old life is saved by none other than Marcus Crassus. For five years, Spartacus serves as trusted enforcer for his long-time boss, Dictator for Life, Felix Lucius Cornelius Sulla during the tyrant's meteoric climb to power. Sulla's henchman would proscribe his patron's vendettas with extreme prejudice for the next decade. But fortunes soon soured for the thirty-eight-year-old mercenary when Sulla's iron grasp relents due to death. In this age, honorably discharged soldiers could expect a pension and land grant. Sulla's untimely demise rendered all promises of compensation to foreign allies void. Rome explodes into Civil War.

The *"...deserter to highwayman"* probably took less than a year. Spartacus, now a forty-year-old fugitive deserter who once bore Rome's most powerful seal upon an agate ring, probably harbored resentment. The disillusioned soldier with nothing to lose, living hand to mouth, makes his robbing upon the roads. Until in a cemetery outside town and passed into oblivion, a drunken Spartacus suddenly finds himself held fast by Roman authorities.

*"...and finally, thanks to his strength, a gladiator."* Every scant historical fragment concerning Spartacus that has survived to modernity describes either his enormous stature or his physical prowess, most times both. In 76, Spartacus stands bound on a podium with a plaque about his neck. Caulked upon the board is his race, age, weight, and height. He has been set apart to be sold last alongside other candidates for competing gladiator academies. From the years 75 to 73, Spartacus would gain adulation in the arena just to spurn it all in a bid for freedom.

This is the world in which we inhabit. Our story begins at the day of breakout in 73 BC, where a clever thirteen-year-old boy, herding grazing goats, falls haplessly into a group of seventy-five escaped gladiators led by a forty-three-year-old living legend. Bear witness to Publipor's experiences through three harrowing years, as he joins a band of ragtag gladiators, and a sorceress, whose force multiplies an army of slaves capable of destroying legions.

# CHAPTER ONE

**"Crucifixes along the whole road to Rome from Capua."**

**—Appian, *The Civil Wars***

_71 BC; 684 auc; anno urbis conditae (year since founding)._
_Mile Marker XLII; Appian Way_

Panic enveloped the heart of every slave as the rolling caravan of cages came to a stop near the monolithic mile marker. Locals lined the cobbled road, applauding and jeering at the condemned slaves. Packed within the press of Roman spectators, a serious young man stood brooding among the mob with what appeared to be his younger sister. Their presence was unnoticed, indistinguishable from the masses whose faces were shaded from the day's heat beneath hooded cloaks. The young man stood steadfast, holding the child's hand as two hearty soldiers carried timber, unloaded from a heavily laden wagon nearby, past them. One legionary held a hammer, the other a bag of spikes, and the timber's weight was slung between them, cradled in rope. The centurion in charge was salty and short on patience; by his shouting, the crowd knew to stay well away from these professionals at work. The man in charge rapped his baton upon the captives' confinement, and terror filled the halted cages.

"Grab the gigger," ordered the centurion to a soldier.

The mature young man of sixteen hard years watched, stone faced for the little girl as they watched captives decide with darting, frantic looks who'd be plucked next from the cage. The slaves' impromptu consensus was the eldest-looking man among them, due to his advanced age and diminutive stature. Having been through this before, the slaves knew to pick someone who'd put up as little a fight possible for crucifixion. Stomachs dropped when keys jingled into the mechanism, turning the lock with a *thunk* that the slaves felt in their bones. Shrieks of horror and grunts of determination filled the container once the clasp became unlatched. Ankles and forearms jammed between bars, jockeying for traction, as the creaking of the cage door opening filled the air. Elbows flailed as grasping hands lashed out toward the victim. The toothless old man with white wispy hair didn't stand a chance when the others pushed him to the door. The little man begged, grasping at forearms with unnatural strength, leaving bloody gouges on the arms of those trying desperately to eject him. The tiny geriatric released them only when stunned by a vicious blow to the head. And then a wicked black hook, secured to an oaken haft, gaffed the ancient little man by his neck, wrenching him from the cage. The door slammed shut with a bang, and soon the lock was resecured to its hasp. The temporary reprieve and relief felt by the slaves was palpable to the crowd once the soldiers moved on. The young empathetic Roman-looking man snarled silently, watching the old man gurgle and gasp.

"Are you trying to kill him?" admonished the centurion over the slave's bloody cough.

"What?" replied the perplexed soldier, holding the shaft with both hands.

"Next time, catch them on the shoulder or an arm," scolded the centurion. "Marcus Crassus will have our ass if he hears we're nailing up corpses."

"He moved," explained the soldier. Both laughed.

"Let's get this shit over with," said the man in charge. "I want to be in the city before dark." The veterans moved with methodical experience, dovetailing timber with swiftly driven nails. Two others, a few paces off, leaned against their *dolabras,* or spades, on either side of a newly dug hole, wagering.

"Mama, or gods?" one asked the other.

"Mama," replied the soldier, confidently pulling two sesterces from his purse.

"I'll take that bet; he's a godly guy for sure," quipped the other as the slave was brought toward them. The conjoined timber beams lay flat and finished, except for the footer, which had to be sized. The young man watched the legionaries splay the trachea-pierced man upon the timber, while geysers of blood spouted from his esophagus with every panicked breath

"Dionysus, save me!" gurgled the anguished, desperate old slave when the first spike pierced his flesh. One soldier gave the other a satisfied grin, extending a palm. The loser grudgingly handed over payment, grumbling.

The slaves stared in horror from their confinement, and by sound alone, it could be told that the spikes were driven expertly quick, with only four blows per hand. The footer was nailed beneath the condemned before the crucifix was hoisted on high. The slave cried out in torrents of blood and screams of agony when his beam fell into the freshly dug hole. The two soldiers had a devil of a time working the beam upright from back to forth and side to side as their *optio,* the centurion, held a weighted string to make certain the beam settled plumb. From the crowd, the sixteen-year-old watched the two hole-digging, gambling soldiers amuse themselves at the expense of a condemned slave. They backfilled the hole with dirt channeled by their sandals while the man shrieked above, all while intentionally over-adjusting the post with relish. It was all fun and games for the pair until the condemned showered both the soldiers below with hemorrhaged blood, cleared from oversaturated lungs with a gurgling cough. The men ran, covering their heads as if escaping a sudden summer shower, to the jaded centurion's chuckling delight. The dying man's last moments were spent trying to claw toes upon a tiny ledge, struggling for air with blood gushing from his neck. Soon, the command to move was given and the line of cages began rolling once more. The young man remained, standing alone at the base of the old man's cross, looking upon the horrific sight of agonizing death. The youthful man held the girl's hand, shaking his head subtly with a straight face for the child to emulate.

This worldly teen had travelled from Capua to Rome enough times and easily counted a few hundred head of slaves crammed in their various confinements as they went. With only ten Roman miles left to go, it was apparent enough: they would run out of road before they'd run out of slaves. The surplus, the young man knew, would be liquidated in the city tomorrow. His mask of apathy contorted to keen awareness upon hearing a familiar, terrified voice escape the rolling confines. The infuriated young man's neck whipped around with sudden recognition. "Va!" screamed a large man from one cage to another. The stern young man helped the little girl mount on the stolen horse before joining her on its back. The youth sat erect with raised chin, staring intently at a very good and loved friend comforting his giant deaf older brother as they began rolling along the Appian once more. The young warrior urged his horse forward, resolved with the thought that the remaining slaves who'd escaped crucifixion today would feed the beasts tomorrow at Pompey's triumph. He decided to follow them one more mile as the small girl swayed silently behind him, resting her head contentedly on his back.

"Like an insatiable stomach that consumes everything and yet remains always hungry...more wretched than all other cities that she was making wretched, left nothing untouched and yet had nothing."

—Orosius, *History Against the Pagans*

73 BC; 682 *auc.*
Capua, Scene of the Crime, Present Day

An urgent message blazes a serendipitous route on an express pony from Capua to the smaller cities of Herculaneum and Nola. Tucked within the young rider's bag are orders to raise Nola's militia and capture the seventy-five gladiators who'd broken loose, last seen heading south upon the Appian, straight for Herculaneum. Another rider races north; he'll exchange three horses and arrive at Rome's Forum in two hours with an alarming message from Capua.

PASTURES, NORTH OF HERCULANEUM, APPIAN WAY,
682 AUC (73 BC)

Goats grazed about me when Marsalis, my friend and a fellow boy of thirteen, came sprinting up the trail with sweat beading off his bronze skin. "Fugitives! Highwaymen!" he gasped, breathlessly pointing down the graveled path. "Come away, Publipor! We must warn the town! People in Herculaneum need to know!"

"And the flock, Marsalis?" I asked, astonished. I was curious as to how Marsalis, who fought wolves with sling and stone, same as I, would be so terrified by strange men that he'd trade the animals' safety for a beating.

"Damn them," replied Marsalis, in a terrified whisper. "Giant cutthroats with knives and clubs—murderous painted furies by the look of them! Seventy or so, moving quickly. They'll be on us,

Publipor; we must flee for our lives!" he spoke as loudly as he dared while bent at the waist and gasping for air.

*We must flee for our lives*—the last words I would ever hear, or never heed, from my good friend after that day. I suppose, looking back these years later, that I was a bit more mischievous than was good for my own wellbeing. By thirteen, I'd already earned an untrustworthy reputation from a few masters and been sold off probably more times than I should've. One taunted after my auction to my new master that I was cursed with the ghost of Pandora. My previous owner wished the new man luck with my willful ways, recommending a shackle at night. I suppose he was right, for just as the cursed woman could not help but look in the box that released the world's misery, neither could I bear to miss seeing these brutes in the flesh for myself.

"Then go," I said, dismissive. "It'd be a blessing if the town were ransacked and our *vilicus* run through. Maybe we'll get a new bailiff."

Marsalis stared, dumbfounded, momentarily blinking before running off as quickly as he'd come. Pandora's spirit of curiosity urged me on to see these ruffians, and while creeping behind a large boulder, I heard men's voices approaching below. Fascinated, I slowly peeked over at the sight of a group of giants, inked brutes walking toward me. I could count a herd at a glance easy enough and saw they numbered at least seventy. Seventy or so of the most frightful, muscle-bound, tattooed brutes I'd ever seen. They encroached armed with butcher's knives, iron skewers, wooden cudgels, and various other handy implements of mayhem. The seventy moved like fugitives on the prowl, suddenly finding themselves set loose. I froze, amazed at the foreign sight.

*Matare potest omnia in die illo* — "Everything can change in a day." Parca, Goddess of Chance, influences even the littlest things in life. Like, say, a nanny goat giving birth to twin kids in spring, and such was the case last season. One kid was born a runt; it was undersized and bullied so much by its sibling that I took pity on it and forced its mother to nurse. When hungry, the animal learned to butt my leg and beg, bleating ceaselessly until I forced his mother to feed him. Since then, the goat never strayed far, remaining underfoot most of the time...as he was now. Goatherds don't usually give names to their animals, but sometimes a few are so outrageous of character that they get named. I called this goat traipsing before me "Useless."

"You think these, the boys, *et rex ovium?*" asked a fugitive, one I'd come to learn was named Vidovic, in his thickly foreign-accented Latin.

"Well, if so, he's a lousy goatherd, leaving them alone like this," replied another escapee, the one I'd come to know as Egus, a man whom Spartacus loved, motioning with a squinty-eyed head and big toothy grin in my direction.

"No, he wouldn't leave a flock this far with wolves and bears about," reasoned yet another, a gladiator I'd come to know as Roc, short for Roucillus. Useless suddenly jumped onto the rock shelf above my hiding spot, bleating unremittingly at my face. I soundlessly shooed him with frantic motions, feeling heat rise to my face with panicky anger, nervous the animal would reveal my concealment. Useless answered my fears by bleating some more, his tongue protruding, our eyes locked. *Damn you, Useless,* I thought. Suddenly, I was ripped from my spot, yanked clear from my sandals, and suspended in the air by one bulging arm and a knife beneath my chin.

"Don't kill it yet, Crixus!" bellowed the voice of authority.

"Damn Italians...all look same, Spar-ti-coos," grumbled the man called Crixus as he effortlessly held me aloft with one hand. Crixus was a huge barrel-chested, red-haired German, mustached and inked with writhing blue snakes all over his body. "What use is it?" he asked in crude baritone Latin, returning his murderous look.

"Herculaneum is warned, every town around Capua warned; all know gladiators escape by now, Crixus," Spartacus dismissed, in passable Latin. "Bring him," he commanded then, motioning with a huge hand. The man named Crixus dropped me and I was immediately shoved forward by a wiry man with ropy veins. This one also had a long mustache running down the corners of his mouth, but his skin was stretched oddly tight about his body and face. He was covered in an intricate pattern of tattoos resembling weaves of a basket. His tall lanky frame failed to signal his great strength. I stumbled when released, then quickly shoved my feet back into the thin strips of worn leather my master called sandals. The lanky brute began laughing when I did so, in a deep, slow drawl with his head thrown back—"*Aw, Aw, Aw,*"—that made his Adam's apple swing up and down. I would come to learn this barbarian named Crastus laughed like that at all things terrific and terrible alike.

"No meat on zis sing, Svar-ti-coos; even za dog, no fight ova zis," joked Crastus in his absurdly deep voice, with an almost incoherently thick northern accent. Spartacus strode toward me, blotting the sun, standing a head taller than even the biggest of the giants. His long black hair was tied like the tail of a horse, and a leather thong at his forehead kept it out of his piercing dark eyes. Tattooed across the man's broad chest lay the image in black of two defiant dueling stallions, rearing with flared nostrils. His massive forearms swelled beneath thick leather wrist guards. Spartacus stood fearsome, holding a wicked black iron blade, the kind used to cleave entire carcasses, slack at his side.

"Name yourself," demanded the giant barbarian.

"P—P—Publipor," I stammered. Some chuckled at the demeaning name.

"Where friend go, Publius?" asked Spartacus, his deep voice stern yet soothing.

"Publipor," I corrected without thinking. The huge warrior shrugged a little before lifting his chin, awaiting my response.

"R...running to w-wa...warn, t-t...town, Her-Herculaneum," I stuttered, while Useless butted my already buckling leg.

"How far?" Spartacus asked.

"Two miles that way," I answered, motioning the direction with my head.

"Publipor hungry?" asked Spartacus kindly. I nodded and without time to jump, the man's cleaver swung in a blur, deftly quick and disturbingly close. Useless' head fell from his neck and rolled silently at my feet. Then his four legs crumpled, his blood soaking the path.

I was paralyzed, adrift in a gulf of silence, when *desiderium vitae*, the desire to live, compelled me to request a knife from a gawking slave nearby; to my disbelief, the man named Vitelli handed one over. With a deep breath and sigh of conviction, I whispered, "Sorry, Useless," to the goat's severed head. I proceeded to gut him on the spot, quickly working the blade, and in short order had Useless skinned. I handed the menacing German a slab of backstrap as a peace offering. The other I gave to a Celt they called Oenomaus, then returned my attention to the carcass, keeping my eyes averted from the menacing men, anticipating a crack at any moment. I butchered my pet's carcass to keep fugitives amused, and I could tell, even in their foreign tongues, they were. After it was quartered, I distributed more of the animal and then went to gather supplies for a fire.

"Where you go, boy?" challenged Crixus' deep, foreign voice.

"Kindling, f-for fire, t-to, roast," I stuttered, pointing to the raw meat held by the men.

"Hurry, boy! I'm famished!" Oenomaus belted, holding aloft

his choice cut of raw goat.

"Boy?" yelled Crixus. I stood frozen and silent, desperately wanting to look away from the fearsome barbarian. "What you tell girlfriend?" Crixus asked, hoisting his portion at the mess that remained of my owner's goat; the men laughed.

"Sorry," I answered, then explained: "I said I was sorry."

"You say more," accused Crixus.

"Sorry...Useless," I replied, feeling foolish.

"You woman, name Useless?" joked Crixus, slapping Crastus' arm. "Aren't they all?" to baritone laughter. Crixus' two front teeth were missing, and when coupled with his awful smile, the remainder resembled awful yellow fangs.

"Yes...No...I—" I stammered.

"Get the wood, boy!" interrupted Oenomaus, with hands full of raw goat meat. "You'd make yourself *useful* if you'd cook me dinner. Crixus, don't harm a hair on the boy till I've eaten," chuckled Oenomaus, in much more intelligible Latin than the others.

*Until I've eaten?* I thought.

In the nearby bramble, I quickly gathered armfuls of crisp twigs and dried grass, returning to cook stolen goat like a poacher. I felt the men's eyes burrow through my neck while I scraped quartz to iron with my back turned; vigor finally produced a spark. Once started, all hands began feeding more wood onto the burning pile of kindling. I pounded two sharpened stakes into the earth on both sides with a rock and requested an iron skewer from a man who was using it as a weapon. I reached out my hand to Oenomaus and he gave me his piece of backstrap. After running the cut through, I did the same for Crixus. Once secured, I laid the slabs across the fire's heat in the crook of the stakes, just above the flames. The smell of roasting meat and the sound of grumbling stomachs made for an awkward wait. "I know where to get clean water nearby," I stated. "I can get some for you." Bladders of all sorts and sizes were thrown in the dirt before me; I stooped to scoop them.

"Oenomaus, go with goat fucker, return before meat burn," ordered Crixus.

"Just make sure you turn *both* portions while we're gone, asshole," Oenomaus retorted. The Celt and I departed. I led him not far to a spring in a cut that flowed from beneath the earth that was cold and clear. Oenomaus soon appreciated my knowledge of the land and the refreshing libation. We made small talk while filling everyone's water, and slowly, I began to realize this was just a man and not a beast at all. The load was heavy, and I was scolded for a breaking a strap on our return, but for the most part, the men were grateful for refreshment. I smiled at a man who patted me on the back after sipping cool water, and I believe he thanked me in a language I'd never heard until then.

The evening was spent reclining with fierce men as they laughed and joked with each other in various foreign languages from all over the world. Thoughts of escape left my mind as they laughed and shared stories, as if I weren't even present. *If they haven't killed me by now, then maybe they won't,* I hoped. Soon, conversation turned to the next city on the Appian Way. Oenomaus used a torn piece of cooked loin to point at me. That's when I learned these seventy highwaymen were, in fact, the escaped gladiators from Capua.

"That's the boy's town, betcha he knows a way round," offered Oenomaus.

"Yeah," spoke Crixus, "a place outside wall, where your kind go make sex with this kind?" Crixus offered his spit of goat as an example. I had to wait for Crastus to stop laughing before I told them how I'd grazed a herd here for years, that I'd been sold four times, and how I knew every stream and valley to the south for miles. When no one interrupted, I continued on about the goat paths and pastures that paralleled the Appian, all the way to Herculaneum's gates. Eventually, the men turned to talk amongst themselves, and I felt pleased to have entertained them with my knowledge. Admittedly, I was having fun; it was a thrilling change of routine over chasing goats around hills, dodging snakes, and running off dogs, only to coax the herd back into fences and return to sleep in captivity. I thought of my *vilicus*, the land boss' bailiff, slapping a manacle about my ankle and turning the key, how angry my new compatriots would be when they learned of it. I entertained thoughts of my new companions rushing to my aid, as if I were one of them, and how they'd exact beautiful vengeance for my unjust abuse...until reality set in.

"So, when can I get back?" I asked, noticing the daylight waning.

"Are you late for a beating?" Spartacus replied, to laughter from the men.

"Probably. I just need to be back before dark," I answered.

"Without a herd?" asked Spartacus.

The loss of the afternoon's work, much less the death of even one goat, would mean bitter repercussions. So, I begged.

"Won't you help me?" I pleaded. "With all the men, we could round and group them enough for me to make it back on time. It'll be easy, I promise, look, look," I said, frantically pulling a reed whistle from my neck. It blew a loud high pitch that was answered with lots of bleating as goats leapt and bounded from all directions, brought in by the call.

"What are you fools waiting for?" Oenomaus asked. "Help the kid round up his kids!"

"You need hurry back to lick you master's ass?" Crixus jested, playing to an audience of former gladiators turned herdsmen. The men did a good job circling goats once I'd called them to group. I was about to thank them when they slaughtered the goats shockingly quick, some with their bare hands. Only a few got away, and I stared, stunned, watching my flock being butchered. Though not known at the time, I would witness this same scene in the near future, played out with men instead of beasts.

"Sorry, kid," said Spartacus. "You tell Roman where slave; so, if let go, must kill you first." Staring into the unflinching black eyes, even as he smiled, made a chill run down my spine. Spartacus suddenly snatched the whistle from my neck, smashing it with his foot. "Stay instead," he winked.

The greaves on Spartacus' shins were scratched and worn, worked in ornate leafing, as firelight played about his stubbled face. Sitting so near, I felt as if in the presence of Mars' mortal form, watching him work a sprig of grass in and out of his teeth, flossing like a mere earthly man. Some of Spartacus' lower teeth were missing and he had the remnants of a vicious scar on his lower jaw, evidence of previous injury. His nose was caved; what was left of his right ear resembled something like cauliflower, and I thought it strange for such an obvious killer to have such a calm demeanor. Spartacus pronounced in tones that soothed, his words leaving me hung on every one of them as he spoke with confident authority. Looking back, I'm ashamed of how eager I was for the praise, but I know it was likely endearing to the men.

As I blabbered about the city of Herculaneum and its surroundings, I noticed a woman for the first time, leaning in to speak quietly into the leader's ear. The wraith whispered inaudibly as I went on about the road leading into town. So engrossed with informing my new masters of its gates and the appearance of its approach, I'd dismissed her as a small, shrouded man up to then—until my gaze found hers. I was struck dumb, unable to look away from the vision before me. I suddenly stopped rambling. The dim glow from the firelight inflamed glacier-blue eyes;

they ran through me, raising gooseflesh. In that moment, time stood still, the earth transformed, and I fell deep into Neptune's watery kingdom at the sight of such a striking color that left me drowning within them. So stunning was her gaze. Her black hair disappeared into the night, making the stars themselves her headdress. I noted her milky white skin and perfect ivory teeth. The curve of her waist and the firmness of her frame were evident even beneath the cloak. She smiled and it felt as if lightning struck; I was unable to move or awaken from the dream that was her, like a mule-kicked man.

"Pick the boy's jaw off the ground, man!" Oenomaus proclaimed, to uproarious laughter from the men. "Best not stare too long; old Spartacus will get jealous. Now, what was that you were saying about the town's gates, boy?"

"I...I..." I began, the stammering evoking more uproar from the fugitives.

"Aye, boy!" yelled Crixus, his stern rebuke snapping me back to sense. "What shape, Herculaneum gate?"

"The gates work, but they haven't been shut since the Italian Wars. The city's for soldiers with sixteen years' service, Roman veterans, that've been granted land in the area," I explained between stealing looks at the woman. "They're old, but armed and armored—men of repute. It also has big slaves from Gaul who are paid to put down anyone who complains."

"So, Latin pipsqueak, have big dog?" mocked Crixus, unimpressed, expecting a reply.

"Yes—erm—uh—sir," I stopped, stuck, not knowing what title to convey to the man.

"Commander, boy!" Crixus admonished.

"Yes, commander," I blurted. My face flushed red after glancing at the woman, who wore an expression of disdain upon hearing the title bestowed onto the snake-covered barbarian.

"How Rome's runts came to rule world, mystery to me," Crixus commented in thickly accented Germanic Latin. Crixus outstretched his arms to address his fellow slaves. "How can it be their stupid gods have so much sway over Odin, while Celts waste time, praying to trees, streams, and fucking rocks!" he bellowed, to audible gasps of the blasphemy from a large number in the crowd. "Fat geezers, lazy off grape, so they got trained dog. I wager, slaves see us, they slit masters' throat, throw in with gladiator." He smiled wickedly and turned to face me. "What say you, boy, how Roman treat their dogs?"

"Like...Romans," I replied. Crixus bore into me with waiting eyes. "Commander," I added, correcting myself quickly. Crixus, satisfied with the answer, turned to the surrounding men and nodded; his hunch was correct.

That first night with the men, I noticed differences between them other than language, hair color, and tattoos. These were slaves from all over the Republic and beyond; just a day ago, any one of them may have had to face the other in the arena to cheering crowds. Even then, I could tell this was an alliance of necessity, born from desperation, a mosaic of men that'd shatter at the first hard blow. But in that moment, I didn't care. I was camped with the God of War and his legion. It was exhilarating, and the rest of the warm night, I stole looks in firelight at the most beautiful woman the gods had ever molded, while Crixus spoke of escape from Capua. Each time I was caught spying on the woman, she'd smirk, forcing me to avert my eyes, embarrassed.

### HELICA

The sole woman of the group—its spiritual leader and Spartacus' wife—recognized the boy from her vision. She recalled the dream clearly once she laid eyes on him in the flesh. Helica was now certain, *this* was the boy who had visited her in a dream the night before. In it, Helica had stumbled upon a boy crying into his knees on a lonely trail. She'd accidentally frightened the child upon approaching, and the boy suddenly transformed into a vulture to escape her. Helica instantly shared his sight once the boy-turned-bird gained height, a thermal catching his long, outstretched wings to soar higher and higher. Once aloft, Helica saw the world below through the boy's eyes. She saw every road, trail, and stream with perfect clarity. In the here and now, Helica remembered the dream. She observed the boy and noted his intelligence as he labored desperately to make himself useful; there was no more doubt in her mind.

This was the boy of her vision.

### PUBLIPOR

I could feel the woman's fierce gaze boring into me, and it seemed I could no longer hear men complaining of noise and hunger. I feared the woman—Helica, I'd heard her called—could read my mind, so I sat frozen as a deer, staring into the fire, trying to think blank thoughts. Nearby, groups began bedding themselves down on whatever handy surface they could find, be it a pile of leaves or scraps of cloth, but most often upon bare ground. I may have heard snoring in the darkness by the time the woman Helica subtly pulled her stare from me, turning to whisper into Spartacus' good ear.

"Oenomaus," declared Crixus suddenly. "Flavius, and that sow of woman, told Cornelius of our plans. I know it!" Crixus furiously jabbed the air. The sudden outburst both startled and puzzled me, but I didn't want to stare outright and incur his wrath, so I watched out of the corner of my eye as Oenomaus replied.

"Flavius is the best suspect of being traitor, I admit, and I hated his every breath, but if he was our rat, then why even come train today?" Oenomaus inquired.

"What choice had he?" Crixus answered. "Had to drill, had to paint the lie. We know it was that shit piece who curdled; if not, gladiator number two hundred now."

Although the details were beyond my knowledge, it didn't take long to realize they were discussing a traitor, one who'd been with them at their training spot—in the *ludus*.

"Wait, you escaped today?" I interrupted, craning my neck in all directions to look at the dozens of men.

"Sure did," answered Crixus. "Be a league from here now, if Crastus stop team from run off with cart." Crixus looked about for his deadly shadow to scold. "Crastus, where in fuck were you?"

Crastus shrugged.

"Should we have built a fire? Shouldn't we be moving?" I asked everyone, fearful.

"All the legions are abroad. There's no way they'd be able to muster anything to catch us ten Roman miles away in just a few hours," Oenomaus replied. "Besides, the people of Capua know us; they'll not be in any hurry to have us back after this morning." Oenomaus raised his brows. "We've made all haste and covered much southerly ground. Light is waning, and we need sleep to move fast tomorrow. Don't worry, Gannicus will watch all night for us."

"What's a Gannicus?" I asked, reassured we'd not be jumped by authorities in the night.

"Not what, *who*," Oenomaus explained. "Gannicus is our *exploratores*, our ranger, our scout; he has night eyes like a cat and ears like a bat." A picture of a man entered my mind, his face human with large black ears and slitted gold eyes. I shuddered with the thought of something like that prowling around the camp at night.

"You!" Spartacus' voice seized me. "Give Roman message tomorrow, or example you be." It was the first order he'd given me and, remarkably, the desire to obey was more overwhelming than his threat of death.

"Yes, lord," I reflexively replied, before the reality of my responsibility set in. The woman walked with Spartacus to lie with him just a short distance away on a spread blanket. I concentrated on twiddling my thumbs, trying not to watch, wringing the excitement from my spirit in an attempt to sleep. But the man named Crixus and our firelight would not relent.

"That piece of shit, Flavius, spilled our plan, Oenomaus. I know it!" Crixus continued, snapping me from the woman's spell, sitting up once more to the commotion. "Bellyaches, sweating, for the gods' sake. Flavius was coward, but none more than today."

"True, Crixus," Oenomaus replied, yawning, "but it's late. I'm exhausted. We've walked many miles and we must sleep." Oenomaus turned and looked at me. "Nothing worse than a traitor, boy, nothing." He stretched to recline.

With a full belly and the crackling warmth of fire, I listened to men of the ring and their muttered fantastic tales. Especially intriguing, and a hindrance to sleep, were the horrifying exploits of Crixus and Crastus, wild Germans from far reaches to the north. I learned that night they were both from the dreaded Cimbri tribe, a dispossessed people wandering in search of a home for many years. When Crixus spoke of Roman treachery and their kin's twice-glorious humiliation of the legions in Gaul, I was fascinated. Both men's moods suddenly soured when Vidovic the Celt mentioned Marius' Mules and the "Savior of Rome," reminding the Germans about the third battle fought in Italy.

"Where you, Celt?" Crixus asked, and cursed the man's race for mentioning the disaster. "Vidovic, you must not been hiding under you mother's skirt...our fathers would have found you," he retorted.

When the man rose to fight, loyal Crastus suddenly intervened with his arm around the man's neck. As the two struggled, a few of the Celt's fellows rose in support as Crastus continued choking Vidovic.

"That, between them...this, between us," said Crixus, causing the Celts to pause. I feared an all-out brawl between my new companions, until Crastus released the almost-limp man.

Crastus belted his distinct laughter, dusting himself off to stand as if relieved of a menial chore. I was bewildered at how quickly the men all milling about moved on from the tense situation, herded into routine by Crastus' awful laugh and Egus' dismissive grin. Crixus didn't wait for the man to fully recover before continuing with his story. That's when I heard about how the two German rowdies had been captured as boys and how they wound up gladiators. Crastus laughed loudly when Crixus explained how he'd saved the man as a boy from his own mother.

Crixus spoke, "She slain the babies and was atop Crixus with a blade when I jumped her." He went on to describe how two ten-year-olds were able to overpower Crastus' mother, only to be captured by Gaius Marius' Mules.

"Yah, she da kilt me, fer sure," laughed Crastus, remembering. "Dear mudder, try saven zie from en zie coward death; Oden keep en zie her," prayed Crastus in a moment of reverence not seen again from him for a long time after. It became easier somehow to understand their Latin as I became more accustomed to the various accents. Crixus was easier to comprehend than Crastus. The red-haired man went on about when they'd first been sold to the *ludis* as teenagers and how they'd been pitted against one another shortly after taking their oaths as gladiators. It was both of the young men's first match, and they fought for hours to a climactic draw, until screaming spectators lost their collective voices. Crixus described Crastus as being fast as a viper and just as terrible, neither able to best the other in the marathon fight.

"Every time, I thought had lanky bastard, he'd move," Crixus mused, to Crastus' roaring laughter. "Stupid fucking helmets, Roman's make us wear, can't see worth a damn under those." Vidovic, the man Crastus had put to sleep, had awakened and was laughing along with everyone by then.

"Du, complainen?" admonished Crastus. "Least you hiden zie shame under zie lid, dress en zie—" Crastus indicated himself by his thumb "—like Pontic prostitute, arm me with fickin fish spear an zie net, first fight look en zie like ass." Crastus the German spoke in the worst Latin I'd ever heard. But I was able to deduce that their reward for the lengthy bout was being sent back to fight another day without either submitting to the shame of defeat. After the match, Crastus swore to the *vilicus* that he'd kill himself before ever fighting as a *retiarius* again. Later, the two vowed a blood oath to support one another outside the arena, but if ever paired again, they'd fight *sine missione*—to the death. Eventually, Crixus' tale arrived at the events of the botched escape.

"Cornelius, zie know, za plan," Crastus mused.

"You see Flavius' melon pop when gate fall, Crastus?" Crixus carried on, standing in the firelight, balling his fists.

"We saw, Crixus," said Oenomaus, interrupting on behalf of Crastus. "You spat on his brains, yes, yes. Now, catch me sleeping while you stop your jaw from flapping, will you?" Crixus grunted, walking away angrily into the night. The day's excitement had drained me and, yawning uncontrollably, I rolled to my side, eyes transfixed on the curve of the woman's hip just yards away. I saw Spartacus roll on top of the woman while covering them both with a blanket. Watching them do it, I pretended to sleep...until finally, I did.

# CHAPTER TWO

**"At the same time Spartacus, a Thracian by birth, who had once served as a soldier with the Romans but had since been a prisoner and sold for gladiator, for obvious reasons; they overcame the guards and armed themselves with clubs and daggers they took from people on the roads..."**

**—Appian, *The Civil Wars***

I was roused awake when Oenomaus woke Crixus with his foot, causing the snake-tattooed brute to instantly jump into a battle stance. His sudden rush of motion snatched me from sleep. How Crixus could be lying asleep one second, then crouched on the balls of his feet, alert, knife at the ready, was astounding. Crixus was assessing his surroundings in the cool early morning before I'd even rubbed my eyes.

"Crixus, save that for the fish-fancying olive eaters coming to put us down," Oenomaus said, showing his palms to settle the startled German.

"Wake the great one, and his *witch*; we need to face this," said Crixus, resentfully rubbing sand from his eyes.

"We're awake," replied the woman, her sultry voice contemptuous. Spartacus craned his neck, stretching, already sitting up as the woman stood dusting herself off behind him. The morning light reflected in her hair; she glided off to squat behind a bush to relieve herself. Quickly, I looked up at Oenomaus to keep from watching her. Unaware then that I'd soon sit in on my first *consilium*—council of war.

"How many, Oenomaus?" asked Spartacus.

"Our scout, Gannicus, says they're about a hundred, more or less, commander. What's the plan?" Oenomaus asked as seventy-five escaped gladiators and one woman began gathering round to listen.

"Roman superior, by a quarter," Spartacus reasoned aloud to himself. "How does Roman march? How many horses?"

"Gannicus reports a row, two abreast; standard Roman gear with short swords, pilums, and shields. One mule cart, no archers, no horses, lord," replied Oenomaus, adding, "The ranger says the cart 'heaps with rope.'"

"Roman will have contempt for slaves," Spartacus spoke to the masses. "They will hold big nose to deal with us. Roman think slave but stupid lamb, in need of shears, so we must not forget even old Roman have sharp teeth. Veterans will have discipline. We cannot allow them to link shields."

"You have plan," sneered Crixus. "Don't need ask *woman* what next?" He flashed Crastus a knowing glance.

"Helica will speak to Dionysus on our behalf," Spartacus replied.

"Boy?" spoke the woman.

"Yes, lady," I responded.

"Helica," she said. "My name, Publipor, is Helica," And for the moment, I was thrilled to realize she had learned *my* name.

"Yes...Lady...Helica," I replied. She smiled.

"Come with me," said Helica, outstretching an arm, her nails denting my flesh as I was led away with a jerk. We walked from the group, just beyond hearing, when she stopped and took my shoulders in both hands. A thin green snake curled around her neck, probing with its tongue to taste the air. "Publipor," stated Helica, "you'll intercept this garrison of retirees coming at us from Nola. You'll be taken to their leader and plead for terms of our surrender."

Helica's words slapped so hard that my eyes immediately watered, breaking my boyish heart. *Is this really the end?* I thought, my mind filled with whippings and starvation, assuming I'd be allowed to live at all. My thoughts raced to what Roman soldiers would do to us when we were caught; everyone knows what happens to fugitive slaves. Thoughts of spikes driven through palms, the brandings on naked rotted bodies in a row on poles outside of town...it was too much. I lowered my face and shook my head in protest as tears streamed down my cheeks.

"Publipor," she interrupted, softly cupping my chin to lift my face. "This is what our god, Dionysus, demands, sweet boy. You'll intercept them, and you'll tell them that we were driven mad by the *ludis'* depredations. When captured, you'll explain to the centurion that Gnaes Cornelius Lentulus, our owner, was a demonic and cruel *ludis magnus*. That Spartacus had no choice but to revolt in order to have strength enough to perform for the coming Great Games. They'll consider it; Romans love to watch their Thracian bloody the sand. They'll also want the accolades that come with dragging our caged champion back alive. You'll wait, meet them, and stand next to the *optio primo,* the first centurion, when we surrender near the gates of Herculaneum. You must find pretense and stand next to the man in charge when we appear. These men may have been soldiers, but they're just militia now. Perhaps their *optio* hasn't earned his centurion's plume. We must know who's in charge from the outset in order to negotiate for the best terms. Do you understand everything I've told you, sweet boy?"

"Lady, they'll each rape you before you're murdered," I pleaded.

"They'll kill everyone without reputation, fix games for those who do, and if I survive my beating, I'll never be trusted off the chain again nor escape a branding this time." I broke off, sobbing.

"Sweet boy, this sacrifice Dionysus demands," Helica replied. "And when the soldiers take you, remember to stay by their centurion's side. Do you understand what I've told you, Publipor?" It was too much; I shook my head furiously at the ground as tears streamed. Helica grasped my face forcefully and froze me in her icy gaze. "You will stand next to their *optio primo* when we surrender. Do you understand, boy?"

"Sa-Sa-Stand...n-n-next to the centurion," I sniffled in a fit. Helica stood upright, releasing me, brushing back her hair to compose herself.

I turned away, forlorn. Terror ran up my legs with every step; I walked in a nightmare, neither living nor dead. No longer on earth, adrift in a fog, my wandering feet found me suddenly surrounded by Crixus, Crastus, and Oenomaus.

"Boy, ready to surrender?" Crixus asked jubilantly in a thick accent.

"Yes, c-commander," I answered, despondent.

"Great!" he exclaimed, thrusting his arms skyward, his exuberance confounding. If Crixus was lucky, he'd find himself humiliated in a rigged fight with an animal. Oenomaus, seeing my stress, handed me a bladder of water; I drank until my thirst was gone.

"Do what the lady tells you, Publipor," Oenomaus reassured. "It won't be as bad as you think."

"It'll be worse!" I cursed angrily.

"Surrender as witch say, or you do without teeth!" Crixus interrupted, threatening, his fist waving in my face. He spun me round, kicking my ass in the direction of an oncoming legion.

Crastus laughed his wretched laugh, "*Aw, Aw, Aw.*"

I ran, crestfallen, until I couldn't anymore.

At a bend, I sat with knees to my chest, crying and exhausted. Yesterday, I was a fugitive in the army of gladiators—today, just a messenger of defeat. Try as I may, I couldn't face it bravely; I'd die a coward. Crying harder, I reburied my face.

The crunch of stone and clang of metal, faint at first, grew louder. I stood, dusting myself off and pretending to be courageous while wiping tears. At that moment, I imagined walking into the arena as a gladiator, like tales heard the night before. Imagining cheering crowds beneath a burning sun, I'd step into its light to thrill and astound adoring fans. Any self-respecting gladiator would never run to a wall, trying to climb out, begging for mercy. From what I'd heard, cowards were ridiculed and died to ringing laughter; shame and humiliation would mark their end. So like those of worth, I tried to be brave like my new gladiator masters, wiping tearful cheeks and forcing my hands to stop shaking while my stomach turned in knots. In that moment, I was more afraid than the day before when I'd been captured by escaped warriors, and the desire to run and hide consumed me; I stood frozen, weak-kneed.

When the former soldiers rounded the bend and spotted me, one held up a fist, halting the column. Old men in ill-fitting uniforms dropped shields to the ground with a thud and crouched behind them. The sound of drawn swords rang, as javelins were readied. Just like they used to years ago, for Gaius Marius, the "Savior of Rome," when life was better fighting in "The Mighty Mules." A once-lauded regiment dissolved by Sulla long ago.

"Boy!" shouted the retired legionary over his shoulder.

"Slaves?" asked what appeared to be the group's leader.

"I don't see any. I don't think so, sir," replied the old hand.

"Seize him!" shouted the retired centurion. Shields parted and a lone soldier emerged, running toward me as fast as his forty-year-old worn-out legs could carry. His scabbard slapped against his leg until he pressed one hand against it while carrying a pilum in the other. The urge to bolt overtook me, but I was still frozen from fear. Putting up my hands, supplicating, I crouched before the old soldier and heard myself say, "*I've a message from the slaves.*" A calloused hand pounded my ear. Hurriedly, he dragged me by my hair back to the column. Shields parted again as he shoved me to the ground. A sandal pressed hard against my back, and I felt iron at the base of my neck while tasting dirt.

"*What* are you doing here, slave?" asked the retired soldier.

"I was taken captive by the runaway gladiators, please help me," I answered, with my cheek shoved in dirt.

"Stand the slave," ordered the former centurion, and I was hauled to my feet. Ashamed, it felt as if I'd already turned on my new companions, desperate just to live.

"I was taken captive, sir," I sang. "They forced me to meet with you, or they'd burn our crops and put our village to the sword. The fugitives wish to surrender, sir. They made me speak terms with you for them, sir," I continued. The veterans all looked late forties, wrinkled and sun-worn, their armor dented, faded, and unpolished, held together with dry, cracked leather. When they laughed, I saw rotted and missing teeth and gray hair beneath pitted helmets. "The slave leader wanted me to relay he and his companions weren't being fed and couldn't perform properly for the approaching Great Games. They—" I tried to continue but was fiercely slapped across the face.

"I didn't ask how slaves were treated, boy, nor do I care. Where are the fugitives and how many are there?" he asked curtly.

Wiping my busted lip with the back of my hand, I tried not to cry again. "Thirty to forty, I think. They said they'd surrender at the marker just before Herculaneum—unarmed, sir," I lied, looking at the ground.

"Forty, huh?" scoffed the veteran. "See why Rome has to pass laws ordering citizens to feed their damned slaves, boys?" Cackles rang out. "They'll have less mouths to feed real soon, won't they!" Their laughter frightened me, and I worried for Helica.

"How far are the barrel scum from here, boy?" asked the war-weary centurion.

"They said they'd wait on the Appian, one mile from the gates of Herculaneum," I lied.

"We got a slog down the road for a few more hours, looks like, boys," the old centurion shouted down the line of retired men. "Damn barn animals have no idea what to do once they're outside the pen. Hunt's over, boys! Idiot slaves can't even take care of themselves or get out of the rain without a beating. You old dregs can march without these damned shields till we get close enough to need 'em." The retired soldiers wouldn't have to carry heavy shields the entire way—an unheard-of practice in an active fighting legion abroad. The soldiers visibly relaxed, spirits lifted with the prospect of traveling unburdened, confident their opponents were merely animals in need of correction. "This way, those of you without any coin to hire a woman will still have the use of your arms...to tug your tiny cocks!" The retired soldiers' conversations quickly turned to *vino*, wine, *tesserae*, dice, and *tabernae*, the tavern brothels of Herculaneum. The old men visibly relaxed as the chore of marching began to feel like an impromptu holiday.

"Slave! Climb up in that wagon and stack shields," ordered a retiree. The short, two-wheeled cart was led toward the column's front by a mule, which was munching inside a feedbag. The men stacked themselves in two-man formations, marching past on either side. Soldiers handed up shields as they passed, and I had a hard time keeping up as they hoisted them at me from both sides. The task was complicated further by balancing on a pile of hemp rope as it tried to ensnare me. Some men even tried intentionally to trap my fingers, and one griped not to scratch his shield, to the amusement of those nearby. Helica's instructions to stand next to their leader was foremost on my mind as we began our journey. Then the idea of an ambush began to sprout. I knew it couldn't be done riding a mule cart from the rear. My thoughts spun, trying to think of any way to get near the *optio* marching ahead of me.

*This wasn't surrender*, I thought. Why else would Crixus be in such good spirits? Why would Oenomaus reassure me that things wouldn't be "that bad"? It made sense: I'd be the instrument of an ambush and keeping me in the dark would make me more convincing. *Of course*, I realized, rolling along. A mischievous voice in my mind said, *Wrap the cord within the shields and bind them.* While riding in the cart following the marching column, I drifted into daylight dreams of dead Romans, stealthily stringing rope through shields whenever no one was looking. The task complete, I fixated on a lie that'd get me next to the centurion.

"Boy, *optio* wants you," ordered a pointing soldier from the rear.

"Yes, sir," I answered, leaping from the moving cart. "You called... for me...sir?" I asked, panting, when I'd caught up to the man in charge.

"I did, slave. Name the animals' leader," he ordered. I wanted then to give a different name, thinking in some childish way it would protect my lord, Commander Spartacus. Instead, I stuck to Helica's instructions.

"Spartacus," I replied.

"Spartacus?" coughed the centurion. "Spartacus! The Capuan *murmillo*, Spartacus?"

I nodded.

"Spartacus, Dictator Sulla's Spartacus?" the centurion went on in disbelief.

I raised my palms and shrugged, unaware of Spartacus' former life at the time. The Roman's face lit in a grin of sparsely inhabited teeth as men marched past. He halted the column. "Boys!" he exclaimed, addressing the veterans as I hear their former commander, Marius, had: self-effacing apologies first. "I've kept a secret from you, and for that, I'm sorry. When the capitol's message reached me, I didn't believe it, and since the Mules of Marius have heard so many hysterical cries from the brats of Rome in the past, I decided not to bother informing you. I'd thought it bullshit, but now we have confirmation, and if this thing's mouth rings true—" He removed his hand from my neck, only to slap me across the back of the head for emphasis and laughter. "Tell my Mules," he coached.

"Tell the Mules wh—" I stopped, slapped once more before finishing.

"Name their leader, jackass!" he snapped.

"The barbarian gladiator, Spartacus!" I shouted, attempting to avoid being hit again. Retired war veterans stood silent as the centurion resumed.

"This errand just got interesting, boys. The dictator's dog is loose," announced the centurion. The collective hated memory of the deceased dictator, Felix Sulla, and his barbarian henchman, Spartacus, descended on the veterans. I'd grown up with stories of Sulla and Marius' clash as a child, and here I stood with men from one side of that legendary clash.

I'd known little of the greater world outside our peninsula before then, but I'd learn later those soldiers weren't allowed to plunder Italian soil anymore. At that same time, unbeknownst to a slave from a village south of Capua, Rome's legions were deployed in strange, far-flung foreign lands. Whilst on campaign with him years later, Spartacus would regale me with tales of pillaged wealth of all the world. He'd speak of Spanish mines spewing silver in Farther Spain and of vast libraries in Alexandria that housed knowledge of the entire world. He'd speak about the Colossus of Rhodes and the Pyramids in Egypt that scraped the sky. I could hardly conceive then how a man could travel so far and see so much in one lifetime. Unlike Egus, Spartacus didn't speak to hear himself or impress others. In time, I'd come to know the man and had no doubt that every word of every deed was true.

While I tended to herds, Pompey's legions were getting rich and famous in Spain, putting down Sertorius' rebellion. In Greece, Gaius Scribonius Curo was laying waste to Rome's enemy,

Mithradates, accumulating slaves and back taxes. Anthony, sailing with Rome's brand-new navy, chased pirates around the Mediterranean in sleek corsairs of Carthage design, confiscating pirate booty. As I chased goats and chafed beneath the rod, Rome flexed, ever growing. Reputation renewed; it was now expanding, marching further on in a series of preemptive wars—unstoppable beneath the *caligae,* the spiked Roman war boot. Spartacus would tell of surviving his first sixteen years, how he'd helped push Rome's boundaries, put in his time, serving, and now it had passed, unrewarded. Spartacus would curse often about confiscated land he'd not received from the late Dictator Sulla for faithful service, and would learn later why. Spartacus commented once, "Veteran colonies fail because those men wielded the *gladius* longer than a *dolabra,* and taking coin was easier than earning it."

These men marching before me, retirees of the lauded General Marius' Mighty Mules, had been recalled by the senate to sweep trash from Rome's back steps. For *these men,* there'd be no reward, only continued service to the city—no slaves, no treasure, no laurels, nor any triumphant return to adoring grateful Romans. This was a shit detail, and everyone knew it as they headed out to recapture Capua's property. Now suddenly, their fortunes had changed. If they couldn't gain wealth, at least they'd earn renewed reputation by capturing the most infamous heavyweight gladiator of the Republic: Spartacus, a horse thief, a cattle rustler, a cavalryman, and a thug. The drunken, suicidal highway robber who finally devolved into a gladiator, who became a famous fighter of enormous reputation, strength, and spirit. The showman people traveled days and waited hours to see; the man I would devote my life to had become *hostem reipublicae*—enemy number one of the state.

"Slave," threatened the centurion, "if just one word proves false, you'll be first nailed up, you got that?"

"Yes, sir, but..." I paused, weaving a snarled web. *Desiderium vitae*; like a hunted rabbit, my mind dashed through a warren of what I'd heard and observed the night before. A loose strand of cohesion was flushed from the depths of fear, scurrying forth from my mouth.

"But, what?" he asked, impatient.

"The slaves' plan a ruse, sir," I spun.

"Ruse?" asked the centurion.

"They've a giant, deaf mute, sir. They plan to introduce him as Spartacus, to thwart their leader's demise," I lied. The centurion rubbed his stubbled chin in contemplation.

"How do they expect that to work, if the man they plan to use doesn't speak or hear?" he asked with disbelief. "Spartacus is the most famous fighter in all the Republic. The fools must know he'd be recognized."

"The man taking his place uses hands to talk with another of them. He's agreed to die for the man he loves. They believe you'll take his silence as defiance, and know it's unlikely anyone will recognize him, because gladiators are forbidden from removing their helmets in the ring," I continued, spinning a thin yarn from scant information acquired a night before. The old soldier nodded; I watched his face accept the logic as he devised a plan of his own.

"You'll walk with me. When we reach them at the marker, you'll point out Spartacus. In return, I'll release you back to your *vilicus*...alive."

We walked two hours; each minute passed as a day. I thought with every footstep that'd be the moment the trap would spring, but each stride brought disappointment. The day wore on and Helios' chariot drove farther across the sky until it finally laid low, casting royal purple and blood red across the entire horizon. Hope began to darken with the sky as my heart, like the daylight, sank with each step. Doubt began to creep; Spartacus, his men, and the woman had slipped away to freedom without me. I'd stuck to the centurion's shadow, just as Useless had stuck to mine, and thought, *Soon, my blood will stain the path.*

We'd reach Herculaneum's last mile marker before evening. I'd schemed to stand close to the *optio* this whole time and now my thoughts raced for any excuse to get away from him as I trailed close behind the man. *He'll order the shields from the cart soon and the soldiers will find my trap,* I thought. As we continued, the path on our left cut into a bluff, to about the height of a tall horse. When a shadow swept over me, my mind dismissed it as a bird, until the sound of wood on bronze rang out.

I turned to see the centurion next to me collapsed, knocked unconscious, his face in the dirt. Spartacus stood before me, his foot upon the centurion's back as all of the wild gladiators leapt from the bluff onto the veterans below. Spartacus winked and smiled, handing me his cudgel as dust swirled. I grabbed it with both hands, but its heft went limp in my grasp. Too terrified to wield it properly, I stood frozen with fear. Spartacus reached, yanking the gladius from the sprawled centurion's scabbard to bury it into the neck of an approaching soldier with one fluid motion. The soldier grimaced, his hand frozen to the sword's handle as his legs buckled. That was the first time I'd heard the noise of warfare, its screams and curses, and I'd learn with time this was no battle, but an ambush—over before it began. Spartacus wanted to take their leader alive; only the fortune of Sulla's dumb luck found me standing next to the man in charge when they pounced.

"Throw down! Sit, now!" Spartacus roared in a booming war voice. The club fell from my hand involuntarily. Oenomaus approached, discarding his kitchen tool in exchange for a stolen sword. He watched, laughing with glee as I fought the overwhelming urge to sit just as Spartacus had commanded the vanquished. Soldiers who'd been able to pull arms tossed their swords and took seats where they stood. Gladiators ran through the ranks, confiscating javelins and swords before any Roman got an idea of trying to use one.

Gladiators disarmed soldiers and sat them with their backs against the bluff. The cart's mule rocked his head incessantly and kicked at the back of the cart with distress until Egus covered the animal's eyes, soothing him in a calm voice. Oenomaus threw a rough hand on my shoulder, escorting me to the cart and pointing to a disheveled, tangled mess of shields, tied one to the other by a single piece of cord.

"Was that you?" Oenomaus asked.

I nodded.

"Brilliant, just brilliant, son. If even a few had formed a shield wall, this could've gone much different." He smiled and slapped my back, and men nearby soon patted my shoulders, grateful as well. The shields looked as though a soldier had tried yanking them from the cart in a rush, like a dog finding the end of its tether the hard way. A few shields lay about with the bodies of two soldiers and lengths of hacked rope interspersed between them. It was easy to see they'd run out of time before being overpowered by angry slaves.

"I need a favor, son," requested Oenomaus. "Can you unbind that rope without cutting it any more?"

I nodded again, beaming with pride, desperate for more praise.

Carefully, I undid each hastily tied knot...when the hair of my arms stood on end. Helica stared at me once again, and her blue eyes set against black hair sent a shock through my entire body. When she smiled, a flush embarrassingly ran through my face; I pretended to concentrate on the rope.

Spartacus and Helica approached me as I unbound the last of it. Helica stood beside Spartacus, beneath his arm. "You do everything Helica ask, Publipor," Spartacus spoke. "Proud, but how you know to hamper shield? Something not told, you do on your own?"

"Your people have nothing but the clothes on your backs and you're armed with kitchen tools—it seemed you needed all the advantage you could get," I reasoned.

"Slave have proper blade, now," commented Spartacus, chuckling. The barbarian tussled my hair with his left hand, smiling. Helica hung under his other, craning to face her husband.

"I told you," Helica spoke cryptically, nodding towards me. "Our way-maker." Spartacus stepped from the woman, reaching into a Roman treasury pouch, and placed two copper drachmas from it into my hand. I held my opened palm and saw the first wage I'd ever earned.

"That, for standing next to man in charge," said the commander, "This, for binding shield with rope." Spartacus reached into the centurion's stolen money bag once again to place a silver sesterce atop the copper drachmas already resting there. The sum of its total, the most I'd ever seen, much less handled.

"I—I've no purse," I stammered, stunned by wealth.

"Buy one," commented Spartacus, with a look to his best man.

"Men!" Oenomaus shouted after a nod from Spartacus, before I could think to thank my lord. "Keep 'em covered till we get 'em bound! Crixus, get some men, strip the dead before they harden, and put on the breastplates that fit each best." To me, he said, "Publipor, give Egus the rope, then gather the swords in a pile over there." He pointed. "Nobody's fighting over swords till we get a count, and somebody get Egus a javelin!"

The captured old soldiers were stripped to their undergarments. Egus helped Vidovic secure the single length of long rope around each neck at spearpoint, one to the other in a long line. After gathering and piling swords, Oenomaus ordered me to cut the soldiers' tunics in lengths to bind their hands.

"Shit for brains!" Crixus shouted to no one in particular. "Publipor!" he specified, snapping my attention to the newly armed and armored duo. The sight of barbarians in Roman gear was unnerving. "Go get Egus, a pilum!" he shouted, making a kicking motion while his hands were kept busy securing soldiers.

"There's nowhere to run, slave," cursed the bound centurion as I went. "Rome will crucify you all." Upon hearing the boast, Vidovic the Celt punched the man so hard in the jaw that I thought he might've died right then. The centurion hung limp in the procession and began to convulse, until the soldier ahead bore the shuddering man's weight upon his back, while the compatriot behind arched his, using his chest to keep the centurion from asphyxiating until regaining consciousness once more. With help from both, the old centurion recovered his feet before being marched, bound and nearly naked, into Herculaneum by dusk. Word that Nola's garrison of veterans was lost had reached Herculaneum quickly, causing rich inhabitants to flee with everything their domesticated slaves could carry. Outside each villa, field slaves stood slack-jawed, watching personally liberated gladiators march bound Romans beneath the arch and straight through the town's open gate.

That evening, our ranks grew by five hundred as downtrodden herdsmen and desperate farm women threw in with liberated gladiators in lieu of a death sentence. With chains thrown off, homes were opened and food handed out; everyone feasted as an impromptu party broke out. Jars of forty-year-old Italian wine flowed like water into the mouth of greedy slaves without dilution. Reverie shone on every face as the night sky raged with bonfires as the town filled with laughter and music. Spartacus bequeathed a quarter of the captured soldiers to Crixus, who was ordered to arrange a spectacle that night for the slaves' enjoyment. I drank my first of many wine cups that night and soon my head was spinning as I cheered on fights and ran around like a possessed ass. By the end of the evening, I was nearing collapse, so I squashed myself between Oenomaus and Spartacus. We sat on a log near a fire, staring at Helica. The woman spun in time to music while Spartacus smiled and clapped before a blazing inferno. Bleary-eyed, I slipped into oblivion, hoping Helica's dress would lift a little higher as the world turned with her.

# CHAPTER THREE

**"But I know not what name to give to the war which was stirred up at the instigation of Spartacus."**

—Florus, *Epitome*

We kept the old, captured soldiers bound and guarded in an abandoned villa with a decorative mosaic floor all night. They lay on the image of a young Roman bride with dark curly hair, holding a lamb, next to her groom with a quill near his lips in contemplation. I awoke on cold tiles, parched with the taste of vomit in my mouth, wondering how I'd gotten there. The soldiers began to stir; outside, a rooster crowed a broken reverie, and for reasons I can't explain, it made me mad that the damned cock couldn't crow correctly. I thought it odd to see Oenomaus sitting nearby.

"Publipor," said Oenomaus when he saw my tired eyes open. "Come with me. I need you." He sat on the short steps wearing a freshly stolen Roman breastplate, his wrists and shins covered with new protective leathers. Oenomaus stood swiftly while I struggled to my feet with a pounding head and terrible thirst—the floor seemed to spin beneath me as I attempted to work out how I'd come to sleep here. I stretched, staggering into the new day with a gaping yawn and wretched breath. The sun assaulted my eyes, and I attempted to cover the blinding glare of Helios' chariot with my hand. We exchanged no words as I strode with difficulty, trying to keep up with Oenomaus' determined pace.

"There's a man," he explained, "prattling at me in gibberish. You're from around here, aren't you?"

"No," I corrected, my entire skull throbbing, "I hail from *Magna Graecia*." Greater Greece.

"Can you speak shit-poor Italian or not?" asked Oenomaus, impatient. After I'd nodded, he said, "You know, you don't have to sleep with captured soldiers just because they're slaves now." He stopped to face me. "You hold a divine place in Helica's heart. Which makes you sacred to Spartacus." No words could have sounded better to my young, drunken ears. Oenomaus turned and resumed his feverish pace through town, so I quickened to keep up. "That one won't stop going on," Oenomaus said upon our arrival at the bath, pointing to an old man sitting at its entrance. "What's he jabbering?"

The old man saw us and began to speak excitedly in Oscan—my native tongue and the rural language of non-Roman Italy. "Boy, boy!" he said, enthusiastically grasping my arm with a gnarled hand. "Inform Spartacus, I've heated the water! His men are welcome. Tell Spartacus the baths are ready for Herculaneum's liberators. Can you do that for an old man, boy?" The leathery-skinned, nearly toothless old man waved his arms to usher us in.

Translating back and forth, from Latin to Oscan, hurt my pounding head and I had to stop him from going on any more by waving a hand and shaking my head. "The old man wants you to enjoy a bath," I translated. "He's heated the water." The stooped old slave gently waved Oenomaus inside with gnarled, crooked fingers. Oenomaus the Celt furrowed his brow, confused, his face a mask of questions. "You submerge in it," I explained, my head splitting as he cocked his. "You sit in water that's hot." I knew then the only hot water Oenomaus had ever experienced boiled his food. I could tell the idea seemed foreign and dangerous to him.

"For gladiators," claimed Oenomaus, "cleanliness came when olive oil scraped dirt and grime from their bodies, the remnants sold to wealthy women as an aphrodisiac or pregnancy aid." We followed the old man, Oenomaus moving cautiously as the wispy-haired slave walked us deep into brick catacombs once reserved only for rich patricians. Inside, the light was let in strategically; the sun's rays penetrated the darkness here and there, slightly illuminating a bench. Fresh water ran from the wall through a stone channel drain, spilling out onto the other side. The effect of the light dancing to trickling water beneath an intricately painted domed ceiling was hypnotic, making Oenomaus gaze about with childlike wonder.

The elderly slave motioned for Oenomaus to sit at the bench. Surprisingly, the grown man looked to me for answers. I made a "go ahead" face, nodding, and he relented. As the bath attendant began unlacing Oenomaus' boots, I stepped out of busted sandals from the dais and onto heated marble. The sensation felt wonderful, but I made no mention of it, mischievously anticipating the Celt's reaction. Once the old man unlaced Oenomaus' boots, he gently coaxed Oenomaus to stand and turn, unbuckling the breastplate. Old, bent fingers, surprisingly deft, unbuckled straps and untied leather laces until he could finally pull off the stolen breastplate. I gazed at all the different symbols tattooed onto Oenomaus' skin as the elderly slave knelt, unlacing the fighter's shin guards. Then, Oenomaus was directed to turn round and face the bricks. The gladiator twisted his palms skyward reflexively and stood with feet apart, head lifted to the ornate ceiling. Having been ceremonially unarmored hundreds of times, Oenomaus eased into vulnerability. Victors supplicate to Nike, Goddess of Victory, after a successful match. I wouldn't know until much later that what I watched then was sacrosanct.

The stooped attendant continued unlacing Oenomaus' leathers until completely stripped. Then the elderly bath attendant respectfully placed the stolen armor on the bench. Oenomaus turned, naked and barefoot, then stepped from the dais onto the heated marble.

As soon as Oenomaus' first foot landed, he jumped completely on top of the bench, spitting at the floor and cursing. The frail old slave, shocked by the reaction, begged forgiveness in the mix of broken Latin that was Oscan. I grabbed my stomach, laughing so hard that I almost forgot my hangover. Oenomaus, at first certain of witchcraft, saw what fun I was having and stared at me suspiciously. His face contorted from fear to embarrassment, then swiftly to anger. I stopped laughing long enough to scramble when he lurched toward me with clutching hands. I leapt into the large steaming pool barely in time, and the echoing sound of splashing water filled the room. Clearing my eyes, I turned in chest-deep warm water, smiling from ear to ear.

"Shit-lett!" Oenomaus shouted, pointing menacingly.

"What?" I asked, shrugging and lifting my palms innocently. Oenomaus surveyed the room quickly, making certain we were alone, relieved his shame was confined to only the three occupants. Grudgingly, Oenomaus smiled and let out a chuckle that burst into riotous laughter. I joined his fit, gasping for air when the old man staggered from the bench with skinny limbs, waving as he breathlessly apologized. When he realized we were laughing, he cracked up in his own wheezing chortle.

"Shit-lett?" I asked the gladiator, feigning shock. "I'm not even the whole thing?"

"You're the piece that hangs on and won't let go," Oenomaus expanded, his laughter waning. "Romans even heat the floors," he pondered aloud, grudgingly impressed. I'd served as a helper at a bath for a previous owner in Magna Grecia and had marveled at the effect warm water had on the body. Now, I watched intently as Oenomaus tentatively placed his foot in the miracle of hot water. I'd been crouched in the bath with only my head surfaced to enjoy the warmth. The rumor was, Gauls hate deep water, and to show the pool was only chest deep, I stood. But Oenomaus remained at the ledge, his foot dangling over the bath.

"Stop doddering like a heifer at the edge," I scolded. "I'm standing. You can't drown as long as you can stand. The mighty Oenomaus, painted savage, slayer of men, is afraid of a little water?" I was playfully walking the fine line between jest and disrespect. I realized then: Oenomaus was the only escaped gladiator I felt comfortable enough to joke with. I wouldn't dare try speaking to Crixus or Crastus that way; I understood then, smiling, that we were friends, but every overindulgence had its limits. So resolved, I waded to the edge and began climbing from the seductiveness of warm water. Tentative at first, Oenomaus began skittering into the steaming hot pool with bushy furrowed brows that lifted with amazement and amusement once he'd entered completely.

"Where are you going, Publipor?" Oenomaus inquired as I grasped the ledge to exit.

"To get everyone else," I replied at the water's edge.

"Fuck 'em," answered a sprawled and contented Oenomaus. "This is ours, until they find us." We spoke of nothing and everything while my hands turned to prunes. Soon, I had to get out and sit on the ledge to cool off when Oenomaus asked, "Hey, if you ran off and were sold so often, how come you aren't branded. Like with an F for fugitive or some such shit?"

"I told them all that they'd get less for me at market if they did," I answered, and it must have stumped the man because he sucked in his chin and scoffed without reply.

"Why did the gladiators escape?" I finally asked. The *ludis* kept gladiators neatly shaven, except for some of the Celts and Germans, who wore distinctive long mustaches, and the beard's new outgrowth began to irritate Oenomaus as he scratched at the scruff on his cheeks in contemplation.

"Why will a fox chew off its paw to escape a snare?" Oenomaus answered the question with another. "You know, I've seen bears break their teeth on iron bars. I've watched panthers pace until they've worn grooves in the dirt. Nothing endures confinement but cows and sheep, Publipor, nothing. That, and the Circus Maximus, the Great Games, of the new year were nearing. The rules in those matches are *sine missione*—to the death. No one would be 'sent back.' That crowd thirsts for blood. The Romans believe it good to sacrifice nearly all to herald a new year." He shook his head regretfully with eyes closed.

"Isn't every match to the death?" I asked, ignorant at the time.

"No, son. Gladiators are expensive pains in the ass, especially the good ones," explained Oenomaus, smiling and wiggling his blonde brows as if to say he was speaking about himself. "No, kid, most times, the crowd is worn out by chariot races and beast hunts. The crowd's bloodlust is usually satiated with condemned criminals by the time we come out. Most times, the people just want to see a tight match, and if you give them that, with lots of exaggerated movements, they'll usually let you live when bested." Oenomaus scratched at both cheeks with wet hands. "Spartacus once spared Crixus in a match where the crowd was howling for his blood." This news was absolutely scandalous, something I could not believe.

"Spartacus disobeyed a *patron*? Can gladiators do that?" I asked, lurching into the pool.

"It was more negotiated beggary, I guess, and no, gladiators can't outright disobey. Only Spartacus could have pulled that off," Oenomaus went on about how Spartacus was able to turn the crowd to his will, thus allowing the *patron* to signal the virtues of mercy for the masses.

"Why not just kill him," I blurted, suddenly surprised by my own ardency. Oenomaus smiled, knowing I feared Crixus terribly.

"If you want to be afraid, take the man as an enemy," spoke Oenomaus. "If you want not to be afraid, take him as your ally," the thought of which was unfathomable to me at the time.

Oenomaus' countenance soured. "But yes, sometimes gladiators die for the spectacle, and we do it as men." I could tell some memory was seared in his mind; a brand from an iron that would not heal. Vanquished faces visited Oenomaus, haunting him, expressionless. Sitting with me, Oenomaus remembered a time he had to give death to a dear friend in the ring.

This is what he told me.

ROME, CIRCUS MAXIMUS, OENOMAUS, 680 AUC

(75 BC)

Oenomaus retired, turning his back, as was custom after wounding an opponent; he'd tried to lay the blade on the man's shield, but his friend had left an arm exposed. The *seconda rudis,* second official, turned Oenomaus to face his opponent with a forceful hand to the shoulder, and that's when he saw the terrible damage done, along with the upturned thumb of the game's *patron.*

Oenomaus looked into his friend's eyes, half-hidden within the visor, and caught him wink with a painful smile. Oenomaus' friend, pale and bleeding badly, threw off his shield and lifted himself onto one knee, presenting his neck by lifting his head skyward. Roars of, "He's had it!" and *"Jugula! Jugula!"*—cut his throat—were almost in unison.

Oenomaus was resolved to end his countryman's suffering quickly. Loud enough for the bleeding man to hear, Oenomaus said, "*Vala,* my friend"—see you soon—before quickly plunging the blade deep down into the man's throat, burying it to the blade's hilt through to the man's ribcage. That strike shut everything down at once, allowing the fallen to instantly join the dead, unencumbered by pain. Oenomaus recalled the odium of waving a palm around the ring to cheering fans.

In a haze, he stepped up to the winner's podium, careful not to disgrace himself by falling. When Oenomaus reached the top, he was disarmed by the *summa rudis,* first official, and rewarded with a bag full of coins. A masked man, dressed as a vulture, rode in on a jet-black stallion. The aberration wore a long black robe that draped across the animal's girth. Oenomaus watched the creature dismount and slit his dead friend's throat, affirming death for a cheering crowd, while Oenomaus held his prize money.

The demon returned to his mount and undid a strap that secured a hooked pole to the animal's flank. The vulture-costumed fiend returned to the body, piercing that most vulnerable tendon behind the heel with his tool. Oenomaus couldn't look away as the demon fixed the pole to the animal and dragged his friend's body beneath the gate's darkness. Oenomaus was failing in his duty to show appreciation, instead watching men rake and turn the sand beneath him. Oenomaus snapped to the crowd's waning cheers and lifted his palm and bag just in time before the audience felt snubbed. The victorious gladiator took one last look before stepping down. Oenomaus' friend, whom he'd trained, eaten beside, and shared everything with for two years, no longer existed. Like that, he was gone, blotted from history to become lion shit.

HERCULANEUM, PUBLIPOR, 683 AUC (73 BC)

Oenomaus hadn't spoken for a while. He stared off in the distance, deep in thought. When he shuddered, I interrupted the silence with a question.

"Where are we going, Oenomaus?" I asked, turning to face him. "If the bear chewed through iron, if the panther found its way, where would they go?" Oenomaus opened one eye, cocked his head, and smiled.

"To where they came from, of course," he spoke plainly.

"You'd walk...all the way to Gaul?" I asked, astonished.

"Must've walked it, to get here," he said, dismissively closing his eye once again.

"Is that the plan? Are we escaping to Gaul?" I eagerly asked.

"We?" Oenomaus scoffed. But witnessing my pain, he softened. "You are much too clever to set loose just yet. We're going to need a hand out of here, and if you don't mind, could you help for a bit more? It might make you rich. Besides, why would a Thracian go to Gaul, and why on the gods' green earth would Crixus and Crastus? My people hate Germans. They'd sell 'em back to Rome for a jug of wine, if they didn't skin 'em first," he explained. "No, I'm afraid there's no plan, boy, unless you call eating, sleeping, staying alive, and corralling a woman every now and again a plan." Unable then to see how any of that would keep me from my flogging and death at Roman hands, I was saddened. Noticing my crestfallen expression, Oenomaus attempted cheer by saying, "All I know is, what brought us here was foreseen by Helica; she prophesied the breakout, and when the opportunity presented itself, we seized it."

"Helica planned the escape?" I asked.

"She had the vision pointing to moments of opportunity when they presented themselves at predictable times," Oenomaus explained. "It's like planting and sowing, she explained, and showed us repeating dates when men and iron were unfettered." Oenomaus arched his brows and went on. "Telling us to note when deliveries opened gates. Helica said the *lanista* put too much trust in *familia gladiatoria,* or spirit of brotherhood, for his own good to keep men faithful." Oenomaus smirked. "But his most fatal mistake was underestimating the cunning of a woman." He winked. "She says Dionysus visited her one night, giving Helica a vision of a key made of flesh that would unlock our chains and blow down the gates with a word." Oenomaus' animated hands leapt from the water. "A sacred symbol was left behind when she woke, so it couldn't be dismissed." He raised his pointer. "A holy mission, given to her by the God of Wine himself. When Helica woke the next morning with her groom, his face was replaced by a coiling serpent. She interpreted Spartacus had been given terrific and terrible power, that only *she* could determine was lucky or not."

"Spartacus was the key?" I reasoned, then wondered aloud, "What was the word?"

"It must've been, 'Kill him, Crixus,' because that's what Spartacus yelled when it all began. Crixus killed the cart driver and reined in the mule team that yanked down the gate. Then again..." he thought aloud, scratching his irritated chin, reconsidering, "maybe it was, 'Yaw!' That's what Crixus yelled when he slapped the ass's rump when the chain was fixed. So, who knows? Many more should've made it out, though—we were betrayed." His countenance suddenly changed as he thought of men who'd been left behind, brothers who hadn't made it. "The spy, whoever the louse was, squealed, probably thinking to save his skin from the coming games. It's fitting that the iron gate crashed down on Flavius, if he was our rat. His brains popped like a squash," he recalled with a vengeful smile. "Nothing worse than a traitor, son. Nothing." Oenomaus spat into the water. Oenomaus had said that twice by then, but I would not fully understand the disastrous effects of what treachery births until many years later.

"Why was a woman allowed to stay with Spartacus in the *ludis?*"

I inquired, finally asking the question in my heart. Oenomaus opened both eyes, turned his head, and smiled knowingly. He'd seen many men fall under Helica's spell of beauty and knew now it worked on boys as well.

"Women make men docile, easier to manage. Lots of gladiators are married with the *ludis'* blessing," Oenomaus answered. "That, and she's a gifted healer. Helica's mother was Scordisci, a tribe known for eastern *pharmaka,* the secret knowledge of plants and venoms. She's got the gift of past and future sight, traveling places between our world and the next. She's stopped many wounds from infection, including mine," he said, jerking a thumb from the water to his upper chest, where an old scar ran long. Hot water loosened Oenomaus' muscles along with his tongue, and he spilled his former life before me.

I saw with my mind's eye as he spoke: a young raven-haired woman in an iron collar and plain hard spun woolen frock. Oenomaus said, "The slaver claimed the Thracian girl was more troublesome than she was beautiful. He threw her in as part of a deal for new fighters, just to be rid of her angst. The *lanista,* Cornelius Vatia, could not believe the deal he'd been given and couldn't have known he'd sown his own demise by raping the girl on her first night in the *ludis.*" Oenomaus shook his head. "The next day, she let it be known that she'd put a hex on him, causing horrible dreams of decay each night afterward. Helica promised to remove it only if he released her. Cornelius, tormented yet cleverly underhanded and morally unable to take a loss, devised a plan to get the most out of a valuable gladiator and a new, young, and beautiful slave. Knowing they shared a language, Cornelius devised a most devious plan to free her without release." Oenomaus continued, barbarically clearing each nostril of dust-tainted mucus, one at a time, into our water. "By giving the woman to the custody of a slave, he owned her now through proxy. The first evening of the deal, Cornelius slept the entire night like a contented baby, believing he could best the boatman out of a ride. He boasted he'd never taken a loss in business and convinced himself that he'd outsmarted a witch. Cornelius shrewdly weighted the scale with every advantage in his favor— he couldn't just give her away without a return. With one look, Cornelius knew the value Spartacus placed on the young woman and schemed deeper. Such was his character. He bargained that if Spartacus won his next match, Cornelius would gift the gladiator his beautiful Thracian prize. Cornelius slept well, believing he'd parlayed advantage over a gladiator and the witch, enriching himself while casting away a curse at the same time. The first night in Spartacus' cage, Helica entered a trance, prophesying our escape and that Spartacus would lead an army of slaves, 'the likes of which, the world has never seen.'"

I listened, enthralled, slipping deeper into the steaming magic of hot water.

"Spartacus' reputation and undefeated record was renowned throughout most of Italy by this time. Cornelius fumed at the odds makers; they made it impossible for him to capitalize on owning the most ferocious gladiator in the entire Republic. Frustrated, Cornelius insisted on turning a profit and tempted the competition by insulting their pride. Cornelius boasted to the surrounding schools, lamenting the only fighters with a chance against Spartacus were in his own stable," Oenomaus explained, clearing more mucus into my water. I'd ignored the first, but this new discharge was notably copious and disgusting. I floated cautiously away from the vile strands to avoid dragging any of its hideous contents across the pool with me.

"Cornelius, tired of Spartacus not earning what he believed was his due, wagered twenty-to-one that three gladiators fighting against Spartacus at the same time couldn't defeat the champion.

Such a spectacle is usually reserved for criminals; it's considered abhorrent due to the bout's predictable outcome. Cornelius gambled, thinking he'd incentivized Spartacus enough by dangling a large enough piece of meat before the barbarian. Confident the bewitched fighter would net a huge payday, Cornelius threw the dice."

I sat with Oenomaus, glued to every word. He spoke over a lullaby of tumbling water that soothed my first hangover, and my eyes soon became heavy. Resting my head and shoulders on the pool's edge, separated by a curtain of steam, I drifted to sleep with Oenomaus' saga of Helica being taken to Spartacus in fetters.

Youthful beauty stood chained before a caged gladiator, the bars between them; the Circus Maximus' crowd groaned outside their stone confinement. The guards unlocked the slave woman; Helica placed both her hands through the bars onto the inked horses of Spartacus' chest. She described an outcome in the privacy of their common tongue, how Spartacus could survive the coming match by abandoning the art of dying well. But the training of gladiators demanded them to go willingly into death, to take the iron without flinching, honoring their sacred oath. Yet victory dictated that the *leges pugnandi*, or "rules" of the match, be discarded. The young raven-haired, blue-eyed beauty had information through her vines that the match was rigged. Taboo dirty tricks would be forgiven, she explained. How disgusted the crowd would be at such a mismatch—they'd demand blood payment for the insult. Spartacus laughed involuntarily when Helica explained the match must not last longer than it takes a mother to scold a child.

"You've never met my mother," jested Spartacus, in Thracian. Unfazed, Helica continued elucidating her vision. He'd have to use underhanded tactics to beat the first two, and the third would draw blood but be struck down by "black lightning." Thunder would herald Spartacus' victory, and he'd sleep, burning for three days before she could bring him back. Trying to interpret the woman's cryptic language confused the giant warrior, until the barbarian accepted it for what it was: the mystery of women. Then came Cornelius' thugs to exchange slaves in the cage at spearpoint. When Helica finished, Spartacus was led away. Helica sat alone, cross-legged, tossing knuckle bones into dirt, awaiting the barbarian's return.

A *tibia* sounded, the horn commencing a match. Spartacus entered the western gate; his oversized dolphin-crested helmet and long, curved blade revealed his identity to the awaiting throng. Explosive cheers quickly turned to a collective groan, then violent curses, as three opponents swaggered in abreast through the opposing gate. The trio of cocksure gladiators taunted the crowd irreverently with palms raised, inviting spectators to jeer, implicating there'd be no need for the crowd's mercy. The middle gladiator was a *murmillo,* another bare-chested heavyweight with a big shield, armed with a curved blade like Spartacus. A gleaming bronze vambrace covered the entirety of his sword arm, his head encased in an oversized and feathered gladiator's helmet. On Spartacus' left, the Roman theatrical ideal of a Thracian with an oversized helmet, short sword, and small shield. To his right, a *retiarius,* an un-helmeted, trident-armed gladiator hovered; the weighted net in his grasp threatened entanglement.

The crowd whistled disapproval when the *retiarius* struck, pitching the lead-weighted net at Spartacus' feet. The crowd went silent, holding its collective breath in anticipation. Spartacus dropped his *scutum,* the large shield's edge, into the sand, trapping the net cast beneath him, and then stepping onto it for good measure. The *retiarius* lunged with a single-handed thrust from his trident. Spartacus lifted the heavy shield from the net, and the weapon struck with a resounding *bang.* The *retiarius* yanked the net, expecting to up-end the *murmillo,* only to pull himself headlong into the *scutum* instead, to the crowd's delight. A puff of dust indicated the trident's fall, coinciding with a hollow thud of bare head on birch plywood. Spartacus tossed the big shield atop the unconscious *retiarius*—an unprecedented move—using the man beneath as an elevated platform, launching himself airborne at the "Thracian" holding a small shield.

The crowd collectively gasped when the outnumbered champion grabbed at the small shield with his bare hand, pulling it down and slashing sidelong with the curved blade once he'd returned to earth. It struck brutally beneath the chinstrap with a sick, fleshy sound. The crowd went wild when they saw the spray of blood drench the opponent's bare chest in torrents. The dying gladiator brought both hands immediately to his neck, instinctually attempting to staunch the bleeding. Two steps later, the man collapsed, motionless, faceplate first in the blood-drenched sand.

The large *murmillo* moved in suddenly from center, attempting to blunt the champ's momentum by ramming his large *scutum* into Spartacus with a bull's charge. It slammed like a brick wall, forcing Spartacus to roll and lose his sword, recovering onto a knee just beyond its grasp. The Circus Maximus responded, one moment jubilant, cursed the next, to the spectacle's ebb and flow. The opposing heavyweight pressed again. This time, Spartacus swung his arm full force at his opponent's eyes. The entire arena collectively gasped in horror as the underdog flung a handful of sand into the *murmillo's* full-faced helmet. Gratuitous amounts of coarse powder found its mark through sight holes, blinding the big man. Spartacus had just spat in the face of *leges pugnandi:* he'd blinded his opponent with sand, the most underhanded and loathsome thing a fighter could do in the arena.

Silence momentarily gripped the onlookers as they processed

the abomination of what they'd witnessed. The *secunda rudis'* eyes shifted to the *summa rudis* for answers on the confusion with the unconventional bout and the crowd's reaction. The officials shot a glance up at the *patron's* booth, both expecting the signal to intervene from the game's producer. Meanwhile, the crowd quickly considered the stakes, collectively judged the circumstances equitable, and, in unison, erupted, cheering acceptance and instantly forgiving the affront. Both officials remained frozen at their posts as Spartacus recovered his giant *sicca,* the curved blade, from where it'd fallen in sand after he'd been bowled over. His opponent stood upright, shaking his head and poking fingers through his helmet's narrow opening, trying to clear sand from his eyes.

The experienced opposing heavyweight *murmillo,* fully expecting the match to be stopped and Spartacus put to death for the infraction, held his shield. Training and muscle memory made the veteran *murmillo* hold fast to his *scutum,* the large shield granting him just a moment's reprieve from death. With eyes still watering, he knew instantly when the *tibia* didn't sound and the crowd erupted that he was in big trouble. The big man just barely braced behind his shield in time when Spartacus charged, sending the skilled fighter reeling. Surprised, the opponent struggled on his heels to keep his feet beneath him. The crowd shouted as Spartacus chewed through the shield with crunching, heavy blows heard even in the farthest sections of the circus. The *murmillo's* ornate helmet sparked and rang as the eastern blade reached over his shield. Spartacus continued furiously as splinters and woodchips flew from the shield like a woodsman felling a tree.

Spartacus pressed hard to shouts of the crowd, until a highly trained, exhausted arm shot out desperately from the side of a battered shield. Spartacus swerved his entire body, almost avoiding the lunge, but the blade bit deep along naked ribs. The crowd cawed when blood ran from his side. Spartacus yanked at the top of the chewed-up shield, pulling his opponent forward forcefully onto his angled blade. It passed through the sternum and into the heart of the *murmillo,* exiting visibly through the back. He fell. The crowd stood mute, absorbing the spectacle they'd just witnessed.

Spartacus inspected his wound in the stillness as best he could through his helmet, catching his breath. The crowd moved its collective head silently. Spartacus noticed movement in the periphery—the *retiarius* had awoken. The wounded, newly conscious man crawled on all fours toward the ring's side to where the *patron* sat. Jutting out his hand with two fingers extended, the signal of submission, the gladiator begged to be "sent back" to fight another day. All eyes turned to the wealthy *patron,* everyone awaiting his decision with a signal.

"*Respectus non leges pugnandi,*" Spartacus heard Helica's voice. Life poured from the wound and pain gnawed at his mind. Spartacus bent, retrieving the discarded trident from the sand. Woozily, he judged the distance and, in a split second, threw the ugly, black iron weapon with all his waning might like a spear. A brilliant bright light of pain flashed like an electric bolt from Zeus, blinding him when he released the rough bolt. Soaring high, it struck the *retiarius* at a perfect arc, exactly in the back of his neck, the bolt swaying upright in the distance.

Thunder exploded as the insane crowd roared with a tumult heard outside the city's walls. Spartacus collapsed. The *patron* read the mob's mood correctly, holding his thumb skyward, forcing a smile. The patrician did his best to appear as though he approved of the killing, even though the sentence hadn't yet been handed out. Beneath wine-soured breath, the wealthy game giver cursed the temerity of spoiled gladiators.

Jumping joyously, Gnaes Cornelius Vatia immediately ordered his ruffians to collect his winnings. Sycophants heaped insincere praise as he happily tallied coins with his mind, until realizing he was unable to reach a sum with just his head. Suddenly, Cornelius' countenance changed—he burst from his seat, angry with fear, yelling for a spot of clay and a stylus. Fearing he'd be skimmed by his own thugs before reaching a total, Cornelius ran frantically after his money before even some of it found new pockets.

In the cell, Helica listened to chaos through confining stone, tearing strips of wool, soaking them in clean salted water and wine vinegar. Crushed herbs lay carefully arranged next to a bed of clean straw, while a thin green snake slithered around her neck. The serpent kissed with a delicately flicking tongue. She smiled, contented her vision was true.

# CHAPTER FOUR

**"The first position which attracted the ravening monsters was Mt. Vesuvius."**

**—Florus, *The War Against Spartacus***

"Who gives a tin cup of shit about Spar-ti-coos, the squalling peacock?" came a gruff voice. I was jerked to the here and now when Crixus and Crastus stepped from the dark, vile aberrations appearing from the shadows into the dim light of the bath. The elderly attendant returned from his boiler just as the duo appeared, looking fearsome in their newly acquired leathers and arms.

The imposing men towered over the frail octogenarian; he stood motionless, goat-stricken, looking like prey circled by wolves. Crixus enjoyed inflicting pain, but what he really, really loved, was causing terror. He smelled it in the prey before him now, filling him with pleasure, generating that awful smile. He craned his neck slightly toward Crastus, never releasing his glare from the frozen old man. "Crastus?" Crixus asked his companion, staring murderously at the old man. "How *long*, you think, hundred-year-old Roman can hold breath?"

"He's not Roman!" I blurted out foolishly from the water, instantly regretting it. Softening my tone, I said, "He's Sicilian." Crixus released the old man's gaze, lost his carnivorous smile, and focused on me with a whip of his head. "A-An islander," I mumbled. Cold fear flashed down my spine beneath his terrifying gaze.

"Crastus, can bucket of piss drown?" Crixus asked, raising thick red brows at his shadow. Crastus replied with only his deep menacing laugh, a sound that I hated then, but came to love in time.

"The old man's mine, Crixus; leave him alone," Oenomaus said calmly from the pool, cooling the tense mood with a carefree tone. "Our man Publipor captured him and forced him to heat the baths for us. Come, man. Join us, Crixus. Get in, Crastus." He invited the pair with only his head and palms breaking the water's surface.

"Fuck, me!" exclaimed Crixus. Distracted by the nearest painted tile decorating a wall, he motioned Crastus to join. "Take look at this, Crastus. He's dog mounted a woman while *she's* holding cup!" he exclaimed in childlike glee. Ruddy Crastus stepped beside red-haired Crixus to get a better look, "No woman living sips wine while *I'm* mounted!" Crixus boasted, slapping Crastus' shoulder. "The tiny-cocked Roman, can't even knock it from her hand!"

Crastus responded by laughing even more slowly in his obnoxious way.

"Are you getting in or not, Crixus?" Oenomaus asked, annoyed. "Your voice is hurting poor Publipor's ears, and you know he's recovering from his first wine binge." His voice carried a tone of mock sympathy, and pangs of resentment for Oenomaus struck me instantly when Crixus returned his ever-furious eyes back to me. I couldn't believe it; after all the time we spent becoming friends, Oenomaus plotted retribution the whole time from his embarrassment in front of an old man. Gannicus later termed it *hyacinthum et vulture*—the blue falcon, the friend fucker.

"Stop fouling my water, you dirty little Italian shit!" Crixus yelled, pointing at me. "Grab loot outside, drag it here, before some spook try and steal it," he ordered. Crixus began undoing the laces at his wrist leathers with his teeth.

The old man, who hadn't moved, tentatively stepped forward from force of habit to help. Crixus growled like a dog at him. I followed the old man to the exit as he turned and shuffled out as fast as his ancient body could take him.

"Gods damn, them! Even the fucking floor, is hot!" Crixus exclaimed from inside. Bringing Crixus his loot indoors brought me to an even more disturbing conversation: "Why you piss in corner, Crastus?" Crixus asked. "Just go here," instructed the German from the water. I jumped into my old tunic and slipped into beaten sandals to escape.

SPQR, 682 AUC (73 BC)

The wealthiest man in all the city pored over meters of fine Egyptian papyrus sprawled over an intricately carved, and equally expensive, ten-foot-long table. There'd been a Crassus dating back to the first senators of the old Republic. The Crassus family was among the first citizens to throw off monarchy, expelling the last king from Rome, but as of late, they had fallen on hard times. A prominent name isn't enough during civil war, and it forced this Crassus—Marcus Licinius Crassus—to claw back from obscurity and near ruin...before backing Sulla. After the civil war, Marcus Crassus shrewdly purchased as much property as he could with every sesterce at his disposal. By age forty, most of the city's poor rented beneath one of his cramped roofs or toiled in the south on one of many rural estates owned by the patrician.

Ensconced at his rarely used palatial Roman villa, Marcus plotted as sunlight glinted off exquisitely polished marble. An engraved breastplate and helmet hung neatly on a rack—

ornaments of authority flaunted on the balcony. Expensive candles burned needlessly in the light of day with the smell of rose wafting through the home, blunting stench from the city below. Distinguished Marcus Crassus wore a toga made of the softest cotton trimmed in purple. Patting sweat from his forehead with a scarf made of oriental silk, Marcus was suddenly interrupted by a knock at the door.

"What is it?" asked Marcus Crassus, annoyed, refusing to remove his attention from the map as heavy, iron-reinforced doors opened with the faintest squeak on oiled hinges. In walked Marcus' most loyal scribe with his usual sense of purpose, holding a wax-sealed letter for his *bulla*, or boss, and former master. Respectfully removing the brimless woolen skull cap of a freed slave and holding it before him with both hands, he stood patiently, then cleared his throat. The man had served Marcus' needs with competent skill in Rome and abroad for over twenty years. Distracted, Marcus Crassus held his hand out behind him and the man approached, attempting to place the letter in his former master's palm. Faltering, he missed the handoff and readjusted. Focused on a particular part of the trail map, Marcus turned to grab at the letter, annoyed at having to divert attention away from his important work.

Marcus huffed his breath and tossed the correspondence in the air, disgusted once he finished reading it. He grumbled, promptly returning to the same spot on the papyrus as before, the disregarded letter fluttering to the floor. His Greek-educated, now-free former slave hustled to where the letter came to rest and stooped to retrieve it, standing quietly and waiting once more. Marcus Crassus' focus remained there for a great deal of time before finally turning to grab another scroll. Suddenly reminded of his servant waiting, Marcus stood erect to face him.

"Why, Merillius, is the senate bothering me with this garbage?"

Marcus asked, dismayed by every word written.

"The third slave revolt—that's what the senate's calling it," answered the free Greek.

"Seventy gladiators run out of a cage, and I have to pay for it?" Marcus asked.

"The senate has assigned the *Campus Martius*, the Field of Mars, to you. As such, they claim it is your purview," the free scholar answered. Marcus' mature freedman, who understood intimately the subtle nuance of senatorial gossip, explained more plainly: "They've trounced a militia of Nola's veterans and sacked Herculaneum. The Pompeiians are screaming they'll be next if Rome doesn't act now. The slaves are led by Spartacus."

Marcus Crassus paused in his work, raising eyebrows as memories of campaigns and previous interactions he'd had with the man flooded back from when they'd both served the late dictator, Felix Sulla. Marcus quickly disregarded the disgraced barbarian cavalry soldier from his memory to focus on the task at hand.

"Good-for-nothings run this fat, lazy Republic, Merillius," Marcus commented. "In the time of our fathers, *centurion* meant *greatest* of a hundred Romans, not *leader* of eighty poor foreigners with borrowed arms." Thinking he was meant for an earlier time, Marcus shook his head, cursing the hated memory of his father's and brother's butcher: Gaius Marius. Marius was the example of what happens to a republic when a *novice homo*, common man, with only two names climbs Rome's *circus honorums* ladder too high. Before Marius reformed the army, Romans were expected to fight for their city. But evidently the wars got too far, and it became much too hard for any self-respecting citizen to be away for so long in defense of an obviously stable nation. Marcus' blood boiled for allowing Marius' ghost to reside duty-free in the estate of his mind, even for the briefest moment. With Roman self-control, Marcus expelled the dead man from his thoughts. "Find whichever snot-nosed son of the next ne'er-do-well is in line and hitch him to this shit show,"

Marcus Crassus ordered, exasperated, throwing up old yet muscular arms.

Merillius, knowing the senate wouldn't listen to the word of a slave, freed or not, remained where he stood, respectfully leading Marcus with his eyes to the stationery and reminding him with a look. Marcus groaned, scratching a quill with ink onto thin parchment, hastily pouring wax, pressing his seal, and handing it back. Marcus Crassus, done wasting time, returned his focus to the table for more important and profitable business.

Merillius took the assignment orders that called for raising a hastily conscripted legion of locals and exited with the same purpose he'd entered. Being a most adept Greek accountant, Merillius knew better than to walk the streets of Rome, jingling and burdened, alone. He retained Marcus' fire marshal, Atticus Fabius, for protection first before opening Marcus' war chest with the key kept round his neck on its silver chain. Atticus, a large Etruscan who'd served Merillius' master as *optio primo,* first centurion, in the army during the wars, had found new employment setting and putting out Marcus' fires in Rome.

The Greek removed his woolen skull cap and re-entered the Forum with his head held high, not just a freed slave with approval of financing, but with the entire sum, along with insurance, to make sure Marcus Crassus' money bought what was paid for. Merillius endured the obstinate fireman on the return trip with private knowledge: Atticus Fabius Dominicus' name was in the letter. *Better hope your blade smarts as much as your mouth,* thought the bean counter with a smirk as the war vet droned on with poking laughter, completely unaware that he'd been drafted.

GLABER, VIA APPIAN, 682 AUC (73 BC)

Freshly appointed Caius Claudius Glaber proudly rode the Roman-engineered, arrow-straight Appian Way south toward Pompeii astride a powerful chestnut mare. Sinuous muscles bulged from the animal's broad shoulders as the horse's coat reflected sunlight like polished bronze. The mare pranced on cobble with iron-shod hooves, a fine specimen of Numidian breeding, while a man with lesser parentage and only slightly better wits rode with chin haughtily high. The praetor's *lictors*, six men appointed to protect the praetor with their lives, walked before him, proudly holding the company *signum*, the legionary standard: a raptor cast in pure Spanish silver, its wings spread wide as victory ribbons blew in the wind on the march. Six silver disks adorned the pole borne by a young soldier, whose helmet was festooned with the pelt of a wolf's head. Heralding their procession and looming above all flew the majestic screaming eagle, the *signum*, or standard of Rome's legions. The soldier holding it marched alongside five others. One held the *fasces*, an axe bound to wooden rods, the holy symbol of Rome's lawful right to dispense punishment and execution.

Young men stepped in time to a drum, marching with pomp and looking impressive as they recruited more soldiers on their journey to put down slaves in the south. They enlisted hungry youngsters eager enough to pick up arms, slip on a breastplate, and join the newly formed regiment of green soldiers as they went. On the day Glaber was finally appointed praetor of the new legion, a cunning senator had whispered deceptively in his ear, helpfully reminding Glaber of Rome's history, explaining in previous slave revolts, Rome had sent four thousand men into Sicily to squash slaves. Dutifully, Glaber parroted what he'd heard as his own opinion, sternly protesting the lack of manpower with borrowed objections like the fool he was. The majority of senators promptly rebuked Glaber as cowardly, threatening him with removal from the command, pounding the rails inside the forum with disgust. Quickly recanting, the thirty-five-year-old, freshly appointed praetor, long on ambition and short on ability, abruptly changed his tune.

Once on the road, Glaber eagerly soaked up the trappings of command on the slow march south toward Rome's seaside vacation villas, barking harshly and throwing threats at new recruits with words he'd borrowed from experienced officers. Glaber enjoyed every envious eye as he rode, dreaming of his successful return. His mind was entranced by thoughts of a gilded chariot pulled by four unblemished white horses, with captured slaves in tow, being showered in laurels tossed by grateful citizens, all of them cheering Caius Claudius Glaber's triumph.

*Favor of the gods finally smiles upon me,* thought Glaber. The new praetor imagined the posting after he'd rounded up all the smelly slaves. He'd show those old men in the senate his true worth. *Capture a few stupid slaves—what could be easier?* he thought, smiling as he rode.

# CHAPTER FIVE

*"...the female sex has a certain sanctity and prescience, and they do not despise their counsels, or make light of their answers."*
—**Tacitus,** *Germany and its Tribes*

I was chasing pigs around their pen with a stick in the early morning, swatting at them for fun and making them squeal, when I noticed Helica. She carried a heavy bucket down the street with both hands, the weight causing her to lean slightly to one side. It bounced from her thigh awkwardly, white powder puffing with each stride. Helica walked through the villa's door where the soldiers were kept for the night. Curious, I jumped a rickety fence and gave chase, following through the shaded villa's perimeter to hide behind a column.

The day before, Spartacus had ordered his men not to kill more than a quarter of the captives, for reasons he didn't explain. I'd heard Crixus and Crastus groan between themselves, but the morning revealed they'd obeyed, despite their homicidal desires. Spartacus had ordered Egus to guard our captives and protect them from the violent citizens. Egus was a bald-faced man with squinty eyes and short black hair, who wore a satisfied, toothy grin for all occasions. He did not move from his position inside the villa as Helica entered.

Helica set the bucket down hard; the sound echoed through

the interior courtyard, and waking captives cracked open bleary eyes at its drop. The villa's *piazza*, its open-air square, had been immaculately kept by slaves. All of the potted plants were lush and well-watered. Hardly a scratch of dirt scraped my sandals; I knew intimately how much work it took to keep such an expanse swept.

The survivors, old comrades made captives, had spent another night bound together; they all wore a mask of disciplined resolve, and smelled of urine. Crouching in shade next to a pot of rosemary, I watched as Helica hitched up her frock and bent, scooping two heaping handfuls of powder used to mark slaves at auction. Egus stood at attention, armed with a javelin, and merely nodded to her. Excess chalk ran through her fingers while she stomped angrily toward the bound men. Helica hurled it to explode at their feet, her voice a demonic shrill.

"Now you are slaves! You, and you, too! You—all of you—are my slaves!" she screeched, releasing years of pent fury onto the captured soldiers.

Recoiling closer to the ground, captured soldiers closed their eyes and held collective breaths as she returned with handfuls more. "I have bought you. My daughter has paid for you!" she screamed.

*Daughter?* I thought, shocked momentarily at such a revelation until an eerie, white cloud of the talc filled the courtyard's center as women, first to arrive at the sound of commotion, watched casually, their security provided by a smiling, armed gladiator. Those first ladies who joined that day would form the core of what Helica called her Cult of Dionysus; but really, they'd just become the Cult of Helica.

"Wake, you lazy good-for-nothings! Your mothers should've tossed you on a trash heap with the little girls!" seethed the beauty. Helica produced a cattle prod, the long, leather-wrapped cane used to coax cows along, and shrieked for them to stand. "Why aren't you working, slaves? Stand up! Why aren't you working? Stand up, lazy! Go lie down in the cemetery if you want to sleep!" she bawled, all while pelting them.

Men raised bound forearms, attempting to deflect the wicked blows Helica delivered up and down the row. Tentative at first, just a few women joined, but within minutes, all adjusted quickly to new ownership with gusto. Grabbing handfuls of fine white powder and flinging it at the prisoners, Helica and the women of her new cult continued screaming. Chalk madness and talc bedlam erupted as Helica regained her sanity, all while the other women, left behind, lost theirs. The momentary reprieve from a vicious beating resumed when Helica passed the cane to an eager, wild-eyed middle-aged woman. The villa's pitch screeched with various female furies all expending years of pent rage on the Roman captives. Pale female faces coated with fine talc beat their former tormentors unremittingly, birthing the most faithful of Helica's cult. Helica stepped, ghostlike, from the cloud of hellish shrieking that continued. She emerged, shaking fine powder from her hair, and adjusted her simple dress with dignity while calmly giving orders to the powerfully built Egus. As she passed near where I was hidden, she announced, "Publipor, come to the bath in one hour." She exited without a glance in my direction.

In town, shackled soldiers were divided into work gangs and set to stripping the town of its wealth for self-liberated slaves. We placed the old centurion with a busted face in stocks, heavy timbers clasped in iron around his neck with only a portion carved out for head and hands. We put him on display in the forum for humiliation; anyone who went to the town's center hurled vile things and insults at him.

"Enjoy every minute off your cross, Publius' *boy*," spat the centurion, defiant to the last as I passed. Great apprehension filled my gut upon hearing my Roman name roll off the lips of an official administrator. *Publipor,* Publius' boy, was what my Roman master thoughtlessly heaped upon me when I was first purchased, a time so long ago I can hardly remember. This *optio,* however, stripped of power or not, made me very uncomfortable. *That man can identify me if he ever gets free,* I thought, and for the first time in my life, I *needed* someone to die.

Slaves with ample idle time for the first day in their wretched lives spent most of it frivolously, like children set loose. Some went to the brothels that miraculously remained open and unscathed throughout the entire sacking. Stealing, by far, seemed to be the most popular endeavor, engaged in by all newly self-liberated slaves. Quickly, word spread through all Campania of our revolt, causing more and more slaves to arrive. Most were shepherds and field laborers, escapees from cities such as Nola in the east, but even as far south as Salernum. Slaves poured in from all over. One group, still shackled and chained by the ankles, walked into the liberated city of Herculaneum, stepping in unison, begging for a smith.

I strode through town a conquering hero, surveying all that was mine. Iron, bronze, livestock...everything was the property of slaves. Amphora jars full of oil and wine were everywhere, and even the presses used to fill them were being carted off. One slave, packing his new mule overloaded with treasure, was forced to choose which items were most valuable when the beast was packed to capacity. He furiously removed an item he'd secured, only to replace it with another thing found suddenly worth more. I thought him silly, repeating the process over and over. I passed the greedy fool, smiling, until Crixus and Crastus, swords in hand, rounded the corner into sight—I felt the sudden urge to pee.

Crastus the German pointed at me with his sword. "Sheezin kompf!" he yelled in some bastard form of busted Latin. To me, his words sounded as if he held stones in his mouth, making correct pronunciation in our foreign tongue impossible. "Gettin ze shit face, heren," he said thickly, pointing the sword at his feet. Both men stood motionless, daring me to run; the pair looked just as shaggy and fearsome in daylight as they had in the dimness of the bath. They'd abandoned the armor from the day's heat and smiled wickedly at me while wearing only boots, loincloth, and belts with huge daggers stuffed through them.

Bulky, snake-covered, and bright red Crixus stood next to lean Crastus, his ruddy complexion tainted with intricate basket-weaved tattoos. They waited for me to make the next move. Two naked soldiers stood tethered by their necks behind them, looking more like paupers than the fierce veterans of yesterday. The captured wretches carried huge sacks of treasure, full almost to bursting, over their bloodied shoulders.

"Tell sound wall make," commanded Crastus. I followed them, not because I understood what they wanted, but because I had no choice. So much for liberation.

Within a few blocks, we arrived at a wall painted with official town business and graffiti. "Maken zie sound," ordered Crastus, pointing his sword at the notices written along the wall's expanse. Official town business, painted neatly in official script, filled its majority—notices for Herculaneum's citizens.

"It says a lot," I answered. With that, Crixus calmly handed his leather strip of leash to Crastus and slapped my head with a heavy palm.

"We know it say more, so don't try trick, *Roman*," Crixus said gruffly over the ringing in my ear as he calmly retrieved the leash.

"It says..." I began, "anyone caught tampering with the water pipe will face punishment. It says, the vote for city council will be held on the twenty-third day of Aprilis. And I'm not Roman," I corrected, rubbing my ear, and carrying on before either could hit me again. I read the notices aloud until, eventually, they bored of it.

"Zis one," Crastus interrupted, pointing at crude scratches at the wall's bottom.

"Lydia's an easy lay," I read, and they burst into laughter. Crixus tugged on his slave's leash, asking where he could find Lydia. Both men laughed obtusely at each other's bawdy jokes. Down the informative wall we went as I read salacious graffiti while they entertained one another in German. While translating for the animals, my eyes skimmed the rest of the news, like notices of festivals or holy days, and who was expected where. What provinces had disease outbreaks, where leper colonies were located, and instructions on the use of a bell to avoid them. There was a table for converting taxes, notices of where, when, and whom to pay. I silently read the important bits while they carried on like hyenas at the nonsense they asked me to read aloud.

"That one," Crixus asked, pointing at scribble, more interested in perversity than news.

"Claudius is a crook," I answered. Luckily a few were illustrated and even Crastus could grasp the lewd depictions without my help. His slow, annoying, deep laugh caused his abnormally large Adam's apple to swing up and down like an olive press each time. Crastus mainly spoke his native German to his fellows, but anyone could tell his mood easily enough. He growled when he was angry and laughed obnoxiously for everything else. I endured Crixus, Crastus, and their private laugh riot with the two least fortunate new slaves in all of Italy. The wall ended at an intersection where a deep-set post stood four feet tall. Tacked to it were notices of the latest official news written on kid leather. I read them quickly, with neither man asking what was written.

"Sheezin kompf?" Crastus asked, slapping my head.

"What?" I answered with attitude, rubbing my head and

making an angry face.

"Vitch wantsin ze bitch at du, zo go, sheezin kompf," Crastus finished, palming my face to push me on my ass. Laughter and pointing ensued between the two as I tried standing.

"It's 'shit for brains,' stupid," Crixus corrected, "not, 'shit head.'" Crastus drank from his wine bladder and laughed louder. They carried on obliviously, each hysterical as they drank, yanking on their slave's leashes. Furious, I rose, brushed myself off, and almost considered cursing them beneath my breath until Crixus' hard, swift kick to my rear jolted me to run away from anything so deadly stupid. "Today, shit mind!" Crixus exclaimed, grabbing the wine bladder from Crastus, who in turn congratulated him for the hilarious new joke as I ran to the baths.

Moving as fast as aching buttocks could carry and hoping Helica could heal bruises, I ran to her with all the official notices etched clearly onto the clay tablet of my mind. The old man watched through milky cataracts as I limped to the bath's entrance.

"The sorceress is waiting inside, kiddo. You're to see her," said the old man, in our language.

"Who's protecting the...enchantress?" I said, using the other Oscan word for sorceress, and felt a tingling sensation across my skin as it left my lips. The old man held up a bent finger and pointed off to the side. Following his ancient, arthritic pointer, Spartacus came into focus.

He sat carving beneath a fig tree, sitting upon a milk maid's stool. He winked at me, smiling in lieu of a wave, and returned his attention to a toy stallion he carved with a large blade. A stolen Roman pilum lay near him, and his newly acquired *gladius* stood upright, stuck into the earth at his right while an enormous Roman shield lay flat upon the grass to his left. I turned to the old man, but he'd vanished and gotten a head start on me down the steps inside. I hurried in after, and he waved his crooked hand to pass when I caught up. Slow efficiency in every movement kept the elderly attendant moving steadily all these years as he mumbled instructions about the bath out of habit, waving at the large pool.

Returning to the baths somehow seemed different a second time. Perhaps it was the *absence* of Romans that made me leery. Paintings, mosaics, and sculptures seemed to watch me eerily as I went; light and water played against ruins of Greek architecture. Sculpted Roman necks seemed to move, turning to follow me on marbled busts. Mosaic, tiled Roman eyes accused as I went, while jet-black creatures slunk in the shadows, disappearing upon closer inspection. Deep inside the narrow hall, the vaulted ceiling opened to a large domed room. Copious amounts of steam rose from the water as I removed my sandals at the dais and placed them beneath the bench. Warmth welcomed my bare feet again as I presented myself at the pool's edge. Water tumbled as auburn lamplight flickered about the ancient room in a voiceless void that lasted so long I thought I may faint.

Unable to take anymore, I blurted, "Whatever it is you want, I'll give." I sounded absurd and felt ashamed for such nonsense once I'd said it.

"I know," Helica cooed. Her voice echoed, betraying her location.

"I have nothing," I admitted sadly. I felt even more foolish.

"Do you have eyes?" she asked hauntingly.

"Yes, lady," I answered, tingling with dread.

"Can I have them?" she dared.

"L-Lady?" I stammered.

"Lift your face, look at me," she demanded softly. Water

distortion thwarted every effort to see her completely; her hair was a shroud dark as night, floating about her. Fleeting glimpses of ivory skin beneath rippling water aroused adolescent desires.

"Your eyes, Publipor, your ears, your mind...will you give them to me?" the siren asked with an icy stare.

I replied by nodding, praying she meant metaphorically.

"Then use your voice now. Tell me what you've seen and heard."

I began by sharing what I thought most important, like official notices on the wall and information written on parchment nailed to a post. Helica allowed me to continue uninterrupted until my memory ran blank. At last, believing everything of relevance had been mentioned but desperate still to please her, I continued rattling like a rock in a box. "There's a trader outside the Capuan Gate, exchanging coin for slave treasure. He—" I was stopped.

"There is, is there?" interrupted Helica, suddenly standing out of the water to her waist. I couldn't help but stare at the black ropes of wet hair, parting behind a long neck, cascading over supple shoulders, covering full breasts. Speechless, I turned to stone with my mouth agape before her radiance. "Publipor, dear boy, please go outside, retrieve my husband, and tell him I'm now ready," Helica directed, releasing me from her spectacle. I turned to retrieve the commander with the image of Helica's femininity stamped onto the coin of my imagination, wondering, *What was she ready for?*

# CHAPTER SIX

"…he held a piece of money from the first payment to his son's nose, asking whether its odor was offensive to him…Titus said, 'No…'"
—Suetonius, *The Lives of the Caesars*

Gavius was born just another poor plebeian making a living off the wealth of Pompeii's patricians. Gavius, a fisherman's son, had a particularly industrious spirit and an unnatural tolerance for risk in business that became emboldened after every successful venture. Gavius began making bricks as a boy, to the consternation of his father, for coins. Using his own forms and formula of mixed straw, mud, and clay, Gavius made bricks in his spare moments between mending nets, leaving them to dry during the day while fishing in the bay of Naples. He sold the catch on shore for his father every evening, only to hurry home and sell bricks at his front door by night.

A teenaged Gavius used his surplus bricks to build a bread oven, and began leasing it to the local baker. Once Gavius' lease earned enough to purchase the amount of flour necessary to turn a profit, he evicted his tenant, thanking the baker for his recipe. Eventually, Gavius' slaves baked enough loaves for him to stop fishing once and for all, to the horror of both parents. Churning out so many, the city contracted with him to pacify masses, hurling Gavius' loaves into the stands between acts. At twenty, tired of being gouged by the local mill, Gavius purchased a stone to grind his own flour at a mill bought with bread and built with Gavius' bricks.

By age thirty, Gavius leveraged his brick business to purchase clay pits on the Isle of Capreae, where he built an industrial kiln and began making amphora transport jars. Soon, the poor fisherman's son had his hand in all sorts of endeavors and bags of coin, producing jars with the initials P.G. stamped into them, filled with olive oil or wine for all parts of the Republic. Gavius' favorite phrase, "Money has no smell," meant Gavius sold without qualm to the capitol and pirates alike. The sayings, "Coins jingle whether minted in Carthage or Rome," and "It's only illegal if you get caught," were often whispered on Gavius' lips.

Word blew like wildfire. Herculaneum had been sacked by escaped gladiators, making the affluent citizens jump in their boats and run to Rome, while those without means ran for escape. In Gavius' mind, the "disaster" citizens referred to presented opportunities. It filled his head with thoughts of asset liquidation at thieves' prices. Gavius would endeavor to exchange easy-to-carry coins that the fugitives preferred for their ill-gotten wares, with a borrowed freeman's slave cap on his head. The cap of the freed slave was his badge, a credible credential for Gavius to steal his countrymen's booty by exchanging currency for fugitive goods, slave treasures like ivory, alabaster, amber, and glass, all purchased for a pittance from smelly, dumb brutes—stupid slaves who had no idea their real worth.

Gavius' enclosed four-wheeled wagon had been parked all day at the impromptu exchange. The crowd of commerce alongside a summer shower tore the earth beneath, tilling it to mud. Gavius tried motivating the mule team with a whip, as fine Arabian rugs tied in bundles swayed awkwardly atop an overloaded cart. Metal clanged as the cart jerked, but the wheels, sunk to their hubs, didn't budge. Tensed wood sang a high-pitched melody of friction, and sturdy muscles shook beneath foaming coats. Gavius thought it odd that slaves would own slaves of their own; a couple of the men held two captives by ropes around their necks. Gavius relented, sitting in the driver's seat, stymied, thinking of ways to extradite himself, when the four new customers approached.

"I'm out of coin, gentlemen," Gavius explained. "As you can see, I'm full of product, but I'll return at dawn with more coin. If you'd be so kind as to help get my wheels started, I'm sure a half-turn will set them free. There'd be a few sesterces in it for each of you," he proposed to the oncoming rabble. Gavius tipped his disguising skull cap, smiling politely to the armed men while hoping they couldn't smell that he was a Pompeiian.

The four menacing men removed hoods and opened cloaks in unison; the two captives made no move to run as the barbarians disrobed. Gavius' eyes opened just a bit wider at the sight of foreign, painted killers. "Wait, sirs, give my mules another chance. Stand back! I don't want anyone getting muddied," he pronounced, stuttering and stalling for time, trying to escape. The lathered team of wild-eyed mules with billowing lungs disagreed. Gavius noticed the blond-haired Gaul with a prominent scar across his chest walk casually to the lead's bridle; he took the animal's muzzle in hand and soothed the beasts with calm tones. Gavius, from the driver's seat, watched a somehow familiar-looking mountain of a man with dark eyes stride alone into the muck, sporting expensive-looking horse tattoos across an ample chest. The lone fierce barbarian held out a hand for Gavius' whip.

Gavius paused momentarily, reservation on his face, then complied hesitantly, handing it down without protest. "I have travel mates waiting for my return, friends," Gavius commented.

"If friend we be, you arrived, *friend*," the black-haired behemoth retorted. "This, your new friend, Oenomaus."

Oenomaus, standing beside the mule's bridles, lifted his chin. "This, new friend, Crastus." Spartacus gestured to the circling lanky, tattooed German. "That, Crastus slave." Spartacus pointed at the captured Roman soldier.

"*Aw, aw, aw.*" Crastus belted his obtuse drawl at the absurdity, following Crixus to the mud hole's edge.

"That, new friend, be Crixus," the leader of the vicious men continued, pointing now to the red-haired, snake-covered clod, "and *his* slave." Crixus clapped his slave's neck.

"Say hello, to *friend*, bitch dog," Crixus admonished the captured veteran. The Roman gravely nodded salutation.

"I am Spartacus. Sulla's dog, the Roman calls me, though not to my face," smiled the massive barbarian, the realization almost smiting the man dumb. Almost. "Have you heard of me?" he asked, cocking his head. Gavius, fully embroiled in negotiation for life, thought quickly through a haze of terror, finally realizing he'd been detained by the famous escaped Capuan gladiator's leader himself: Spartacus of Thrace. Gavius' mind flashed to a spectacle he'd seen from the stands just a year prior, where he'd watched this very man penetrate armor and win handily in a very quick, unsportsmanlike match. His concentration returned to survival as cold, black shark eyes stared unremittingly into his.

"Yes, uh hem," Gavius squirmed. "Well, it's an honor, Spartacus, a most prestigious honor, sir." Crixus exhaled a huff and groaned, rolling his eyes in an expression of disgust.

"Just lick his ass already, Roman," demanded Crixus, disgusted at the pandering Pompeiian. Crastus belted laughter at the quip.

"But gentlemen," begged Gavius, "I must return to my children. I'm a widower, you see, and they could starve." Gavius fumbled with his woolen skull cap crumbling through nervous, fidgeting fingers.

"Yes, children must eat," Spartacus reassured, nodding. "You master, he must be most...benevolent." Gavius looked confused upon the driver's seat while processing the comment. "Have callous not on wrist, not on neckline. You head, you hand—no owner mark," charged Spartacus in workable Latin.

"I...uh...hem—my owner, he, he shackled, only the ankles," replied the terrified swindler. The barbarian reached up to the floorboard and lifted Gavius' long tunic. "It's, it's...on the other—" Instantly, Spartacus pulled Gavius violently down by his ankle into the muck. Oenomaus calmed the frightened mules as Crixus and Crastus flanked the mudhole, swords drawn.

"Please!" the mud-covered man pleaded, sitting in the muck. "I'm just a slave, recently freed. I didn't know..." he exclaimed, wailing for life.

"Freed, from where?" Spartacus asked. Gavius flashed frightened looks to Crixus and Crastus, grateful they preferred to keep their *caligae* dry. "How long, you free...and by who?" Spartacus repeated, standing to his shins in mud and holding the filthy man by his hair. Gavius' eyes rolled side to side as incoherent thoughts raced. His mouth motioned while words stumbled from his lips. Gavius looked into Spartacus' unflinching black eyes and knew the man saw through him. Gavius closed his, weeping for a quick death.

"Frau!" Crastus hurled his worst insult from the muck's edge.

"*Mollitia Romanista!*" Crixus spat the Roman slur for 'softness,' in its feminine suffix, while pointing his sword at the man.

"How long?" Spartacus asked again, deliberately slower, wrenching Gavius' hair harder in his palm.

"I'm not a slave...I-I'm a businessman. P-Please, s-spare me," Gavius squealed, praying truth would finally bring mercy.

"From where you come? And address me as *lord*," Spartacus corrected, inches from the terrified man's face.

"P-P-Pompeii! L-Lord!" cried the merchant, sobbing.

"Pompeii, say you!" exclaimed Spartacus, cheerily. Spartacus released the man's filthy hair, asking, "Why not you say so first?"

"Who gives a cow shit? That fucking cart's mine!" Crixus snarled. Raising his sword, Crixus glanced at Crastus, who nodded in agreement. Oenomaus stepped beneath the mule's neck and drew his own sword from its scabbard; Spartacus subtly shook his head.

"Crixus, will you slave carry everything you steal?" asked Spartacus, bobbing his head at a wretch holding a canvas bag over its shoulder.

"If they want life," answered Crixus, jabbing toward the captive soldier with his sword.

"You make yourself—shepherd of men? Watch that many slaves, carrying all that shit up the Alps?" asked Spartacus. "Get more in coin over mountain, besides, you make self storekeeper, try sell all this shit on other side?" Spartacus turned to Crastus and said, "Crastus, you believe Roman survive climb? Think they make other side with all you trinkets?" while pointing at the wretched, naked captive. Crixus and Crastus looked at one another in wordless reasoning, lowering their swords. Crixus angrily pointed with his unarmed left.

"I do it with that fucking cart, *Thracian!*" threatened Crixus, and spitefully, he spat on the ground. Spartacus dismissed the German, extending a helping hand to Gavius.

"Sacrifice, for Dionysus," Spartacus commented to Gavius. "Before slaves travel west, Pompeiian join slave, feast this night? Maybe in need of coin, after all." Spartacus helped the man to stand. "Roman coin, no northern counterfeits." Spartacus raised his brows and bored into the man for understanding. The merchant watched, stunned, as the blond, mustached gladiator tilted his head, mouthing the words, *West, into the sea?* with raised palms at Spartacus. Then Gavius looked to see the lanky one covered in weaved tattoos unsuccessfully work out with long fingers how many coins a slave could carry before giving up. Then Gavius watched with terror as the big red brute, Crixus, eyed his mired cart. The filthy swindler stood with help from the barbarian, bewildered just to be alive, wondering how he'd become a guest of slaves and not another captive in their possession for amusement.

Everyone was confused—everyone except Spartacus.

### A BOY EMULATES HIS HERO; 682 AUC (73 BC)

Carving a lump of root beneath the shade of a fig tree, I sat upon a three-legged milking stool with a Spanish sword stuck in the dirt to my right and a small shield lying to my left, playing watchman. I pretended to guard for Spartacus and the Pompeiian as they used the bath to talk business.

Sitting vigil at the bath's entrance, the old man slept in sunlight with his arms crossed, while a girl ran past with a skin of wine. Shaking my head, I chuckled at the old man's ineptitude as a sentinel, and was suddenly startled by an unseen voice asking, "What are you doing, boy?"

I froze and turned to look.

It was just Gannicus, a Roman ex-slave with dark hair and olive skin from Capua. He was not a creature with bat ears or cat eyes at all. I exhaled, relieved.

"I'm guarding the door for Spartacus," I said, feigning indifference.

"You sure you're not trying to open a vein, fumbling with that?" he asked, motioning his head at the lump of root that had no semblance of a horse. Gannicus sat on his heels in front of a mulberry bush, examining me.

"I'm ready to die for my commander," I said, foolishly.

"Looks like that's *all* you'll do," he retorted, remaining

completely still.

"Where's your pilum?" Gannicus had sized me up too well; I'd looked for a javelin all over, trying to imitate Spartacus, but they were all being hoarded. I attempted to carry off a large shield as well, but gave up, wondering, *How can a man carry something so heavy, much less fight with it?*

"I don't throw spears," I said, haughty, pretending to know the business of arms at the ripe old age of thirteen.

"You don't know much," quipped Gannicus. "Besides, I can't teach a 'know-it-all' anything." He dismissed me, stood, and turned to leave.

"I know plenty, Gannicus, just ask Spartacus. He'll vouch for me," I replied, invoking my lord's name.

Gannicus turned to face me once more. "You are amusement," he said, "useful for the moment. Helica sees some kind of purpose you'll serve, but once that happens, you'll be discarded." His words stabbed like a dagger and my anger swelled, causing me to shake involuntarily.

"I hampered the soldiers' shields!" I shouted, rising to my feet. "I serve Helica's cult." I was on the verge of tears, incensed.

"Yesterday is worth shit," replied Gannicus. "Today is the day you must pay, *boy*." My heart pounded; irrational fury overtook me to the point of trembling. "Are you an officer, *boy*?" he asked.

"No," I answered, frightened and fuming.

"Then why the sword on your left?" Gannicus inquired. *It's what Spartacus did*, I thought, immediately recognizing the childishness of the answer. I remained silent. "Battles are won with shields and men, *boy*," continued Gannicus. "Roman soldiers lock shields with their left and stab with the right. The army with the most men should always win, except we Romans fight outnumbered...why?" He paused for an answer he knew I didn't have. "If you can't hold the big shield in the left and stab with the right like the Hoplites of old, then *you're* useless." His words ignited my shame. "We aren't too proud to steal what works from any enemy. Our swords and horses are Spanish or Numidian; our shields, our ships, Greek. You name it, we got it somewhere else. The city itself was settled by Trojan refugees and even our first women were taken from the neighbors." I'd calmed a little from listening to the brief lesson when he began to jab at me again. "So, can you?" Gannicus asked.

"What?" I said, like an imbecile.

"Hold a shield and *othismos* within the cohort?" he asked about "the shoving" of shields, then spoke aloud to himself. "I think Helica might be wrong about you, kid."

"No. Can you?" I retorted, sick of criticism.

"No. The difference being, I don't pretend that I can," replied Gannicus, with sober, sad brown eyes. A long silence enveloped the moment until Gannicus broke it. "Spartacus is shifty," he added.

"Shifty?" I asked, wondering if I should be offended for my lord.

"He can change hands in the middle of a fight," Gannicus explained. "And by the way, you can't hide worth a damn, either."

"What?"

"You can't hide from a chalk-blind woman, and you didn't see Crixus until he held you like a kitten. You couldn't see Spartacus sitting in the shade until an old man showed you, and you don't even know that I watch you." He counted my inabilities with his fingers.

"Well—I—" I stammered, stunned stupid.

"How's your night vision?" Gannicus interrupted, changing the subject once more. "I've seen you try to make me out in the dark. Other than the dogs, you've gotten closest to discovering me coming into camp at night." Suddenly a compliment? I couldn't get my bearings with this man.

Gannicus asked about my ears with a whisper, almost inaudible.

"I have perfect hearing, *Roman*," I replied, smugly determined not to be bested at the game of wits any longer. Gannicus straightened his face and stepped toward me. My fear returned as he approached.

"My name is Gannicus, little shepherd," he challenged, but I remained steadfast, unflinching, no longer rising to the bait. "If you want to play barbarian, hurry up and die, and stop eating our food." Gannicus paused a moment when I held my ground, then softened. "You've a good sense of direction. I've seen you mark time with shadows, heard you count steps in town to keep from getting lost. I've seen you read two languages and heard you speak four. If you want to serve a real purpose, lay off the un-watered wine and come with me tonight."

Eager to change the subject, I asked, "Why do Romans dilute their wine with water, but the Gauls don't?" Gannicus' countenance seemed to change and he refused to face me.

"Because only Gauls and *fools* take Dionysus' spirit straight to the head."

"What about the festival of sacrifices and feast in the *piazza* tonight?" I asked, selfishly childlike, stopping him.

"I'm talking about after. Meet me at the Capuan Gate tonight," Gannicus replied over his shoulder. I stepped back toward the stool once more when he'd gone, and turned to sit, when I was suddenly confronted by the old man standing silently before me. Startled, I tumbled, landing on my back. The old man gummed a smile, fanned his arms, and rasped a wet laugh at my awkwardness.

"Did I sneak up on you, kiddo?" the ancient playfully asked in Oscan.

"I just didn't want to break your little bird bones," I answered angrily. The old man laughed more and began hacking a cough, reaching with a gnarled arthritic hand to offer help that I waved off; the old man labored to sit instead, patting my leg.

"Never thought I'd be free twice in my life," mused the old man in my parents' language, wistful beneath the fig tree's shade.

"Were you born free?" I asked. The old man hooted, waving his leathery hand to indicate he hadn't. Light danced across his wrinkled and spotted face.

"Oh, no, child. I was born a slave to slaves on the island of Sicily, ages ago," he stated, staring with milky eyes into thin air in the afternoon's warmth.

"What happened? Did you earn citizenship and lose it?" I asked, working the puzzle.

"Oh, no, kiddo. My father and his fellows threw off the Roman overlords on the island when I was about the age you are now." An almost toothless grin overtook his face as he spoke. "We took over the estates. I slept in a bed with furs and stole a pony." He chuckled, remembering fondly.

"What happened?"

After a time, he answered, "The Romans took it back."

"And?" I asked, captivated.

"My father was crucified, my mother...buried alive...then they took me," the old man replied, patting my leg again and straining to stand.

"Will you come with us?" I inquired as he straightened with great effort.

"Oh, no, kiddo. Twice lucky is plenty for an old man."

"What will you do when we leave?"

"Die free, I suppose," said the old man, shuffling away.

I took my seat again and quickly found myself stewing from Gannicus' rebukes, oblivious to what the old man had shared and the implications his words would have in my next three harrowing years. At that time, I couldn't see past the petty anger of the moment, promising myself never to have anything to do with Gannicus from then on. I'd no idea then how close to Gannicus I'd become, nor all the close calls and bloody adventures we'd have together. It's funny how we don't see the impact people have at crossroads in our lives until years later. Though I'd never have believed it at the time, Gannicus and I would become thick as thieves, and I'd eventually know things about the man that he would never share with another soul. Gannicus confided once that his brother Va, a deaf eunuch of substantial girth, worked the *ludis* of Capua as a trainer. I'd learn how Va had held a shield for men as they broke themselves upon it in training at the school. I'd hear how Gannicus fetched water, straw, and maintained the *ludis'* needs, while his brother Va, a completely deaf and mostly mute giant who made only one sound in exertion, came to the *ludis*. The noise became Va's name; men shouted it lovingly from the benches whenever Va bested a man in practice. "Va!" they screamed, I was told, in affection for the big man, yelling each time the eunuch grunted. Gannicus confessed one day that Va, the eldest, and he were born to prominent Capuan rose dealers and about the guilt Gannicus carried over squandering his brother's inheritance.

I knew babies like Va were usually left exposed or sacrificed. They were considered a curse from the gods—punishment for sinful parents. Fortunately for Va, mothers can't see deafness in infants and most fathers don't waste time looking, unless the baby lives a few years. In time, it became apparent that Va couldn't hear and would never speak. Va's parents took him to Rome as a boy, where he was castrated by the Virgins of Vestal, forever ending the family curse. Gannicus explained how responsibility of the firstborn now fell upon the second: him. He told me about how he efficiently ran the family business until the time of their father's death, when, unexpectedly, their mother, a harsh taskmaster, died soon after. Gannicus explained how, without her constant nagging, he quickly lost interest in being up to his elbows in manure, feeding roses and constantly hustling them north for Rome's tedious celebrations.

Gannicus confessed to discovering Capua's lavish nightlife, soon preferring to drink wine and attend orgies at the palatial Capuan homes while entertaining fellow merchants. Instead of tediously working, Gannicus enjoyed wearing expensive, loose-fitting togas, eating exotic foods, and spending extravagantly to impress his peers, even going so far as to become a fish fancier; a raging fad among Romans at the time was to see who could support the most lavish aquariums.

Within two years, Gannicus lamented, their business began to falter with neglect. The parties soon became boring and friends became as sparse as profits. Gannicus was reduced to stumbling into brothels that quickly stripped him of his last coin and tossed him out. Gannicus confessed that Va carrying him home in the mornings, smelling of fermented fruit and vomit, became a local Capuan fixture for a time. Until, finally, the day of destitution arrived. With nothing left to leverage or borrow, they were forced to forfeit their parents' home. Va's once-profitable fragrant rose business had been run to stinking ruin by Gannicus the second-born.

Toward the end, Gannicus sold himself and his brother into slavery for a jug of cheap wine, foolishly believing their new lives would resemble his parents' pampered domestic slaves. The moment Gannicus' new owner found it necessary, they were both liquidated to the *ludis*. Gannicus sobered for good, cleaning latrine buckets while his sweet-tempered, giant brother Va became a practice dummy. Even knowing all of that about the man, I loved him, and would never have survived the war without Gannicus Varinius' training.

# CHAPTER SEVEN

**"He also celebrated the obsequies of his officers who had fallen...and ordered his captives to fight at the pyres...a giver of shows."**

—Florus, *The War Against Spartacus*

The smell of roasting meat filling the air made me salivate as blazes, bright as the sun, lit the forum like daylight. Slaves played tunes of their regions with strange wind instruments while women danced around various pyres. Every conceivable food was available to everyone, offered on long benches and tables set all about outside in the warm starry night. Pigs on spits turned and glazed crisp while entire sides of beef with tripe and sweetbreads were laid out in various cuts for the picking. Exotic *hors d'oeuvres* of mice and voles, salted anchovies, olives, dates, and honeyed figs were on display for everyone's enjoyment.

"Sheezin kompf, zie drinken!" Crastus shouted as he emerged from the throng, handing me his bladder among the pressing masses within the amphitheater grounds.

"I can't tonight, Crastus," I pleaded, refusing with a palm.

"Vas ist vong? Du vooman partz zie bleeden, sheezin kompf?" asked Crastus at the slight.

"Stupid! I told you already, it's 'shit for brains,' not 'shit head,' in Roman girl talk," Crixus interjected, correcting Crastus in their shared language, while disparaging Latin. "You say what in skull, not what Pube think," Crixus explained, this time butchering Latin for my benefit, pointing at his own head.

"Drinken zie, sheezin zought!" yelled Crastus, attempting the insult once more in his terrible Latin. Crixus shook and then slapped his own head at the depths of Crastus' density. I escaped their routine by quickly walking away.

At center stage sat the table of honor. Above a crowded heap of people, Spartacus sat in the table's middle with Helica to his right. Oenomaus, dining to Spartacus' left, waved for me to approach. I ran to him, stopping abruptly with the stage up to my chest, gawking at a row of demigods above.

"Will you sit with me tonight, Publipor?" Oenomaus shouted from his elevated seat upon the theater's stage.

"I will," I said, smiling.

"Have you eaten?" Helica interrupted.

"No, lady," I answered.

Helica straddled the long bench and rose to her feet, walking around where I stood below. She stopped to gather items from the table, handing a terracotta plate down with polished utensils. Oenomaus washed his hands in a large basin, rinsing them in clean water before returning to eat. Spartacus smiled down and winked, dining with utensils.

The image struck me. *These men, they aren't slave-like at all,* I thought. The gladiators I knew spoke respectfully and shared everything with humble dignity...mostly. Spartacus drank, washing his food down, then called out to me. "Publipor, go with Gannicus tonight. Listen, do what Gannicus say, please," he commanded from his perch.

I nodded, secretly hoping to avoid the task as Helica held my hand beneath the plate, when she produced a small bowl, pouring a fragrant paste with a mischievous grin. *Garum,* or fish sauce: the most delicious addition to any food I'd ever snuck. My mouth watered at the pungent smell of fermented fish innards. I couldn't wait to get something to put it on as Helica crumbled salt onto my plate and released her grasp. Helica stopped me with a finger before I could run off. "Eat figs, olives, and bread, not just meat," she instructed.

"Yes, lady—Lady Helica," I replied, excited by her touch and attention. Helica stood and returned to the table, retrieving a sheathed dagger and a large flagon for water. Helica stooped to drape a sling about my neck, handing me the sheathed dagger. I set my plate down nearby to admire the blade wrought with engraved grapes along its length. The large brass-hilted dagger had a leatherbound handle and was sharp as sin upon my thumb. Helica knelt even lower, reaching for the cord of rope used to hold my garment closed. Pulling at it, Helica untied my tunic nearly to opening. A flush ran through my loins, causing me to instinctually recoil. Helica giggled.

"Keep it wrapped tight, Publipor," Helica instructed, smiling wickedly. She tucked the blade behind the cord and tied it firmly. "Sharpen the blade constantly and keep it oiled. It'll be useful for a long time." The woman kissed my forehead, then stood. When Spartacus, Oenomaus, and the Pompeiian raised their mugs in salute, I lifted my flagon, returning the gesture. Donning the water flagon and grabbing my plate, I went to find a spit of meat. Unfortunately, I ran into the jackals instead, as Crixus and Crastus sauntered past to their place among the table of honor.

"Hey, stupid," Crixus said, chewing a tongue sandwich. *Damn it,* I thought as the duo noticed me. I saw they ate with filthy hands.

"Yes...commander?" I asked, pretending to be tasked with an errand.

"Little Pubes, don't let Gannicus pregnate you tonight in forest," said Crixus, releasing the punchline as Crastus laughed, while thrusting his hips at me.

"Yes, commander," I replied, running off back toward the theater before either could attempt a kick.

Mount Vesuvius loomed above all, blotting out huge swaths of stars low on the horizon as Herculaneum burned all around. Exhausted slaves camped upon the road for the night, trundled up bedrolls instead, following Herculaneum's welcoming beacon. The slaves came in sporadic groups and were welcomed with hospitality as they entered the city's opened gates. Sitting on side steps, shoving fish-paste-slathered meat into my mouth with both hands, I noticed a familiar face.

"Can you ride?" Gannicus asked as he approached.

I nodded, chewing, regretting not lying that I couldn't.

"Meet at the Capuan Gate tonight, after the last sacrifice," he said. "Dress warm, be armed, and bring water."

I nodded again, thumbing the sling on the new water flagon wrapped about my chest. I chewed my mouthful slowly, hoping he'd leave. Loud drums suddenly boomed, commanding attention to the amphitheater's stage.

A throng of slaves packed the stone steps, and four slave leaders stood on a stage where Greek tragedies had played just a day prior. Oenomaus walked towards the stage edge, a commanding presence, his golden hair catching the moonlight.

"It appears we've worn out our welcome," announced Oenomaus, arms outstretched before the masses. The crowd laughed heartily. "A real legion," he continued, "four cohorts of two thousand men, has been detached from Rome to kill us and take back the city. It'll be here tomorrow." He let the stark revelation sink in with a pause. A hush overtook the once-rowdy crowd as the decree's reality began to take hold. Oenomaus continued, "Come morning, we take the trail to Vesuvius' summit. Those able are welcome; bury your treasures and ascend with all the water you can carry. Each of you is charged with bringing a bundle of straw and extra clothing. Those infirmed or unable, fill your bellies, be our guests, and may Dionysus find you hidden well on the morn."

The masses sat silent as Spartacus stepped forward. "Up there," Spartacus announced, pointing at the mountain. "Roman approach will be visible from that perch. There! The few count as many, up there, slave find way out," proclaimed the giant. "Slave climb heaven, demand gods deliver slave from Roman chains! This night, eat, drink, have joy, for tomorrow, slave may die!" The crowd screamed in rapturous approval as Helica sauntered across the stage wearing an ivy headdress and a linen dress that flowed with every step. With a live snake wrapped around her neck and a pinecone-tipped fennel staff in hand, Helica moved to address the crowd. I followed the wiggle of her breasts when she raised her arms; silence gripped the crowd. Helica began singing praises to her god in an exotic language with high, haunting tones. The woman sang a song of pain and hope, beautifully matched with a single flute played by Egus, revealing yet another of his seemingly never-ending hidden talents. Emotion moved me, though I didn't know a single word from the forlorn song. Slaves sat frozen, mesmerized, wanting more.

"Slaves! Foreigners! Women! People of Dionysus!" Helica proclaimed when she'd finished singing. Using the snake to point at the dark mound looming above, she said, "Vesuvius, the mountain where Rome's Jupiter surpasses Apollo's Olympus." She paused. "That is where Dionysus will plead on our behalf! We'll present the Hercules of our age to the gods!" Helica shouted skyward, "Here, at the bottom of Jupiter's Mountain, we start our pilgrimage in gratitude to you, O God of Slaves! We climb steps to your chamber and ask that you hear our cry for deliverance." Helica bowed, and the women of Dionysus' cult bowed with her.

"Help us, Dionysus, as we offer you these gifts." She suddenly stood erect once more, the throng of female supporters rising with her.

The entire mob, on the edge of their seats, listened intently.

"Anoint the Hercules of our age!" screamed Helica, to raucous roars. "If you supported Mithradates in the past," she screamed, pointing at the mob, "then fight for Spartacus now!"

The crowd erupted rapturously as the cult of women genuflected while singing praises to their spiritual matriarch. The women departed when Spartacus, Crixus, Oenomaus, and Crastus stepped forward abreast, facing the frenzied mob filling the amphitheaters steps.

Silence overtook the crowd when Spartacus spoke. "Herculaneum, slave army, I promise nothing, offer only freedom, here, now. If join, you may get bloody, you may die, or could even—get rich." Spartacus raised his chin. "Either way, slave free now." Spartacus dropped his gaze, scanning the crowd. "Slave, understand not a word of *home*. Most you slaves, born slaves here, but new world to north, to east, where Roman number few. A place, slave know not. We plan to return there, free men. Slave scale Alpines, slave become free. No Roman catch slave up frozen pass. Once we cross, we separate, become, slaves no more." Spartacus' jaw clinched, balling a fist that became a pointer. "Oenomaus take Celt to Gaul." Oenomaus, the blond Celt, saluted with his sword from the stage. Spartacus continued, "Crixus lead Germans cross Rhone, to Germania." The tattooed Germans punched their fists in their palms, snarling. "Italian free to go as they wish," continued the commander. "Italian, find maroon colony, outside of Roman influence in Toga Gaul, hide in hills with Samnites best bet, I say, for Italian slave. People of the East, with me!" Spartacus boomed, thumping the inked horses on his chest. "We slaves demand, this night, on Roman shrine, that we make altar to Helica's god, the

God of Wine, the God of Slaves. We drain Roman blood this night, to you, O Dionysus! May this sacrifice intoxicate you and make this our freedom's offering," Spartacus proclaimed, clenching his fists to the sky. "All you immortal gods of Mount Olympus! Hear us! We demand this!" Spartacus sprawled his fingers, addressing the crowd. "Today, slave run, but tomorrow, slave open enough Roman throats; make every Roman pay slaves—" Spartacus' rage was painted upon an angry face, "to leave!"

The crowd's eruption continued as Crixus and Crastus worked them to a fury, pumping muscular, tattooed arms skyward while whirling swords danced to booming stolen drums. In the periphery, slaves produced a filthy, naked centurion from the stage's side steps. The formerly imposing man, now bent with weight beneath his stocks, appeared wretched as he was forced to the stage's edge.

"Grateful slaves!" Crixus antagonized. "Show *producer,* proper gratitude." He mocked, introducing the pathetic centurion in a game of farce, nearly shoving him with a kick from the stage's roost into the murderous throng below. "This, *optio primo,* the sergeant major, to Gaius Marius, the Savior of Rome!" Crixus proclaimed in his very best Latin, drawing out the exaggerated title in mock Roman pomposity. "Rule over game, and judge for you, 'the great unwashed,' who shall live, and who shall die," concluded the German, raising his thick red brows, panning for effect.

An enraged mob hissed and whistled, screaming at the bound centurion with blind hostility at the demeaning proclamation. The starved centurion tried eating the rotten food thrown at him while pinned beneath the crush of heavy stocks. Crastus forced the kneeling man's head up by his hair, encouraging the mob to jeer further. I laughed out loud when one slave pushed his way to the front but was unable to urinate a stream high enough to reach the captive. Spartacus walked Helica from the dais to her seat in the front row, holding her hand the entire way. Before sitting, Helica ran her hands beneath the dress, daintily regal. Oenomaus handed Spartacus a huge, orange terracotta mug as I ran to cash in on the invitation Oenomaus had made earlier. The Celt sidled over, making room. Spartacus leaned behind Oenomaus, handing me his mug, and when I refused, Spartacus winked and smiled, nodding approval for passing the test.

"Next fight good, you like," Crixus promised the crowd, working them on stage with Crastus, his ever-present, wicked shadow. Self-liberated slaves pushed ex-soldiers, naked and bound, onto stage left. "From Roman shit ditches herself, we present to you, this dickless eunuch!" Crixus shouted, extending an arm at the condemned man thrown on stage. More free slaves pushed his opponent and former comrade onto the opposite side with the centurion framing the foreground, still trapped in his stocks. "Versus, this worthless pile, hailing from Roman cesspool of his mother's crotch." Crixus continued, this time speaking seriously to the combatants, "Winner, we award food and freedom." He bent to a blood-soaked basket laying at his feet. In it was a huge cow's liver. Crixus lifted the beef organ with both hands, licking his lips with mock delight. The crowd rewarded his hijinks with uproarious laughter. "Crastus, pick *felix* Roman!" Crixus beckoned Crastus to pick a lucky winner.

On cue, Crastus tossed his sword sidelong in the air to land with a metallic *clank*, grinding to a halt on lime-based cement, its point halted stage right. "Dickless, win knife, good end!" Crixus exclaimed, cutting loose the bonds at the man's wrists. Turning, Crixus walked to the opposite man, cutting loose his bonds as well, leering with his hideous, yellow-fanged smile. Crixus placed the knife into the condemned man's palm, daring the Roman to use it. The former soldier refused Crixus' bait. Soon the gladiators

Egus and Vidovic were prodding at the men with spears, forcing former comrades to close ground for *damnation ad gladium,* condemnation by combat.

The armed man weighed his options momentarily, then lunged suddenly at his unarmed compatriot. "Got money on you, Dickless. Do not let me down, or I kill you twice," joked Crixus. Worthless grasped Dickless' hand mid-stab, sweeping his opponent's leg behind the knee. Falling together, Worthless struggled to control Dickless' wrist in a deadly stalemate. The crowd hooted with pleasure at the life-and-death contest playing out before their eyes. I bounced on the edge of my seat, spectating from the front row next to Oenomaus, watching then what I thought at the time was my first gladiator match.

Worthless somehow managed to turn the knife away onto Dickless as they struggled. Slowly, the knife inched closer to the neck of the man on bottom, the blade shaking violently in both of their hands; it began to pierce. At that moment, I placed myself inside the losing man's skin and became angry with the crowd rooting for death. The sadness of being murdered by a friend brought a tear that I wiped quickly before anyone saw it. Dickless gutturally groaned, then relented, allowing the blade into his neck. Blood sprayed from the wound onto the winner, painting everything with dark crimson. Choking spasms quickly stilled in a dark red pool of slippery stickiness, draining onto the stage in rivers.

The crowd exploded exuberantly over the man's death. Satisfaction hung on Helica's face, as did the enjoyment with which Spartacus watched the bout. It saddened me further, wondering what these two had to have endured to hate so deeply. *How many friends has Spartacus had to kill? What had they done to her?* I wondered.

"Don't worry, son," said Oenomaus, interrupting my thoughts.

"We're just doing to them what they'd do to us. This is for all the men who didn't make it out." Oenomaus could tell by my expression that I struggled with the concept, so he lightened the mood by pulling two coins from his purse. "Bet that guy wins his next match, what say you?" he asked, sliding two sesterces between his thumb and pointer. I had that, plus a silver denarius; I had no idea of its value, but didn't want to lose it.

"I don't have any coin," I lied.

"What?" Oenomaus exclaimed, pretending surprise. "Did you not earn pay for the raid?" he asked, fully knowing the answer.

"I-I don't want to lose them," I admitted, not wanting to be caught lying to Oenomaus again.

"You'll have four, if your man wins," explained Oenomaus.

"I'll have none if he loses," I said.

"Clever boy," Oenomaus commented, smiling. "Nothing wagered is nothing gained, boy." He rasped the coins together again, tempting me.

"That guy?" I asked, pointing at the wretch.

"Nope, that's my guy, take the fresh one," Oenomaus winked. I took the man's measure standing above me; he looked sturdy but exhausted.

"All right, the fresh one then," I agreed, "but the winner just won...won't he be set free?" I reached into my new purse, careful not let Oenomaus see my lone silver piece.

"Do you really think Crixus will let that soldier go?" asked Oenomaus, stacking his two coins on the stone between us. I placed my two on top of his and waited with vested interest for the next match. Crixus triumphantly walked across the stage, emptying his mug onto the centurion trapped in stocks.

"What use, have you, Roman?" Crixus asked, cursing the captive to return his attention once more to the crowd. "Lousy contest!" he proclaimed. "No sport, whatsoever; but every champion is due, victory's spoil." Crastus tossed the cow's liver, and it landed in a wet sop at the winded man's feet. The starved soldier-turned-slave bit greedily and chewed his prize. "Now, Roman eat, is time for freedom," Crixus announced.

The crowd jeered disapproval while the blood-covered victor looked dubious. Crixus stripped the knife at sword-point. "There, I free you...of knife!" he yelled, delighting the mob. "Crastus, champ, need new challenger!" Crastus grinned and nodded, to roaring approval.

The inequity of it turned my stomach. The man had been offered freedom if he bested an opponent. Exhausted and disarmed, the ex-soldier was thrown back into combat. Though I'd hoped to win the bet, the cruelty was sickening. I looked again at the two men I respected and the woman I adored, hating the enjoyment plastered to their faces. *What horrors they must have endured to derive pleasure from this?* I thought again, when Crixus introduced a fresh captive on stage to jeering from the mob of spectators cramming the amphitheater.

"How does a field slave know how to read?" Oenomaus asked me suddenly, over the din.

"My owner thought I was smart enough to be domesticated," I replied, turning from the spectacle.

"Then why turn you out into the fields?" Oenomaus asked.

"My owner said I was...*too* smart," I answered during a lull. Oenomaus scoffed appreciatively, tossing back a drink. On stage, the champion retained his title handily as the challenger slipped while trying to grasp a blood-slicked opponent. The winner, stripped of his knife once more, had a new opponent introduced. I suppressed my feelings of pity for the man and for my lost fortune.

"Gannicus is smart," added Oenomaus, over clamorous noise, gathering up the four sesterces to hand them to me.

"What?" I asked, prying my attention from the combatants long enough to take the money without thinking. I'd heard what was said, but I fished for further explanation and a reprieve from the depraved spectacle all while holding Oenomaus' winnings in my palm.

"Gannicus is...*very* smart," Oenomaus reiterated, buzzed from alcohol. "Many of us think you'd be useful to our cause, if he trained you." He took another hearty swig as a buxom foreign woman with hair the color of cornsilk batted her eyes and filled his mug. Oenomaus smiled, holding the mug steady while they flirted with their eyes. His gaze continued to follow the woman as she moved down the row, pouring wine for others.

"Trained for what?" I asked, dismayed by the stack of coins now resting in my hand.

"*Exploratores*, scouting and wayfinding, that sort of thing," Oenomaus answered, distracted once more in the search of the serving woman. "Listen to Gannicus, learn everything you can." His gaze stayed on the woman while the exhausted, blood-soaked, naked soldier on stage was again stripped of the knife and a fresh opponent was brought forth. Crixus created another degrading description for the new challenger. This time, when goaded by spears, the champion grasped the opponent's blade hand, guiding it to fall upon escape. Crastus angrily put three coins in Crixus' palm—the same three they'd already exchanged. Their wager, now a wash, made Crastus laugh terribly.

"Oenomaus, I lost," I admitted, reminding the Celt of our own wager. Oenomaus raised his blond brows and looked into my hand.

"Doesn't look like it," he replied, closing my hand with his.

Fires were fed more of Herculaneum as the intense blazes illuminated the amphitheater's stage bright as day. "Why does Spartacus act so...Greek?" I asked.

"Greek?" Oenomaus scoffed.

"He eats with utensils," I explained. "He has manners; even tries to talk like them."

"Spartacus' spirit has more *mos maiorum* than most Romans. Spartacus is what Romans aspire to be, and it disgusts them to see nobility in someone beneath them," Oenomaus explained. "His father was ordered to submit hostages when his people were conquered. By twenty, Spartacus was already a knight. *Equites,* your people call them," Oenomaus added in his Gallic-accented Latin, taking a long pull from his mug.

"καβαλάρης?" Cavalry, I clarified my query in Greek.

"Exactly," affirmed Oenomaus in Latin. "Spartacus led a detachment of Roman cavalry for eight years. Our man was Sulla's deadliest hand. Most of Pompey's boasts against Mithradates were Spartacus' accomplishments." Oenomaus bragged reverently of our commander's former life. "Spartacus returned with Sulla to kill Romans in Rome. It was Spartacus who gave the Colline Gate to Sulla, not Crassus. A barbarian outwitting the children of Mars," Oenomaus mused, shaking his head. Drinking deeply, upending the cup, Oenomaus continued, "Sulla could never have won the Civil War or seized sole power without the barbarian."

Within Oenomaus' description, I pictured a twenty-something Spartacus in my mind: the image of a youthful foreigner, shaving twice a day to look more Roman. Oenomaus described a motivated young man, so eager for citizenship that the barbarian shone above ranks of ardent, brave counterparts. With my mind's eye, I saw Roman-cropped black hair, with an eagle stamped prominently on his breastplate, thick oiled leather lined in leopard fur with a polished Spanish sword, worn on the left in an ornate scabbard. His nose wouldn't have been caved yet. His ear would have been whole and his mouth full of teeth. A man of unyielding determination and loyalty, an outsourced foreigner conscripted to subdue a republic for Rome's first *dictator ad vitam*: *Felix Sulla*—Sulla the Lucky.

"What happened?" I asked. Oenomaus turned up the large mug, finding it empty.

"Sulla died a year after retiring." Oenomaus looked for a hole in the bottom of the mug, then pitched it down. The Celt rose, frustrated and dry, staggering away in search of the pale woman from Gaul armed with a pitcher. The crowd hawed briskly when another veteran killed his comrade on stage for the amusement of slaves. The tired spectacle had quickly become tedious, and I grabbed my midsection as I was seized by gut-wrenching pain.

"Sweet boy, you have no need to feel sorry for these *Romans*," Helica reassured. "They are wicked, damnable servants of evil; they're the enemy of mankind. It's necessary we give them to the gods, so they'll take notice of us and intercede."

"It...it's not the sacrifice, Lady...Lady Helica," I stammered, clutching my stomach with a grimace. "I've never eaten...so much before." My guts churned aloud. Helica reached into her bag to pull out a sprig of herb.

"Chew this, drink water, and go move your bowels," Helica spoke, over the crowd's jeering of combatants on stage. "You should be well enough to ride tonight, but if you aren't, go with Gannicus anyway."

"Yes, Lady Helica," I answered, making sure I had all my money and gifts before running off to the toilets.

# CHAPTER EIGHT

"...the failings of the human character, which is restless and untamable in its struggle for freedom, or glory, or power."

—Sallust, *Histories*

The toilet was crowded, and I stood queued long enough to risk blowing out right where I stood. Painfully running from the toilet's stench, bent, and clutching my belly, I hurried to the nearest dark alley. Ripping off my undergarment, I hoisted up my tunic just in time before my insides burst out in a hot, putrid spray of filth. Crouching in the darkness and burning from the ass, I whimpered from the dual sensations of pain accompanied by relief. My stomach settled as the churning of my belly stopped. I spit out the herbs, chewed to a pulp, as the horrid smell made me wretch, waddling bowlegged in darkness. Without the aid of a rinsed sponge, I wiped with my undergarment before heading for my rendezvous with Gannicus at the Capuan Gate, feeling much better and enjoying a breeze.

The suntanned gladiators, Roucillus and Egus, manned the gate, armed with swords and pilums when I arrived. They both wished me luck before opening the heavy wooden gate just enough to let me through. Outside, the sky glowed above Herculaneum's palisades, and hearing the timber beam fall back into its iron cradle aroused sensations of isolation and vulnerability.

I squinted as I walked, trying to find the ranger.

"Own a sling?" asked an elevated shadow from the darkness. As I blinked, Gannicus slowly came into form. "It's the bonfires. They ruin your night eyes," he explained, appearing from the night as I stood dumbly, attempting to regain my vision. Feeling about with my hands, seeking to find the pony Gannicus promised was straight in front of me became frustrating until it nickered. I reached and touched her. Soon, darkness cleared enough to make out Gannicus mounted on a similar dark-colored mare nearby.

"Of course," I answered. Asking whether a shepherd owned a sling was a question too stupid to be asked.

"You said you can ride...right?" persisted Gannicus. I answered with a perturbed look beneath the moonlight. "Then grab her mane and mount up. We need to go."

"Go where?" I asked, squaring up on the animal.

"North."

"Why?" I asked, bouncing twice before jumping.

"Scouting."

"For what?" I pestered as my filly checked her head and neighed, stomping the ground.

"Scouts," Gannicus answered. I'd finally mounted when the hot-blooded little filly whinnied and kicked, throwing me. Slamming into the ground set my ears to ringing as pain shot up my back. Angrily, I stood as Gannicus rode up and blocked the riled filly with his mare, snatching the beast's mane to press its muzzle against his own mount, quickly calming the animal. "Let her settle. We'll set out in a minute."

"How am I supposed to ride her if she throws me?" I asked, embarrassed and pointing accusingly at the animal. Gannicus mimicked my perturbed expression from earlier.

"What do we do when we get thrown?" challenged Gannicus.

"We get back on," I finished, resolving to remount.

Squaring back up on the filly's left, I bounced twice like before, leaping onto her back. The pony accepted me as I grabbed handfuls of her mane, heeling my female forward. We walked them a great deal before Gannicus allowed us to canter and make some ground. I tried to gallop but Gannicus slowed me, saying, "If we have to run them, it'll be in the opposite direction, and the horses will need their fastest legs then." We trotted an hour until finally slowing to a walk. The beasts caught their breath and cooled from the sweat pouring from them in rivers, but my filly checked her head, wanting more.

A quarter moon shone without a cloud as we made our way into the chilly starry night. Once my eyes had adjusted, it was possible to see for quite some distance and we made great pace on the straight, smooth, cobbled Roman road. I put my filly behind Gannicus' mare to calm the beast and pulled over the hood, tightening my cloak, settling into routine. As we rode, rhythm, silence, and time took hold as my eyes began to stay shut a little longer between blinks. Soon, silly thoughts started swimming, images disappearing when my eyes reopened. Snapped awake, I'd catch myself before falling, then quickly settle back into sway to doze off once more. It became torture to remain awake; desperate thoughts of dismounting to lie down on the side of the road to sleep tempted my dreams. With buried chin, I dreamt of a shepherd's daughter I'd coaxed into a woodshed once, when my pony suddenly stopped. Smashing my nose into the horse's neck jarred me awake. The animal whinnied as my bearings recovered. The stars in my eyes gave way to the ones in the sky as my head settled, and I realized I was still with Gannicus upon the Appian.

Gannicus leaned from his mount to read the gigantic moonlit mile marker. "We need to get off the road," stated Gannicus, motioning the direction with a hand. "There's a stream about a quarter of a mile that way. There's a ford. We'll water and hobble the horses there, then circle back to the road farther north and see what we can on foot."

We stepped our horses over the curb and onto a dirt path, walking them toward the sound of trickling water. A small stream shimmered in moonlight as my filly passed Gannicus' mare on the grass to get at the water first. The little brown filly trotted out to the stream's middle. I asked if the horses were cooled enough to drink, and Gannicus said they were. I stopped fighting with the parched pony, relinquishing mane, letting the animal's head drop to drink. The pony gulped greedily. I had to resume our argument when I jerked the animal's hair to stop her from gulping too much before becoming waterlogged. Once on the other side, the animals began grazing. I watched Gannicus tie his mare's front forelimb with just enough rope to step. Gannicus wrapped and tied a blind around both horses' eyes, while I hobbled my pony's forelimbs the way Gannicus had.

Gannicus then crouched and dipped his hand in the mud along the brook's bank, extracting a palm's worth, then began smearing his face with it. I mimicked without question. "We must stay together," Gannicus whispered. "It'll be impossible to find each other if we get separated, and if we do, it'll mean things went very wrong. Whatever you do, don't cry out—make frogs chirp instead. Follow their sound, to the one that croaked first." Before I could ask, Gannicus retrieved two round river stones from the ground and began banging them rhythmically. Slowly at first, Gannicus increased the tempo until speeding to a sudden, silent stop.

"What in Hades are you—" I began, until interrupted by hundreds of chirping frogs croaking up and down the shallow gully in reply. Gannicus handed me the stones when they eventually stopped. I mimicked, and again frogs called out in unison for a time before quieting.

"If the horses are gone, parallel the road back, and for all the immortal gods' sake, stay off of it," instructed Gannicus. We walked north, then east, back in the direction of the Appian, through wild country. We crouched in a depression where Gannicus stopped our progress with an index finger over his lips to communicate silence. "Stay here," he whispered, slipping away alone.

I sat in darkness for what felt like forever, as shadows played tricks on my eyes once more. Time and again, I focused on movement and waited, when something else would distract me to wait once more in vain. Attacked by relentless yawns, my eyes became heavy while crickets chirped a lullaby. I was startled and my slumber interrupted when Gannicus suddenly appeared in my lap with eyes like lamps against a darkened face. Sweat dripping at the corners of his ears and breathing briskly, my mentor spoke with quiet intensity, "Romans, camped along the road. Stay behind me. Step from heel to toe and you won't snap twigs." He handed over a pouch full of oblong lead weights.

"May Helica's god help us if we need to use acorns," Gannicus spoke. Even at my young age then, I'd known the heavy little lead projectiles could kill rabbits, stop a bird, break a rib, or take an eye. The missiles were used by soldiers and shepherds alike on everything from wolves to cavalry; the deadly little acorns could catch a meal or spook a horse. Often, insults were etched upon them. *Up yours*, read this one in Latin.

My tunic's cord got crowded with a sling draped next to the dagger alongside a pouch full of acorns; I made room. Gannicus took my hand, having me grasp the back of his cloak before heading out together. We crouched in moonlight, moving quickly, and in an unsettlingly short amount of time, the glow of a campfire and the sound of voices were seen and heard. We skimmed the ground, moving uncomfortably close to voices over a snapping fire.

From concealment, I watched four soldiers pass a skin of wine between throwing *tesserae*, the dice, at a plank of wood laid upon the ground. The men laughed loudly, oblivious of being watched. "If that twit Glaber," boasted a soldier, "thinks I'm drawing guard duty all night and marching all the way to Pompeii first thing in the morning, he can take that switch and shove it up his ass." He drunkenly gathered dice at his feet for a re-toss.

"Don't be stupid," announced another. "Glaber won't march until he humps that laundry hag he keeps in the baggage. Besides, all you have to do is say, 'Night duty remains with the baggage while marching,' and that dummy will believe it." From the darkness, we watched them tumble dice while wagering and drinking on duty.

We hugged the ground, listening for truth between lies, and Gannicus whispered, "How many?" I held up four fingers. Gannicus shook his head, then held a thumb up to his eye, blocking the campfire with it. I mimicked, darkening the fire's glow with my thumb. When two more soldiers appeared in the distance, having been previously obscured by the blinding glow coming from the fire's light.

"First thing I'm doing when we catch these animals is get me a slave girl and relieve this horrible itch at my balls!" shouted a boastful young sentry, grabbing his crotch.

"They need to drop first, pup," admonished an older soldier. The circle of men laughed at the youngster's expense. "Besides, you'll have to wait for twenty-three hundred men to finish first, kid," joked the old hand, who had clearly been sent along to keep wayward boys out of trouble. The junior soldier processed his response through a wine-hindered haze, thought better, and remained silent. Lewd jokes and drunken challenges continued until finally, Gannicus touched my arm to slowly crawl away.

"What did you learn?" Gannicus asked, washing his face clean once we reached the brook.

"They're less than half a legion," I replied.

"What else?" asked Gannicus.

"They probably won't head out until late morning," I answered.

"What else?"

"Their leader's name is Glaber, and they speak ill of him," I continued.

"That sounds important. What else?"

"That more men could be present, even if they're not seen," I answered, unsure how to articulate aloud everything I'd observed.

"Come on, Publipor, you're mentioning everything obvious," admonished Gannicus, his face completely clean now. The horses were found grazing together in the moonlight, not far from where we left them.

"I learned how to 'hobble' a horse, how to make frogs 'chirp,' how to darken my face," I continued, hoping I'd gotten to the answer.

"Publipor, you can do better than that, can't you?" pleaded Gannicus as we mounted, walking our horses back to the road. We stepped over the curb once more as hooves clopped on cobblestones back to Vesuvius.

"They have no fear of us," I said to myself.

"What makes you say that?" Gannicus asked.

"They're drinking and gambling, when they should be watching for an ambush," I answered.

"Very good," Gannicus encouraged, emboldening me. "Why?"

I took a minute to answer. "They don't respect us because they think we're asses muddling through an open gate," I reasoned.

"Now you're rolling along. Go on."

"They seem very, very young. Not much older than me, except for the one older soldier," I observed. "I think, since all the armies are abroad, they conscripted youngsters, threw in a smattering of veterans to drill them and throw at us." We walked the horses side by side in moonlight. Gannicus nodded his head in agreement, remaining silent, so I continued. "I think we're walking back to Herculaneum because you're timing their march," I surmised; Gannicus smiled.

Walking the horses in the night breeze, I pulled my cloak tight and listened to Gannicus explain how to estimate the size of an enemy. "A centurion's responsible for eighty men. Count six plumed helmets and you've got four hundred and eighty men. Just round to five hundred. It's always better to *over*—rather than *under*—estimate a head count. Five hundred men is a cohort; ten cohorts are a legion. Now, what do we estimate Glaber's strength to be?"

"Twenty-three hundred," I answered.

"Make it twenty-five since we didn't actually see any of them. What would you tell Spartacus they measured?" asked my tutor. I thought for a minute.

"Half a legion. New recruits with few veterans. Bad discipline. Two or three hours away, well-armed and heading south. They'll probably arrive at Vesuvius after noon with full baggage, cavalry, and archers." I finished, then decided to add, "And if things go sideways, always have a backup plan."

"Helica might be right about you," Gannicus said, impressed. "Publipor?"

"Yes?" I answered.

"Your name means 'Publius' slave'?" Gannicus asked.

"I guess so," I reasoned, shrugging.

"Want to change it?" asked Gannicus. For a moment, I thought of grand names.

"Nah," I declined. "Probably wouldn't answer to anything else, anyway." We plodded along, walking our beasts back into town. As the sun chariot rose, Helios lit the edge of the world, chasing away the heavens. We walked our mounts beside each other to the closed gates of Herculaneum. Egus peered over the wooden palisade to find returning friends, acknowledging our arrival with his distinct toothy grin. Egus motioned Roucillus to unbar the gate; the heavy beam lifted, and the gate opened enough to enter single file.

"Your kingdom, my lords," chided Egus, bowing grandly and grinning from ear to ear as we passed. "Bet little Pube-i-por, killed 'em all already, Roc," Egus poked at his companion.

"You save some for us, kid?" asked Roucillus, a blond-haired Gaul everyone called by his nickname.

Behind a re-barred gate, we walked into a ruined and abandoned Herculaneum to a rooster's crow, a dog's bark, and smoke rising from smoldering heaps of ash. The soldiers' bloating bodies were piled in front of the amphitheater's stage as vultures circled overhead, awaiting the corpses buzzing with blowflies. Scrawny dogs with bald patches greedily chased off crows for ample souring scraps. A boy took our horses as Gannicus and I walked to the villa used by Helica and Spartacus to give our report. I stood behind Gannicus and kept my mouth shut as he went on undeservedly about my abilities during each phase of our outing, and I blushed. After dismissal, Gannicus ordered me to find a place to sleep, but there was no way I could, not with all the frenzied activity about to be unleashed.

I woke that afternoon in a bed of furs, drooling into a goose down pillow, surprised that I had slipped into such fitful sleep after all. I looked around and vaguely recalled wandering into a random home. I rolled from the luxurious bed to the balcony to urinate. Helios was directly overhead. The realization that I'd slept the morning away was suddenly paramount on my mind. Gannicus estimated the arrival of the Romans to be this day, during this afternoon. I gathered my things and went outside to look for news. A lone dog slunk past. *The town's deserted,* I thought, rounding a corner.

The stench of death and a pestilence of flies assaulted me as I retched, fighting the urge to vomit. Large buzzards hopped about on rotting carcasses, cawing, wings extended, their menacing claws and beaks establishing pecking order. Perched ravens picked eyes from an impaled head while dogs growled and snapped. Two older women argued in the afternoon's stench, stopping to stare as I passed. I returned to the Capuan Gate to find the same two men, Roucillus and Egus, joking while they stacked piles of flotsam before the heavy gates. They'd both clearly been at it all day. Egus still had his distinctive giant grin plastered on his face and only stopped toiling long enough to chide Roucillus.

"Well, I sure am tired of doing *all* the work around here, little Pube-i-por," commented Egus, his tongue twisting sideways in a silly expression.

"*Dentatus!*" Big teeth, insulted Roc. "Egus, you're a lazy son of a bitch," he retorted. "If my foot wasn't in your ass all night, you'd be talking to Spartacus right now with empty excuses and a back full of stripes, you ungrateful runt," Roucillus continued, laboring. Egus wagged his brows at me with delight at Roc's annoyance.

"Where is everyone?" I asked the gladiators between their banter. Vidovic, a quiet Celt working alongside them, pointed at the mountain and returned to piling the town's jetsam in front of the gate without a word.

"Well—you better get your little butt up that hill, tiny man. Them Romans are comin'," Egus joked through big teeth. Peering at the mountain, I saw a long line of humanity ascending the trail with huge bundles of straw strapped to backs. I ran to the open Pompeiian Gate to find Gannicus sitting in the sunlight, sharpening his dagger and wiping it with an oil-soaked rag.

"Good morning, ranger," greeted Gannicus.

"Are we all right? Have we overslept? What's our plan?" I asked in rapid succession.

"Take it easy. The Romans are moving slow, like you said they would," Gannicus spoke. "They aren't in a hurry. Trying to recruit more boys, no doubt. We'll be the last up. Fill your water and drink miserly—there'll be none where we're going, so take as much as you can carry. Everyone's going to bring as much straw as they can. Might as well snatch as much bread as you can find as well. I'll be here setting the fields ablaze until you return, and we'll run off the horses before we go."

# CHAPTER NINE

"...being a Thracian mercenary, had become a soldier, and from a soldier a deserter, then a highwayman, and finally, thanks to his strength, a gladiator."

—Florus, *Epitome*

While I was at the well filling my flagon from a bucket, the old bath man approached, shuffling along, accompanied by a young girl. She looked to be about eleven years old, dressed in a plain wool frock full of patches. With wild, unkempt hair and bare feet, she peeked out from behind the old man. A *pupae,* or dirty straw rag doll, was held close to her chest. "This is my granddaughter, Pila," said the old man, introducing the girl in Oscan. "Publipor, let an old man die knowing his kin will live a bit longer. She's not a useless mouth; she can shear sheep, spin wool, and she knows how to butcher and tan hides." The girl stood by quietly. The old man carried on at length about the girl's abilities, until I interrupted him with a palm, apoplectic as to why a father would name their own daughter *Pila*—little spear.

"I can't take care of anyone," I explained. "I'm not trained—I'm not even *exploratorae*." I went on, without any pretense of bravado, listing reasons why I should *not be* strapped with this burden. The old man looked through me sadly with milky white eyes.

"I've kept her hidden, kiddo. Her father is dead; she has no one to look after her. I'll be dead soon and she has yet to fulfill her life. Take this girl. Please," he said, pushing the girl forward. "I won't be able to keep her hidden from the soldiers and you know what they'll do to her." I hadn't the heart for denial, so I became angry.

"She needs to carry her own water and a bundle of straw. It's cold on the mountain, so she'll need warm clothes," I demanded, squirming. The old man smiled, swinging a pack from behind his shoulder that struck dirt with a slosh. The girl peered at me with wary eyes, clutching her *pupae*. "I can't babysit. When we get to the top, she's on her own." The old man walked up and patted my shoulder gently as the girl buried her face in the old man's belly with arms wrapped tight around his midsection. The old man indulged the girl for a great deal of time before finally wiggling free of her clasp.

"Her name is Pila," the old man repeated. He turned to his youngest family member. "Little spear, go with Publipor, make yourself useful." On bended knee, the grandfather spoke gently to her tear-streamed face. The old man explained the need to leave and why the girl had to run as far as possible to escape Romans. "That's a clever young man," said the old bath attendant, pointing at me. "The gods speak clearer to old men, and Dionysus has shown me this boy will get you clear of here." The small girl holding her doll looked resentful, defiant, and angry at me by the time he'd finished.

"He looks like Pan, Umpapa," Pila squeaked. Pan, the Greek god of shepherds and flocks, the child of Hermes who had horns and legs of a goat. A lyre-playing, troublesome, ugly half-breed is what she called me. I said she looked like Medusa, which made the girl cry.

At the Pompeiian Gate, gladiators and slaves continued upending carts behind barred doors. We planned to climb the walls out. Spartacus ordered a withdrawal to spook the half legion with a quiet, locked city. Gannicus explained they'd be wary of a trap and trench on the way in, giving us time to get everyone to the top of Mt. Vesuvius. An old woman smiled, waving goodbye, while an older man sobbed. My heart sank thinking of elderly people hiding babies, both wandering toddlers, doddering into wolves' teeth.

Gannicus led his mare and my filly out so we could turn both loose and run them off. Gannicus shouted, slapping both horses hard on their rumps to make them bolt. The pair galloped furiously a furlong when, inexplicably, mine slowed and stopped to look back as her stablemate disappeared over the rise. Pila, stunned by the power of the beasts, clutched her *pupae* tightly when the small horse began walking back.

"We must," Gannicus spoke to me, winding a loaded sling above his head, then turning to the trembling girl. He didn't seem surprised at her presence, but with his skills of observation, I wouldn't be surprised if he'd known of her existence long before the rest of us. "The beasts can't climb and we must not leave them for the Romans." I could tell the girl hated to see the animals harmed, despite reassurance of the necessity. I loaded my sling and ran at the filly, screaming, releasing the acorn on the exact trajectory, but with lackluster force—it fell short. The missile tumbled impotently before the horse as the filly approached, sniffing turf.

"Yaw!" Gannicus screamed, running past to strike the two-year-old with a lead pellet to its rib. The female leaped; kicking and whinnying, she bolted like lightning over the ridge as Pila wailed. "It won't kill her, and she'll stay away from people for a while. We can leave no aid," Gannicus explained to Pila once more, pointing at walls of smoke billowing in the afternoon fields of wheat, spouting gouts of flame. I ducked just in time for the stone Pila threw at my head to miss.

"Nice," remarked Gannicus, admiring either my reflexes or Pila's pitch. Pila bent for another; I ran at the girl, wrapping my arms around her before she could throw another.

"They'll use that pony against us!" I yelled, Pila's face inches from mine. Red, defiant eyes pierced me from her small, smooth, youthful face. Pila lifted her knee into my crotch and I collapsed, cradling my privates and groaning. Gannicus chuckled, herding a crying Pila, while I clawed at dirt and fought for breath.

### RUNAWAY SLAVES ESCAPE BY ASCENDING THE HEAVENS, 682 AUC (73 BC)

A quarter of the way up Mt. Vesuvius, Pila began to struggle. I transferred the girl's bundle of straw to mine and found myself climbing with a four-foot-high bushel, piggybacking comically as I went. We were promised that the only trail eventually meandered into cool mists of a bowl-shaped summit. When breathing became difficult, I carried Pila's water. As the sun blazed, I looked back as Herculaneum lay below, small and insignificant. *Is this how the gods see us?* I wondered, drinking.

"They don't waste time, except to swat at us," Pila panted, and I realized I'd spoken the thought aloud. I cocked my head, curious at the bizarre response, before continuing up the steep incline once more, sweating and gasping for breath.

"Helica...promised...Dionysus, will help us...escape Italy," I labored, leaning forward, burdened and trudging, reassuring myself as much as the girl.

"Helica, Smellica," dismissed Pila. "Dionysus, Schmionysis," she mocked between gasps, childishly rhyming nonsense while leaning against the incline to brood. "There are no gods, only cruel men."

*Pessimistic Pila*, I thought, thinking better than to say it aloud.

Helios dragged the sun, setting our horizon in flaming red, as

I looked down at the tiny city below, watching miniature soldiers approach. The Romans arranged themselves in tight little squares, three rows behind shields, moving as one toward the Capuan Gate. It was fun to watch them use so much caution on an abandoned city. More tiny men hid, mounted, off in the trees, while tiny archers followed in a neat row. I thought of the old man from the baths, Pila's grandfather. I regretted not learning his name. When asked, Pila's only response was, "He was Umpappa."

Our long caravan stopped at last and we began to settle in for the evening. There was a series of soft *thumps* as bags, rucks, and flagons hit the ground.

I took out my water flask once more. "What are you going to drink later?" asked Gannicus when he caught me gulping.

"I'm thirsty," I replied, frustrated.

"Will you be thirsty in an hour, when it's gone?" Disappointment clear on his face, he turned and walked away. Sweating and exhausted, I reluctantly put the water away while fires were kindled as dusk gave way to night. Pila and I walked the crater's rim by moonlight, surveying below. We found a spot and lay upon our bellies at the crater's southern edge, watching the torches of Pompeii below.

The city carried on as always, I assumed, relieved upon hearing word that the Roman army had finally arrived to recapture us fugitives. I'd heard rumors of Pompeiians feeling safe from us freed barbarians behind their army and high stone walls. Pila shivered inside my cloak as we huddled together for warmth, staring at the pile of straw amassed in the crater's center, which got taller with each new arrival; the material was hauled up en masse by the slaves to make straw men. It gave me an idea. Paltry fires were rendered useless by crowds and the fight it took to get close enough to make any difference in the cold wasn't worth the effort. Instead, I waited for the straw to become unwatched.

The girl's teeth began to chatter. When the time was right, I grasped Pila's hand and dove headlong into the pile to burrow deep within. Inside, it was black as pitch. We arranged ourselves parallel, setting into the crackling, almost dusty scented material. Pila's teeth ceased chattering as it slowly began to warm. She whispered, "Do you have parents?"

"I guess, I must have," I replied in a hush. "They must have died, I can't remember them."

"Maybe they sold you," she said softly.

"Maybe you were sold," was all I could muster in return.

"Oh, no," Pila refuted quietly. "I had a good Mamma and the best Pappa."

"If they were the best at being good, then why were you being raised by your grandfather, huh?" Pila couldn't see my scowl, nor my bruised pride.

"Umpappa helped Mamma when Pappa died fighting for Silo," recalled the tiny young girl in darkness. Even a goatherd from outside Herculaneum knew of Silo. The exploits of the Samnite leader Silo were renowned amongst all non-Romans. The once-loyal Roman subject, who'd fought on the side of the Romans for decades, one day decided his people would no longer do so without the vote. Silo declared the Samnites wouldn't fight for the wolf people, nor participate in putting to heel any more Italian tribes, without representation in government. I'd learn three years hence it was Spartacus' urging of Pompeii to attack Silo's flank that saved Sulla's army from the Samnites in the battle for the Colline Gate. Silo's Samnites, Rome's deadliest opponents, fell that day—including Pila's father.

"At least your mother is still alive," I tried helping, "isn't she?"

"Mamma showed Umpappa that the Romans had poisoned our well."

"How?" I asked, impressed and curious.

"She drank some," whispered the girl, clutching me now. We lay together silently in darkness until we finally slept.

That night came to me a vivid dream about a boy, long ago and far away, in a place I knew not. The boy in the dream walked before a cowering army, boldly winding a sling overhead. Outside bowshot stood an armored, eight-foot giant, removing a plumbed helmet in disgust. The giant Philistine ridiculed the opposing ranks for sending a boy as their champion to die alone. Goliath removed his helmet and stood bare-headed.

"May this paltry boy," the Philistine spoke contemptuously, "be what Judeans consider a champion?" Goliath sneered, daring the boy to release, when the stone struck his temple.

I woke up, scratching an itch in my warm cave of straw as Helios' light worked its way deep within. Pila lay on my chest as sweat ran down her cheek and onto my stomach. Muted sounds of people milling about tumbled into the interior of the now-stifling straw cave. I went to peek for a way out, and got shoved out by an errant kick from Pila. I toppled out onto the ground, landing near a large slave woman with warts who was stuffing hay into clothing. The disfigured woman jumped, surprised, but soon the row of women stuffing clothes, relieved at the sight of children, began laughing. Especially so after Pila popped out with straw stuck in her hair.

"Look, Crastus. Rats in straw," commented Crixus, pointing. Crastus laughed his stupid laugh. The pair sat sharpening poles along with a large group of men near a fire. By the time we'd brushed off and stood, a woman grabbed Pila's arm, conscripting the girl into manufacturing straw men. Pila stuck out her tongue as I ran away.

"Pube, Gannicus looken zie for du," Crastus spoke with a straight face. "Mit think he want...more of du bung." The German laughed accursedly, edging Crixus with an elbow. I left them to find Gannicus. The crater was bustling with activity; men drilled with iron swords and wicker shields all about, while others threw javelins into the soft embankments for practice. Some men got knocked on their asses in the crater's center, bowled over by Va, the enormous, deaf eunuch holding a giant *scutum* and yelling the only word he ever uttered: his own name.

The haggard centurion, dragged up the mountain and bound by his wrists, lay upon the ground, praying for death as throngs of fugitives worked together on the necessities for survival in the bowl of Vesuvius' summit. Women and children pruned long lengths of wild grape vines growing everywhere, weaving them into baskets and makeshift shields. Helica sat hooded on the ground, rocking and chanting, cross-legged in a trance; it was disturbing to see the whites of her eyes rolled up in her head like that. "Staring at gods," she'd explain later. An acrid smell boiled from the small tin pot smoking before her.

"Leave her," Gannicus whispered, naturally spotting me long before I noticed him. He placed a hand on my shoulder and steered me away to follow him into a haunting fog. "We'll take the trail most of the way down," he explained, "below the mist. Drink hearty, but keep your water here. We'll parallel the path down when we find their probe." My heart jumped a bit at his words, which could only mean we were going to find the men sent to find us. Standing at the mouth of the path, Gannicus turned to me and secured the things inside my old, frayed cord belt, tying everything tightly before releasing me.

"You need a proper buckle and belt," Gannicus said, feeling five acorns in the pouch and handing me a few more. Pulling my dagger, Gannicus inspected its edge before sliding it back. "If we get separated, get up on the path as fast as you can and keep going until you find the others...but don't get separated."

## THE ROMAN ARMY ARRIVES AT VESUVIUS, 682 AUC

### (73 BC)

*Optio Primo,* Sergeant Major Atticus Fabius Dominicus, a trusted fifteen-year vet, gave his horse a pat on the neck as they watched the newly appointed Praetor Caius Claudius Glaber preen on his expensive mare. They were concealed within the trees just outside Herculaneum's Capuan Gate with the rest of the calvary.

The veteran had been sent along by Senator Marcus Crassus to drill green soldiers and keep an eye on Glaber, the untested praetor. Atticus knew without seeing the man's face that Glaber was smirking; he clearly thought the army's approach was stunning. Atticus rolled his eyes, shaking his head imperceptibly at the green men before him.

The Mithraic War had brought Atticus rank and renown, for himself and Commander Marcus Crassus. He remembered then in the surreal moment, watching fledglings press forward, of earning garlands in the battle for the Colline Gate against a formidable, deadly, and determined Italian Samnite army long ago.

It bitterly reminded him that his oaths to Marcus Crassus, the richest son of a bitch in all of Italy, were Atticus' only insurance against reprisals after Sulla's death. Meanwhile, Spartacus, Dictator Sulla's "loyal dog," was "shit out of luck," as the saying went among the regiments after the tyrant's death. Atticus knew that Sulla cheating Spartacus out of his retirement would make the man a murdering, suicidal, drunken highway robber, and it did. Atticus had heard the big news when Spartacus was finally caught napping and condemned to slavery. He had even been in attendance the day his comrade's feet were chalked; the infantryman had seen firsthand the furious bidding war between rival gladiator camps over the new hot commodity. Now, the war veteran looked up at the mountain between the trees, wondering if it really was the old cavalryman Spartacus who'd taken all those slaves to the ultimate high ground.

The old vet stifled a sigh as he watched amateurs try and keep formation in the assault against Herculaneum. The cohort marched at full step, and the proximity to the city's walls at that pace made Atticus cringe; it put soldiers beneath walls, butting them against immovable stone in very short order. The disaster took its course, and soon Glaber's first row of shields buttressed the city wall. Atticus watched helplessly as men in the rear kept piling on fallen men like asses, continuing for several rows, until the inept young men finally stopped advancing due to a lack of real estate. Despite their best efforts, a few soldiers were injured inside the press of razor-sharp blades. Atticus swallowed his contempt for the patrician in command, hiding disdain behind a mask of professionalism. Lesson learned. Atticus shouted his orderlies forward to staunch bleeding from the new men downed against Herculaneum's wall with forceps and sewing kits.

"No one seems home. Shall I assist the men, sir?" Atticus addressed the officer without a whiff of contempt. A dismissive flick from Glaber's wrist granted the centurion authority to restore order. Atticus grumbled into his cheek pieces as he rode to disentangle the inept praetor's toys. Atticus looked up, trying to catch a glimpse of an old friend, straining to see Spartacus in the clouds.

# CHAPTER TEN

"Then Clodius the praetor was sent out from Rome against them with three thousand soldiers, and laid siege to them on a hill which had but one ascent, and that a narrow and difficult one, which Clodius closely watched."

—Plutarch, *Life of the Caesars*

We followed the steep path as it zigzagged down the mountain for a very long time, and I wondered if going down wasn't more difficult than going up. At one point, there was a transition so steep that steps had been carved. Gannicus stopped as I gasped for breath.

"Help me gather stones about this big," Gannicus instructed, holding a rock the size of a melon with two hands. A vulture blew past on a thermal, inches from my face, and I wanted to join it in flight instead of wasting time stacking stones with an ex-drunk.

The idea of flying like a bird reminded me of a lesson from my Greek instructor about a man named Daedalus and his son, Icarus. Daedalus, the father, made wings of wax stuck with goose feathers for both to escape a prison. Daedalus told his son not to fly too high, for the sun would melt the wings, nor too low, for the sea would swamp them. Evidently, Icarus couldn't escape fast enough; his wings melted climbing too high, too fast, and he crashed to the ground. When asked what it meant, I concluded it was a cautionary tale about men who reach beyond their station. The tutor beamed with pride when I'd answered correctly, but quickly soured when I'd added that I, too, would've tried to escape. I was subsequently whipped so hard that, at seven years of age, I stole a horse, got caught, and was sold off in an afternoon.

I thought about that day while gathering stones and piling them atop the carved steps, when another huge black vulture flew by on a thermal up the mountain. I thought it a strange coincidence at the time; now, I know better—the birds always circle when armies gather, waiting for a banquet of corpses.

We went for a time further, then slowed, coming to a long stretch of path that switch-backed down the mountain for a mile. I thought of my abandoned water when my mouth dried from the labor of piling stones and climbing. The going became difficult once we left the trail and had to use the wild vines clinging everywhere to help traverse the rugged terrain. Finally concealed at a spot slightly elevated in a sparse patch of woods, we disappeared into shade overlooking the path below. There we sat for a great length of time, until finally, the Romans appeared.

Tiny, light infantry soldiers walked warily up the steep incline, shields strapped to backs, their swords drawn. Gannicus quickly showed me the best way to count them, testing me between the rocks as they grew in size upon approach, explaining how he'd come to a number of sixty. Gannicus claimed these Romans were just a probing force sent to test Spartacus' reaction.

"Climb to the steps and start hurling rocks when you hear me signal," ordered Gannicus.

"How will I know the signal?" I asked, confused.

"You'll know," Gannicus reassured, "and get the big ones rolling first." He encouraged me to depart with a subtle push to my chest, and I went back the way we'd come. It was far more treacherous ascending off the trail alone. I used the grape vines strangling rocks to navigate the places most precarious. By the time I'd climbed the hewn steps to where our rocks were stacked, I was exhausted. *What can a few rocks do to soldiers?* I thought, impatiently wondering what Gannicus' signal could be and about which stones should be released first.

From below, Gannicus shouted, "Now, Publipor, now!" as he came bounding up the trail.

I hesitated; the prospect of killing Gannicus with a stone was very real. When Gannicus shouted curses, I began hurling rocks down carved steps. They tumbled, thudding heavily upon descent, gaining deadly momentum with every bounce. I watched a stone fly directly at the scout below as he slung at Romans with his back to me, and I thought, *I've just killed Gannicus.* The deadly missile accelerated with every bounce directly at him. Miraculously, Gannicus noticed it in time and fell flat. The rock zoomed over top and thudded sickeningly into a young soldier in pursuit. The stone struck square in the soldier's face and his helmet flew skyward, disappearing in a red mist over the ledge.

"More, Publipor, more!" Gannicus implored, breathlessly bounding up the carved steps while dodging released stones. Quickly and heedlessly, I began hurling larger rocks. When Gannicus climbed to my side, he began flinging stones as well. I'd no idea how much energy a rock could carry down the steep grade, but soon learned when they arrived for soldiers below. Light infantry formed up behind their shields, four abreast—all that could line in a row on the steep and narrow path. A soldier below took a big rock to his shield; the stone punctured his *scutum* made of glued plywood birch. Dismayed, the young man lifted up his rent shield as if it were busted sackcloth.

Another stepped up to replace him, relocking shields to fill the gap as a deadly hail of flying rocks assailed them. We were like cyclopes hurling boulders, striking men down in a vicious storm.

The Romans retreated beneath our torrent; down the graveled path they withdrew, backing behind their shields, their arrows falling short due to the steep angle.

"Get up and warn the commander! I'll be right behind you!" ordered Gannicus. I'd almost forgotten my thirst until the excitement wore off and my mouth reminded me that I was completely parched. I climbed without a glance back until my chest felt like it was set on fire and cramps pierced my side. My every thought was consumed by the water I'd left at the summit. I struggled with it now, desperate to quench my thirst, but when I arrived, it was gone. My head spun, too dehydrated for tears.

"Here," said Pila, holding our flagon of the precious liquid in small hands. She'd seen me leave the water and evidently had taken it to Helica to be refilled. Greedily, I snatched it from her, gulping huge amounts between labored breaths. When I could finally speak, I told the fugitives waiting what was happening while pointing down the mountain. Armed men assembled and slaves headed down with stolen Roman shields to help Gannicus repel the Roman incursion.

"Don't drink so fast—you'll get cramps," replied a squinty eyed, smiling Egus behind a big shield, holding his pilum. I eyed him sidelong as I gulped, daring him to try and take it, when Pila gently reached up and slowly pulled it from my lips. There, shaded at the base of a little tree, Pila, her doll, and I sat silently until excitement waned and my eyes became heavy. I woke later near dusk to Pila scolding her straw *pupae* quietly, like a stern mother.

"Are you hungry?" asked Pila when she saw my eyes open. She produced a hunk of hard bread. It crunched in my teeth, which made my mouth dry once more. Pila gathered our things with her doll head locked in an armpit while situating our belongings and placing the leather strap of our water skin around my neck.

I finished tucking the dagger inside my crowded cord belt as we walked back to the crater. I kept the impoverishment of my old tunic to myself, adjusting my many things behind the old, frayed cord once again until I could replace it. Pila noticed me feeling at the new purse strap hidden beneath my wretched rags. "You need a proper belt, and shouldn't you be getting paid like the other men?" commented Pila, unwittingly mimicking Gannicus.

At the top of Mt. Vesuvius lay a mass of straw men stuffed in clothes, resembling dead men. They lay stacked atop one another and placed near the ramp leading out of the crater, reminding me of the heap of bodies left at Herculaneum. I found Oenomaus reclining against the crater's embankment, sharpening his sword with a stone. The light-haired serving woman from the city sat next to him, stitching a garment in the chill night. Pila and I joined them at their small fire as wind whipped flames.

"Gannicus is fine," answered Oenomaus, reading my thoughts. "Our ranger says you set up an ambush, killing many Romans that sent the rest back beneath flying stones." Pila could not see it due to the fire's glow, but redness filled my cheeks when she turned her head to look at me, silently impressed by what she'd heard.

The thought really hadn't entered my mind until it was spoken into reality. Gannicus heaped the entire credit for routing the incursion undeservedly on me. A dark thought took root: *I'd killed a man—at least one.* The image of a young soldier's smooth face burned into my mind. I can still see him, before his face was ruined, and still hear the sound of impact, the spray of blood, haunting my dreams to this day.

"Spartacus is extremely proud of you," Oenomaus said, yanking me from the disturbing memory. The woman smiled, reaching gently for Pila's doll, but Pila wrenched it to her neck in whining protest. The light-haired Gallic woman persisted, smiling reassuringly, until Pila finally relented. Oenomaus' woman used a large needle and quickly stitched a busted seam, returning the doll with a smile. Then the woman ladled two bowls of vegetable broth, handing them to us and returning to the crook of Oenomaus' huge arm.

"Very impressive indeed, boy," Oenomaus praised, after she'd settled in. "There must be at least two thousand slaves up here with us." He looked around at the mass of milling slaves in the moonlit crater. "How many men do you think they have, Publipor?"

"Gannicus says there's at least two thousand five hundred," I answered.

"How many say you?" Gannicus asked in his Gallic-accented Latin.

"The same," I answered.

Oenomaus took the measure of the masses before him once more and asked, "Do you think we can beat them?"

"Maybe," I shrugged, lying for Pila's sake. Oenomaus laughed and we talked into the night, feeding our campfire when it dwindled. Whispering, I asked the unanswered burning question I'd had for days: "Why don't Spartacus and Helica have children?"

Oenomaus thought for a minute and replied, "Helica got pregnant quickly after being given to the *ludis* when she first arrived. Spartacus married her, claiming the child, even if some whispered Cornelius had gotten in her first. Cornelius had her flogged once when Helica was very big; the stripes became infected and she nearly died of fever as Spartacus tended her. The orderly at the *ludis* claimed that she and the baby would probably die that day. Spartacus sacrificed everything he could get his hands on with every *sesterce* of winnings to appease the gods so they would save her," Oenomaus remembered. "It must have been enough, because Helica recovered, birthing a dead baby girl. Helica wailed for the girl's body upon hearing that a dog from town had carried it off our rubbish heap. She'd lost so much blood, the orderly said that if she lived, she'd never have children—and the attendant was right. Spartacus had a fan kill the dog and burn the girl's body with a drachma in her mouth. Since then, Helica no longer goes in season; she's barren," Oenomaus concluded. For a split second, I wondered why a man would keep a woman who couldn't have boys, then remembered: the woman was *Helica of Thrace.*

The light-haired woman on Oenomaus' arm stripped lengths of wild vine, snipped them clean, and quietly began weaving a basket in fire light. Remnants of ancient lava flows ran down the crater all around us, resembling ropes. Pila shivered at my side. Staring at the jumble that was becoming a basket in the blonde woman's hands and the hardened ropes of stone flowing from the crater's walls like vines gave me an idea; I excused myself to explore.

BAY OF HERCULANEUM, BENEATH MT. VESUVIUS, 682
AUC (73 BC)

Most of Atticus' morning was spent drilling mistakes out of green soldiers. Two had been disabled, cleaved by accident in Glaber's ill-advised mosh. He'd watched in disbelief as Glaber assembled light infantry off in the distance. Light infantry, the most athletic and adept boys at soldiering, were sent by a buffoon, leaderless and outmanned, up a choke point.

Before long, young strapping men came back dejected and beaten, returning to camp with the dead stretched upon their shields. Atticus had to get away from this fool, deeming the commander unworthy of advice and incapable of instruction. Glaber would no longer find any support from his *optio*, Sergeant Major Atticus Dominicus, ever again after that day. In the command tent that evening, oblivious of the loss, Glaber reclined with officers dining on rations and plans for tomorrow's assault. Officers pandered between bites, commending their commander's brilliant plan of storming heights and overwhelming the vermin come morning. Eager young men nodded in agreement, arguing which man would earn the honor to be first to lead the army up Vesuvius. Atticus silently eyed his youthful peers as the other veteran scoffed at foolery being spoken aloud. Thankfully, the other man broke with disgust before Atticus did.

"Oh, for the immortal gods' sakes, we know where they are! They can't fly away!" the veteran said, exasperated, trying to introduce some common sense into the discussion. "Have you heard of a mountain lake around here? Me neither. They can't have much water—assuming the stupid animals didn't drink it all on the way up."

Glaber listened intently as the young officers stopped braying long enough to hear from the wise old soldier. Atticus noticed the young commander's eyes squint slightly smaller with every word; he kept his mouth shut, almost feeling sorry for his jaded old comrade. "Our guys would be fighting uphill, two abreast, the whole way up a damned mountain, for Jupiter's sake," reasoned the centurion. "We saw what a few big rocks could do to your best boys." The old man pressed too far by pointing at Glaber.

"Seize him!" yelled Glaber to his *lictors* in an unusually high-pitched screech. The officers rushed, disarming the slightly drunk, surprised *optio dio* at sword point. The grizzled man apologized profusely, begging clemency while being removed. Atticus was relieved the other man blew his top before he'd done the same. The smug little bastard of a commander had turned his attention to the only other veteran who hadn't agreed wholeheartedly with the earlier plan.

"Perhaps," said Atticus politically, "what my undiplomatic colleague advocated, sir, was a blockade."

"Go on," said the young commander.

"Our wise commander," Atticus flattered, "surely knows the only way to the summit is the path. We've enough men to garrison Vesuvius' slope; all other ways down offer only deep crags or sheer cliffs." Youthful lieutenants began nodding agreement in consensus. "Let the animals starve and go without water for a few days. They'll come down on their own, begging for a shackle." A dozen heads nodded like birds before he concluded with the distinctly Roman axiom: "An army wins with the *dolabra* before the *gladius*, sir."

Later that morning, Glaber announced his new battle plan to troops from upon a dais. The men were ordered to begin trenching and surveying for a camp. Glaber ordered that timber collected from the woods be hewn into planks and set into earth. With divine wisdom, Glaber had switched the operation to a blockade of attrition, sparing men the rigors of an uphill fight. The boys heralded his genius, applauding with gratitude as Atticus' brother centurion was placed in stocks outside. "*Qie dubitat*"—"pessimist"—was painted in white across the beam. Atticus congratulated himself for his skillful army politicking; he stared at the mountain once more, thanking Mars there'd be no fight against gladiators while climbing Mt. Vesuvius.

In the evening's waning light, Atticus fixed his gaze toward the summit, focusing hard through eyes that weren't what they used to be, when a tiny man standing perfectly still appeared. Atticus stared for a long time, so long that other tiny men came into focus. *Something's off,* he thought. The more he stared and the harder he concentrated on the mountaintop, the more certain he was that the tiny men hadn't moved, but when Atticus brought it to Glaber's attention, the commander rebuffed the sergeant for being too skittish. He decided then he'd hitch his packed horse outside the tent tonight and sleep armored. Just in case.

Atticus tossed in his bunk, dreaming of the east a lifetime ago, when he'd served Commander Marcus Crassus beneath General Sulla. In this dream of the past, a youthful Sulla watched from a hill surrounded by *lictors* as the armies crashed below. Sulla had finally persuaded the easterners to engage in the perfect place after harrying and starving them for weeks, even depriving the enemy horses of fodder by burning entire pastures. During that battle, Marcus Crassus had experienced a much harder time than young Pompey.

"Stand and live, or run and die!" Atticus shouted, as he had years ago, trying to bolster the nearest youngster.

Fear was painfully evident in the young man's eyes, so he encouraged continued defense. The cohort's men, replaced twice already, were running out of replacements. Atticus felt strength wane and luck run dry while struggling in a muck of blood and shit, when a blade suddenly poked through the shields. Atticus held the youngster's gaze.

"Hold the line!" he shouted, thrusting his blade over the wall of shields.

Tired and short of breath, he quickly stole a glance to look for Sulla. *Surely he'll send reinforcements to us by now,* thought Atticus, trying hard not to spread doubt to his young counterpart. Quietly, Atticus prayed to both Jupiter and Mars, secreting a coin between his cheek and gum for the ferry he was certainly soon to take. In memory, Atticus didn't hear hooves nor the crash and shouting of men, only experienced a sudden slack in his shield— he nearly tumbled forward as the enemy dropped their defense to run routed. Atticus stopped the young man from giving chase by blocking him with his sword's broadside. "It's a trick," he explained, shaking his head. "Don't pursue. They'll spring cavalry on us in the open if we give chase."

"Our Thracians have punched their flank!" someone shouted.

"The day is ours!" screamed another, pointing a sword upon the plain of galloping horses as cavalry struck the fleeing foe. In dreamy recollection, Atticus watched a mounted barbarian with fine Roman armor free a man of his head in a single stroke. Great and powerful was the arm, and broad were the shoulders almost completely tattooed with the image of a horse's mane flowing from beneath polished bronze scale plates. Atticus remembered Spartacus wheeling around, and his first sight of the barbarian reaping a terrible harvest of men. The great shout that went up for the foreign cavalry saving the day from certain and humiliating defeat still rang in his ears.

Different shouts filled Atticus' dreaming ears, until he was awoken enough to discern the tumult just outside his tent was happening right now. Atticus rolled from his bunk and out the tent's flap. The sergeant's horse whinnied, startled by the sudden appearance of a man under hoof in darkness. Atticus mounted quickly, straddling the already packed horse, and instantly kicked it to a run. Atticus thundered past a soldier struggling with a blond slave over the alarm bell's mallet and caught a glimpse of another running a javelin through a big naked slave's back. The soldier wrenched at the pilum with both hands, trying mightily to dislodge the weapon, spilling entrails with every gory attempt. *Too late, they're inside,* Atticus rationalized, speeding for the opened gate flooded with a horde of attacking slaves and fleeing Romans. Atticus trampled a slave who'd stepped out to stop him while a second—just a boy—leapt clear barely in time.

# CHAPTER ELEVEN

**"...and issuing forth by hidden exit, seized the camp of the general by sudden attack, which he never expected."**

**—Florus,** *Epitome*

Slaves heatedly discussed different ways of escape from the half legion below. Pila and I remained seated on the outskirts, longing for a meal. I regretted drinking so much water when I shook the nearly empty flagon; I handed the remainder to Pila. My mind drifted to the overabundance of the feast just a few days prior, but instantly wished that I hadn't when my stomach growled. Pila took another bite of our hard bread, handing me the heel. We sat in the sun's warmth, listening to men decide our fate.

"The faithful will pray to Dionysus; we will consecrate the crater tonight with blood," announced Helica. "I'll study the death spasms after opening the centurion's entrails. If nothing else, his liver will give us the answer."

"Yes, dove," answered Spartacus.

"Why wait?" blurted Crixus. "We slide on guts? Swing like monkeys, huh, witch?" He waved his arms in a monkey-like pantomime and it made me think about the ropes of braided wild grapevine. Crastus began belting his awful laugh as I remembered the ropes and what I'd discovered a night before.

"Why," I announced, "don't we just make rope from all the

wild vines and climb down the sheer side?" Crixus, Crastus, Oenomaus, Helica, and Spartacus all gazed at me, then to each other, wordlessly blinking, everyone wondering why no one had thought of it already.

Every hand set to making rope that night; men gathered vines in large bundles, while women and children stripped and braided them in long strands inside our crater. Moonlight illuminated our expedition down the sheer side of Vesuvius. Stakes were secured and vine ropes dropped along the cliff's various shelves. My fear was abated by confident men; I did what they asked and they kept me from falling, and before long, I was descending with their same confident proficiency. We tested rigging, making improvements on our ascent. Gannicus shook my shoulder appreciatively upon returning to the summit. I felt like a necessary cog in the wheel of rebellion.

In the crater's center, Helica had our captured centurion's skull strapped tightly against a lone tree. Spartacus stood behind the bound man with blade in hand.

"*Gaula commada,*" the centurion spat. *Long-haired Gaul*; the worst insult a Roman could give a foreigner. Spartacus the Thracian ran his sharp blade across the man's throat effortlessly, while Helica read the former *optio's* chokes and spasms. Helica concentrated intently as he died, suddenly casting a worried glance to Spartacus when the man passed on to the underworld. Pila stared unflinching when Helica sliced the dead man from pubis to sternum without nicking an intestine. The centurion's guts spilled like a split bag of beans as Helica rummaged through them, up to her elbows in gore. Casting a frantic look to Spartacus, Helica muttered beneath her breath, her hands searching within the Roman's contents upon the ground.

"I can't see it," Helica pleaded, her voice quiet but betraying distress. She snatched a smaller knife and returned to the soldier's carcass, where her hands disappeared inside him once more. The woman worked the blade quickly to remove the liver as the large, gelatinous organ spilled wetly onto the ground atop a heaping pile of entrails. Helica stared at its steam intently, apprehensively flashing another worried look to Spartacus. "I can't see," she repeated quietly.

The sorceress' eyes closed in frustration, then reopened. She spoke aloud to everyone, and I knew her well enough by then to see that she was not confident.

"Spartacus' great and terrible power," announced Helica, "revealed by Dionysus in Capua, is enough for now! Never forget: as our commander lay dying, our god, the God of Slaves, raised our champion to deliver us from bondage through an earthly instrument!" she screamed, pointing at Spartacus. "The serpent, coiled above his face, witnessed with mine own eyes, kept death at bay." She continued about the vision of an army led by Spartacus to dispense Dionysus' justice upon wicked Romans. Helica's cult ushered prayers back to the outlawed god of the destitute, the poor, the slave, the woman. Dionysus, God of Wine and Fertility, would receive his due praise as Helica whipped the masses into raged frenzy. By the time she finished, desperate slaves were ready to run down the mountain and slay whomever they first laid hands on.

"This night!" interjected Spartacus, raising palms appealing for silence. "Slave place straw men. Light fire outside crater, Roman think slave fixed for night, with luck, Roman *will* lull. Second watch when men get sloppy, slave strike Roman then." He emphasized with clenched fists. "Roman camp, one acre, in perfect square, will be walled with wood and trenched. In center, be largest tent, command tent; we squeeze it first. Oenomaus, you quiet bell—bell must not ring. If just one man, ring bell, no more stabbing sleeping babes but smash by anvil." Spartacus spoke in a parable, so that even the most simple-minded shepherds understood.

Everyone listened intently to Spartacus, captivated by his voice of confidence, all praying our leader would deliver us from death as wolves circled below. Commanding attention, Spartacus drew himself up to his entire height, declaring, "It is better to die by iron, than of starvation!" Everyone, myself included, screamed enthusiastic agreement and set to work defeating the Roman army camped below.

"She doesn't know," intoned Pila, speaking privately to me as the uproar died out.

"Know what?" I asked, clueless.

"Helica can't tell if Spartacus is lucky," said Pila. "I heard them." Horrified, I flashed Pila an angry evil eye.

"Shut up," I demanded, "you're just a scrawny Samnite girl. What would *you* know about eastern sorcery?" Pila's lip curled, the doll fell to her side, and her head cocked.

"The gods don't care," she continued, "because they're not there." I shoved an elbow in her ribs and she stomped on my toe; we endured our equal pain silently, listening in the dark.

I let Pila drink first when we returned to the crater, then took a meager sip myself from our dwindling water. Fugitive slaves carried wicker men stuffed with straw to the crater's rim, planting them into loose soil with poles and silhouetting them against the coming evening sky. An entire army of straw sentries were posted against the side of the mountain before dusk, while an army of desperate slaves spilled quietly over on ropes made of wild vines. One old woman, unable to rappel down, agreed to stay at the summit and stoke fires to thicken the deception.

Pila balked at the ledge when we approached, begging me to let her stay with the old woman. The girl trembled, holding hands over her eyes as I lashed her onto my back in order to climb down. Slaves helped one another descend, while a separate contingent of experts concentrated on silently lowering weapons. We continued through dusk, traversing down into the night until safely reaching Vesuvius' base.

### INSIDE THE ROMAN CAMP, 682 AUC (73 BC)

The second shift was deep into their second hour as men settled into the routine of an uneventful night's watch. The hammering had stopped hours ago, and exhausted, snoring men slept contented in their barracks, insulated from an autumn chill. Proper watchtowers would go up tomorrow—for now, men perched precariously high upon temporary stands. Eight young men stood in three-hour shifts, keeping the camp safe while their brothers slept. Guarding the command tent stood a single soldier beside a post where a warning bell hung. The night man remained awake throughout, in charge of keeping shift changes on time and waking camp before dawn. Next to the large iron bell, the dutiful soldier held his mallet, ready to alert the camp in the event of danger.

### VESUVIUS, 682 AUC (73 BC)

We left our women beneath a ledge near the mountain's base, but some of the more manly women protested and came to fight. The majority of females stayed behind and were told to run if no one returned by morning. Helica kissed Spartacus farewell, wishing us luck. I turned to Pila, who crossed her arms, doll flopping over one elbow, daring me to try the same.

"If no one comes by morning," I told Pila, "run to the hills and hide. Get away from the group and get alone. Whatever happens, Pila, don't let them get you."

Pila put the doll behind her back, softened her smooth face, and kissed me on the cheek. "They won't," she replied.

That autumn night, we jogged without a word in the cool air along a gravel path with shields strapped to our backs and swords in hand. In a brisk pace around Vesuvius' base, nearing the city, we slowed and crouched up a ridge, slinking on our bellies to survey below. I sat just outside the circle of men as they decided what to do next.

"I need the boy," I clearly heard Gannicus say to the men. "He's quick and lean, he can keep up, and he'll know how to get back if I can't."

"Take him," replied the commander.

I nearly spat out my drink of water. We scurried off, crouching as close to the ground as possible along the ridge side, concealing ourselves with sea dunes.

Circumventing and redirecting inland, we approached from the sea with the Roman camp silhouetted behind moonlight. Using mounds of sea dunes, we sneaked from one to the other and approached their camp, our steps concealed by the sound of crashing waves. The dunes broadened into a narrow plain, forcing us to crawl for quite some distance to a trench and a tall, neatly arranged palisade of wooden planks.

My ears believed we were making enough racket to fill a circus, though in reality we made less than a mouse. Inching along, Gannicus finally stopped in the darkness as Vesuvius and the heavens loomed above. He pointed at men standing on a raised platform behind the wall. "There'll be a ditch as deep as your knees along the bottom," whispered Gannicus. "We need to crawl through, if it's not staked with lilies, and find a way in."

*Lilies,* I fretted, silently fearing staked impalement. Unfinished construction forced the two sentries to stand exposed on a stand with only a rail to keep them from falling. The two looked uncomfortable, peering over us and out to sea. The Romans expected us slaves to take the path down and beg for food when we tired of freedom. They certainly would never have considered a threat coming from the sea by slaves trapped up a mountain. The men guarding above faced the camp's rear; they were posted out of bureaucratic habit, not military necessity. I watched one head bob slightly, while the other leaned against his spear as they wrestled with the constricting night.

Rolling into a thankfully un-staked ditch, we crawled up to planks driven deep into the fertile black earth. Crawling behind Gannicus and sneaking peeks between slats, I caught brief glimpses of tied horses munching hay behind neatly arranged tents. Gannicus nodded for me to look through a knothole, so I put my eye to it and saw the outline of a soldier standing next to a bell at a large tent.

"How?" I mouthed, motioning to the palisade. Gannicus shrugged. My mind raced like Mercury thinking of ways to enter the camp, knowing we'd been at it way too long already. There seemed no way and, frustrated, I grabbed a handful of earth, crushing it between angry fingers as it poured through my grasp. My hands soon became spades, easily moving vast amounts of rich, volcanic earth, silently digging like a mole at the board's base.

Gannicus began helping and, before long, we sat in a deep indentation within the trench. Deeper and deeper we dug like dogs, until the plank's end became exposed. We worked our hands beneath and it popped like a child's tooth, nearly falling inward. Gannicus snapped to a knee, grabbing it with all his strength, and I quickly helped to keep it upright with a sigh of relief. Gannicus smiled in the dark at the close call, gently setting the board against another without them clapping. Peering through the breach revealed sentries up close in their battle with the night. Gannicus flashed a knowing look, setting the plank back loose, before crawling away. Quick as silence allowed, we raced back, trying to take advantage of a dozing night's watch before shift change.

An army of fugitives huddled in darkness beside a road on the outskirts of town. Gannicus heaped praises on me while describing the situation to impatient men. There in the darkness, Spartacus devised our final plan against the Roman camp. Gannicus was ordered to take a contingent to our new back door, silence the bell, and open the gate. Gannicus emphasized the gap's narrowness, advising that only spry men would make it through the opening. Asked whether or not Oenomaus would fit, Gannicus shrugged. "Without armor, maybe," he advised. Oenomaus immediately peeled off his breastplate, declaring to make himself fit. Spartacus ordered Oenomaus and Vitelli, a lean and muscular shepherd, to concentrate on the bell while everyone else opened the gate.

Once again, we snuck around within the dune flats, finally crawling back to the spot where a loose plank waited. Gannicus slipped through first and I went next—to see men in stands staring directly down at me. I remained motionless until one inhaled deeply, half asleep in the moonlight. Slowly, I regained enough confidence to move again when Oenomaus began slipping weapons through the gap from outside. Vitelli was big, but in the tall, lanky way; he was able to wriggle through. Oenomaus' build was different, and when he tried squeezing through the planks, he became stuck on his broad chest. Oenomaus exhaled all his breath and got scratched up shoving his massive form through the gap as we pulled at him with all our might. Oenomaus was halfway through when he became hung on his girding's buckle. He silently wrenched himself back, bruised and bloodied, to strip naked. Wearing only sandals, he struggled once again, this time completely nude. We pulled him through.

Like Greeks of antiquity, we slipped silently from the belly of our wooden horse to open our Troy. Gannicus and I ran along the fence's perimeter toward the gate while Vitelli and a naked Oenomaus veered to silence any alarm that may ring. Our men stabbed unsuspecting soldiers posted at the gate's entrance—they hit the ground dead while I strained alone with a huge beam slung in an iron cradle. With help, we set down the heavy beam, opening the gates for silent killers seething for sleeping soldiers.

Spartacus, Crixus, and Crastus were running for the command tent when a horrible, frantic ringing broke the silence. The soldiers posted on stands, suddenly startled alert, broke from stupors to look down, nocking bows from quivers hung full of arrows. Without thought, I flung an acorn at the guard as he drew, hitting him square in the face. The soldier shouted in pain, tumbling backward to be stabbed by an awaiting slave.

"Ambush! Inside the fence, ambush!" screamed the other, being pulled down to the clang of a bell. The terrible hacking and stabbing of iron into flesh thrummed from various tents within the camp. Hooves thundered beneath a lone rider galloping headlong at me for the open gate. Reloading and unable to wind, I jumped barely in time as the mounted Roman trampled the man nearest. I was oblivious then that I'd just locked eyes with Marcus Crassus' *optio primo*—the old centurion stared at me as he sped past.

Guttural groans and unearthly screams of the fatally wounded filled the night. Frightened young men begged for their lives, crying out for mothers as the walls crawled with attempts to flee. A few made it, but most did not; the majority were cut down before they knew what hit them, reminding me of the time gladiators fell upon my goats. The following silence after the bell's ringing amplified continued slaughter as I ran to the command tent where Oenomaus lay. The Celt panted for breath as I fell to the ground before him, his face a mask of intense pain.

Oenomaus' hands worked at stuffing coils of intestines back into his belly. A slain soldier held a bent javelin in a death grip next to us, having been cleaved to death by my friend. Oenomaus had killed the sentry after being run through the back by a soldier's *pilum*. Most of the terrible damage was done when the javelin became stuck as the young soldier tried in vain to dislodge it from my friend with strenuous wrenching. Mighty Oenomaus killed the assailant, only after his midsection had been ripped to pieces by the javelin's bending mechanism.

"Get my people...over...mountains," Oenomaus grunted, between gasps of blood spilling from his mouth. Crouched near him, I was lost in the depths of sadness and confused as to why Oenomaus could possibly think that I had that kind of power... until my lord answered from behind.

"I swear it, by your gods and mine, dearest friend," vowed Spartacus softly into our friend's ear. Then he thrust the sharp dagger between Oenomaus' ribs, freeing our friend from pain as I held him. Spartacus shook his head, muttering, "The man, I cannot afford to lose, lost already."

He pointed to me and ordered, "I give you, Publipor, this honor: you will wear Oenomaus' girding and buckle in return for burying this...most powerful Celt." Spartacus gave Vidovic a stern look. "Vidovic, you will give no aid to the boy with the hole. The boy must earn a death's wage that Oenomaus has paid with his life." Spartacus saw the pain he caused the shocked Celt Vidovic and softened. "Oenomaus will take what he needs with him into eternity, my brother. Vidovic, help the woman prepare his body." Spartacus abruptly turned to Crastus. "Take horse, hunt down and kill that rider, before he warns Pompeii." Crastus nodded. "Gannicus, retrieve women, before they go to ground." Everyone abruptly departed, complying with Spartacus' instructions.

The War for Herculaneum was over before sunrise beneath

Vesuvius, while Caius Claudius Glaber, the newly minted praetor, lay dead in his bunk with the camp's laundry woman. Spartacus walked away in the new light of day, shaking his head and mumbling, "Too soon, Oenomaus. Too soon..."

I dug in loose soil until the grave was up to my shoulders. Oenomaus' yellow-haired woman sobbed and sang, lovingly washing the body with a sponge beside me. Helios finally broke the horizon, and I'd run dry of tears when Helica walked to the edge, casting her piercing gaze at me.

"Oenomaus enjoyed your company," said Helica. "He gave you many compliments in life. Our Celt's grateful you toil for him now. This isn't punishment, you know; it's a high honor to bury such a man. It means you are family, entitled to inheritance. His sword, his scabbard, his armor, will be entombed in Celtic custom." She paused. "But this...this is gifted to you," Helica handed me Oenomaus' buckle. With dirty, blistered palms, I admired the screaming eagle cast in silver with outstretched wings and grasping talons.

"Skin these dogs," yelled Crixus, breaking the surreal moment, "before they harden." He wanted to harvest all the valuable armor before rigor mortis made the task gruesomely difficult. Helica helped me climb from the pit while three Celts, along with Vidovic, lowered Oenomaus' freshly shrouded body into the grave. Bound in linen from head to toe, Oenomaus was interred as his buxom woman wailed into unbound hair. Vidovic and his fellow Celts interred their barbarian chieftain with every tool he'd need in the afterlife, except one. Helica had snuck a coin into his mouth, against their custom, before he was wrapped, just in case. Oenomaus' woman inconsolably sobbed as I helped backfill my friend's grave.

Helica swabbed a salve on my blisters after the ceremony, reassuring me that it made my hands tougher. Once the Celts were finished with all their rites for Oenomaus, Helica handed me a bag of olives and we sat chewing and spitting pits. The snack slaked both thirst and hunger.

"Where is Pila?" I asked.

"Pila went to her grandfather."

"Is he alive? Did Umpappa survive?" I asked.

"No, sweet boy. Pila's gone to place him on the pyre and give ferry payment." I was relieved that Pila was safe, and it allowed me to take a step back and see the bigger picture before us all. I thought of a comment Gannicus had made on one of our outings: *"Roman soldiers don't take a shit without written orders,"* he'd said. The thought seized me that if I could just read to Helica what was written, maybe she could give Spartacus a leg up on our next foe.

"We need to grab the Romans' correspondences," I told Helica. "Their orders will have information we might need. I can read them to you."

"Smart boy, you're going to come in very handy," Helica commented, cupping my chin.

Helios dragged the sun directly overhead by the time our dead were burned or buried in a hasty memorial. Crastus returned with news that the mounted soldier who'd escaped rode north to Rome, not south for Pompeii, buying us time. Spartacus ordered the captives bound and their camp seized before riding off with Crixus to speak privately of fortune.

# CHAPTER TWELVE

**"No man ever had a better friend, nor worse enemy..."**
—*Tomb of Felix Lucius Cornelius Sulla*

I've never been to Rome, but if I imagine what it looks like, I think it'd look like Pompeii. Located in Campania, the heart of Italy's grape basket, a one-day ride from the city, is where wealthy Romans retired beneath Vesuvius' shade. Foremost of all Campania's triple resort cities was Pompeii, but all were great, successful, well-greased money-making machines. Most estates were owned by wealthy previous consuls and senators, aristocrats with rank. But, just as Heracleum was rich, Pompeii was wealthy. Where Heracleum was fancy, Pompeii was extravagant. The villas were larger, the mosaics bigger, more colorful, and ultra-realistic. The art, with vivid reds and yellows painted upon architecture of stone craft, was second to none. Pompeii boasted four baths, a forum, an amphitheater, its own *ludis,* ten *popinas* or bars, and several *tabernae*—brothels. It's where Spartacus took the most magnificent black stallion, Pegasus, from an elite stable full of hotblooded, imported sporting horses. Spartacus commandeered the most expensive stud in all the world, previously owned by Marcos Meteli himself; we helped ourselves to everything else. My purse bulged heavy around this time, along with Oenomaus' giant silver buckle, and my beat-up old cord belt felt its strain.

While Herculaneum received warning of our coming and most had escaped, the Pompeiians weren't so lucky. Citizens of Pompeii were told their army had the slaves trapped and contained on Mt. Vesuvius. Correspondences from Glaber to Pompeii gave assurances the rabble would be rounded up within a week. Pompeii's high, sturdy stone walls and well-maintained gates hadn't been needed since the civil war years ago. People of Pompeii hailed what they assumed was the victorious approaching Roman army, certainly dragging bound slaves to the arena's cages where they belonged. Pompeii's Herculaneum gate was held wide open; it teemed with people shouting patriotic approval of the army's success, welcoming them to billet in the town.

"*Fugitavi!*" shouted someone too late. Our horses, walking a few paces behind an army of slaves dressed as soldiers leading phony captives, rushed for the open gates. Screams filled the afternoon as the city erupted in terror. Pompeii's citizens realized too late that they'd been duped by disguised slaves. Slaves resembling soldiers from a distance ran through a cloud of dust, rushing to support their mounted forerunners. I ran with everyone else, watching Spartacus and Crixus ride beneath the heavy iron portcullis when it fell. As Spartacus passed beneath, Crixus followed, but the gate fell with heavy iron spikes. Rusted metal dug deep into Crixus' stolen stallion's rump, violently nailing the beast into the earth. Crixus skidded several feet across cobbled stones as the horse kicked helplessly beneath cruel iron. The large horse labored to rise as shock set in. We clamored beneath the heavy iron gate, partially wedged open by the animal's huge carcass, thrashing the last of its death throes while pinned to the earth.

Crixus shook off the fall quickly, giving iron to anyone near, as Crastus rushed the gear house, killing everyone and raising the heavy gate himself. There, at the gates of Pompeii, I witnessed murderous debauchery beyond description, a whirlwind of murder and rape that consumed the port city. Once-docile slaves dragged their former owners out into streets as blood offerings. Slaves sacrificed their owners' wives and children outside front doors in uncontrollable riotous rage. Sewers ran red through the streets as blood from Pompeii's people flowed. Glaber's confiscated baggage train was finally pulled through by our women as screams of terror and groans of pain echoed from every wall. I was watching the wealthy citizens run like chickens from a cook pot when I recognized the pitch of a particular girl's scream.

*Pila!* I thought, running to the sound, afraid for her. My feet found me flying up marble steps, every other stair skipped and untouched beneath me. Bursting through a door, I saw Pila being pushed down to the floor by a toothless, dirty, wild-eyed slave with long, frayed hair. The attacker's member was stiff, and he was attempting to force himself inside the tiny girl as I ran at him. Pila screamed, pushing him away with all her might as he continued trying to violently rip off her tattered wool dress. I was on him, jabbing at his belly in a flash. The wretch grasped my blade with both hands as it sank, and we locked eyes before I yanked the knife back. For just the briefest moment, deep furrows appeared in his flesh as the sharp blade exited his grasp. I caught a glimpse at white of bone, my view instantly obscured by rivulets of blood streaming through filthy hands. The wretch turned and ran, spouting a crimson trail all through the extravagant home to an exit. I breathed a sigh of relief. Pila hugged me while straightening her dress and crying.

Noises from the underworld engulfed Pompeii. Pila grabbed her *pupae* from the corner of the room and put her hands over her ears while closing her eyes. I grabbed Pila's wrist and we ran up more marble steps together into a master suite. We ducked through fine curtains, where an ornately carved wardrobe stood big enough for us both to hide next to a bed. I helped Pila into it, and we spent the day hidden from horror until dark. Eventually, thirst and hunger drove us from hiding to timidly feel around the strange home, and eventually to tiptoe out onto strange streets. A cloudless sky filled with stars from end to end and a golden waxing moon illuminated the carnage. A mumbling woman and a sobbing man quietly lamented the night at different parts of the street.

Drums, horns, and jeering crowds broadcast up the thoroughfare from the amphitheater. The city of Pompeii rose from the bay and was built on a steep angle upon Mt. Vesuvius' base. The rise in elevation and torches, alight in the Forum, illuminated the metropolitan horizon above. Taking Pila's wrist and leading her up the hill toward the light with my massive, grapevine-wrought knife, I passed all manner of absolute horror on our way to the Forum. When we arrived, Spartacus and Helica reclined on couches at the place of honor, while Crixus and Crastus were absurdly dressed in improperly adjusted togas, feasting and living lively. The bonfires were even larger than before, and music I'd never heard made beautiful girls in colorful dresses dance seductively. Pila glared angrily, no doubt thinking I stared at the dancing women, but I was suddenly lost in thought over my friend Oenomaus.

The world went on. Our plight continued. It hadn't ended when Oenomaus was run through the back and his stomach torn open. The finality of it struck me. I missed my friend, and I was saddened by the fact that I'd never see him again. Tears welled in my eyes watching everyone carry on like he never existed or that this young girl hadn't just been attacked. Seeing them oblivious to it all made me resentful. A stunning assortment of treasure in different forms was piled high in the theater's center—was it worth as much as the girl or my friend? I saw intricately carved ivory and polished silver placed atop heaping chests of jewelry and coins, along with blocks of salt or Eastern pepper. Barrels of vermillion—enough to paint the town red twice—were stacked as high as pyramids. Crowds in the amphitheater entertained themselves with Pompeiians, roaring disapproval over a current match in the background. The futility of it all sickened me.

It was Herculaneum multiplied. Helica spotted us first, waving us to her with a smile. Upon closer inspection, Helica's smile was lost as her fingers snapped, recognizing intimately Pila's ragged condition. The striking woman demanded a meal and bath be prepared for the girl quickly. We were soon eating ravenously, and I purposely avoided *garum*, fish sauce with un-watered wine, remembering what curses it brought last time. When Pila could eat no more, Helica sent us to the bath with two attendees to get clean. The women of Helica's Dionysus cult brushed and trimmed our hair after we were scraped clean from our bath. I could tell Pila's nerves had settled, which made me happy.

SPARTACUS, A BARBARIAN OF THRACE, REMEMBERS
674 AUC; (81 BC), AN EXCEPTIONALLY BLOODY YEAR

*I did not want any of this,* Spartacus reflected. *All I wanted was to make my father proud; now, I can't let the men down,* he thought to himself in regret, standing beside the door in a room full of important men. General Felix Lucius Cornelius Sulla sat between two capable commanders: twenty-four-year-old Pompey and thirty-year-old Marcus Crassus, in the six hundred and seventy-fourth year since the city's founding.

I watched the room where busy administrators passed sentence on the recently apprehended. They'd all been searched for hidden arms and interrogated long before I had anything to do with them in my dealings as Sulla's personal bodyguard. The traitors looked roughed up good after having been milked for co-conspirators to add upon the lists. When we'd won the Civil War, Sulla's title of Felix, or lucky, was decreed to be officially affixed onto his civic name, having it bestowed upon himself—by himself. With my help, Sulla subdued the senate; now he pursued retribution by releasing me and my men to hunt traitors with impunity. Sulla had Pompey, the young phenomenon, sit alongside him between the older wealthy rival, Senator Marcus Crassus, I knew in order to keep proceedings civil. The separation sometimes quelled their constant bickering that I thought was funny, though neither of the bitter rivals knew I thought the powerful men of Rome both small and petty. They'd smartly backed Sulla over Marius during the civil war when fortunes weren't as clear. The lucky schmucks hedged bets and were now being paid dividends. I once respected the fact that all three were veterans of foreign, domestic, and even, civil wars between Italians. Those glory days are just memories, and to know what these men had become is to despise them now. Together with bribe, carrot, stick, and sword, the three, along with myself, tamed the Italian tribes, forced an eastern king to sue for peace, and saved a republic from itself. Those three Romans gave me and my men such a taste for riches that we all went east once more in search of wealth, the amount of which defies imagination. That is, until the newly elected Proconsuls, Marius, and Cinna stole control of Rome in a coup, while we fought with Sulla abroad for gods and country.

We were in Illicium when word reached my commander, General Sulla. Our praetor insisted on oaths of loyalty from everyone in the field right there and then. I was just a young warrior of some repute by then. "Just another Thracian, handy with horse and sword," they'd say behind my back. And on that terrible day, upon my home shore, I spoke a vow that would bind me to a madman: Lucius Sulla, *Dictator ad Vitum*—till death.

This day's order of business, like all others since thwarting the attempted coup, was handling those who'd conspired with Rome's enemies. Marcus Crassus sat next to his new Greek slave, Merillius, reading the names of those who had large enough estates worth confiscating. Crassus introduced new names upon Sulla's lists: citizens with better plots. The proscription lists detailed patrician families summarily marked for death after backing the wrong side. Most were names of Marius or Cinna supporters and their families, ancient names of Roman clans that I helped confiscate lands from and eradicate. Some, guilty of only being cursed by the immortal gods with prime real estate coveted by powerful greedy men. Crassus grumbled at Merillius, a trusted slave and accountant, about Sulla giving the city of Nola and its surroundings to Pompey. Crassus seethed at the thought of so much fine property lost in deference to a man who'd never even held office. I thought it funny when Crassus declared once in jest, "Pompey the Great," insulting the young upstart. I thought it even funnier when, to Marcus Crassus' disgust, the moniker stuck, going so far as to be used earnestly by Sulla. I once heard Crassus whisper Pompey's darker nickname in private: "Butcher's Boy." The baby-faced commander had earned the title by being the son of Pompieus Strabo, the man who put already-conquered Spanish towns to the sword, or more notoriously, tainting wells.

Pompey yawned at the proceedings served by his Greek attorney, Cicero, giving no thought to old Marcus Crassus whatsoever. All while Sulla poured over lists of senators, noble class *equieties*, and merchants who'd backed the wrong political faction. I personally posted throughout the countryside lists of condemned names, outlawing entire households for summary execution. I knew Sulla's family were murdered by Marian supporters while on campaign, and also knew the man would take retribution in copious abundance. Sulla had escaped the first bloodshed as a youth, and he now exacted adult revenge with my hands, making me stinking rich in the process. It was Sulla's striking, manly looks which made him so popular among acting troops while in exile. Sulla cut quite a manly figure and made such promises of wealth that it attracted men of all sorts, including an impressionable foreign mercenary like myself. In all my time with the man, Sulla never lost his taste for theater life nor bawdy jokes, but, like Janus, he could turn a face murderously serious whenever necessary.

## THE FIRST TRIUMVIRATE

"Neither of you seem up to the task," remarked Sulla, "so, I've outsourced." His way of saying that he'd hired a bounty hunter: me.

"What care do you have for this pup, and why bother?" Marcus Crassus asked, disgusted, knowing the young Julian's family was on the path to obscurity anyway. Marcus tried reasoning with the Dictator once more, not wanting to invest any more money on a goose chase for some boy priest who didn't even own property and would probably wind up just another failed Caesarian.

"The boy is Cinna's nephew," Sulla insisted, "and he's married to Marius' niece. He'll divorce the girl or be judged dissident." Sulla looked at both men. "Either way, any child of that woman is forfeit. Marius' line ends here and now, forever, immortal gods damn him," grumbled the dictator. A bored Pompey wished to leave while Marcus weighed lives against silver as Sulla plotted bloody revenge. In the interim, Sulla released me, his trusted hound. Inevitably, I'd earn my pay and the boy would eventually be his.

SPARTACUS RECALLS MEETING JULIUS CAESAR AT
THE TEMPLE OF JUPITER IN 674 AUC (81 BC)

I was partially delayed by a priest in a pointy felt hat at the temple's entrance after dismounting and securing my horse to the post. The priest moved quickly, trying to thwart my entrance, when I strode toward him.

"You cannot enter Jupiter's temple, barbarian," hectored the priest, scattering sacred chickens.

"Why not?" I asked in my best Latin, which never felt natural on my tongue.

"Your luck will run out and your horse will burst from Jupiter's bolt," declared the priest, attempting to block the entrance once more.

"Show me," I said, challenging the robed boob. I turned at the doorway to wait for my expensive horse to explode.

"He won't do it now," stated the priest, exacerbated by my heathen ignorance.

"Why not?" I repeated, leaving the priest to stammer incoherent gibberish as I continued beneath the temple's arch unimpeded. "Can man hide here?" I asked, changing the subject and slapping the waist-high oaken offering box's side; my golden agate ring caused a heavy thud.

"Of course not," answered the stunned priest. When I pulled my short *gladius*, the dull rasp of my blade leaving its scabbard silenced his petulant protesting.

"Bet this aureus..." I wagered, displaying a gold coin with my free hand, "make boy jump from box if donate to Jupiter, to God of Gods." I knew he understood my rough Latin. The priest trembled wordlessly as I held my blade over the slot, slowly lowering the sword. A scream from within revealed a fifteen-year-old apprentice priest, struggling from confines to extradite himself, before I pierced him.

I snatched young Gaius Julius Caesar by his ear with my hand and led him out by it. I returned the aureus to my purse, anticipating another once I'd returned the boy to the *bosa*.

"I told you both," Sulla gloated, upon hearing of my arrival, "my dog would catch the boy." He chuckled as the three deciding Rome's fate watched as I led the boy, Julius, by the neck, shoving him forward once we'd entered.

"Gaius Julius Caesar, you've been accused of conspiring to overthrow the Republic in a seditious plot to crown Gaius Marius King of Rome. How do you plead?" asked Cicero, Pompey's prosecutor. "I'll remind the accused: punishment for sedition is summary death." The sound of men being throttled in an adjacent room filled the otherwise silent chamber.

"I thought I stood accused by you, Sulla, not this...Triumvirate," spoke the intelligent young priest, gesturing at the men seated on either side of him. "How can a young bride's groom threaten 'The Dictator for Life?'" argued young Caesar boldly. "If love's a crime, then I'm guilty. Guilty of loving Rome with all my heart." Marcus Crassus rolled his eyes with disgust while Pompey admired the boy's guts as Sulla barely restrained his natural homicidal tendencies. I grasped my sword's hilt, waiting for the nod, but Sulla closed his eyes, exhaling instead.

"Please, kid," pleaded Sulla, "we're not in the mood for oratories or made-up religious omens. What we need is for you to divorce." Caesar, about to interrupt, was quickly silenced by Sulla's palm. "She's a Marius, and if you plant a baby in her, it will be a Marius; his line will not continue," Sulla threatened, emphasizing his meaning with a determined face. "*If,*" continued Sulla, "she were to be divorced by her husband, and *if* she joined the order of virgins, then *maybe* she'd live. I divorced my wife while she lay on her deathbed, son. This one divorced for money," Sulla pointed at Marcus Crassus. "This one divorced—now he's a Meteli," Sulla reiterated, pointing at Pompey, then turned his palms skyward. "So, come on. Divorce her. The Tibris *can* hold more bodies. And another thing," added the dictator, holding up papers for the young man to see. "When I pass these legislations, even *you* might one day have a senatorial seat."

"A senator beneath tyranny; how enticing," Caesar replied, flirting with death.

"Stupid," Sulla stated. "I'm going to retire, when I'm sure another Marius can't try to usurp our Republic ever again." His patience was nearly spent.

"Like you?" asked a fool-hearted Julius. I tightened my fingers around the handle, aiming for the boy's scrawny neck, anticipating a nod from Sulla signaling death. Surprisingly, Sulla exhaled again instead, waving the young priest away. I released my sword, using the free hand to grasp the luckiest young priest in Rome by his neck and leading him out with it...still attached.

I was thinking of all my killings while escorting the young patrician from the premises when the impertinent upstart asked, "How did Sulla get Mithradates to sue for peace?"

*"Veni, vidi, vici,"* I mumbled, my thoughts consumed with trying to avoid killing the boy's woman—I hated killing women.

"What?" Caesar hectored.

"I went, I found, I killed," I menaced. "You remarry, divorce wife. Don't want to kill you, nor her, no want kill women...or boys," I implored. I'd learn years later what an indelible mark I'd left upon the young Caesarian. After releasing the boy outside, I returned to Sulla's chamber to stand guard inside the door.

"That one's trouble," Sulla mentioned of Caesar before returning to writing legislation that forever ended any prospects of another civil war and ceaseless dictatorship.

"Please," interrupted Marcus Crassus, "no one can hear anything that boy says past that funny-shaped head of his.

Besides, who ever heard of a *Caesarian* accomplishing anything in over two hundred years?" Marcus Crassus dismissed the youth as a waste of time, desperately wanting a return to the profitable business of proscription.

"I could use a young man like that," schemed Pompey.

"I told you my dog would find the little dolt," Sulla gloated, pointing to me. "No, Marcus, and you're wrong, Pompey; that little fool would give away the grain stores for a few votes. Anyone with eyes can see he's another Gracchi." Sulla then prophesied a curse to Pompey that would someday come to pass. "Have your way and take him; only bear in mind the boy you are so eager to save will one day deal the deathblow to the cause of aristocracy, which you have joined with me in upholding; for in this *Caesar* there is more than one Marius."

After I'd been relieved, I paid a man to read the notices tacked to a news post. The man counted acres doled out by Sulla to his supporters and veterans for the past year. When he was done, I thanked him with payment, dreaming of a day I could retire and raise cows. *I'll buy a pretty Thracian, marry, and plant lots of boys in her on an estate of my own.*

Though I knew most merely referred to me as just a Romanized barbarian, I worked for a dream, so I could one day purchase a life of my own.

POMPEII, PRESENT DAY, PUBLIPOR, 682 AUC, (73 BC)

"Watch out, shit for brains!" yelled Crixus, driving a four-wheeled wine cart with two yoked mules too fast. Iron-shod hooves pounded sparking cobblestones as the cart flew at me, going the wrong way down a one-way street. I was pushed against the nearest wall by some strong figure. Crastus sat next to Crixus, bellowing, "*Aw, Aw, Aw,*" while several men in the back sat upon a wine skin so large it took up the entirety of the wagon's cargo hold. I watched them blow past while men shared drinks from a hose. I'd been pushed to the wall by Egus, who raised his brows and smiled broadly at the close call, his arm still across my chest.

"Spartacus looks for you," said Egus. "In the House of Faun, near the big gate. 'Faun' is etched on its front; can't miss it." I nodded my thanks to the squinting toothy man and ran to find my commander. "Where is your woman?" Egus shouted after me.

"Pila's helping in the forum...and she's not my woman," I corrected, yelling back as I went to find the House of Faun. It didn't take long, though I was momentarily confused by its entrance. Instead of a house, it looked like a row of retail shops with a green door in its middle, forcing me to do a double take at the curb's marker. "Faun" was unmistakably etched there, so I decided to enter the green painted door.

The interior sprawled before me for an entire block with exquisitely painted walls trimmed in gold along its entire length. Tiny painted cherubs frolicked throughout the home in silly depictions at odd places as I entered the home's atrium. Inside, along with the sound of tumbling water, came laughter—deep belly laughs that started and stopped in fits and pauses, then resumed. The kind of laugh that makes you involuntarily smile without even knowing what's funny. Spartacus belted another fit of laughter from his seat on a bench as I approached. Drawing closer, I saw a large orange kitten padding about, marking the huge man with its cheeks, frantically vocal. It paced back and forth, rubbing its chin on ornate greaves, meowing incessantly, begging madly for more of the salted fish Spartacus fed to it. Spartacus let the cat lick his salty fingers clean, laughing heartily at the tiny creature, entertained.

"You called for me, commander?" I interrupted.

"I did, thank you," Spartacus said in his deep voice, breaking more dried fish apart. "You miss Oenomaus?"

I nodded, suddenly saddened with the memory.

"Me too. Man of his word is rarity, son," Spartacus continued, scratching the greedy kitten on its head. "Lost few that night, Publipor—lot less than I thought we would." He shook his head, remembering the raid. I followed his gaze to the floor, where I noticed tiny colored tiles. My eyes shifted to focus on them.

An enormous tile mosaic scene of war, with crashing horses and lowered spears, sprawled before me. One man in the scene had long flowing hair like that of a Greek, while another was hooded in strange foreign garb. "Alexander the Great, defeating Persians," Spartacus explained when he saw me transfixed. "Persian beat, horse is turned," he pointed. I could see the logic in it as the cat lapped at his extended finger. I'd no idea who Persians were, but they looked flamboyant, and the one on the turned horse clearly had fear tiled onto his face.

"You read...please?" Spartacus asked. I'd still not become accustomed to being asked politely—it made me work harder to please him. Realizing I'd not answered the man, I nodded. That's when Spartacus threw the salted fish out a window and the noisy cat followed. He washed his hands in the fountain. "Gannicus watches you, tells me things; he says, you good ranger, real good," he declared. "Gannicus *also* say Publipor have woman." Both proud and embarrassed, I blushed.

"No, I...she's just a girl," I said. "The bath man's granddaughter. The old man made me promise to look after Pila—short spear, that's her name—before we were overrun."

"You man of you word?" asked Spartacus, pointing now to a small, opened chest full of papyrus. I retrieved it instead of answering and began reading. It was a ledger of payroll for soldiers and itemized amounts of inventory. I read the confiscated correspondence clearly and loudly for my commander as he listened silently. Spartacus had me read the letter from Marcus

Crassus twice, which informed Glaber that a second force would be raised by month's end. Crassus wrote, excoriating Glaber that a blockade for a "pack of runaway slaves" was shameful, instead ordering a frontal assault once Praetor Varinius arrived with a fresh legion.

"This...Varinius, will conscript youngster on way...like Glaber had," Spartacus reasoned.

"It says here that Lucius Furius, Varinius' *legit*, has departed already with another two thousand men, completing Glaber's half legion," I read. "Furius will be here any day."

"Furius too late. We ambush *new* Romans, where we kill *old* Romans," he concluded aloud, working the logistics of it with his mind. "Slaves celebrate lost, sacrifice this night in *palestra*. I will have plan then, share there. Find Gannicus; we go to Herculaneum," he ordered, then stood, stopping me with a palm. Spartacus eyed me up and down, standing massive and thumbing Oenomaus' silver buckle, which was hung at my belly behind an old, frayed cord belt. "That not, how you wear it," Spartacus spoke, kindly. The bare-chested man bent to open a nearby trunk and looked at me.

"I...don't have a belt," I explained.

"How long, you wear same clothes?" Spartacus asked.

"We get a new tunic every year," I explained, suddenly ashamed of my rags.

"Here," Spartacus said, tossing me a new linen garment, then tossed another from the opened trunk. "Give other to woman. Come here...please," said Spartacus, motioning for me to follow. Rounding the fountain, I changed tunics and came upon a set of armor racked neatly before me. "Roman armor, child armor, but it work," explained Spartacus. "Look size, gift from Helica, try on." I couldn't believe my eyes nor ears. The breastplate was a tad big, but Spartacus explained that I'd grow into it and having it loose was more desirable than going without one in war.

The helmet sat well as I strapped the leather skirting about my waist; meanwhile, Spartacus replaced the buckle on the sword's belt with Oenomaus' silver eagle. I'd put on my new greaves and wrist leathers by the time Spartacus finished looping the short sword onto the belt. He flipped it to his other hand behind me, buckling it tightly at my front. Stepping back, Spartacus looked down at me with his hands on hips, smiling like an approving god.

"Publipor, you look frightening," said Spartacus. "Be even scarier, if sandals, not look about to come apart." I down looked at the thin strips of leather with holes, barely clinging to my feet. "Go to Roman house, find sandal, find you woman sandal," Spartacus ordered. I was too far over the moon to correct him about Pila not being my woman; I simply nodded.

Standing at the pool, I saw myself decked for war and enjoyed the power reflecting back. I pulled for the sword, but my reflection was reversed and I grasped the wrong hip; confused, I turned to Spartacus.

"Publipor, right-handed," Spartacus explained. "You wear sword on left, not going in shield wall anyway. Publipor, eyes up— reflection opposite. Not *look*," Spartacus said, reaching for his own sword to exemplify, "but *feel*."

I reached again, this time *feeling*, without a look at the reflection. I pulled the short sword reflexively.

The blade felt great in my hand, perfectly weighted with a lead pommel. I looked like a free man holding the sword, a man who would never take another whipping. "I hear you have good aim with this," Spartacus said, stuffing my pouch of acorns into the girding of the leather belt he'd gifted, next to Helica's dagger and the heft of my bulging purse. "This, handier," he continued, picking up a nut wood bow strung with sinew and showing it to me, along with a quiver full of iron-bobbed arrows. "What Helica, say gift, I call wage, son. Wage earned." He handed everything to me. I'd never felt happiness like that before and I didn't know how to react, so I sheathed the sword to take up the bow. "Mind, little bow punch armor not, but take eye, maybe. Remember," said Spartacus, wiggling the sword's pommel at my hip, "stab, not slash...and here, this week's pay." Spartacus reached back into the box and placed five silver sesterces into my grasp. The realization that I held enough in my hands to purchase a horse or two struck me silly; I wouldn't have to steal them if I didn't want to.

Eager to accomplish my duties as a paid soldier, I told him, "I saw Gannicus earlier, but I'm not sure where he is now." I stuffed my pay away. It felt strange to be wearing so much of anything, let alone polished metal and leather. I was heavier, slower, but more protected. And most importantly, I looked the part of one of Spartacus's men.

"Gannicus is at *tabernae*, down street," Spartacus replied. I stared blankly, blinking in response. "Is across street, temple Fortuna Augusta, walk behind, go block, then turn right." I mumbled what he'd said in the wrong order. "Yeah, all right, just come along, then." We exited to the street, where Spartacus made a chopping motion with his hand in the brothel's direction. "If Publipor get lost, boy just follow cock and balls carved into street," Spartacus finished, pointing at the paving stone in the middle of the road.

There, chiseled into paving stone, was an image of a penis and two testicles pointing in the direction Spartacus indicated. "Tell him: come quick," Spartacus added, and was chased noisily back into the House of Faun by the perpetually hungry juvenile cat.

"Yes, lord," I answered, following carved cocks, breaking in new leather, and armed to the teeth, all while marching like a soldier on busted sandals with holes in their bottoms.

# CHAPTER THIRTEEN

**"...who could believe that an army of Amazon women, or a city, or a tribe without men could ever...not only organized but make inroads upon the territory of other people."**

—Strabo, *Geographies*

The same phallic symbol carved in the street was rendered on a wooden sign above a brothel's door, adorned with wings jutting from stone by a metal pole. I stepped beneath the curtain to smell incense and exotic aromas. A lyre-playing man stopped upon seeing me enter with my armor, sword, and bow. After a brief inspection, the musician returned to playing, disregarding me completely. Ladies plied their trade in stalls or waited for customers on each side of the room as erotic noises of ecstasy bounced from every wall.

My task to find Gannicus was interrupted by an attractive woman with unbound hair and excessive jewelry. The tall, fair woman ran her fingers across my breastplate. "Looking for some action, soldier?" cooed the prostitute. She walked on, chiffon swaying, laughing as I stammered a reply. As I tried to refocus, I caught my first glance of the much-rumored warrior witch Shixa, who was seated across the room. Even in the brothels' din, I could tell Shixa was a very powerfully built woman with hair like snow and pasture-green eyes. The warrioress reclined beneath lamplight, obviously from northern Gaul, identified by their distinctive white hair. The outline of a striking serpent was marked on both sides of her face; long, blue, tattooed fangs ran from her temples, framing a predatory appearance. This topless, platinum-blonde witch with emerald eyes entertained both terrible Germans; she stared at me unsettlingly while they drank together on an oversized sofa.

"Sheezin, face!" exclaimed Crastus, following her gaze. "Comen zie join." He patted his hand on a cushion, welcoming me onto the sprawling couch.

"I can't. Spartacus sends me to retrieve Gannicus," I explained. "Have you seen him?"

"Don't know, just got here, is possible. Ask Shixa," said Crixus, mocking. "Shixa? You see brown shit piece, stand yea tall?" he asked, holding his hand away from the couch, low to the ground. "He'd be asking for boys to plug," Crixus continued, grinning at Crastus, "and he smell of goat. You smell man like that, Shixa?" Crastus laughed, filling the room with his pestilence.

I'd soon learn that the white-haired witch was a druid from northern Gaul who specialized in telling fortunes, interpreting bird omens, and manipulating stupid men. Shixa smiled ominously, exposing unnaturally large canines, playing along with the brutes. "We had someone like that earlier," hissed Shixa. "We sent him off with a billy—he seemed satisfied." Shixa shrugged as the girls lying about with them laughed.

"Where you get ridiculous clothes, shit face?" asked Crixus.

"Pube, du looken zie like Ee—ta—lee—on monkey-ficker," Crastus added, chucking a coin at me. I dodged as it whiffed past my head to ring against the floor. Several girls leapt up and ran, fighting, after it.

"Another two-thousand-man army," I explained with importance, "is headed to Herculaneum to link up with Glaber as we speak."

Both men laughed.

"Might be bones not burned left on pyre, Roman can link up to," Crixus quipped.

"There's more. More Roman soldiers coming," I berated, "and more besides them! Three thousand—maybe even more than that!" I was shouting, frustrated with their indifference.

"That it, sheezin kompf," declared Crastus in his busted Latin. He stood to eject me. I grasped my scabbard and motioned my right over the sword's handle as he approached. "Pull, I kill you," Crastus promised, closing the gap and grabbing my ear before I did anything stupid. Crastus pulled painfully, kicking my behind out of the brothel and sending me sprawling on my belly in the street. The lyre player held the entrance curtain aside while Crastus threw my bow upon my back, laughing his stupid laugh, before both returned inside.

"You trying to find me?" asked Gannicus from the shadows.

"Yeah—no...well, Spartacus is," I answered, grimacing and rolling over onto my back. "He wants to set an ambush on the Appian, north of Herculaneum, at the place we captured the militia." I suddenly worried about scuffs on my brand-new breastplate. I felt gouges left by the street with my fingertips. Gannicus helped me to stand and together we retrieved my arrows that had scattered about, placing them in the quiver one by one. The music from inside stopped long enough for the curtain to be pulled once again as another man was tossed out onto the same spot where I'd landed. A grunt from impact with the street was his only sound, and all of us were motionless until the silence was finally broken by Gannicus.

"I heard about your armor, but not the bow," Gannicus commented. "Have you ever shot one?"

"Never," I answered.

"All right," replied Gannicus, cheerily smiling and slapping my shoulder as we walked together downhill, back to the House of Faun. When we reached the estate, I stopped, wondering if the man who'd been tossed in the street was dead or just unconscious. Inside the house, Spartacus dismissed me to speak with Gannicus privately; I went to find Pila.

Fresh water seemed to pour all about from everywhere in Pompeii. The walled port town sloped downward from its highest point where the amphitheater and vineyards were, all the way down to Venus' Temple, where the water finally drained into the suburban baths and out to sea. *Via Formani*, read the sign, leading onto the straight, steeply sloped street that channeled the rivers. Outside the temple, slaves threshed chaff from wheat, and there I found Pila sitting backwards upon a donkey with a whip, walking the animal in circles around a millstone. Pila was under the direction of a band of women, the cult of Helica, preparing provisions for our departure at Gavius' bakery. The bored little girl slapped the ass on its rump to get it moving when it tried to stop. "I have to find you some shoes, but here," I said, handing her the gifted, clean yellow frock.

"You'll be helping bag flour, youngster," demanded a large woman from Helica's cult.

"I have orders from the commander," I protested, lying, "to bring this girl to Helica now." I pointed at Pila, mustering authority.

"I'm ordering *you*, to bag *that* flour, before I knock your face off your face," ordered the woman, hands on hips. Pila suddenly popped her donkey whip at the woman and hit the ground running, grabbing my arm.

"Run!" shouted Pila, and soon we were splashing across a flooded street. We held hands and laughed as the woman shouted threats. Walking along *Via Stabina*, we both began to notice that Pompeii hadn't been completely sacked after all—it'd been harshly subdued. We'd made it to the *Stabian* baths by the time Pila asked to sit complaining of sore feet. We sat outside watching Pompeii return to life in the brightness of the day after having been trampled a night before. Completely empty streets a day prior began to sprout people like weeds from between cracks of paving. Life jutting forth, defiant of circumstances, even if only for life's sake. In the moment, I thought of that fateful day when my new slave masters slaughtered my old master's herd. My mind ran to those animals who'd bounded in escape, which made me think about the soldiers of Glaber's camp. Though most were killed, I remembered those who'd scaled sheer walls in complete terror to get away. I thought of the soldiers who fought each other with only the scantest hope of life, then of the old centurion who trudged up a mountain in stocks refusing to die.

"What?" Pila asked, when I'd mumbled something under my breath.

"The indominable human spirit," I repeated an old lesson from another life so that she could hear this time. "Just something an old tutor taught me once," I dismissed with a wave.

"In—don—man—ble?" inquired the girl.

"It just means 'untamable' or 'unstoppable,'" I explained, "like a horse that won't be ridden or a girl named 'little spear' who won't do chores." She smiled. "I thought we'd killed everyone," I commented aloud, proven wrong about Pompeii's destruction while watching a shopkeeper right his tables and chairs at a *tabernae* across the way. "Looks like it was all partisan," I commented, peering up and down the long thoroughfare as it stirred along its entire length.

"Party sands?" Pila asked.

"Like," I put my finger to my chin, thinking of how to explain. "You know how there are two different kinds of Romans?" Pila, a rural girl, looked at me as if I were crazy, shaking her head, believing there to be only one type: the despicable kind. "Do you see here?" I pointed to various citizens all attempting normalcy. "These you can see are called 'plebian,' and they do all the work like tending to land, slaves, and animals. They own all the shops, run all the *tabernaes* and *popinas*, all the restaurants and stalls, all the stuff in the cities," I explained.

"How come *these* pleb-ens didn't get murdered?" asked the inquisitive girl in our language.

"I guess they hadn't owned any slaves to kill them," I shrugged.

"If pleb-ens do everything, what does the other kind do?" she asked in Oscan. I scratched my head.

"Patricians?" I asked to make sure; Pila nodded. "I don't know. We don't really rub elbows, Pila," I joked. Pila giggled when I prodded her ribs with an elbow for effect, realizing then that I hadn't seen too many patricians in my lifetime either. Pila certainly never had, aside from watching them hidden within their fancy litters parting crowds with foreign slaves through busy streets. "We saw a few yesterday's evening," I reminded her.

"We did? Which ones were they?" Pila asked curious.

"The ones being murdered."

"Oh," Pila said, averting her bright brown eyes into the street, unable to forget. "You can start to smell them, when the breeze blows right," she trailed. We sat silent for a while as Pompeii recovered all around us. After the initial shock of our revolt had settled, local freemen and plebeian shopkeepers cautiously came out to do what they had always done: provide goods and services in exchange for profit to make their livelihood. To say the brothels and bars were first up and running would be misleading, because I never saw one shut down.

Pila was silent and didn't notice Crixus and Crastus round a busy corner across the street to harass a sharpening cart's proprietor. They were too far to be heard until Crixus yelled, "How about I hack you, with dull end then?" he admonished, menacing with a drawn *gladius* as his lanky shadow bellowed bellicose laughter, quickly ending negotiations. Soon the vendor's foot swung in a pedal, sending a large round stone flying in circles on a workbench, rendering sparks. The fearful plebian tradesman honed iron edges to perfection for both former slaves. I broke Pila from her stupor with a finger to warn her of the Germans nearby. She quickly recovered her feet again to stand, brushing herself clean, nudging us into a narrow alleyway before either German noticed us leaving.

As we walked more streets of Pompeii, it was the same everywhere in the city: food vendors seemed to be the first ones who returned to their stalls, followed by hungry tradesmen. Spartacus paid a local smith to remove iron shackles from slaves' wrists, ankles, and necks. Pila and I watched, amazed at the inferno of coal as it turned bright red within the smith's shop. We watched the apprentice work bellows and felt its blast of heat on our faces, fascinated with white-hot iron being pulled from Hades by tongs. Sparks rang as iron bent to the will of the skilled smith and his helper with every hammer blow. We were both amazed as an iron collar was quickly pounded into a horseshoe. The smith's right arm was bigger than his left, and he wore a leather apron pockmarked with burns. The two craftsmen worked perfectly together without a word between them, efficiently accomplishing their task of wrenching iron.

We moved on in search of shoes for us both up an arduously steep slope until making a left on *Via del' Abbondanza*. This road had a sidelong and more gradual ascent, making the climb much easier. While we rested on a sidewalk, letting water run over our feet, a custodian with a manure cart stopped to scoop shit.

"Come on," I said, trying a door to escape the cart's pungency;

the door opened without a key, and we entered. Pila gasped audibly at the floor's mosaic when she saw what was tiled. There in the entrance was an image of a Numidian slave holding two oil lamps, dragging a massive penis. "That's not real—they don't get that big," I reassured Pila, wondering if indeed that was the case. Pila stepped around the mosaic like hot iron as we entered the multi-level home, which was adorned with marble statues and extravagant paintings. It was hard to concentrate on our search for shoes with all the distractions. We were both struck dumb, mesmerized motionless by one particularly bizarre painted image.

Painted along an entire wall were images of tiny African tribesmen riding a giant spine-backed lizard. The group of black-skinned men painted on the wall resembled children, with short limbs, enlarged heads, and potbellies. They appeared to ride the lizard with bit and bridle while collectively holding the reins. An even more horrific beast, big as a cow, capsized a dugout canoe and was devouring a lone, tiny man. The attacking animal wore pink skin and had a bullfrog's mouth full of boar's tusks.

"It's a hippo," came a voice in a strange accent from the darkness. We turned to see a Numidian boy around our age. "Those are pygmies," explained the dark-skinned kid, pointing. "The rich buy them, to show they rich. The lady here had tree," finished the African boy, holding up three fingers.

"Three hippos?" asked Pila, amazed.

"Tree pygmies," corrected the boy, laughing. "Hippos hard keeping, very spensive, very mean, take a lot a water to keeps them wet. Got a Nile Dragon, though, want to see?" asked the boy, excitedly pointing at the pygmies' mount painted in the image. Pila nodded and the boy waved for us to follow him into the atrium, where a green pool lay in a depression. The boy opened a nearby chicken coop, reached in, and grabbed a protesting hen by its legs. The bird squawked and flapped as murky eyes opened from moss growing in the dirty stagnant pool. Pila stepped back instinctually as water stirred; the boy ripped flight feathers from the bird's wings. The kid flung the bird, and from the depths of a nightmare rose a huge, ferocious beast with crushing teeth. It engulfed the chicken with two terrible snaps and returned to its depths just as quickly. Pila screamed and shook with fright while I worried if I'd pissed the front of my brand-new tunic. The boy with a broad nose and hair like wool laughed at our distress. When Pila and I finally gathered our wits, we were abruptly joined by three of the strangest-looking Africans I'd ever seen. They resembled the painted tribesmen depicted riding a lizard on the painting inside; shorter than me, but fully grown, the men were small-framed, with short limbs, large heads, and potbellies. They looked wary, and were dressed in exotic garb, festooned in feathers. The boy spoke to them in a singsong language and they seemed to relax enough to talk.

The boy introduced himself to us as Lelu, son of the town's *bestia tracto*: beast master. Lelu explained that his father had been held by Pompeii for an animal's poor performance in a recent match. "Is not his fault. Spooked cat, crawl the wall; loose cat do what he want, when he want."

"Umpappa shoos cats with a straw broom," commented Pila.

"Not cat, cat. Pantera, bigger than a man," Lelu explained, making claws with his hands.

"Is your father still caged?" I asked.

"Who know what bardarian do with them?" Lelu said sadly.

"Probably set them free," I retorted.

"Haven't left the house since you peoples got here."

"Let's find him," interrupted Pila.

"You're safe with us," I implored. "Where's the *ludis?*" Then I remembered my other task. "Wait, first, I have to find shoes."

I pointed at the girl's bare feet. Lelu spoke to the tiny painted bushmen and they replied back in a strange tongue.

"The woman here had children that had shoes," said Lelu when they finished.

Soon, Pila and I were lacing new sandals on our feet, provided by recently dead Romans.

We arrived at Pompeii's *ludis* of thick stone walls and iron bars as windows buzzed with flies and the place stank of toilet. Entering the anteroom revealed a loop of keys hung on an iron hook set into a wall. They chimed in my grasp as we walked further into the cell's darkness. A stench assailed us as we approached condemned prisoners sitting along the cell's walls. With grim faces, they assessed what fate was about to befall them.

Lelu's father rushed the bars upon the sight of his son, and they embraced lovingly, speaking to each other in a common language.

"Get a load of this shit," commented a filthy wretch, sitting against the wall. The condemned prisoners sat bewildered, watching suspiciously as a boy verging on manhood walked to the lock, followed by a budding-breasted girl and a squad of pygmy house servants. The prisoners had heard the night before that the earth had opened up and swallowed howling Romans.

"The commander, Spartacus of Thrace," I announced in my best grown man voice, turning the key, "invites you to join the celebration and sacrifices tonight in Pompeii's liberated amphitheater. Find new clothes, enjoy the baths, and feast with us tonight." The men cheered as I pulled the hasp open to their cages, releasing them from the stench and filth inside. Thankfully, the shoulders of my breastplate turned out to be amply padded, as they were tested in abundance from grateful men. Out into sunlight and fresh air, we exited the *ludis,* when suddenly, I was hoisted upon men's shoulders as the liberated began singing an old jig, "Conquering King," aloud. The unlikely procession wound up Pompeii's main thoroughfare, continuing onto *Via Del' Abbondanza,* all the way up the steep street toward the city's amphitheater.

### HELICA

In the city's assembly, Helica pointed for Va to set a huge table down. "Va," The large deaf man exhaled his name out of habit when the heavy table hit lime-based concrete with a thud. Helica turned towards music when she heard it coming up the street; Va looked to see what held her attention. Both watched the impromptu parade marching up main street with a small soldier hoisted on the shoulders of filthy prisoners dressed in rags. Va and Helica stood mesmerized at the sight of tiny adult Africans shaped like children, blowing pipes, followed by a girl with messy hair, in a new dress, carrying a *pupae.* The bustle of activity in preparing for festivities scheduled that night came to an abrupt halt as everyone stopped to watch our bizarre triumphal approach.

Helica watched the poor goat herder hoisted on high, forcing her to contemplate her own life. Helica's every thought and action since capture had been consumed by escape and revenge; those achieved, Helica now found herself adrift. *We could sail to the east, reclaim Spartacus' inheritance, and become vassals of Mithradates,* she reflected in the surreal moment. This incarnation was the most rational extension for their lives. Helica saw in her mind's eye herself as a chieftain's wife, standing in an earthen hall, surrounded by frolicking, black-haired stepchildren. The woman knew then what the vision meant and what had to be done to make it so.

### THE SCOUNDREL

Gavius wore a disguise beneath his cloaked hood on the way

to the celebration in Pompeii. Gavius knew it was of utmost importance that he not be recognized by anyone inside the city. His very life depended on deception while attempting his biggest gamble yet: brokering the sordid old saga of Romans cheating Romans. Gavius sent couriers to the ports of Crete with cryptic messages that only privy persons could comprehend. The merchant planned to help the slaves as long as it benefitted him, and so far, it exceeded his wildest imaginations. The gladiator matches between pampered aristocrats was lacking in excitement, especially after the sporty performance of retired soldiers exhibited back in Herculaneum. However, Gavius found it difficult to discuss business with the escaped gladiator's commander. He seemed incessantly involved in a match of pitted Romans or spoiling his wife with attention. And when Spartacus finally did conduct business, his terms were ridiculous.

When Gavius took a seat at the feast, near enough to Spartacus so they could bargain together, Gavius got the distinct impression the barbarian leader had been double-crossed by pirates in the past.

"I was told they'd arrive today," Gavius protested. "Helios is not yet down," he proclaimed, pointing out the setting sun.

"Can trust pirate, with only two things," said the tattooed barbarian to the capitalist.

"What's that?" asked the scoundrel.

"Pirate always try to screw."

"And the other?" Gavius asked, curious about the line's punch.

"Pirate will keep trying, till done," Spartacus answered.

## THE COMMANDER

As I piled savory meat onto Pila's plate, and extra helpings onto my own, I watched Spartacus and the cloaked man argue, both keeping an eye out to the sea, where dark clouds gathered.

The freed slaves ate like ravenous beasts, some made themselves sick, reminding me of my own first festival with them all. I sat proudly next to Spartacus at the table with the men, until I had the saddening revelation that I sat in Oenomaus' place.

"That, what happen," joked Crixus, pointing a roasted goose leg at the dining pygmies, "when man, mate with man." Crastus' absurd laugh caused the pygmies to pause, until he finally stopped, and they quickly returned to eating with tiny hands. "Which of you hatch them?" Crixus jested, pointing accusingly at Gannicus and me with the bone.

"Enough," Spartacus suddenly interjected. "Crixus, we nip this force, led by a Roman no one, in the bud. Before they join with other Roman, make them harder killing. Sick season soon, need south place, hold up for winter."

"Why not stay here till spring?" proposed Crixus, who was clearly comfortable in the port town.

"Too much wall, for not enough men," answered Spartacus.

"We be ten thousand," Crixus reasoned. "One wall worth hundred men." Crastus nodded agreement.

"More reason, to leave, look around, Crixus," Spartacus said, panning his hand. "No commerce here, Crastus—cows slaughtered, fields burned. If Roman siege us here, trapped rats, we be. Eating belts by spring, probably, eat ride...long before then," he concluded, pointing at some horses on the horizon, enjoying their own feast of hay.

"We won't let them besiege us," spouted a youthful new slave in haste. "We'll fly out the gate and smash them." He pounded the table, causing mugs to jump.

"Will you suck sea dry then, slave?" inquired Spartacus, boring into the young man with all seriousness. "Tell us, how slave stop Roman ships from pouring in bay?"

"Why can't we just hire these pirates to sail us east?" interrupted

Helica. The pleading in her tone surprised me; I wasn't sure why she'd want to travel there, but she clearly wanted it desperately.

"Because, my doe," Spartacus explained, trying to be patient, "I swear oath to partner, help Oenomaus' people get home, to be free. Cannot sail away; must face this man one day and answer for what is done here, my brightest wife." Helica turned away from her husband, stabbing at the fish on her plate with vitriol. She knew better than to press again, although she clearly hated his answer. I stuffed some honeyed bread in my mouth, mulling on Helica's reaction. I'd been around enough of the world by then to realize that as far as Helica was concerned, her deal with Celts, Gauls, and Germans ended when she broke them out.

*"Damn the man...and his oaths,"* I thought I heard her murmur as lightning slashed across the sky.

"Crixus believes Jupiter's bolts are sparks from the anvil of a god's son," she said directly to Pila. "Isn't that preposterous?" Spartacus gnashed his teeth; at the time, I thought my lord's anger at his wife was for bringing attention to herself while the warriors plotted fate. But Spartacus would share later during a ride that it was the temptation he felt when presented by his wife out loud to abandon his oath to Oenomaus and become a man not of his word. Saying then that it was something he was inwardly desperate to do, but would not permit his living soul to carry the shame of in death and into the afterlife—where Oenomaus surely waited. I understood, then, why Romans didn't allow women to council—and then reveled in the uniqueness of Helica's position amongst this band of barbarians.

"Speak not now, woman," Spartacus spoke sternly. Just then, Jupiter lit the evening bright as day, suddenly illuminating ships docking below. Everyone turned to watch the two long warships with sharp bronze rams protruding the water line row to port with sails furled tight along their mast. I was near enough to hear

Spartacus whisper, "Will listen open ears, in private, my dove, tonight."

I stood to get better vision and to investigate what sweets and pastries were laid out at the end of the table. We all watched as the boats' long oars were hauled in and the ships were tied to piers jutting from Pompeii's shore below. Strange foreign men disembarked, exotically dressed, wearing long, braided hair intertwined with glass beads and gold rings. The pirates were ferried by wagon through the Marine Gate, and everyone watched as they came into view after making the left on *Via Palaestrania*. From my angle, I could see Spartacus' jaw stiffen as he balled a forty-four-year-old fist under the table.

Spartacus squinted through a furrowed brow, no doubt trying to discern the sailors' faces. When the foreigners hopped off their ride and approached the amphitheater's edge, Spartacus shook his hand loose before grasping the captain's forearm for a shake.

"Welcome, Heracleo," announced Gavius, standing from his seat, having jettisoned his cloak, now certain he was only in the company of co-conspiring accomplices. The captain returned the greeting with a nod. "Have you brought the money?" Gavius inquired.

"Ah, now why would I be here-a, if I did not-ah?" retorted the captain with disdain obvious in his passable Latin.

"Enough," Spartacus interrupted, and I could tell he was annoyed with Gavius' Roman need for immediate negotiations. Spartacus veiled threats within his admonishment of Gavius. "Bargain not yet struck, Gavius. Crixus, must overlord weight, quantity, quality of weapon. Crastus, need watch count, guard exchange." The commander then addressed the captain, Heracleo. "Treasure count, in Palestra." He motioned to rows and rows of stolen tents housing the town's wealth from the coming rain below. In daylight, the Palestra was an open grassy expanse where citizens went to make verbal contracts, witnessed by others, to one another. At certain times of the year, pens were erected as citizens performed their sacred duty, meandering through to cast their vote without a spit of shade. At night, the Palestra was where Romans came to celebrate their numerous holy days and holidays with extravagant bazars, complete with fire breathers, jugglers, and performers of all manner. This night, in the city and at this luxurious venue, slaves would sacrifice for the gods' favor. Upon the Palestra's dais, Spartacus waited for thunder to quiet after another blinding flash of lightning. "Done tonight, but not now. Now, fill mug, eat. Pompeii, welcome to all!" shouted Spartacus, addressing the pirates and waving them to banquet first.

Heracleo smiled with black teeth, nodding appreciation and thanking the commander.

"Arranged," Spartacus resumed, speaking to the captain as the pirates formed the start of the line at the buffet tables. "Pirate stay in estate of Lucky Julia." Spartacus motioned to his right at the largest palatial estate next door, overlooking the amphitheater and the Palestra's tent-filled expanse. Heracleo raised pierced and studded brows, impressed, while the other pirates nodded contented agreement to one another. The liberated slaves of Pompeii took turns offloading bags of coin and all manner of goods from the foreign ships after everyone had eaten their fill.

We carried treasure of all sorts: thousands of bricks of salt, bags of amber, piles of ebony, and enormous tusks of ivory from something Gannicus called an "elephant." We exchanged goods stacked higher than a horse's bit for large, metal-rimmed shields, sharp iron swords, and bags of coin. I personally transported bundles of perfectly straight, lathe-turned, iron-bobbed arrows, fletched with goose feathers. In another trip, we brought long ash poles with wicked iron tips, alongside assorted heavy scale, plate, and ring mail for our men. Pirate booty once bound for Pompey in Spain would be used now to kill Romans in Italy.

I'd never seen such an accumulation of wealth before in one place. Gavius affirmed he hadn't either, and he owned part of an island. Bags of labeled coin lay in piles, enumerated and sorted by type: A for gold aureus, D for silver denarius, S for bronze sesterce, and the majority inked with the Greek letter ϙ for copper quadrans. Spartacus lavished coins on the masses during the banquet, to the consternation of Crixus and the pirates—both considered paying slaves a waste of money.

Spartacus had no problems figuring numerals; he just needed me to read what commodity was listed on the manifests, using his hands as an abacus to quicky tally sums. I read them aloud in front of pirates without shame. In this way, Spartacus let it be known that he'd not tolerate cheating. Spartacus scratched blades with a file, or peered down the spine to ensure straightness, or thumped a shield at random while I read aloud. The imposing man was just as intimidating with his mind as he was with a sword, and the pirates dealt straight, respecting his prowess.

"Where's all this stuff going?" I asked Gannicus on one trip to load ships, referring to all the goods that couldn't be used to kill a man without extreme creativity.

"To Roman ports, for resale," Gannicus answered. "A Roman will sell you the rope to hang him with."

"I understand trading for weapons, but why keep so much in coin?" I asked, ignorant of why so much was in currency and what purpose it served for war, since not even I could keep all my coin on my person by this time. I even buried a few stashes and had forgotten where by then.

"Look around," Gannicus answered, gesturing. I saw faces of slaves in the city around me; they laughed in merriment, most experiencing joy for the first time in their hard lives. Fat stomachs and jingling purses walked the lamplit streets of Pompeii all around—most were ready to die to keep it that way. We passed a young couple passionately kissing in the shadows of an eave. "Because for us," commented Gannicus, "every day is Saturnalia; that's why." He spoke in reference to the Roman holiday of slaves trading places with their masters for one day a year. I looked down when a single raindrop struck my arm, and more began to fall upon my head.

"We'd better get back," I told Gannicus, worried for little Pila. We ran and another flash of light was followed by a deep, menacing rumble as torrents of rain suddenly fell in buckets. Slaves threw every scrap of wood onto fires, attempting to keep them blazing. The liberated slaves of Pompeii quickly carried food beneath tents to shelter it from the downpour's onslaught. Pompeii's combatants of the arena received a reprieve when the games were stopped due to poor weather. Spartacus shouted for the new arrows to be taken indoors to prevent them from warping, and that's where I found Pila, looking like a lost, wet kitten, shivering in an empty tent.

"Ready to go?" I asked. Pila nodded with chattering teeth. The influx of fresh water to a town awash with fountains and channels made already-inundated streets turn to raging rivers. We carefully made our way back to the villa where we'd spent the first night hidden in a wardrobe by jumping stone blocks to cross the flooded streets. Opening the unlocked door, I lit a dolphin-shaped oil lamp and pulled my dagger noisily, loudly announcing that I was armed. Pila's teeth were the only reply from inside the abandoned villa, so I barred the door behind us. I found a blanket draped over a chair and threw it over the wet, freezing girl. We retreated upstairs to the master suite, and I dumped oil from my lamp to start the brazier. It was fashioned in the shape of a hippo's gaping jaws and I laughed aloud, realizing it to be something I'd not known of just a day prior. I told Pila to strip from her wet clothes and get beneath furs. Once I'd heard her retreat, I turned to Pila so she could hand over her soaked garments while clutching the covers. I placed them over a chair to dry and was about to leave in search of a bed of my own when her tiny voice pleaded.

"Publipor, stay," peeped Pila.

It took me longer to undress, fighting straps at the breastplate's rear without help as Pila giggled. I pulled the leather over my head and smelled why men didn't wear them all the time. Once stripped naked, I climbed into the down-stuffed mattress beneath plush furs. Bare skin warmed mine and we fell asleep clutching one another, exhausted.

### SPARTACUS MOUNTS A NIGHTMARE FOR A FAMILIAR RIDE

That night, Spartacus lay with his wife in a similar bed in another part of the city. He'd been grateful that he hadn't recognized any of the pirates and been subsequently forced to kill them all. He'd been double-crossed in the past once while on campaign with Sulla, years before. Being cheated over some horses made Spartacus lose face momentarily with Commander Sulla and he never forgot the culprits' faces.

Pleased with the trade, he'd fallen asleep easily that night to the rumbling of thunder and torrent of rainfall. The old warrior was visited by a familiar dream that returned to him often. In it, Spartacus was a boy again, standing in his grandmother's pigsty at the farm back east. As a boy, Spartacus loved the winter feast of Yule and the delicious dish of suckling pigs that accompanied the special event every year. The part young Spartacus didn't care for was the job he'd had since turning twelve. In order to have suckling pigs, you have to slaughter piglets, the task he faced now in memory. In this nightmare, the winter litter of piglets squealed and ran in circles around his ankles, desperate for escape. The boy Spartacus had discovered a year prior that by grabbing both hocks and dashing their heads against the stone barn, the horror was quickly silenced. After a couple, youthful Spartacus got into a rhythm, and before long, the squealing had stopped and the task was gratefully finished. Only now, within this recurring dream, Spartacus was no longer a boy of thirteen on his grandmother's farm. Spartacus was twenty-one again, with his regiment, campaigning in Illicium with Sulla. The warrior was startled by Atticus, who peeked around a corner, staring at Spartacus' hand.

"Pompey says we're done here," Atticus spoke flatly. "We're moving out." Spartacus followed the man's eyes to look at his own fist. He was clutching a limp baby's ankle; he saw the devastation to the child's head. Spartacus released it to fall sickeningly atop a sopping wet pile of babes. Then he woke. The dream came so frequently, Spartacus hardly stirred anymore; Helica snored uninterrupted upon his painted chest.

### A NEW DAWN FOR PUBLIPOR

Pompeii, sanitized by the downpour a night before, no longer smelled of low tide, death, and sewage when we woke the next morning. The deluge washed away everything, from manure in the streets to the filth stuck in drains—it even pulled the mounting bodies out to sea. So much so that the public toilets were scoured and fertilizing oyster bays. I blinked awake next to Pila with a painfully erect penis. I ran quickly outside and awkwardly urinated, hoping it would go away before Pila woke. Our army was to meet outside of town later that day with fresh horses for the long ride back to Herculaneum. I left armed to the hilt except for my new bow and quiver; those remained for safekeeping with Pila. The dagger I left for her safety.

"Stab, don't slash with it," I reminded her before leaving, making sure she had coin enough to buy whatever she needed while gone.

*"Vala,"* Pila said in Latin, *See you soon,* waving goodbye as I left with the men. It was great that Lelu was allowed to come along; he'd convinced Spartacus that his father would be a perfect steward for the horses if the men had to fight dismounted. We rode north with Mt. Vesuvius on our right and the sea to the left all day, until the sleeping volcano began shrinking to our south. The ride seemed to pass quickly as Lelu and I shared stories of our pasts while the old man grinned in nodding chuckles with every translation. Before realizing it, we'd already returned to familiar terrain, we approached the land near where I'd run off with the fugitives just a week prior. Ironically, in the exact place where the old vets were ambushed is where Quaestor Lucius Furius and his men were killed.

Using a clever system of fresh horses left on the Appian, we exhausted their mounts, leading cavalry ever further from the infantry. Spartacus pounced on the poor cavalry after their horses were spent, while Crixus and Crastus ambushed a surprised and unsuspecting green infantry. I felt bad for the stripped young bodies we left for birds, and used a large portion of my coins for the dead. With that deed done, we headed southeasterly, this time putting Vesuvius on our right while traveling south on the *Via Latina*, a road of Roman engineering leading arrow-straight to the metropolis of Nola.

# CHAPTER FOURTEEN

"...they ravaged over the whole of Campania, laying waste to Nola, Nuceria, Thurii, and Metapontum with terrible destruction."

—**Florus,** *Epitome*

The second-angriest I'd ever seen Spartacus was in the city of Nola, the one town Spartacus made sure burned completely, beginning with Sulla's estate. Nothing was spared devastation, and it was the only time I remember Spartacus not telling the slaves to hurry in their mayhem. Nola hadn't fallen for the farce of Saturnalia like Pompeii. Soldiers parading as captives and captives pretending to be soldiers didn't work this time. Spartacus was left bargaining at the gate with the terrified inhabitants inside, until a drunkard from within hurled an obscenity. I stood in horror, watching the foolish man interrupt negotiations by upending his toga, exposing himself, and cursing.

"*Galla Commada!*" screamed the inhabitant, ignorantly disrespectful. I turned to see what my commander would do.

Without word or expression, Spartacus lackadaisically signaled by wagging two fingers. I abruptly scraped quartz to iron, sparking a dried bird's nest and blowing spark to flame, then tossed it, igniting a bucket of pitch. Fire sucked air and whooshed to life as skilled bowmen passed before me, taking turns dipping wool-wrapped arrows into flaming tar. Within minutes, archers set the gates of Nola ablaze from a distance. Attempts to douse flames by the inhabitants were quickly dissuaded by perfectly placed goose-fletched arrows upon their person. Spartacus let the gates burn long enough for greedy, wild-eyed slaves to be able to plow through their ashen husks. Man and beast alike felt the hatred our leader had for poor Nola and the victims of his vengeance. I remained in a cloud of dust, afraid to move, as Pegasus, Spartacus' stud, bolted past me with our commander aboard. I felt pity at the sound of screams coming from within when our mob stormed in.

The slaves who remained outside were mostly women and children, or men who had no appetite for any more wanton murder. Gannicus explained as we stood outside Nola's walls that the city was Sulla's conquered region, the place promised long ago to loyal soldiers or allies who completed their contracts, but it had all rotted now from Sulla's deceit. A once-cheated Spartacus now settled his debt with interest from the long-dead dictator. I would see later that Sulla's statues had been toppled and smashed to bits, the only such display of uncharacteristic pettiness I'd ever witnessed done by the man. Later, when the rest of our tribe arrived, Pila and I walked privately to a hill overlooking Nola and sat beneath the shade of an oak instead of participating in the looting. We rooted for escapees, making for the woods, when Helica appeared alone from behind the massive oak tree.

"The screams must have been heard in the heavens enough to have gotten at least one god's attention by now," Helica claimed, sitting cross-legged to join us as Nola burned below. "It's appropriate for my husband to have revenge on his birthday." It made me wonder when my birthday was, other than thirteen springs ago, so I asked the date. "You know good and well it's been six hundred and eighty-two years since that fiend, Romulus, founded his horrid city. Our commander was born forty-five-years ago today, in the east, *Novembri sexti*, beneath the scorpion," Helica spoke reverently. "We'll return to Pompeii and prepare for winter to the south. We're too close to Rome in Campania. Besides, we'll attract more slaves in Lucania. This way, the Germans and my husband can drill new men till spring, when we break out." Her voice struggled to rise over the groans from below. "We must escape before the legions of Spain and Greece return to Italy."

"Helica, won't the Gauls just kill us anyway when we arrive?" blurted Pila, gesturing to herself and me. "Even if we make it to their side of the Alps?" She was desperate to know if the rumors we'd heard were true.

"Of course not, sweet child," Helica lied, stroking Pila's hair. "The least of our pressing worries right now are Gauls, sweet Pila. At present, our concerns are the Romans." Helica turned and fixed me with her icy stare. "You'll have to keep an eye on this..." Helica thought for a moment then continued, "Varinius, and this *other* legion, Publipor." Drowning within Helica's eyes, I vowed to watch Varinius' army like a hawk. Pila glared and we left, but for some reason, Pila stayed angry without a word all night.

Our slave army spent a month playing hide and seek with Varinius' soldiers in the shadow of Vesuvius. Gannicus and I watched Varinius' scouts watch us, each content knowing where the other was without forcing a fight. On one of my first outings alone, I spied an armored, mounted boy staring back at me from a hill. I could tell he was young, not fully grown, but sporty and armored, like me, on his mount, alone. As far as I could tell, the only difference between us was for which cause we fought—his *civitas*, mine *libertas*. It wasn't worth the arrow it'd take just to loose a potshot at him, though the thought crossed my mind. I'd seen him before, around Nola and Herculaneum, when I'd scouted with Gannicus before. Here, outside Pompeii, we were alone at last, and I prayed to Dionysus for strength to kill him, hoping to the god I'd never have to try.

*He's bigger and older, but so is everyone...except Pila,* I thought. Each taking the other's measure, we sat motionless as I relaxed on the mount, pretending to be an old hand, disinterested, all while at the same time trying to puff in my breastplate and appear larger, acting as if I'd seen him first. The armored boy nodded before turning his horse. I nodded reflexively in return, unable to stop myself. *Had I won the battle of salutations?* I wondered, as butterflies filled my stomach at the notion of fighting him with unsheathed blades.

I rendezvoused with Gannicus at the appointed place, and we shared what we'd seen before briefing our commander and heading back to the field. This went on for some time, and before long, I found myself alone farther afield on increasingly important business. By year's end, I'd become one of the best eyes in the army; when Spartacus burdened me with the big job of fooling a Roman commander named Cossinius. Spartacus packed our stolen camp and moved us south with the women in a train, ordering me to travel with them, making sure we clanked and clamored as loudly as possible the entire way.

Cossinius' scouts watched our army of slaves attempt to escape south to Sarno, on the *Via Annia,* to my homeland, Magna Graecia—Greater Greece. They should've watched longer, because when their scouts broke off, I signaled with a banner for our men to pounce. I knew what would happen and had no need to watch, so I went ranging instead.

Again, I found the armored boy. He reminded me of myself; I drew my bow and aimed at the back of his head. Inexplicably, as I calculated the distance, a flash of sweating fever struck me before releasing the shaft of bobbed iron at him. The familiar twang sounded wrong, and when the sinew slapped my wrist guard, I could tell it was off. Slowly the ashen shaft bent, wobbling at the armored boy while time stood still. Practice and pointers from Lelu had made me good enough to stop birds in flight now, but the missile flashed beside the armored boy's face. I knew he felt its breeze. Our eyes met. My hands shook as I tried to reload, thinking the armored boy was about to turn his horse and charge me. Thankfully, he kicked his horse away instead, and I caught my breath as he rode out of sight.

We charged the ranch villa outside Pompeii with a roar, banging swords on shields and cursing as we went. Cossinius, caught completely unaware, ran frightened from the bath and leapt aboard his mount, completely naked. We'd surprised the dupe with his toga off. Slave warriors pulled Commander Cossinius naked from his horse and stabbed him. Romans quickly dropped and ran upon seeing the fearsome barbarians and furious slaves charging for blood. We'd beaten another army. Everyone rejoiced, but Spartacus shook his head, mumbling. One day after all of this, I asked my lord why he did not exult like the others in the victory's thus far; this is what he said.

"Children of Romulus have gone fallow with *mollitia* in city of leisure," Spartacus used the Roman word for "softness" in describing our enemy. "Slave think all legions are such. Soon, they will learn, not all legions cut and run..." he looked square into me. "Too late—I fear—they will learn, is my concern."

THE COMMANDING GENERAL OF ALL ROMAN FORC-
ES IN ITALY THINKS OF EXCUSES, 682 AUC (73 BC)

Varinius sat at a field desk encamped somewhere in Campania with his last piece of papyrus. The quill's feathered end shook spastically as the newly appointed praetor bantered the right words about in his head. Varinius wondered how to ask for help from the senate and explain that the two newly raised legions had been lost by Cossinius' carelessness. He had difficulty formulating the right words to avert blame, resulting in a pile of expensive papyrus sprouting about his feet like tumbling weeds. Within Varinius' ranks were remnants from the armies of Glaber, Furious, and Cossinius, survivors of Spartacus' reign of terror upon southern Italy. Shame of defeat hung on them all like a thick fog. Young men with reputations to rebuild begged for a second chance at the rabble. Soldiers lamented aloud about all the underhanded and devious schemes used by scum to achieve their inglorious victories. Romans swore to avenge themselves and restore the domestic legion's honor before the fighting season's end.

That patchwork legion stalked the slave army warily through southern Italy, waiting for a mistake.

### VARINIUS KEEPS AN EYE ON THE SUN DIAL, 682 AUC
### (73 BC)

*No more waiting, no more hesitation,* thought Varinius, knowing his time was short. It was almost year's end, and with winter approaching, that normally meant it was too late for fighting. With the senate up his ass, he had no choice but to make a move now. Luckily, his patience appeared to finally have paid off; there was no way he could pass on such a ripe opportunity given by dumb brutes. Varinius' highly motivated young men vowed *non receptum*—no retreat—once again. Confident of redemption, Varinius stroked his figurine of Mars for luck while watching camped slaves in a valley wide enough to form ranks, hopeful the slaves remained unaware of his army's presence. A smirking Varinius planned his pincer for daybreak, thinking, *They've gotten too uppity, too confident.* He listened from the tree line to the banging of pots used to make breakfast for ten thousand fugitive slaves. Smoke rose from their camp in the early morning light.

Varinius knew they were fixed and unaware.

Varinius had to pounce for the sake of his reputation and that of his men. The chance had to be taken now before it slipped away again, like every time before. Varinius mustered the men and began speaking to them while mounted in the tradition of Hellenized Roman peptalks, attempting to motivate an army by insulting their manhood.

"I'm afraid," began Varinius, "they may be too much for you, my beleaguered troops. I've received word from many mothers, wishing their little boys' safe return to the city at once. Who of you will return in shame to mommy's blanket before winter? And who of you will stay with me to save our country's reputation?"

Soldiers cursed and begged to attack slaves, swearing victory or death, tearing clothes to express their deep desires at redemption.

Varinius, satisfied he'd worked his men to an adequate frenzy, unleashed them.

### PUBLIPOR

From on high, I watched Roman soldiers form ranks and charge our slave camp. Varinius believed he'd forced us to give battle and could probably smell victory as his men got close enough to throw javelins. From my vantage point, I saw their commander's frustration when the first ranks paused. Then his fear at discovering that our sentries were dead men propped on pikes, holding wooden spears and wicker shields. The old woman knew what she was doing when she volunteered to bang pots, but it was still hard to watch what they did to her. She laughed as the soldiers killed her, pointing her gnarled hand at a ridge of horrid barbarians riding wild ponies and pouring out of the hills from all directions.

I sat mounted beside Gannicus, watching slaves bound from our ridge and onto the legion below. That was the first time I'd seen a proper shield wall. Armed slaves thundered toward the legion, threatening curses and banging swords upon shields held high. Then, at fifty paces, men hurled javelins toward one another. Briefly from my perch, it appeared the Roman's might succeed in sustaining our onslaught, until our cavalry joined the fray.

Spartacus, Crixus, and Crastus rode pell-mell on proper horses into the broken legion. Spartacus' war voice boomed orders in the valley below, bolstering former slaves and ex-gladiators. Vanquished Romans fled the field. Slaves received no rest until they'd achieved total victory in our commander's eyes. I remained on the ridge with Gannicus, like I was told, desperately wanting to go down and prove myself upon the retreating forces. We watched slaves pull the red-caped soldier off his mount from our vantage. Then, helpless, we witnessed the desire to capture Varinius alive dissolve into a fight over a glittering bridle and an expensive horse. Slave greed saved the Roman. Desperately, Varinius broke free and ran possessed, gaining enough ground to be collected up by the armored boy. I watched amazed as the boy ran his thundering horse alongside the fleeing Roman. The armored boy grasped his commander's arm and used the animal's momentum to swing Varinius upon the horse's rump. They escaped over a rise on the overburdened animal together. *Could I do that?* I wondered, with grudging respect.

After collecting the victor's spoils, we left enemy bodies to rot beneath circling vultures and took advantage of Roman paving. Upon the *Via Annia*, we made incredible time, quickly arriving at *Campus Atinas,* a very small town, in no time at all. Gannicus and I were hardly in front of the army when the little village with no walls saw us approach. I felt sorry watching them run in panic, secretly hoping they'd have time to flee before the rest of our army arrived.

"Chase a dog and it'll run, but run and it'll chase," Gannicus taught. We watched the smart ones flee with keys to locks they'd never reopen and witnessed the stupidly greedy with all their belongings, get bit by foaming, vengeful slave jaws. Our numbers grew beyond counting with all manner of slaves there. Spartacus shouted, trying to rein in the behemoth army of slaves brimming with new people to no avail; even he couldn't stop the tempest this time. After the slaughter, Spartacus had five men throttled for raping or killing our own.

"Man with no discipline, while foraging," admonished Spartacus, "have no discipline, in fight!" He dispatched a brigand by his own hand after passing the sentence.

The rest of the oath-breakers were forced to kneel, bound by wrists. I recognized the dirty, toothless man with bandaged hands begging for mercy. It was the man who'd tried to rape Pila in Pompeii. Quiet Vitelli, Spartacus' bodyguard, throttled the condemned in seconds, and I hated the cretin...until I noticed the markings on his body. The rapist's forehead was branded with the Greek letter A, probably his master's first initial. The dead man's entire back was a heap of healed calluses, and a tan line around his neck showed years in a shackle. From my bank, I placed a copper coin in his mouth before his body was impaled and left at the intersection. From that day forth, our commander balanced men's greed upon the scales of harsh discipline. When I asked Gannicus why men perpetrated such cruelty in pursuit of material possessions, he said: "Greed is like fire; essential, but ruinous if left unabated."

On our way to the Gulf of Tarentum, we helped ourselves to whatever Salernum and Picentia offered—by taking it. When we reached the region of Lucania, even more escaped slaves of all sorts joined our cause in droves. Fieldhands, shepherds, and vine tenders all united in ransacking Foman Popilii, Atina, then

Tegiamam, all the way to the crossroads of Grumenium. There, Crixus had a man drawn and quartered for insulting Shixa, sanctifying yet another intersection for safe passage. It took an entire week to pass through all of Lucania into the region of Bruttium, as slaves indulged themselves gluttonously the entire way.

At the border town of Nerulum, etched above its entrance arch, was the inscription, "You are now in Bruttium." It took three hours for all our numbers to pass beneath those words. We continued south through Bruttium, leaving Nerulum in our wake to reach the old Greek city of Thurii by nightfall. The Romans tried changing the city's name to Copia, or *abundance*, when they conquered, but everyone still just called it Thurii. The ancient town was abandoned and unlocked when we arrived, except for eager slaves thirsting for the vague idea that was freedom.

We spent that mild winter foraging towns in the regions of Bruttium and Lucania, always using ancient Thurii as our springboard. Slaves from the countryside drilled for war between pillaging Magna Graecian abundance, including Lelu and me. When Lelu wasn't teaching me how to shoot, he was helping his father with the animals, once rustling an entire herd of wild, shaggy ponies into a ravine. Lelu's father had an ingenious way of breaking the stubborn little horses quickly. He'd make the beasts unsure of their footing by having them stand in a dry creek bed littered with loose stones. The animals didn't dare buck or kick and risk a break in the ravine. Lelu's dad first blanketed their eyes; next, he placed a pygmy to sit on the animal until it calmed. When the pony became accustomed to the weight, he'd add another small man, repeating until it equaled the weight of an average Italian. Lelu's father finally placed bits in the little horses' mouths, and by the time we walked them out, the temperamental ponies no longer thought for themselves.

"What use could these stubby things possibly have?" I asked Lelu, knowing full well the little ponies couldn't outrun real horses and that our men would probably drag their feet trying to ride one. Not to mention, they were prone to biting; mine even tried scrubbing me off with a tree.

"This pony go, where the horse can't...you'll see," Lelu answered cryptically.

In school long ago, I'd learned that before Romulus and Remus ever suckled the teat of a wolf bitch, Thurii was a thriving Greek colony in southern Italy. Now in ruin, the ancient Greek buildings stood as a testament to superior design and construction. The old city, overgrown and long since put to heel, was once the hub of Italy—before refugees from Troy came ashore, changing the country's orbit forever.

In Bruttium, I'd studied Pythagoras as a small boy, before being sold for horse thieving and running off. I was thinking of those days when Pila suddenly came running at me, pointing to the coast and announcing the arrival of five ships. Warships of Carthage design rowed into port with bronze rams slicing turquoise water and there they docked. Gavius disembarked with Captain Heracleo, grasping forearms with Spartacus, Crixus, and Crastus. They left the wharf to speak privately in a nearby *tabernae*. Pila and I followed. We listened from outside an open window as they argued about money, plans, and women.

"It a-getting harder for ah pirate to sail-a these days," Heracleo explained. "Antony's navy, she getting a-better, not a pushover, like just ah year hence. I think they hire the a-Carthaginian, teach-a them to sail," bemoaned Heracleo. "The crafty sons of bitches, come up with ah dastardly thing only those-a *bastardi* could-a devise," he lamented. "Once-a they ram-a you, they drop ah plank with their ship and ah hook, then run across like-a furies, and a-swamp the ship with-a men. Seen them do with-a me own eye,"

Heracleo explained, as sailors nodded. "Don't care, how much a-money you try bait-a me with, can't spend in a-Neptune's Hall."

"So, they have diving boards," replied Gavius, dismissing the pirate's concerns. "Are you telling me, the pirates of Cypress are afraid of some land-lubbing Romans in dugouts?"

"Ah dugout," Heracleo scoffed. "You have no idea, what you talk about-a, brickmaker," the pirate captain insulted with his rolling tongue. "Not a-run anymore of these trinkets-a north to those a-spoiled *bastardi*. You Romani act-a like they do *me* a favor, stealing from-a *their* own countrymen; look down ah big nose," spoke Hercleo, incensed. "No, thank you, brought-a de payment as agree. Now, me and de boys, we sail-a home, while still-a can."

"More arms?" interrupted Spartacus.

"Me men-a, we appreciate de wealth-a, commander, ah really do," Heracleo spoke, genuinely changing his tone to one of respect for the renowned gladiator. "But you must understand-a, not like de old days, these Romani, they become-a deadly on da water too," explained the pirate captain in a thick accent. "Dey sink a-two of my ships and capture ah third—those-a men, dey-a *crocifigerre*," bewailed Heracleo. Spartacus nodded with understanding while Helica shook her head with frustration; even I knew the woman would be unable to convince her husband to board the vessels. Matters settled for a bit, until bags of coin came up, along with Crixus' greed.

"Spar-ti-coos, you want give treasure to voomen," menaced Crixus, "give yours. Me and mine, we keep ours...Is decided." The two Germans nodded to one another in agreement.

"Money just litter to carry our plans, Crixus," explained Spartacus. "Men have wife, wife make child. Paid men fight, broke men run."

"Then, they die poor. Look at that," said Crixus, pointing outside at the pygmies loading a cart nearby. "Not dodging blades for those things." Upon hearing the slight, Crastus began laughing in a full roar, head back, while his Adam's apple traveled the length of his throat. "When spring come," Crixus added, "I raid, burn, rape, then take it all north. We not take weak freeloaders. If want to escape with millstones around you neck, do it alone. We agreed to leave Italy, not take in strays. I fight not for useless old women, or their droppings." Crixus pointed to a local woman and her baby. "We take fierce, get rich. Not home, to be poor like fathers." Men and women of his ilk nodded, murmuring agreement in German and Gaelic. Shixa stood with her fearsome ladies and hissed at Helica. Helica stared stone-faced in defiance, restraining her cult of women with a hand. Crixus and Crastus rose in unison, grasping swords. Spartacus made no motion as they menaced, while Gavius, Heracleo, and the other sailors sat quietly, as tensions built in the dim light that fought through a missing roof tile above.

"Crixus, you are right; it best we split," reasoned Spartacus. "Too many here, and separating will confuse next Roman sent against us. Yes. Good idea." It was one of many times I'd heard Spartacus take the unseen path with calm decisiveness, instantly soothing any hairy situation. By appropriating Crixus' idea, Spartacus left the German flattered yet confused. I peeked inside the open window and watched Spartacus stand to look the German in the eye. Then Spartacus did something I could not foresee. "How old when you *captured*?" Spartacus asked Crixus, using the German word that had a dual meaning for coward all while closing the gap between he and Crastus in three quick confident steps. Spartacus did all this while smoothly moving his hand on his sword's grip to stand over the lanky German.

Crastus froze in place, while Crixus stood back and pulled his blade.

"When Butcher Boy, arrive with Lusitanian," Spartacus

addressed Crixus calmly, inches from Crastus' face. "Work together or die apart, Crixus," Spartacus turned his head to face Crixus all while continuing to menace over a very tall Crastus. "How long you think Roman leave slaves to run loose? How much money Roman lose? What Roman do, to make stop? Old men, boys, fought so far. But Roman get *real* legion here, real soon." Spartacus' tone tensed. "When Pompey comes, over Alps better you be, son."

Crixus and Crastus remained still, with only one sword drawn between them, when Spartacus suddenly took a step back, changing his tone to speak with the room.

"I have seen forty thousand Romans, cross mile-long pontoon in two days. I have seen Roman march thirty miles, build at night, fight all day, tear down, do again next day," he explained. Crixus lowered his sword; Crastus inhaled. "You won't stop Roman with wicker. You think Roman chisel those for fun?" Spartacus said, pointing to the carved round stones used by Romans in siege engines scattered about the quarry outside. "Slave drop *fasces,* little rod-bound hatchets, and stolen silver *signum* they preen with when that stone starts to fly," Spartacus returned his attention to Crixus. "Agreed, we split, confuse Roman, but make haste, Crixus. Best shot out, slave work as one." Finished, Spartacus pulled his *gladius* in a blur and tossed the sword to stick into the table, jarring those nearest. Spartacus then offered his forearm to Crixus before Crastus. They received it in turns by locking arms in Roman fashion before their heavy drinking resumed.

I would ask my lord later why he menaced Crastus first and not Crixus, since he was the one most threatening. "Because Crixus will not fight me alone, but Crastus will fight anyone who fights with Crixus," he clarified that day. In time, I'd see it many times myself.

Pila, Lelu, and I soon bored of the incoherent boasting and

futile arguments about money that was in greater quantity than we could ever spend. Beneath a burning sun, we left to see the amazing sights of the ships docked at port. We were quickly shooed away by impatient sailors who had no time for children mucking up their carefully orchestrated operation. We were forced to gawk in awe at the bevy of materials offloaded from the ships and stored on shore. Lelu highjacked a metal loop and we chased it with a stick down the beach with laughing children in tow. Pila had her straw *pupae* stuffed into her belt so that she could have use of both hands while overtaking Lelu's control on the hoop with a stick of her own. It was fun to play like little ones again and we forgot for just a moment that the world wanted us dead. We disobeyed and returned to the port just to rest and watch, but while there, Pila and I couldn't help but gaze in wonder at all the pigeons kept in cramped wicker cages. The colorful, red-eyed birds cooed nervously with tiny little pouches secured to their legs by a miniature shackle; I wondered what they were used for and asked Lelu.

"They take message," Lelu pointed at the sky and drew a slow imaginary line. "A—a—all the way across sea," he exaggerated.

"Yeah, sure," I answered dubious. Lelu liked to tell tales, just to see if I believed him.

# CHAPTER FIFTEEN

"After this, still greater numbers flocked to Spartacus till his army numbered 70,000. For these he manufactured weapons and collected equipment, whereas Rome now sent the consuls with two legions."

—Appian, *The Civil Wars*

CATO THE YOUNGER FINDS AN ALLY IN THE SENATE
OF 683 AUC (72 BC)

In Rome's new year of 683, the senate elected sixty-two-year-old Lucius Gellius and the more reasonably aged forty-three-year-old Gnaeus Cornelius Lentulus Clodianaus as Rome's dualling councils. Gellius, a man of wisdom but well past his prime, quickly appointed Quintus Arrius, a former boxing champion, as his commander to pursue actions in his stead. The senate's first and most pressing order of business was the slave rebellion burning out of control in the south.

It had grown from nuisance to national embarrassment, and was now a full-blown emergency. Couriers were sent racing to Pompey, campaigning across Spain through a system of relays. Pompey would receive the message in an astounding ten days and could reply in a fortnight. Rome had begun to awaken and Spartacus, wintering in the south, felt them stir.

"Send Varinius the reinforcements he needs in total,"

proclaimed a rotund senator from the rostrum, "not this piecemeal fashion. That's what's killing us."

"Send anyone other than Varinius," announced another. "Obviously, it's gotten out of his grasp as well. He's just not up to it."

"Send him, send them—why not send yourselves?" Cato the Younger intervened. "That's what you should be asking, my esteemed citizens. This is what happens to our Republic when its citizens shirk responsibility." Cato the Younger, the embodiment of old-fashioned, simple Roman values, silenced the senate to shame...almost.

"Pray, will the pious younger Cato," asked a senator, dripping with sarcasm, "be volunteering himself for military service?"

"Yes, I will. Will you?" retorted Cato. The elder politician coughed, clearing his throat to purchase time, eventually spouting about a time long ago in Spain. He sat to jeers.

"I intend to do my duty," Cato continued, "even if it means stooping to capture runaway slaves. Because Romans need do what Rome needs in times of peril. Not for laurels or triumphs and not for higher office, nor position, nor for wealth, but because it is our duty to the ancestors who built *this* city for us," Cato concluded, pounding the rail.

Marcus Crassus, stirred by the younger Cato's patriotism and his own fierce desire for higher office, spoke next. "Austere men of prestigious lineage, younger Cato is right: we cannot wait for Pompey, or some other *great* man to return, all while our country burns," said Marcus, using young Pompey's moniker sarcastically. "It's said, 'No man is truly rich until he can finance his own army,' and every senator here knows I hold more land and have amassed more wealth than my grandchildren could ever spend. I've done it with my own means, afforded to me by this great city, and I intend to pay it back. If both consuls will grant, I request the title,

Imperator, for a fixed time, just to settle the matter." The request would grant him limited dictatorship. Some senators grumbled, others delighted, as powerful men weighed the city's options with Sulla's memory looming like a thunderhead.

"What do you mean, 'settled'?" asked a senator for clarity.

"I mean, utterly destroyed and made an example, a display any illiterate slave can easily understand," Marcus Crassus finished. The senators debated for hours while Marcus spoke privately with Cato. By session's end, the consensus was that the shadow of Sulla cast too near for most; they could not give complete control over to one man again so soon. Senators decided instead to send the dual consular legions of Lentulus and Gellius, with Arrius, the former boxing champion, to command elder Gellius' troops in the field. Infuriated, Marcus used his lauded self-restraint long enough to make it home before expressing his displeasure upon shatter-able furniture in private.

BREAK OUT, BREAK UP SUMMER, 683 AUC (72 BC)

Spartacus commented once, "Whenever men gather for war in winter, more die of cough, than from iron," and that winter I saw exactly what he spoke of. Southern Italy in winter is chilly but mostly mild, but that year the wind lashed, bearing cold rain. People coughed and died from fever, and even I'd gotten sick and remained so for an entire week. Fretting Pila brought me hot broths and herbs from Helica, dabbing sweat from my head and emptying my bucket. When at last I began to feel better, I was able to return the favor for the girl. I worried Pila would join Oenomaus in death as she lay in fevered torment on her twelfth year of life. I sacrificed a dove privately and prayed earnestly for the first time to Helica's Dionysus.

When the weather broke and spring arrived, Pila had recovered, and we both escaped the pyre. With almost all the food stores depleted, it was time to forage as gaunt horses and fugitive slaves rejoiced at warming weather. The gladiators of Pompeii and Capua drilled slaves, while Va wore new men out with a giant *scutum*. Crixus and Crastus hurled repetitive vile insults as they trained the new slaves.

"Stab! Don't slash, you Greek, goat-fucking, whores!" Crixus yelled. Pila was amazed watching manly women train with their long-hooked spears. We watched them thrust their poles over and under shields while practicing. Shixa's shrill scream could be heard over her counterparts and her lean frame proved very powerful indeed. She hissed frightfully at us when she caught us staring; Pila edged us elsewhere. We found the precious few *pilums* that had been doled out only to strong men who showed a talent for throwing them while practicing on hay dummies. Archers were given a few practice arrows and I guarded mine greedily while Crastus kept the rest locked safely away. The army of slaves finally started north, more than forty thousand strong—a lean beast spoiling for a fight.

Spartacus' spies said that throughout Italy, *conquisitores*—army recruiters—scoured census lists while roaming the countryside, conscripting military-aged males for Rome's four new legions. Their tale told that when patriotism didn't work, Rome used pain of punishment for encouragement. One way or the other, Rome would have its new legions raised from Italy's bounty.

"Publipor, you scout for Crixus," Spartacus announced, breaking my heart. "He need your eye. I need know where Crixus go. With Gannicus, work out how," he finished, throwing an extremely expensive shirt of mail at me. I was left wrestling with thoughts of being cast aside and being gifted something so precious all at once. My mind conjured every reason why I'd been condemned to this torment, feeling worse than the time Helica had me surrender long ago. Desperate, I squirmed from it.

"What about Pila?" I voiced the only protest I dared.

"Pila, safe," answered the mountain. "Harm girl is death!" he shouted, pointing to her. I fought tears by blinking and turning away, completely crushed by the terrible order, even with the public declaration of Pila's protection.

"Don't worry, shit head," Crixus commented, "we send you back tattling to man-lover Gannicus, whenever we can. Is right, Crastus?" He elbowed Crastus, who laughed cruelly as I ran away with a heavy mail shirt rasping in my hand.

"Sheezin kompf!" Crastus belted, punctuated with more of that, "*Aw, Aw, Aw,*" of his.

Later, when I thought I was alone at the stream refilling my water, Gannicus approached to hear me grumbling beneath my breath. "Spartacus will take the majority of slaves up through Samnium and Picenum, via the Apennines," he spoke, detailing the two nearby provinces and a small mountain range running up Italy's central spine. "Spartacus knows Crixus won't hurry," continued Gannicus, "and it'll buy time for us to make a run at the Alps."

"Great! Have fun!" I shouted, aggressively passive.

"You're looking at this all wrong, Publipor. Spartacus sees you as capable. He knows you don't need me anymore. Spartacus trusts you." His words made me proud, until I thought of who I'd been forced to go with and whom I was leaving behind.

"Then why is he casting me aside, to those, two...two...vipers and that bitch?" I asked, flailing my arm at the Germans and their woman off in the distance.

"Crixus is hasty," Gannicus explained. "Crastus is reckless. They'll make such a racket the Romans can't ignore them. You're going to be our decoy. Spartacus trusts Crixus to lure the Romans away from our families. Spartacus hopes you'll keep the fools from falling into any traps until we can get away. You're protecting your woman, more than if you were with her," he flattered, emphasizing the importance by grasping my neck and touching foreheads. "If Crixus gives them a fight," he said, "both of you run straight to us."

"She's not my woman," I corrected, then paused. "Both of us... who?"

"Lelu volunteered."

At the last cold snap, Crixus broke out with a ruckus, making sure Roman scouts watched our direction. *"Vala,"* Pila said in Latin, blowing kisses and waving when we went. I returned the gesture, embarrassed as Helica watched with interest.

*Fuck 'em,* I thought, as Oenomaus would've said. So, we lingered.

Afterward, from the shadows, Lelu and I watched Spartacus, Helica, and Pila, along with the families, slink away quietly without us.

## SECURE FORTUNE

The Roman woman knew moving to this backwater city of Herculea with her husband was nothing but trouble. In this foreign place, surrounded by strange cultists, the terrified woman cursed her husband while digging with a hand trowel behind their home. As his bad choice bore down on her, the woman covered the hole with dirt. Buried beneath was her favorite terracotta jar, filled with silver coins and a precious gold jeweled necklace that'd been in her family for generations. The Roman woman would be damned if some dirty slaves would have it; she stole a look around the corner. The woman's husband had already run, leaving her to toil alone to bury their fortune. The sight of growing dust signaled the slave army's approach, validating the horrific news that had reached the woman a day prior. Every terrified tongue flapped of slaves ravaging the countryside. The woman cursed her luck again, running in the direction her husband had gone without her.

### LELU AND PUBLIPOR

Lelu and I watched with horror as the wayward Germans and their ilk slayed everyone in their path with impunity. I wondered what the purpose of having scouts was if you didn't use them. Lelu and I left to wash in the sea, hoping they'd get done soon and finally turn north. *Spartacus is long gone with Pila by now,* I thought, while Crixus and Crastus burned the coast eastward, ever burdened by more and more treasure. On one particularly hard slog and against Lelu's advice, Crastus tried to steal an entire herd of cattle, finally giving up and killing them, leaving their carcasses to rot out of spite.

### ARRIUS

The Roman Quintus Arrius was a famous retired boxer. He resented having to command elderly Gellius' troops in Italy, but he'd do it if it meant being appointed Governor of Sicily. It would be Arrius' just reward for having to deal with all this unseemly business of runaway slaves. The famous boxer couldn't wait to attend parties and squeeze locals for taxes on the luxurious island once all this horseshit was concluded. Thankfully, Arrius had been assigned an easier task of destroying the smaller force, led by two reckless German gladiators renowned in the arena. The old fighter's new scout estimated their force to be ten thousand, much more manageable than the thirty thousand fast-movers Lentulus had to chase.

### GREEDY SLAVES GET GREEDIER, 683 AUC (72 BC)

It took an eternity to make it along the gulf coast to Metapontum on the Pompitian Way. We skirted an old city's walls to avoid trouble; they wouldn't dare send a garrison once they saw our fearsome numbers. At an old creaky wooden bridge, we crossed the Bradanus River into Apulia province. Then Lelu pointed him out—the armored boy. He was a good scout, and where there are scouts, there's always an army. When I, in turn, pointed out the armored boy to Crastus, he squinted in the direction, then waved away concern with his hand and scoffed. We continued along the gulf coast, relinking with the Appian, only to cross the damned road heading further east, toward Neapolis. To my dismay, Crixus had heard of a rich city south of here from someone stupid and wanted it checked out.

The entire Gulf of Tarentum and I breathed a collective sigh of relief when we moved off. I scouted the town with Lelu and watched them prepare. I feared the twosome would turn and try for it. Somehow, between the two of us, we convinced Crixus that it'd be "too tough a nut to crack," and thankfully, it persuaded them to pass. Crixus sent us out ahead eastward instead, seeking the juiciest targets of easiest opportunity. All the while, Lelu and I schemed together to led the Germans eastward, tempting the pair with tales of towns that moved us ever toward the sea. *If I could just get to the Adriatic, we can start north—finally,* I thought. Pila was paramount on my mind around then and I dreamed of her more often than I'll admit.

Finally, we arrived to Mount Garganus standing vigil over the entire Garganum promenade. The jut off the eastern peninsula was often referred to as the "cock's spur" by sailors, for the way it appeared on nautical maps by extending into the Adriatic. The locals deceptively named their mountain Mt. Garganus, which was ironically nothing near the size of Mt. Vesuvius. Mt. Garganus rose gradually to a plateau; it was easy to climb and overlooked all the coastal cities of Asenestae, Merinum, and Urium. The promenade was dotted by prosperous little villages all along its peaceful bay. The mountain gave tremendous views of all the headwaters in every direction, and for the life of us, we couldn't understand why the Germans wouldn't order us up to watch it.

Instead, they spent all their time filling carts with treasure or drinking stolen wine and humping Shixa and her women. None of the other men complained, busy amassing fortunes that would soon kill them. We stuffed limestone caves full of goods all along the shore while paranoid slaves returned over and over, checking and rechecking their cache. Crixus, drunk on victory, boasted continuously of his generalship, or ranted on Roman ineptitude, until he eventually even fooled himself.

One morning, while on patrol in the valley with our shaggy ponies, Lelu and I talked of everything and nothing at all. The camp's drunken laziness had rubbed off and we slacked from a lack of discipline; we chattered like birds, mounted beneath the shade of an oak.

My pony shifted one ear left and I leaned forward, asking, "What is it, Dummy?" The sound of punctured leather, followed by Lelu's gurgling, made me sit up. I saw the bolt, intended for me, sunk deep into my friend's neck. We stared at each other, realizing what had just happened. Lelu's eyes quickly turned bloodshot; he opened his mouth, clawing at his neck, wheezing for air.

To this day, I've never forgiven myself for running away and leaving Lelu to die alone. Dummy reared at the sound of the bow's twang, saving me from another deadly shaft zooming where my head would've been. I traced its track back to the armored boy, standing beside his mount, as he nocked another arrow in his bow. I kicked Dummy as the armored boy ran an arm through his weapon to stow it and mounted his proper horse in pursuit. All this occurred as Lelu squirmed to death on the leaf-littered forest floor. I was barely able to focus from the stumpy gallop, but Lelu's voice suddenly spoke to me from death: *This pony go, where the horse can't...you'll see.*

Stealing a look, I saw that the armored boy had pulled his sword and was gaining fast on his Roman-issued mount. I turned Dummy up toward the mountain, fearing a dismounted fight, when I heard a horse's whinny. The armored boy's stallion buckled trying to keep pace with my sure-footed little pony up the grade. His mount collapsed backward on its haunches and he leaped from it, cursing in Oscan. Dummy continued to claw the slope like a goat with the same jaw-breaking speed as on open ground. Halfway up, Dummy began to tire, and I knew he'd start protesting soon. *I have to warn Crixus and Crastus,* I thought. My mind wished for the old whistle Spartacus crushed a year ago, or anything that would make noise besides my own cursing of luck alone upon the heights. Frantic, I brought Dummy to halt and gathered kindling, desperate to start a fire and warn my army below, simultaneously wondering how I'd tell Lelu's father what had happened to his son in a language I couldn't speak.

### ROME 1 VS. CRIXUS 0, 683 AUC (72 BC)

Quintus Arrius' scouts ranged all over the promontory, searching for fugitives. They'd found a few hauls of hidden treasure within caves, but so far, the slaves had eluded him. One of his capable young scouts walked a lamed horse into camp, its sweat-damp head dipping with every step. The champ wouldn't wait for a report; he'd get to the bottom of this right now. He followed the young man into the paddock, and after speaking to the Samnite, Arrius instructed the eager youngster to find another mount. Arrius mobilized his forces, asking the scout to show where he'd been thrown. Smelling salty air, he visualized himself in Sicily already. The only thing left was to kill these Germans, thumb that old man Gellius in the eye, and be on his way to a lucrative new island post.

### CRIXUS' AFTERNOON GAMBLE, 683 AUC (72 BC)

Crixus threw dice with Roucillus, a slave from Gaul, and accused him of cheating soon after realizing they'd run completely out of wine. Out of patience as well, Crixus decided to nap instead, until noticing smoke billowing from the mountain's side.

"Roc, who's the dumb shit, lighting fires?" Crixus asked, angry someone would be so stupid as to give away their position. Roucillus shrugged, upending an empty wine skin that refused to pour. He tried another. "Send Publipor to find out," ordered Crixus, laying a swirling head in his hands.

"Publipor out wit dat Afcan," Roucillus replied in busted Latin.

"Crastus?" inquired Crixus, sitting straight up, suddenly sober.

"You send him wif da boys to knock around Urium an go to da bay ta get mo wine from dem pirates," Roucillus answered. Crixus ran to his sword quickly, pulling on armor, yelling the call to arms.

### PUBLIPOR

Trail dust rose in the valley below as carrion birds circled above, and all while Dummy calmly munched on the bright yellow flowers painting the entire slope. I removed his blanket and used it to stifle, then fan the fire, sending abnormal plumes skyward. *Someone has got to see this.* The rush of air really got the fire going, and I fed the inferno greenery, trying to make as much smoke possible. Coughing, I turned from the belching plume to see Roman cavalry riding on the trail below. *They'll be on top of my men,* I thought, worried about the obnoxious, snake-tattooed clod. Setting ablaze a particularly bushy branch, I turned the entire mountainside into an inferno. Then, cinching my helmet and tightening cheek pieces, I kicked the sure-footed pony to Urium's Bay before the fire engulfed us both.

It was awkward riding down a steep slope for any duration and my balls were in my stomach by the time we reached the bottom. The squat pony made amazing time without stumbling once. I couldn't wait to dismount—my privates were pulverized. The sight of pirate ships in the bay made me recall a time when Spartacus had once referred to pirates as "notorious cheats and sodomizers." But still, I ran desperately to where they were loading up on the pier.

When I asked for news of Crastus, the sailors, toiling in a rush, said that he'd sped off with fifty riders after the mountain caught fire. With news of Romans nearby, the pirates worked swiftly to load up their sleek ships. I breathed a sigh of relief, thinking, *Maybe I warned them in time.*

The prayer written alongside the ship's bronze ram read, "O Baal, bury me deep and make a big hole." I thought that was a reasonable request for a warship, and turned to find Dummy eating the bush he was tied to. The thought of running the temperamental little bastard made me wince. But before long, the hungry little black pony trotted angrily, unable to dislodge the pest on his back; I bounced along, resenting Crixus for allowing our cavalry to forage so far.

## CRASTUS

Crastus the barbarian rode the magnificent Spanish mare so fast that time stood still. Giant muscles wrenched long, powerful legs; sure hooves grabbed ground unrelentingly, tearing earth beneath her. The mare's dilated nostrils piped vast amounts of air through gigantic lungs, pumping gallons of blood through an enormous laboring heart. The tall, lanky German sat calmly in the flying beast's maelstrom as the trail blew past. Loyal Crastus raced to aid his brother with desperately needed, deadly hands.

# CHAPTER SIXTEEN

"But some of them the slaves stupidly trusted in the forces which were coming to join them and in their own fierce courage; others dishonorably neglected their country of origin; and most with the true character of slaves, sought nothing but plunder and savagery."

—Sallust, *Histories.*

THEIR SIDE, 683 AUC (72 BC)

Quintus Arrius' new Samnite scout, the one awarded a commendation for saving Varinius, told Arrius that the slaves' cavalry was at least an hour away in Urium Bay on the other side of Mt. Garganus. The champ knew he had to knock out this splinter army quick. The plan was for Arrius to help Lentulus by herding the Thracian's larger force northward into a trap *after* defeating the separatists. The seasoned sportsman had heard of an oak in southern Sicily that never lost its leaves in winter; he hoped to see it before then. Here, Arrius knew the ground favored the barbarians, with rolling hills and a ready-made mountain to run up. As with any bout, he knew that if a man in the ring drops a hand, presenting his face, to always lead with a right cross. *The fools sent their best to forage an hour away,* thought Arrius, *leaving the infantry with a shit-ton of baggage.* Arrius grasped the initiative, closing the gap on the slaves so quickly that they didn't dare show him their backs. The talented old boxer slipped inside his opponents' range.

"Form up, by the Old Gods, damn it!" shouted Crixus in his war voice, banging sword to shield. The centurions of Crixus' ten-thousand-man army were mostly ex-gladiators with a couple tough shepherds and one Marian vet. Self-liberated slaves aligned quickly next to the man they felt most comfortable with. "Shield mates are best mates," went the saying. They'd drilled enough to know what to do as each man lined up in a row to the best of his ability. Before long, they'd aligned two rows of three, almost matching the Romans *homo hominis.* Crixus knew he'd have to bunch the men tightly to check the superior Roman numbers. The barbarian now regretted sending Crastus and the boys for more wine. Crixus resolved himself to fight without fifty of his deadliest men, knowing he'd crippled himself for grape spirits.

Crixus was a man who kept coins in his purse and not in dead men's mouths. He didn't pray or see superstitious things other men saw. He knew from experience that strength won and courage decided fate. Resolved, Crixus kissed his sword and grabbed Shixa by the back of her neck, tonguing her mouth. Shixa returned the gesture until they finished, then she screamed for blood. Her fierce green eyes were wild; wisps of her bound, blonde hair wafted in the crosswind. The woman had fermented breath and held a long-hooked spear, seething for a fight.

"Get up your shields, goat-fuckers!" ordered Crixus to everyone. *Too late to run now,* he thought to himself.

"They look pissed-off and tired of getting their asses kicked!" piped up the Marius vet on the right. "At fifty paces, they're gonna throw and go!" He meant they'd use slings, arrows, and javelins at fifty paces, before charging at a run. The veteran didn't bother explaining the rest—everyone knew this was a fight to the death. No quarter would be given; surrender only meant humiliation before an agonizing demise. None of the former slaves were going anywhere unless it was through the Romans.

THEIR SIDE, 683 AUC (72 BC)

Whenever Arrius faced a southpaw, he'd switch to their stance, knowing they'd be unaccustomed to boxing that way. The hills belonged to the savages, but Arrius knew their cavalry was too far away to help, thanks to a talented Samnite scout. It seemed fitting to an old fighter that the slaves should receive some of their own medicine by now, almost resenting old man Gellius for getting any of the credit. *It's worth it to get out of this backwater of shit stalls and bad attitudes. The sooner the better.* He nodded for his sergeant to commence. *Catch the whole damn mountain on fire,* he thought, not caring anymore who was warned or what the fire on the mountain was all about. Arrius' men were close enough now to hurl curses.

ALONE WITH DUMMY, 683 AUC (72 BC)

I wanted to rip my helmet off and throw it in the ditch after riding for the longest miles of my life on what felt like a hammer. I slowed Dummy to a walk; it was no use trying to make time on the path with this thing. Dummy tried craning his neck to bite me as we walked. I couldn't be mad for long, since the pony saved me twice and reminded me of Lelu. I fed him a tuber as we went walking along together on the shady side of a sun-dappled trail. Suddenly, Glaber's chestnut mare, the one Crastus loved to ride, came charging up the way toward us, riderless. I got as small as possible behind Dummy's neck and saw the reins thankfully drooping toward me as she dashed toward us. The big, lathered female asserted her dominance over my shaggy little pony, slowing long enough to put her big head down with ears back. The beast stomped, snorting at Dummy to move, now.

This big female was not a horse to play with. I knew I'd only have one chance to catch her before she tried to kill me. Like a lightning bolt, the broad female reared when I leapt at her bridle from beneath Dummy. Whinnying deafeningly, enraged, the beast thrashed her forelimbs to trample me. Her teeth flashed, along with the whites of her eyes, and with both hands, I yanked myself up by her mane, using the animal's power to propel me onto her back. I gathered the reins before the big mare could protest and yanked her sideways hard, moving her face with the bit in the right direction. The animal turned, I kicked her, and we ran back to the sounds of war, leaving Dummy to munch all that he could, unmolested and alone on the trail. There, one hundred light infantrymen ambushed fifty mounted ex-gladiators in the hills west of Mt. Garganus. It would've been a slaughter, but the inexperienced Romans hadn't accounted for the speed of their opponents...or how quickly gladiators adapted to change.

### OUR SIDE, 683 AUC (72 BC)

The Roman infantry approached, cursing and catcalling, uncustomarily banging swords on shields with a ruckus. The *signum* for the new legion stood on a hill with its command head and retinue of bodyguards watching from above. Missiles flew into the barbarians while acorns bounced and struck home; iron javelins impaled oak to flesh on both sides. Pilums bent, rendered useless by design, encumbering the unlucky men who caught them. The horns blew, sending Romans to run headlong at slaves behind heavy shields.

### ARRIUS

Arrius anticipated the slaves to charge and blunt his men, but curiously, they remained fixed.

*Fuck me,* he realized, too late.

## CRIXUS

Crixus watched the Romans advance from over the top of his shield and prayed to his mother's god for the first time in twenty years.

"God of Thunder, aid me in triumph...and Oden take me if I don't," whispered Crixus. "Now!" he belted, the first row folding behind the second at the last moment. Iron pilums planted into earth raised to meet the Roman onslaught, tips first. The familiar wooden crash of heavy shields was replaced by a collective groan from punctured men instead. The impact of coming to such an abrupt stop affected the entire Roman front row. The beleaguered Romans unfortunately recovered quickly to put up a wall.

## SHIXA DANCES WITH ROC, 683 AUC (72 BC)

Roucillus strained behind his shield at the Roman line pushing his feet backward against his will. Roc caught his breath as the man opposing let up to do the same. The former gladiator made it a point of pride not to be replaced until he'd worn out at least two rows himself. The Gaul thought he'd bit a man with his sword; unsure, he stabbed again over the shields. Roc was about to relinquish his place in the cohort when Crixus' woman, Shixa, Druid of the North, appeared. The seasoned gladiator and friend of Spartacus stayed in the fight just to watch. Shixa dropped her long shaft over the top of Roucillus, pulling and screaming. The fighting woman gaffed the top of a Roman's shield. The man called Roc by his friends ran the man opposing him through the neck and stepped forward.

Crastus sped past before any Roman could pull the rope taught. He turned the animal and charged headlong into the ambush. The Roman light infantry was composed of athletic young men who excelled at soldiering; they were dispatched to set a trap. Though the Romans had the jump on the slaves, the young Romans had mucked it up nonetheless from green application. It didn't take long before slaves had the confusion back in hand as outnumbered barbarians recovered, flying back at Romans like maddened hornets.

The young men from Rome strained to work their plan, while former gladiators forbade them. The slaves penetrated Roman lines, changing the contest to individual brawls where a gladiator was worth three soldiers. Somehow though, the best young Romans hung in long enough for outnumbered slaves to finally let loose. The winded, battered young men from Rome allowed slaves to retreat for respite. Crastus laughed his terrible laugh, yanking a shaft from his thigh, angry the exchange was at an end. Recklessly, Crastus the German turned to look for more trouble when he was punched in the stomach.

## THEIR SIDE

Quintus Arrius hadn't pulled his blade in over a decade, and he'd be damned if a bunch of slaves would force him to do so now, even if it was touch and go. Normally, the old fighter with the caved nose would follow military doctrine and have had his reserve, the light infantry, flank the opponent by now, but they'd not returned.

"Archers!" screamed Arrius, pulling one last rabbit from his hat.

## OUR SIDE

Crixus couldn't believe his luck. When today began, it'd just been another day of doldrum, until everything was suddenly flipped on its back by the Northern gods. Here he was, right where he belonged, about to snatch glorious victory from certain defeat. Crixus challenged the Romans, backing their shields to individual combat and accusing them of homosexuality...when he felt something bite his leg. The German bent to remove an arrow stuck through his shin when his air was punched from a blow to the back. Crixus gasped for a breath that wouldn't come. Knowing he was a dead man, Crixus grabbed his sword firmly and stabbed a nearby Roman.

Arrows pierced men all over on both sides. Combatants released each other to recover from the volley. Crixus caught three—they stuck from his back, with two in the lungs. Shixa watched Crixus fall and knew he would never stand again. The Celtic druid resolved to take as many Romans as she could, making slaves of them for her man in his Valhalla. Shixa wreaked havoc with her damnable pole-armed spear until the Roman archers loosed again. The volley, heavy as rain, struck her all over; everywhere else, men fell beneath its fury.

The slaves held for a bit after dealing terrible butchery upon the Romans even after their self-appointed chieftain, Crixus, had fallen. The real slaughter had begun with a look of doubt and subtle body language, quickly infecting anyone near as former shepherds thought, *Maybe I'll make it if I go now.* Soon, the sound of shields hitting dirt filled men's ears as they fled for safety they would never reach, running with backs exposed to die in droves.

Sprouting with arrows, Shixa caught a deserter; she tripped him with her hook and was run through for her trouble. Shixa, a wily woman who studied stars and bent men with easy guise, died screaming in agony atop Crixus in a heap of gore.

## THEIR SIDE

Arrius couldn't believe they'd lasted three hours. He'd never seen two armies clutch each other for so long and with such vigor. The contest with these slaves was getting too close. *Why hasn't my light infantry returned?* Arrius thought. If he had them now, it'd be over. The old fighter suffered his men being ground down with clenched teeth for hours before attempting to squash the stalemate with a volley. The commander could explain later, "It was for their own good," because very soon after, a slave dropped his shield. The champ noticed the slaves break in panic and flee, dropping protection only to die.

## ON THE TRAIL WITH PUBLIPOR, 683 AUC (72 BC)

Crastus had a shaft in his belly. He was holding it gingerly where it entered his abdomen when I found him. Woozy-looking Crastus smiled with glassy eyes, running red from the middle, watching me stop his favorite horse on the trail. Using a sword to stand and slurring incoherently in German, Crastus staggered toward the animal. He spoke affectionately to the hot-blooded war horse as if it were a woman, scratching its jaw lovingly as bedlam raged all around. Crastus was aided in mounting by his men. Tenderly, they lifted the lanky giant in his dream state, unbothered by the protruding arrow. Those loyal men then strenuously encouraged me to take Crastus and escape.

The tall German sat before me as we rode double on the enormous animal and I had to peer around him to see where to go. The first part of escaping was spent just trying to keep his hands from the reins. We rode from the trail and deep into the woods, until he finally stopped mumbling for a sword dropped long ago. The second part was keeping his tall frame, leaning harder and harder against me, from falling—until I couldn't any longer. Crastus began to slide, so I used my body to break his fall, trying my best to keep him from slamming into the ground. Setting him down gently, I laid him on his back, trying not to disturb the wound.

After a while, the Marius vet who had escaped the battle found us in the ravine and began dressing Crastus' wound. The Roman outlaw explained that he'd been an orderly as a recruit. He worked on Crastus, showing me how to stop bleeding at the German's thigh with rags and stitches. Crastus had ripped the arrow out himself and I expected the veteran to administer the same treatment to Crastus' middle. The outlaw used shears on the shaft instead, cutting it clean with just enough remaining to grasp, but leaving the arrow buried. The man splashed Crastus' wound with wine vinegar before wrapping it with clean wool, covering the exposed shaft completely in a protective cocoon.

"If I take that out, he'll bleed to death before you can get him help," explained the outlaw veteran. The vet recounted Crixus' lost battle while showing me the best hope for saving the German. Working together to mend an unconscious giant, the veteran said, "That's got to come out within four days or he's going for the ride." While scrounging for anything we could use, I produced a half-licked brick of salt—the one Dummy had stolen and had been unable to finish—from my kit. "Mix some salt with boiling water, clean the wound, and change the dressings every day," explained the Marian supporter. He said the wool wrapped round the shaft was only there to protect it from moving and prevent more damage, and he warned that the bandage would become "sticky" if left too long, and that was bad.

I offered to walk and let Marius' former Mule ride while dragging the German. The unscathed war vet declined, stating he was on his way to allies in North Africa instead. I thanked him before departing, dragging the huge German out of a gully on the Marian's bedroll strung between poles. Through the woods, we slowly went, and I thought how ironic Roman politics were that the Marius vet, who fought against Spartacus long ago, fought for him now. Crastus interrupted my musing with a feeble version of his laugh when one of the poles jostled over a stone.

### CRIXUS VICTRIX, 683 AUC (72 BC)

The Valkyrie who'd lifted Crixus up disguised herself as an owl in case the warrior tried to ravage her on his ascendency.

Crixus' storytelling made Crastus tilt his head back and roar with laughter, especially the way Crixus told his tale in German.

Crastus hadn't tasted mead since he was a child, but he now toasted Thor, God of Thunder, with a horn of the most delicious barley malt. Crastus feasted, listening to Crixus describe the battle that'd killed him. Oden had watched with his one good eye as the hero fought to his last. "I'm sorry for sending you out for more wine," Crixus apologized in the language of their birth.

"It's okay, my friend. I wanted more wine, too," admitted Crastus, laughing heartily and enjoying the banquet that raged with storied warriors in an earthen stag horned adorned hall.

Now, Crixus leaned toward him, his face serious. "I'll tell you straight: you're here because I asked for my man," stated Crixus.

Thor raised a cup as Crastus looked sideways at his longest, best friend, confused.

Crixus broke the news bluntly. "This is my feast—you've not been chosen."

A chill ran down Crastus' spine and he became angry, his hands clenching into scare-knuckled fists.

"Wait! You've still got a chance, friend," said Crixus, grabbing Crastus' shoulders to confine the fury. "That's why you're here, man! Thor's worked a deal with his father: if you die in battle next to Spartacus, you'll be chosen," Crixus explained. Releasing Crastus, Crixus spread his arms and grinned in body language that read how easy it would be. "And don't go jumping on any blades, 'cause Oden will know."

CRASTUS AWAKENS, 683 AUC (72 BC)

Oden raised a tankard once more, then Crastus awoke, angry. He wished to be back in Asgard with old friends, drinking mead in a massive hall. Instead, he was stuck in Midgard, with slaves again in a post-surgery delirium. Thirst assailed him in the darkness of a hospital tent. The German felt at the bandage on his stomach where an arrow had been before losing consciousness once more.

# CHAPTER SEVENTEEN

"One of them overcame Crixus with 30,000 men near Mount Garganus, two-thirds of whom perished together with himself."
—Appian, *The Civil Wars*

All spring and most of the summer had been spent scouting for the pair of Germans in southern Italy. We harassed Arrius' forces just to make them dig in somewhere so we could disappear again. I smiled, thinking of all the times I'd outsmarted the armored boy, until remembering what he'd done to Lelu, and that made me angry, so I thought of something else.

Five long months dragged on, and we barely moved. I feared forgetting Spartacus, or worse, being forgotten by Pila. Dealing with stuck, overladen wagons with broken wheels had gotten mundane, and hiding forgotten treasure became tedious. Most of my time then had been spent luring legions away or just watching them. The entire fighting season ran in circles—terrorizing or liberating, always just one hill away from Romans—until the day I slouched on the job, got my friend killed, and my army crushed. Lelu and Crixus were dead, and now I dragged Crastus to die. Guilt weighed heavily on my soul while stopping to hoist the huge man back onto the bedroll stretcher, made more difficult with his fever sweat. Burning one minute, Crastus kicked off furs, only to shiver with chills the next. At a brook, cleaning his bandages, I tried calling frogs again with stones on the warm day. Fall hadn't completely arrived yet and they croaked loudly in chorus each time I banged the round river stones together.

Four days I spent trying to find Spartacus, and I was becoming discouraged, when finally, the frogs returned a random call downstream. I ran to the sound, leaving Crastus' linens to search frantically for Gannicus. I almost cried with relief when I saw him standing there, with frogs loudly croaking all around his ankles.

Gannicus spoke in a hushed voice, "Lentulus' men are nearby; it's a miracle you haven't been discovered." Gannicus dropped the stones as I approached, patting my shoulders, glad to see me unharmed. He ushered for me to follow him off to camp, but I stopped him and spoke of Crastus. When we reached our injured comrade Gannicus said, "Stay with him. I'll be back as soon as I can." He helped me gently lower the litter's poles from the animal's rump. Gannicus jumped aboard Crastus' captured mare and thundered northward, leaving me hidden trailside with the wounded German.

Sometime after, while rummaging through the bag for something to eat, I heard a horse walking the path. The clever armored boy walked beside his ride, following tracks to where they stopped. Standing this close to him, memories assaulted my mind. An arrow for me lodged in Lelu's throat; the shock and fear on his face made my chest heavy with pain that quickly turned to rage.

The armored boy hadn't seen me while unholstering his bow from the mount. My thoughts went to Oenomaus and his agony on that horrible night, when his insides came out. Fury won out over grief.

Twenty paces from the trail, the armored boy's head scanned the trees before him; I could tell by the way he moved he felt like he was being watched. I remained crouched, motionless, covering the German with my body, holding my breath to conceal my patient. Dragging Crastus for days, cleaning wounds, keeping him safe, and chasing off wolves would be for nothing if the boy's arrow found its mark again.

My heart pounded, fixated on the armored boy's unseeing eyes, knowing any moment he'd either hear my beating heart or my laboring lungs. The armored boy's gaze found mine; our eyes locked. Seething, cinching my helmet with one hand and grabbing my small shield in the other, I ran at him from the woods. Then I pulled my *gladius,* my every action swift and flawless. Baring teeth and blade, I closed half the distance on the armored boy before he had decided what to do. My enemy switched to sword after releasing a hasty shot from his bow. With soul-killing hatred, I charged him.

Catching the arrow with my shield seemed too easy.

"For Lelu!" I may have snarled, without a crack in my voice. The armored boy had two options. He chose life by leaping on his mount as I ran on his heels. The bow slipped from his grasp while mounting and I read his thoughts through his face. The scout contemplated retrieving the expensive weapon from the ground—until his eyes met mine. My feet flew and I was ready to pin him to that horse the instant he tried. Instead, he leaned forward, kicking the Roman-issued stallion hard. Retrieving what was discarded, I notched a new, lathe-turned Roman arrow into my newly acquired, very tight nut wood bow. Aiming the weapon high, I released; the armored boy flashed a surprised look back when an arrow struck dirt before him. My unprotected wrist bled from the exquisite weapon's recoil, and I was impressed with its range.

I hurled every curse word Crixus had ever taught me as the boy ran off. "Goat-fucking, Greek homosexual, Italian girl, coward!"— things like that, I think. When the hatred wore off, I vomited.

Pila came to mind while I awaited the results of the race between Gannicus and the armored boy. I sat with the infirmed man, ready to be killed or rescued, whichever came first. While inspecting the redness on Crastus' belly, which crept outward like a flower bloom, I was startled by the sound of hooves, then relieved; they were coming from the north. I waved Gannicus to a stop before he passed us by. His eyes widened when I explained what happened, as the horse stamped in place.

"Our people aren't far behind," Gannicus assured, pointing north and then kicking his steed south, in the armored boy's direction.

In time, a cart finally came squeaking down the grooved path, yoked with two mules. It was driven by a young woman with a familiar, attractive face. She was surrounded by Helica and her cult, along with several horsemen. Spartacus' big black stallion was dressed for war, as was he. The young woman pulled the hay-stuffed cart's handbrake. The mounted commander nodded to me as if to say, "Good job," as horsemen circled round, ready to fight.

Pila had changed a lot while I'd been away; her breasts felt fuller as they pressed against me during our embrace. Her face looked leaner, and when she turned, I saw her butt was in the shape of a woman's. Pila was as glad to see me as I was to see her, and distracted with our reunion, she was scolded by Helica for not helping tend Crastus properly. The women of Helica's cult loaded the wounded German as Gannicus came racing back in a cloud of dust on Crastus' spent, lathered copper horse.

"They're coming," he announced solemnly.

"Gannicus, show Publipor to camp," ordered Spartacus. "Riders! On me!" Eager men, spoiling for a fight, followed their commander toward the pesky legion that'd been stalking them for months.

RE-RETIREMENT, 683 AUC (72 BC)

The former boxer, Quintus Arrius, decided Sicily was much too hot, full of slaves, and not worth his life after all. Arrius resigned in correspondence rather than wait to do it himself in person. Old Gellius wrote back, congratulating Arrius on "their victory," perfuming the stench of Arrius' resignation. To Arrius, Gellius seemed too shortsighted to see that the legion had been cleaved by more than a quarter. *Any more "victories," like that, and we'll have to make citizens of everyone,* thought Arrius, when he'd read the correspondence. The old fighter had sent his regimental *fasces* to Gellius, who accepted the rod-bound axe from a courier, thereby restoring power back to the elder statesmen. Then, quickly and without ceremony, Gellius passed along the holy symbol to Lentulus, right there on the spot of the senate floor, thus transferring Gellius' newly reacquired legion to Lentulus and thereby coalescing the strength of both—and doubling the size of the former's division.

There was no way sixty-year-old Gellius could physically prosecute a war. The two consulars agreed to combine forces, allowing forty-three-year-old Lentulus to squash the rebellion—which everyone insisted on calling a war—with *both* legions. The former boxer hadn't the stomach for another nailbiter after barely escaping the last fight; he contented himself with a humble post back in Rome instead of the lucrative one in Sicily. Quintus Arrius, upon arriving home, replaced all rusted door hinges and window iron on the first floor, whispering for extended family to do the same and warning them to lock their slaves at night.

PUBLIPOR ADMIRES THE FEMALE FORM, 683 AUC (72 BC)

Standing beside the cart, I stole looks at Pila while Helica carefully undressed Crastus' wound. "You were right not to remove this without help," Helica commented.

"Crixus' centurion, the outlawed Roman, dressed it for me and told me what to do," I admitted.

"Just the same, clever boy. It'd be beyond my help if you hadn't kept the puncture so clean," complemented Helica. Pila smiled.

"Will he live?" I asked.

"We'll know after it comes out," Helica replied. "Crastus will be tested hard by the gods for sure, and we can't stay here long. He'll need to be stronger, now more than ever, and it won't happen before winter."

We traveled on rutted farm roads in a small caravan, winding through a valley in the Apennines, threading mountains through central Italy. Beneath a canopy of trees tucked on a cliff's shelf, we arrived at the camp of stolen tents, while Spartacus lured Romans further away before killing them.

Helica and Pila had men place Crastus inside the hospital tent on a table. Mortar bowls of crushed herbs and mushroom caps lay nearby, along with saws, tourniquets, and cauterizing irons needed for surgery. The two women poured wine vinegar on the wound, rinsing Crixus after a hot sponge bath of salted water. Pila showed Gannicus and Vitelli how to hold the straps for immobilization. Crastus, a sweaty mess and hot to the touch, mumbled until Pila placed the leather-wrapped rod between his teeth.

Helica had me fetching water and stoking the fire beneath a pot. It took an exhausting amount of effort and if I wasn't running for water, I was fetching wood. Crastus let out an inhuman yowl inside the tent when Helica pressed white-hot iron to the wound to cauterize it. Helica cursed at men to hold Crastus still as they strained to keep the nearly dead German motionless. Pila's little arms tensed with young muscles from beneath the operating table, hanging by the biting rod wedged in Crastus' jaws, desperate to keep the man's head immobile. Putrid smells of burned hair and charred flesh fouled the confined space. Crastus appeared dead—until I saw his chest rise and fall, slightly. Pila smiled, relaxed, relieved the man was finally unconscious, as Helica ushered everyone out except the young woman, whom she ordered to stay behind, then closed the tent's flap to tie it shut behind her. "Now we let him rest as long as we can," she concluded, washing her hands in a basin outside.

"Why does Pila have to stay in there?" I asked, disappointed. Helica fixed me in her blue-iced gaze and cocked her head.

"The wound needs air; it can't be covered yet," explained Helica. "Pila will swat away flies while it dries so it's not corrupted. Publipor, Crastus will need more caps for pain. Come with me, please." She straightened herself from washing. We walked the shaded side of a hill near a brook, inspecting cow patties in the mist. Helica bent, placing mushroom caps in a bag hung on her hip. She asked me, "Publipor, are we animals?"

"I guess so," I said. "We eat, sleep, and breathe; we're born, we grow old, and die like animals."

"What about the living part?" Helica asked.

"Living part?"

"Do we live as animals, outside in the weather, constantly looking for food?" Helica inquired.

"No, we can build and store," I reasoned.

"Aren't slaves just animals to a Roman?"

"To Romans, I guess so."

"Are you a slave?" Helica challenged, causing me to pause.

*I was free, until they caught me,* I thought.

"Not at this time," I answered instead.

"What makes you free?" Helica quizzed. Stumped, I pulled my *gladius*, the short Spanish sword, halfway from its scabbard.

"This?" I asked.

"And this," replied Helica, nodding and placing her finger gently to my temple. "Do you believe in the gods? Do you worship Dionysus?"

I believed the gods were petty snobs who favored the wealthy and didn't waste time on mortals, unless for macabre amusement. As far as I could tell, and from everything I'd seen, the gods were bigger pricks than Crastus and Crixus.

"Yes," I answered instead.

"Good. Yes, we think of what's after life and many other things animals can't," Helica continued, "and to prove to the Romans we're not animals, we become husband and wife. Just humping on whatever walks through the barn only proves the Romans right." I wondered where Helica was going with the line of questions when she sprung her trap. "You and Pila will be married tonight, after our commander returns," she stated, plain as the day.

"I-I..." I stammered.

"Aye, you will be. We can't have you two running off into the bushes every chance you get. She'll remain pure, and you'll stay honest. We're not having romantic scandals, nor are we running a mobile brothel for teens," she concluded, abruptly ending the discussion.

"Yes, lady," I answered, stunned.

"Pila has gone in season; she's a woman now and your actions will have consequences. Do you understand?"

I nodded, dumbstruck.

"And Publipor, try not to stink on your wedding night," finished Helica.

The afternoon was late when Spartacus returned with everyone unscathed. Pila was finally replaced by another girl in the recovery tent, while I scrubbed with lye and lavender in the valley's river with Gannicus. Gannicus rubbed me with rosemary as we finished, even putting sprigs of the fragrant herb under my armpits. After drying, I dressed and thought of what it meant to be married. *I'm supposed to feed her and keep her indoors...I can't even do that for myself,* I thought, contemplating my fate.

# CHAPTER EIGHTEEN

"Spartacus was a Thracian from the nomadic Maedi tribes and not only had a great spirit and great physical strength, but was much more than one would expect from his condition, most intelligent and cultured, being more like a Greek than a Barbarian."

—Appian, *Civil Wars*

[...according to law, males having reached the age of puberty (14) and females of marriageable age (12) whether they be *sui irrius* or in power...and the intention to live together as husband and wife. *Married Women (IV)*—The Digest of Roman Law.]

Gannicus suggested I air out the breastplate and let him oil my mail while I married. "You won't need it where you're going," he said.

While I was combing my hair in the river's reflection, he asked, "Is Pila pregnant?"

"Gods, no," I replied, fairly certain.

"Well," said Gannicus, "it happens just the way puppies are made, so you'd know." We made our way back to camp, where I waited like a billy goat in fall.

"Ready," asked Spartacus, "to take oath, to ancestor, to Helica's god, and to me?" The legendary man, towering in a fine toga, lifted his chin, expecting a reply.

"Yes, commander."

"You know meaning and weight of this?" Spartacus pierced.

"Yes, commander."

"You man of you word?" inquired the giant. I realized in that moment I'd soon swear an oath to a man who'd enforce it.

"Yes, commander." Spartacus motioned for me to open my hand, and there my lord set a golden aureus.

"Come," said Spartacus, gesturing for me to follow as I stood frozen, staring at the coin.

A corridor of bodies opened for Spartacus as he led me to Pila. Helica stood before an entire army of slaves with all their wives and families. A child running underfoot distracted me—until I saw her. Pila, wearing a bleached white dress, stood waiting beneath a canopy of trees, holding a bouquet of wildflowers. The young bride's hair was tied and embedded with spring flowers that'd be "let down tonight," as Gannicus had joked earlier.

Pila, scared and excited, waited with a bouquet shaking with both hands. I could tell, behind her thin smile, that she was happy. *How would I keep her that way?* I wondered as I walked. I'd not heard the music until it stopped when Spartacus walked past me and turned to face us both. The commander's hair was cut square in Roman fashion. He was magnificently dressed in a toga and clean shaved. To me, Spartacus looked able to decree anything into law then by word alone.

"Pila?" Spartacus spoke. "Promise not to shame this man, give him respect and children, if able?" He spoke in thickly accented Latin.

"I do," Pila replied.

"Publipor, promise to protect woman, discipline with patience, and feed the children you have together?" Spartacus asked.

"I do," I answered, while Spartacus bound our hands in yellow ribbon.

"You both, this day, enter contract, witnessed and vowed before men," Spartacus announced. "Have children, with each other only, unless one dies, or woman cannot. Bring no shame to the man, and honor your ancestors with sacrifices. *Tallasio!*" Spartacus shouted loudly with arms wide, concluding the ceremony as the forest erupted in cheers. I leaned forward to kiss my bride as commanded. Two men carried Pila on a chair to a tent—a gift for us—on a hill just outside camp. A procession of people played music and sang, while carrying the newlyweds to their new home. At the top, our people gave us earnest and strenuous goodbyes, leaving with tremendous noise to let us know they'd gone. Pila and I eagerly celebrated nuptials inside our tent beneath bear furs and goose-down pillows.

### REV. 19:15; "COMING OUT OF HIS MOUTH IS A SHARP, DOUBLE-EDGED SWORD..." PILA DREAMS.

That night, in a prescient dream, Pila was whisked across Alexandria and flown past Egypt to the edge of the world. Pila was cognizant that she'd been taken to a nearing future, somehow knowing what she saw had yet to pass. There in the night, a light shone brighter than a harvest moon. The girl knew intuitively what she couldn't. High in the sky of her dream, an unnatural star cluster shone on a stall. Pila knew, somehow, these were Hebrews from Judea, here for the Roman census. Illuminated beneath the light's beam, Pila watched as a family with a newborn was visited by exotic aliens of the east, proclaiming kingship and bearing tribute. One of their strange, hunched beasts of burden bellowed.

Pila, who normally would've thought an animal shed a very odd place for a young mother to give birth, somehow knew she was watching fugitives. Pila remained ephemeral, an unseen specter, until the dark Persian gifting myrrh beckoned her forward. The new bride approached the infant, asleep from nursing, lying in a feeding trough as a cow lowed. Pila walked closer to see the umbilical cord wrapped with twine by its stepfather as a proud, first-time mother—the same age as Pila—smiled, waving the pregnant girl to see a miracle. Pila stood over the trough lined with straw, gazing at a newborn, when the infant turned its head, unsettlingly adultlike, from where it lay. The baby peered directly into Pila's eyes when a sword suddenly came forth from its mouth. Pila woke trembling.

### AESOP'S MOUSE HELPS THE LION WITH A SPLINTER WHILE HIDING FROM A CAT (72 BC)

Quintus Servilius Caepio served as junior officer under Arrius, until he was suddenly promoted to praetor in the field when the commander inexplicably quit. Servilius' younger half-brother, Marcus Porcius Cato Uticensis, known to everyone as "Cato the Younger," thought Arrius a coward for relinquishing command of the only victorious army Rome had fielded so far against the slaves. Cato believed Arrius quitting with the knowledge that Lentulus' entire army blocked the road ahead was unforgivable. They'd successfully trapped the slaves between two better-equipped and well-fed armies, and still the old boxer retired. Disgusted, Cato spat on the ground, cursing the man for throwing the fight after such a tough contest. With an open revolt running out of control and out of patriotism, Cato swore allegiance to the new field commander of *legio meridiem*. That new general just happened to be Cato's beloved elder half-brother, Servilius. Cato had rushed south to restore the republic he loved by crushing a slave uprising with his brother's army.

### LENTULUS

Lentulus, commanding *legio septentriones,* felt preparations adequate to repulse slaves and planned for offense instead. The filthy Samnite scout, dressed in ill-fitting armor, had assured Lentulus that the new field general, Servilius, was driving slaves northward into the snare despite setbacks and resignation. Upon hearing that the army was victorious, Lentulus had no more time for an Italian. He dismissed the boy. *Rome may consider them citizens now, but never I,* thought Lentulus. He had no time to listen on about how bruised and bloodied the southern army was, especially not by a dirty foreigner. Lentulus knew he'd be the anvil and this Servilius, a hammer. Together they'd achieve success handily somewhere in the middle.

Deep in thought, Lentulus pressed his thumb to the edge of a magic blade forged from a new material called *chalybs.* The oriental emissary who'd gifted him the blade hailed from the land of Alexander the Great's demise: Parthia. It was longer than a Spanish sword but not as broad, and the new metal gleamed with an unnatural sheen. Lentulus could see the value their ambassador placed on Roman friendship by gifting ten trained elephants and this exquisite blade. The dark-skinned exotic man claimed sorcery had been folded into the blade, allowing it to bend where others broke. The blade was made for Rome with an eagle's head pommel of ivory and a leather-wrapped oaken handle. It held a fine edge without a single blemish—not a pock of imperfection along its entire length. Lentulus loved the sword so much he had αστραπή—the Greek word for lightning—pounded into its brass hilt.

## PUBLIPOR

Keeping Crastus stationary for a week helped, and we were able to get some of his color back. The gaunt German's reddened belly looked painful where the cauterization took place, but I could tell it was healing. I now recognized that Crastus' body showed healed remnants of this cauterization process all over: his geometric tattoos disappeared into puffy scars. I was glad to see him sitting up and sipping bone broth by the time we forced him to move.

I thought of Crastus' quick healing as I sat on my mount beneath a tree; the armored boy kept a respectful distance. We nodded to one another from across the field. *I really don't have time for your shit today,* I thought. The annoying task of throwing the armored boy off my tail would take hours and probably require getting wet, but it had to be done. So, I crossed the river, making sure to leave hoof prints on the opposite bank as an invitation. Then rode into scrub, upsetting my mount with scratching thorns for longer than either of us cared to endure. While hidden, I listened to him storm off in pursuit of me and I was able to return back across the river in the direction I wanted. I had no reason to disguise my tracks doubling back; by the time the armored boy got wise, I'd be long gone. Eventually, throw him I did, but it was annoying to ride so far in the wrong direction. Gannicus, I knew, was out there somewhere, unencumbered by the pest and probably getting better results. I'd been sent north to take the measure of an impressive-looking army blocking our way. When I arrived, I stayed hidden, making squares in my mind and counting, multiplying the number of men in each square by the total number of squares then rounded up for good measure, to a tune of ten thousand. Rome had sent ten thousand soldiers, ordering them to take no prisoners and humiliate slaves upon their death for its glory.

Gannicus and I rallied in the ravine and were headed back to camp by the end of day. He had gone south, measuring the remaining forces of Arrius after the close fight with Crixus. Gannicus learned from townsfolk that Rome's commander, the one who'd defeated Crixus, had suddenly resigned. Gannicus gave

Spartacus the location, numbering their force at five thousand and dragging a mass of wounded. He claimed that the expensive victory made their forces wary, that they'd been gut-pierced by Crixus, but their morale had been restored by a new commander promoted from within their ranks.

Gannicus finished and Spartacus listened to my report next. I told of being hampered by my run-in with the armored boy.

"I ask for information, you bring...excuse?" tore the commander.

Terror gripped me and my stomach dropped. Stammering and stuttering, I eventually explained that I'd gotten rid of the prying eyes and that the army blocking us was ten thousand strong.

"Just say that, then." Spartacus admonished. "Now—kill scout," he ordered, flippant.

My commander had just given me a direct order. As the initial fear of his rebuke subsided, it was replaced by apprehension of a new directive. *Yeah, I'd tried to kill him, but he had me cornered and I was protecting Crastus,* I thought. *Or I'd lost my nerve.* Either way, the thought of seeking him out for murder was something else entirely, especially since really, I was afraid of him—and besides, the first time I tried putting an arrow in him, I missed.

"What wrong?" asked the commander, reading my face.

"I...I don't know..." I stammered.

"Don't know what?" Spartacus demanded.

"If...if, I can...kill him," I admitted, ashamed.

"Why not?"

"He...he's bigger than me and...and...I don't know if I can..." I trailed.

"Can what?" interrupted the commander.

"Murder him," I admitted, with head down.

"Hah, murder!" Spartacus scoffed. "We don't murder enemy, any more than we murder chickens." He waved dismissively.

"We kill, not murder," Spartacus corrected, with Helica nodding agreement. "As size go, boy cannot be *that* big, if he keep up with you." His words brought laughter from men nearby.

The commander lowered his forehead to mine and said, *"Credo te ipsum." Believe in thyself.* I'd been tasked with killing the armored boy and the realization weighed heavily even before I'd been dismissed.

Pila attacked me when I returned to our tent, and it helped me forget the job...for a while. Later, Pila cried after burning our dinner, even when I'd told her that char settled the stomach. She stormed off and I lay alone on my back, handling Oenomaus' buckle above me, admiring the eagle trapped in silver. I wondered what Oenomaus would say about the whole thing and began to laugh, remembering him screaming in Latin: "Stop flailing around and stab, stupids!"

*Now, I'd almost lost both Germans,* I thought, admitting to myself that both men saved my bacon more than once while on campaign. Though crude and wild, both lived by a code that I eventually came to respect. They always tried to take on large men first, neither killed or raped children, and no two men would you want more on your side in a fight. Both truly were "long-haired Gauls" in every sense of its meaning. *When in time had this many legendary athletes ever been thrust together in one place to change the world?* I wondered.

I woke to the sound of my wife cursing after dropping our water just outside the tent. The leaves were dark and ready to fall; we rolled up our bed in autumn's nip, between kisses. I had to find a way around the legion in the north if I was to escape with my new wife. A snow flurry of scattered thoughts blanketed my mind and somewhere between all that, I'd have to kill a scout. Pila broke my train of thought, handing me my things after I'd mounted.

*"Vala,"* she said.

# CHAPTER NINETEEN

"They attacked Spartacus and were beaten. Spartacus even captured the horse of Varinius; so narrowly did the very general of the Romans escape being captured by the gladiator."
—Appian, *The Civil Wars*

Cato walked alongside his older half-brother Servilius with the army on their way to reinforce the Roman General Lentulus. Arrius' scout, now working for Servilius, told how the larger group of slaves were hiding in Samnium, jumping along the Apennines, desperate for a way north. Servilius and Cato took notice that the little Samnite seemed to live on horseback, and both were confident the bold little scout would soon locate their fugitives.

Cato wished for Rome to continue in their grandfathers' ideals of rugged individualism, free market trade, and private property rights, all essential for a healthy Republic.

"Rome before Greece or Carthage," said Cato the Elder about all things. Cato's grandfather, "Patron of the Senate," ended every argument with, "Carthage must be destroyed," no matter the case. Cato the Younger, at twenty-three, began his second military career late, re-entering service for his half-brother Servilius. Cato was proud to have taken part in the first victory over the slave perversion sacking the land. He'd seen the hideous barbarians, with all their hair and gaudy tattoos, fighting like possessed animals. Especially disturbing was the red-haired, snake-tattooed giant leading the horde, who was accompanied by a white-haired witch in that last harrowing battle. *What a horrible world it is outside Rome*, thought Cato, praying for a return to conservatism and an end to all the abominable foreign influence to his nation.

## LENTULUS

Lentulus was tired of waiting, digging, and hammering from this side of the river. The commander of the northern Italian forces watched his breath in the morning and knew time was running out. He knew the big army of slaves was headed straight for him, all while Servilius harried them northward, or so Servilius' dirty little scout said. Lentulus had to admit, the old boxer had really given it to a splinter force of Gauls by killing their chieftain...if the report by an Italian were true. According to Servilius' scout, only nine hundred of the original smaller army's ten thousand were captured alive—a testament of ferocity. The scout described the victor's mood as "proud of the victory, but fearing another like it." A fight so brutal, claimed the scout, it convinced the governor to resign; shameful for anyone else except the beloved famous boxer. The young scout went on *ad nauseum* about the quality of the slaves' cavalry and their "invisible" scouts.

"Nothing escapes their eyes," remarked the small Samnite, with a little too much regard. Lentulus listened to the boy, wondering if the young hand admired fugitive slaves more than Roman soldiers. The boy's description of barbarians was disgusting; having intimate knowledge of their different cultures and tribal names bothered the commander. A Gaul was a Gaul to Lentulus, whether from Germany or Thrace. Lentulus wouldn't be bothered learning barbarian "culture," and the young man's knowledge of such things deeply disturbed the commander. Proconsul

Lentulus was supposed to send the boy back across the field to Servilius with instructions about the coming fight. Lentulus mistrusted this scout; he ordered the boy north instead, with a sealed message for Commander Cassius in Mutina's outpost. The armored boy, unable to abandon his new battle-tested field commander Servilius, disobeyed and rode loyally south to his new commander, knowing full well the consequences of such a choice.

## DECISION TIME FOR SPARTACUS

"Must be over before *Decembri,*" said Spartacus to me in confidence. It was that or wait until spring again, and even I knew that was time we didn't have. Hiding in Cisalpine Gaul, by way of Sabini, we slipped into Umbria, giving a wide berth to the capital city. We passed the beast on the Apennines Trail, while the city and the surrounding countryside held its breath to let us pass. Around this time, linking with Gannicus became more difficult; the northern climate stopped frogs from chirping, and we missed each other several times, making the ride into camp very anxious. Eventually, we'd debrief our commander by reporting enemy movements, interpreting their numbers, and describing the terrain—then we'd receive new orders.

During our war planning at Spartacus' *consilium,* he used a stick to draw in the dirt for his leaders. "We here," he said, pointing. "This, Lentulus," Spartacus marked the spot with an X, then drew a line. "This, the river, Scultenna. Here, only bridge across." He erased the line with dirt to represent Stone Bridge. Spartacus scratched another X below the first. "This, the brothers, Crixus has lamed," he explained, drawing an arrowhead indicating their direction of travel. "Lentulus will want Roman half-brothers, to push us slaves onto the plain, with backs against river. There, Lentulus, won't move." He looked around at everyone. "We must, *force* him. Gannicus says, two brothers move slow, towing wounded, no doubt. That make two brothers, ones to hit, but mistake not," Spartacus paused, pointing at the arrow that represented Servilius' troops, "that dog, bites."

"There aren't any other fords across, Publipor?" Egus interjected.

"Here and here," I answered, poking holes in dirt representing the river crossings with my finger. "This one's too deep for wagons, and they're both far. Maybe a two-hour ride."

"Lentulus, will want his fewer numbers to last long, here," Spartacus spoke, pointing at the X above a scratch that was Stone Bridge. "Roman intend to choke slave on bridge, force two-side fight near water's bank." Spartacus scratched his chin then gave the answer: "We pull north legion out of position first instead, then turn, ambush brothers." Our commander paused. "What say you?" he asked his men.

The sergeants who'd served him knew Spartacus fair and open to suggestions. Half wanted to turn and take on the wounded legion serving beneath an untested new field commander named Servilius. Others wanted to outrun the small force and concentrate on punching through Lentulus' dual-proconsular army in a run for the Alps.

Spartacus let every man finish speaking before deciding. "Must think when fighting, two against one," he reasoned. "Should kill strongest first; we finish what Crixus started after handling larger legion." Most of the slaves were excited—the ones who really never intended escape—while some resolved to follow orders despite their desire to leave the peninsula and return home.

Later that night in our tent, Pila secretly shared her misgivings about leaving for an unknown land of frightening rumors. I suppressed my own, trying to convince her into going. We spent the night lying in our tent, unable to sleep from worrying over our future. The memory of Lelu drifted in and out of my mind. I woke to the cool before dawn and stepped from the tent to stare at the heavens and escape those thoughts. Pila joined, wrapped in our blanket. "You're going to have to stay with Helica," I quietly told my wife as she covered both our shoulders, "in the baggage train, when we engage."

"Yes, we'll stay near to tend the wounded," Pila spoke softly into my ear.

"These are two proconsular legions, Pila," I said, and her face twisted quizzically. "Rome elects two leaders every new year," I explained, "like a chieftain or a king, but Romans don't call them that, since they're chosen from among the people. They call them 'consuls' and each is appointed their own legion." Pila began to nod and I'd hoped I made my point about the danger until she quickly furrowed her brows once more.

"How does anything get done if the two kings disagree?" Pila wondered.

"I think that was the point," I digressed. "Gannicus says one console is supposed to keep the other from doing anything stupid, but that hasn't been the way for decades now. Now, one just tells the other where to go. Look, Pila," I turned to my bride, relinquishing the shared blanket to drape it over her shoulders while watching one another's breath comingle in the new dawn. "I promise to teach you all I know about how the world works, my little spear, when we have the time." I lowered my head level with her pretty brown eyes. "Four thousand five hundred; do you know how much that is?" Pila's eyes sharpened as she thought.

"A legion," replied my bright young bride.

"Now double it, like I showed you," Pila worked the numerals the way I showed her in both hands, returning her astonished gaze to me once she'd reached a total.

"Nine thousand," she reasoned.

"Nine thousand, Pila." Caressing her cheeks in my palms, I whispered, "I say this not to frighten nor to brag, my beloved wife. I tell you true only to clear your vision and steel you for what's to come." I looked from side to side in camp to see if anyone was listening nearby. "One's already killed Crixus, and I've seen them fight. If it weren't—" I blurted, louder than I should have. "I let down my guard and got lazy," I confessed, lowering my voice, saddened by the memory of Lelu grabbing at his neck...before I had run. We embraced. "You must escape," I said, tearful. "If we lose, get alone. Get away from people, get as far as you can from Helica's cult, if—" Pila disengaged our embrace to place her finger over my lips for silence.

"Each day is a gift, husband," Pila reminded. "Now, why don't you go find our way around these *two* Roman armies and stop worrying?" Newly educated, Pila beamed contentment. I told her I would, and we kissed.

At daybreak, as Gannicus and I were readying to leave, Pila handed up my remaining things after I'd mounted. *"Vala,"* Pila said with a wave, implying that she'd see me again soon, smiling as I rode away.

Spartacus made a huge production of our departure, lining all the carts and wagons in a row, fully laden. The plan was to feign a return drive south at the two half-brothers, Servilius and Cato, thus exposing our rear to Lentulus' entrenched army across the river to urge them out. Spartacus' objective was to dangle a juicy worm at the bigger fish, making a proposition so enticing that the enemy couldn't refuse. We loaded everyone's treasure onto wagons and pulled them with lumbering oxen completely uncovered. For good measure, Spartacus had all the women unbind their hair and ride in the back of all the carts including our wives. My queen and my spouse—chum for sharks.

Gannicus rode south to locate the force led now by Servilius,

Cato's elder half-brother. My job was to signal the cavalry if the bait worked, or protect the baggage if it didn't. That done, I was supposed to look for a scout to kill. By now, I knew most plans dissolve once people are added into account. I'd also learned: always have a backup plan. We'd conspired to trick Lentulus from his entrenchments behind Stone Bridge by baring our juicy butts while appearing to roll south and attack the southern commander's battered army. If that failed, we'd just fight everyone and let fate decide. We'd pull Lentulus from the superior position or attack a weaker army; either way, we were going to fight today.

Selfishly, I hoped Lentulus wouldn't fall for the trick if it meant less risk for Pila. I saw exactly what I feared come to pass: Spartacus' guess proved right once more when Lentulus rushed for the easy pickings of our lumbering baggage. First, their cavalry charged over the sturdy Stone Bridge, followed by a legion of infantry. The narrow crossing funneled soldiers like sands through an hourglass, hampering ten thousand men to a crawl as the confined space clogged with humanity. I mounted my gelding, riding hard to the relay while waving a banner. In turn, another scout rode to a separate ridgetop to wave his own. I watched in horror from my vantage as Roman cavalry rode hard toward my wife. Helpless, I kicked west away from my woman, trusting Spartacus' trick would work by obeying my commander's command. I forced away my gaze and left them to fate, following a hunch.

IN THE NORTH, 683 AUC (72 BC)

*Thank you, Jupiter*, thought Lentulus. Servilius' foreign scout told him that the enemy had been packing to move again, and the little, Gaul-loving Samnite was correct again. Lentulus had his doubts about the dirty Italian, but he'd be damned if the little bastard wasn't right once more. The commander's focus was on the rump of this gazelle; extending his claws, the Roman pounced like the lion he believed he was. The Roman commander was flabbergasted that the stupid slaves would give their backs to him while dragging so much baggage. He was amazed by the ineptitude of his previous counterparts for giving such rank amateurs so much respect as they had to these slaves. Did they really believe he couldn't redoubt from this blocking position to attack them? Did the scum really think that his Roman legion dug in from fear? He'd show these barbarian brutes Roman military doctrine: attack always.

Lentulus pulled Lightning from its scabbard with his red cape flapping, inspiring men from atop an imported stallion. Rearing for effect, Lentulus charged headlong after his cavalry in a flash, all while his bodyguards struggled to keep pace upon the congested Stone Bridge.

### TO THE SOUTH, 683 AUC (72 BC)

Cato the Younger walked north with his half-brother, Servilius, the brand-new commander, alongside a tight-knit band of battle survivors. Servilius swore to his new men that as long as he commanded, he'd never allow another discharge of arrows like the one Arrius had loosed onto them in the previous fight. A soldier pointed for the brothers at birds circling and smoke rising off in the distance. Servillius' army had seen this play before, and Cato agreed—dig in and wait.

### LENTULUS THE LION ATTACKS, 683 AUC (72 BC)

Heedless, Lentulus continued to ride, chasing after his cavalry, caught up in the heat of the moment. His standards, bodyguards, and command head were far behind by the time he noticed a mass of mounted slaves along the entire ridge. The Proconsul, Gnaeus Corneilius Claudianus Lentulus, promptly dropped his priceless blade to tumble end over end, flinting light magically until coming to a rest in the grass. The Roman traded the long sword for two handfuls of reins instead. The Proconsul's red cape flapped in the wind once more, this time in the opposite direction. Swordless, Lentulus sped back in terror for the protection of his infantry, begging Jupiter to keep his stallion from stumbling.

## SPARTACUS SHEARS LENTULUS THE LAMB, 683 AUC
### (72 BC)

Spartacus saw the banner and walked his horse to the ledge, tightening cheek pieces as he went. From high ground, the old warrior, about to kill the men below, reflected on all the times he'd been here before. *Someday this will end*, Spartacus told himself, thinking then of his mother and father; he hoped they were old and still alive. There was a time, not long ago, when Spartacus had been ashamed of being Thracian. The younger man couldn't abide by their simple ways, couldn't get far enough away from their ridiculous superstitions. Now, he just wished Rome never existed and that he'd never left home. Spartacus missed the smell of his mother's stove and longed to be back as he watched another red-cloaked fool outpace his ability and run for life. Signaling horsemen, Spartacus watched the commander drop a polished blade in the grass as slaves ran down the Roman. Spartacus' cavalry descended and crashed into the line of horses below, scattering them to the wind. Blade met shield. Romans defended their lives from the slope as barbarians poured in on top of them.

Spartacus knew nothing spooked infantry more than seeing their own horses galloping toward them for safety. Especially if one was wearing the red cloak of command and screaming "Attack!" while retreating. Drills were one thing; watching thirty thousand barbarians come with hatred in their eyes was another. The new men formed a wall out of habit and froze until the hollow sound of abandoned shields hitting the dirt filled the line. Next, hundreds of shields began tumbling and it became another route as men fled desperate for life in all directions. Most bottlenecked the bridge again, except this time in reverse. The unruly press clogged unshielded retreating men who were in turn easily hacked and stabbed in the back. The slaughter was terrible, Spartacus shouted to his army trying to remind former farmhands to "stab, don't slash!"

Archers rained death from above onto men who thought they'd made it safely to the other side. Lentulus trampled his own men beneath the iron hooves of his fifty-stone horse, trying to cross back over the narrow bridge to safety.

Driven mad with victory and bloodlust, former slaves gave chase to hated Romans. Some eyed abandoned wagons loaded to overflowing, while most purged old grudges with new Roman proxies.

Spartacus walked his horse to the spot where he'd seen the glimmer and dismounted where a blade lay. He bent to retrieve it and was struck momentarily blind by a ray of sunlight glinting from the blade. The former gladiator was astonished by the light weight of such a long sword. It was balanced exactly off its pommel and felt perfect to a man who'd held plenty. This was surely the sign his wife had been waiting for. Spartacus stood, admiring the sword's straight spine, wondering what the Greek letters written upon the hilt read, when battle noise reminded him once more of the fight; Spartacus signaled his bugler.

"Leave them!" Spartacus' war voice carried like a drum across the valley, echoing from Stone Bridge where his army stood victorious. "Release the beaten for those yet to be," Spartacus pointed south with the stolen sword. "For Crixus!" the warrior boomed, rearing Pegasus, the priceless black stallion from Pompeii with the magic blade held aloft. The commander turned south, letting loose the vanquished legion to now lead an attack on two troublesome brothers once and for all.

# CHAPTER TWENTY

"We are told that from his very childhood Cato displayed, in speech, countenance, and in his childish sports, a nature that was inflexible, imperturbable, and all together steadfast."

—Plutarch, *Parallel Lives*

I had a hunch the armored boy would cross this shallow ford; I was right. The detour took a long time, and if I was wrong, I'd have wasted all of it for nothing. My mind stopped wandering to Pila and her fate once I saw the scout riding toward me. I tied the horse, unholstered the armored boy's stolen bow, and scurried for a shot with no time to tighten my wrist guard. My aim took a lot of lead as the armored boy charged past on a fast mount. Events unfolded quickly and time slowed while I visualized a bolt through the armored boy's neck. *Can't afford to miss,* I thought, lowering my sights for the unarmored portion of his ribs. The quick tempo of events hadn't allowed for any second thought or apprehension. *Must not miss,* I thought, crossing into what Crixus called "the zone," where every movement was precise with foreknowledge of the opponent's intentions, a place in the sand where time slows and no mistakes are made. Through that funnel, I released before the fleeting moment passed—to see the bolt sunk deep into an unsuspecting horse's neck. The creature's forelimbs buckled, sending the animal tumbling at a run. The armored boy's unstrapped helmet flew from his head as he soared through the air like a bird. I dropped the bow and drew my sword, watching the armored boy put up his hands just before impact. The mammoth beast rolled, kicking, exploding a cloud of dust. I ran at the armored boy to finish the job, then slowed, astonished to see him stand.

### GANNICUS

Gannicus rode Crastus' horse back in the direction of Spartacus with the forest engulfed behind him. Spartacus curbed Pegasus to a thunderous stop as the animal labored, its obsidian haunches glistening. Gannicus' eyes were drawn to the unusual sword held by the warlord when they met on the road.

"Two miles," informed Gannicus. "Drawn up for battle on the fire's other side."

### HALF-BROTHERS TAKE FULL MEASURE, 683 AUC
#### (72 BC)

Cato's elder brother, Servilius, posed a question in the formal old tongue his brother preferred: "Pray you, brother, may the fire be but distraction? Do birds circling for Lentulus leave us duped to inaction?"

"Aye, brother, make haste to our countrymen!" replied Cato, in the nostalgic fashion of classical Latin. Servilius ordered his men to strap shields onto their backs and jog double-time through smoking embers. The half-brothers shelved their many wounded along the roadside, vowing to return once the battle was won.

### NEMESIS

The armored boy coughed blood while his horse's head flailed in pain as it kicked and bucked, running off to die somewhere away from us. I approached cautiously, watching the armored boy struggle to remain standing. My counterpart gingerly drew his sword after fiddling with a wonky scabbard. A pebble lodged in his face fell to the dirt; his eye was bloodied and purple, already swollen nearly shut. Blood ran from the armored boy's nose all down his front. He stood, slightly bent, no doubt from a broken rib. I wondered how he could even stand, much less spoil for a fight. The armored boy limped toward me, armed, unable to bend his knee; I felt pity. Throwing my shield on the path and pulling my dagger, I approached the armored boy with two fists full of iron.

"Surrender, captive!" I ordered in authoritative Oscan, and by his reaction, I could tell he understood.

"Come make me," he replied in our language with a bloody mouth.

"You're a Samnite, not a Roman," I reasoned, ever approaching.

"More Roman than you, scum," the armored boy replied, spitting a tooth and limping forward, bloody and broken, but defiant.

"Our people have resisted for generations. You can join us," I implored in our parents' tongue. I was within feet of him.

"Join you in crucifixion?" the armored boy scoffed. The image of Pila nailed to a beam flashed through my mind as he lunged. The taunt would've worked if he hadn't been injured and so slow; I stepped easily aside. The armored boy groaned like an animal, staggering through the failed, labored lunge.

"Please," I pleaded, instead of thrusting for the back of his neck like I should've.

"Was that," the armored boy taunted through busted lips, "what your monkey said, when my shaft found his throat?" The insult and sexual innuendo infuriated me. The armored boy turned slowly to face me once more and spat on the ground. "I was there, at your wedding," revealed the armored boy. "Did you see me?

Are you sure...you're the first...to be with her?" Blinding hatred filled my soul, swelling from sorrowful confusion at the inability to reason with him. "Doesn't matter; we'll get her, in the *end*." The armored boy sneered, pleased with his double innuendo in our language.

"So be it," I may have said, as Crixus yelled from the grave: "*Don't slash! Stab the fucker!*" I lunged. The armored boy unexpectedly circled his sword deftly quick, parrying my thrust to the side. He fooled my sword hand, but the dagger in my left sunk to its hilt through unprotected leather beneath his arm. When I pulled the blade, the Samnite exhaled inhumanly from mouth and armpit simultaneously. The armored boy slumped to the ground, bleeding badly, and then rolled to his back, staring at the sky while laboring for breath. I sat with him and our eyes met. "What's your name?" I asked.

"Marcos," he rasped, his good eye dilating. I realized then—by fifteen, I'd become a married, wealthy killer. I rested Marcos' head in my lap while he died. Reaching into my breastplate, I pulled a coin I'd earned from the Germans.

"I've got the toll for you, Marcos," I said, holding a fortune in silver where he could see it.

"Wha—" *cough, cough*, "yours..." gurgled Marcos.

"Publipor," I said. Marcos smiled a bit then winced from pain.

"Pu—Publius?" Marcos coughed up blood as I shook my head no.

"Sh—" *cough, cough*, "should be..." He smiled up at me again. Marcos and I knew this would be the last dealings we would have with each other on this side of life. The young scout peered up into my soul. "Did...good. You...got me...Publius," he got out before his opened eye turned glassy.

When the last of his breath left with a rattle, I told him he was brave, and then said, *"Vala."* I'd forgiven the insults after my hate was gone; I knew Marcos only said those things to hasten his end to pain. *It was his job to kill me,* I reasoned, *just like mine was to kill him.* I sat with Marcos in my lap long enough for my leg to tingle, then noticed a red wax seal on the scroll from his bag that had been tossed in the crash.

Certain Marcos had gone, I put the over-payment in his mouth and set his head down gently. While retrieving Marcos' belongings, I went about preparing to leave and realized I had no time to bury Marcos. Instead, I decided to burn him quickly with the intense heat of evergreen branches. It wouldn't burn long, but it'd burn hot, and though it wouldn't reduce him completely, it was the best I could do for him at the time. With my silver in his mouth, I set Marcos alight in his breastplate and holding a sword, just in case. For a time, Marcos owned all my thoughts, until concern for Pila returned once again. I gathered my things, shaking off what I'd done, then untied the big mare and took us both for a drink. In the water, a killer washed blood from his face, glaring at me from a rippling reflection.

## PILA

Pila nervously drove the maddeningly slow cart as the Romans charged across Stone Bridge after them. She beat the beasts until her arms ached, but it did no good. *We may as well drag stones while we're at it,* she thought, disgusted with the pace. Helica rode in the back with a blade, tending to Crastus, who lay on an oversized wool blanket covering straw. Pila looked again when the horns blew and saw the entire event happening again, this time in reverse. She watched as men jostled with one another back across Stone Bridge to their side of the river for safety. The young woman sat amazed as a thick volley of arrows rode like a cloud, shading earth below. Pila couldn't peel her eyes off the sight of so much destruction befalling their hated enemy. The girl's mouth fell agape as she watched so many men in the distance cram themselves within the same spot, all attempting to flee with their lives back across the river. She giggled, watching excess soldiers fall comically from either side of the bridge. From where Pila sat, it wasn't long before she couldn't see a single remaining enemy soldier standing upright. The young married woman burst out with relieved laughter as she watched the huge warrior Spartacus race past on his black horse, riding south and dragging dangerous mounted men with him. With the battle won, and while stripping the dead, it struck Pila that the landscape was reminiscent of a busy tailor's pincushion; she giggled to herself at the macabre thought. Pila sobered suddenly, staring forlorn into the basket of bloody arrows that she held at her waist, deeply worried for her new husband.

## CATO THE YOUNGER

Servilius and Cato ran blind, expecting the young scout to have returned with word from Lentulus by now. Their soldiers outpaced the burnt landscape, trotting on foot to Stone Bridge as vultures circled above. Servilius slowed his men a step, fearing there'd be a fight waiting at the end of a long jog. The jaunt left him winded, and smoke from the fire didn't help either—if command felt the strain, so did the men. Servilius slowed them to a walk before the line checked itself as the whole column came briskly to a halt.

"Slaves!" rang the dreaded shout.

"Shields!" Cato and Servilius ordered in unison, the line stretching to fill a narrow valley's width. Roman soldiers locked shields and readied javelins for a wall of barbarians blocking the road ahead. Slaves made lewd gestures with their hands and cursed Romans, who returned in kind, tongues and asses out, one line taunting the other into making the first move.

"Get to the city, brother!" shouted Servilius. "Regale them of our deeds at Mount Garganos and return a day that is not lost." Servilius had served in Gaul long enough to know when three thousand weren't enough. In desperate trouble, Servilius became ashamed at his attempt to keep his half-sibling safe within his legion; the thought made Servilius loathe the irony and curse fate.

"Lentulus will send reinforcements," implored Cato the Younger. "We need only hold out!" Servilius grabbed his charge, Cato, lovingly behind the neck, forcing him to his brow.

"We are the reinforcements," Servilius broke the dire news to his ignorant little brother. "The only ones coming for us...are them." He forced Cato to look at the vultures above. "I can't tell Mother, when I see her in *Elysia* today, that I got you killed. Please, Cato," Servilius begged. "Someone must tell the city. Run before the men see—go before it's too late." Cato's elder half-brother, the newly field-promoted Praetor Quintus Servilius Caepio, fully expected to be in the underworld before day's end, but he wanted to save his kin first.

"I won't abandon you, brother," proclaimed Cato. Servilius took a step back, bringing the point of his *gladius* to a familial neck.

"You'll die by my hand, so help me Jupiter, before I'll let slaves do it," Servilius promised. "You wanted to join the army. You're a soldier; now follow my orders." He put the sword down to kiss Cato's brow with tears in his eyes. Cato ran to the woods while men jeered from across the line. A "man of the people," Cato always walked everywhere like the ancestors he revered. Walking that day saved Cato's life. If he'd ridden like an officer, he would've run into Spartacus charging the back of his brother's line.

## OUR SIDE

"Now!" ordered Vidovic for men to throw. The slaves who

had toiled in tanneries and stone quarries a year ago proved more adept at hurling javelins now. One slave said the "trick" was height. "Ta higher dat pilum fly, ta harder she falls," he said. "Heavy metal," what soldiers called the javelins that men stuck and bent in shields. Timed right, they'd help pull down parts of a wall just when the men arrived. Vitelli, Spartacus' Italian bodyguard, took advantage of a Roman soldier struggling with the weight of a pilum stuck awkwardly into his shield. The powerful former herdsman stepped on the angled iron shaft, levering a Roman forward. Vidovic took the opportunity to run the Roman straight through his rawhide breastplate with a single lunge of his *gladius,* the Spanish short sword.

The armies crashed, men grunted, short swords stabbed. The slave army's rows were deeper in the confined valley, unfortunately aiding the Romans. They were hemmed in and unable to come around despite the greater manpower. But sooner or later, outnumbered four to one, eventually everything grinds to a nub—even an entire Roman legion.

Luckily, Spartacus didn't have to mill the enemy that way. Using Gannicus' smoke, Spartacus concealed the horses' dust and rode behind the Romans to charge their rear.

## PUBLIPOR

I was exhausted and wanted to sleep, so I let my mare meander through the woods. I looked for circling birds high above to get my bearings whenever there was a clearing. I'd read Marcos' newly unsealed secret scroll five times. My horse's ear moved and we both watched silently as an exhausted Roman officer jogged by, oblivious. *I could sink one in him right now, before he knew what hit him,* I thought; then, remembering the letter, I let him pass. Twenty-six years from that moment, that man, Cato the Younger, would plunge a dagger into himself, rather than live beneath

Caesar's Empire.

### SERVILIUS BLOWS HIS TOP

"Hold!" Servilius shouted; his *optios*, the centurions, passed the message down through the ranks as Servilius heard hooves beating behind him. After Servilius' head left its shoulders, he heard nothing else, forevermore. His red cape was radically re-dyed in the surreal moment; Servilius' head fell beneath Pegasus' hooves. Cato's elder half-brother, whom he revered, lost his head that day in Nowhere Valley for a slave uprising that Rome's citizens preferred not to admit was even happening.

### THE HARVEST

All three moved in tandem—Spartacus, Lightning, and Pegasus swung as one, mowing men like wheat as the magnificent beast leapt in and out of the line with ease. Soon, Romans ran through the woods shield-less, hoping someone else would catch it in the back before themselves. The formerly victorious Romans dissolved, recoiling from the slaves' fury. The army of slaves freed their hostages, re-running a chain from shackled slaves onto soldiers, quickly exchanging bonds.

### PUBLIPOR RETURNS FROM A MOST TERRIBLE MISSION

When I arrived, men were stripping the dead of everything but flesh.

"Glad, you could make it, lord!" shouted Egus sarcastically for the benefit of others.

"Nice afternoon stroll, lord?" Vitelli jested with laughter, struggling to remove the bronze scale from a dead man.

*We've done it! We beat them both!* I thought.

"May I check on my wife, commander?" I requested first thing.

"No, she is dead or not; we find out when done," answered Spartacus, then gruffly tasked me with gathering arrows, acorns, and pilums. He laughed at my silence, ribbing me, "Don't you trust me?" After I nodded, he then asked, "You kill, that scout?"

I nodded, staring at the ground. "Good, that scout get under skin," Spartacus commented. "Woman fine, probably," he declared, smiling at me with a wink. I thought working the entire day and fearing for Pila was exhausting until I experienced Marcos' death continually re-entering my mind.

# CHAPTER TWENTY-ONE

**"...The son had a lean and hungry look."**
**—Description of Young Cassius, William Shakespeare,**
*Julius Caesar*

Gaius Cassius Longinus, Provincial Governor of Cisalpine Gaul, or "Gaul, this side of the Alps," and sometimes, "Toga-wearing Gaul," cleared his throat to read aloud the correspondence to his son. Ordinary Romans romanticized the outpost for the girls as a wasteland full of barbarians, but really it was just a sleepy weigh station for green soldiers headed to Gaul or war-weary vets returning from savagery. The lone outpost was used by aspiring politicians and slave traders alike. It was the last Roman outpost, the final hurdle for anyone not authorized to leave. "Let them leave, Papa," implored nine-year-old Cassius to his father, Governor Cassius, after hearing what was read.

"What would happen, son, if we just let slaves run off whenever they feel?" Cassius reasoned with his namesake.

"They would," answered the clever boy.

"They would," praised the father, "and what would they be, then?"

"Free?" answered the youngster. Cassius Senior, proconsul two years prior and master of mint before that, laughed with joy at the insightful boy he'd raised in the godsforsaken Padus River Valley.

"If Daddy doesn't stop the bad slaves, then other slaves will think they can run, too," Cassius Senior explained patiently, so the lad could understand. Soon thereafter, younger Cassius went with his mother back to Rome before the slave army crushed his father's outpost. Years later, a grown Cassius would conspire with Brutus to backstab a friend—for the good of his country.

## PUBLIPOR

The Padus River Valley stretched in the distance from trailhead to forever and then some more. Out of the Apennines, down it went until the heavens fell flat upon the earth, farther than the eye can stretch. Pila wore out the hand brake on our wagon during the descent and we had to stop and apply more rawhide after chalking the wheels with rocks. Once we got going, Crastus moaned, holding his wound as the cart swayed, and wind whipped all around the desolation. It wasn't until we were finally near the valley's bottom that it became clear. The heavens weren't laid upon the earth forever; instead, the earth reached straight up to the heavens in a wall of mountains so high they became clouds. I'd seen mountains. I'd climbed them. These were nothing my mind could fathom, nor gods could create. Unless I'd seen them with my own eyes, I'd never believe such things existed.

Adjusting my crotch on the horse was difficult, since the only direction we went all day was down. By darkness it finally leveled off and we struck camp. I was erected soon after the tent; Pila succumbed before the flap was secured.

I woke with my bride snoring and drooling onto my chest in the bleak northern morning. This was not a land of figs, olives, and wine like where we were raised. This was a cursed place of cow shit, horseflies, and abominable cold. *Why would anyone live in a place of such frigid temperatures?* I shuddered, fearing what waited on the other side when I heard footsteps approaching our abode.

"The commander wants all scouts to his tent now," said a former slave. I nodded from the tent's flap, barely escaping Pila in time for the summons.

Gannicus and I weren't the only *exploratores* sent to scour ahead for the army by this time. We stood at attention with new scouts standing in a row beneath a stolen tent, before the commander and his wife. Pegasus snorted from a corner; the black stallion would've been invisible in the dark if not for the whites of his teeth munching hay. Spartacus reprimanded or commended scouts for their previous actions in both battles—either instance was motivating. We were then excused to brush and water our horses for a reconnaissance mission. We were tasked with the nightly reconnoiter of the provincial governor's outpost.

"Publipor, stay," ordered Spartacus. "You too, Gannicus." Helica, lounging on fur-covered straw nearby, handed her husband Marcos' letter. Spartacus unrolled it to stand beside a tall, ornate lamp for light. "Read, again," asked Spartacus, calmly tapping paper.

"As to your prior correspondence," I read aloud, "negative. We're in no need of your standing army of five thousand." I cleared my throat to continue. "In the unlikely event the eels slip past, you will be the only dam to stop its flow. As to your current concern: yes, Pompey has sent word to Rome that he will be on his way from Spain after winter with his legions. Pompey intends to quell the slave revolt and claim credit for the whole affair. I must reiterate; we must stop this escape from happening or that carrion, Pompey, will claim undue credit once again for himself, becoming unstoppable in the senate. I'll do the arithmetic for you," I read, feeling Roman contempt waft from the page. "Pompey's twenty-nine. We could spend the rest of our days in the Butcher Boy's dictatorship." I paused, knowing Spartacus became inflamed last time at this part. Helica nudged me on. "Lastly, 'Pompey the Great' decrees: citizenship for any Spaniard or Lusitanian who commits conspicuous acts of valor and joins him to save Italy." I kept my eyes locked on the document in fear. But Spartacus remained silent, so I continued, "Could there be anything more conceited and abominate? I've already informed the senate, who'll be to blame if slaves escape the peninsula, so don't even try a go around." I finished the dead man's threat, lifting my face.

"Pompey's legion won't mow easy," reasoned Spartacus. The commander disparaged men from the armies we'd faced thus far, then of the matter at hand, he said, "We kill outpost, not trap ourselves in pass. Slave army kill Roman here—now."

### GANNICUS WAITS ON PILA

"Come on, Pila, I don't have time," I pleaded, as my woman struggled to undo my undergarment. I'd gone to our tent to get help dressing out for the mission, only to be undressed completely by my spouse. "Gannicus is waiting," I protested, squirming from my determined young bride. I finally made time while Gannicus waited, watering our horses.

We rode, then walked, and eventually crawled to the spot Gannicus had found. *They have no horses*, I thought, from our ridge watching the outpost nestled in the valley's bottom. On our stomachs, concealed in grass, we spied on them. I was shocked at how few steeds they had; certainly not enough to match ours.

"They know we're fresh off our victory from Stone Bridge," Gannicus whispered. "Romans embellish," he explained. "I'll bet they think our tangle with four legions will keep us at bay. They assume we'll skirt past and dash for the mountains." The commander wouldn't allow the little Roman dog to nip at our heels up the pass. Spartacus intended to kick it to death right here, right now; Gannicus and I showed him how.

"Roman, will watch slaves, make for pass," Spartacus announced, mustered in a clearing. Men flashed knowing glances to one another in the moment, all knew we'd be harassed backwards, watching our asses the whole way up. "Roman will tar Roman who let slaves escape," Spartacus explained to the laughing masses. "Roman will climb wall to get at escaping slaves; we kill Roman then." Everyone stood deadly silent, intent on every word. "In dark, we stash horse, come light, wagon women, bang pot, wave hair, show ass," the commander concluded, speaking simply to erupting laughter from the men. "For Crixus, we this name fight, the Stone Bridge—bit," he spoke, impersonating Crixus for effect. He let the snickering wane before continuing. "Tomorrow," the warlord paused, then boomed, "the Crixus, Maximus!" The crowd went insane in a lust for more gladiator contests between Roman soldiers. "We send, Crixus, Roman slave! Roman home! Roman women! Burn all!" he screamed, to the army's roaring approval heard all the way in Mutina.

In the morning, some prayed on homemade altars as others performed superstitious rituals, while everyone drank stolen wine. Over the last two years, I'd learned, un-diluted wine feeds the fire needed for most men to face a wall of blades.

OUTPOST MUTINA, WILDS OF NORTHERN ITALY, 683
AUC (72 BC)

Governor Cassius watched the rabble stumble by on foot with busted, creaking wagons pulled by lumbering oxen. "Where are they going?" Cassius asked his accountant, Cnaeus Manlius, from the outpost's wooden palisades. It seemed the slaves wouldn't attack at all and looked as if they thought they'd just roll on past the fort unimpeded.

"To the mountain pass, sir," replied Manlius. Cassius looked sideways at the bean counter.

"Manlius?" Cassius asked.

"Sir?"

"Did your mother have any live births?" Cassius concluded.

### PILA MAKES A BREAK FOR THE PASS

My stomach turned in knots as I watched Helica and my wife roll so slowly past the wolves. I felt sick when the gates blew open and five thousand soldiers poured out at them. The governor's men ran on foot, gaining ground quickly and shrinking the gap until slaves leapt from concealment. Slaves unhitched wagons, quickly upending them to release arrows from behind cover into an onslaught of unshielded soldiers.

### A BUREAUCRAT GOES TO BATTLE

Manlius' front line dropped, grabbing puncture wounds as the Roman accountant stood stupefied. Manlius was impressed with the height and speed of a javelin plummeting toward him. He watched amazed as the heavy iron punched through plywood and into the flesh of a man on the line. When Manlius finally realized that the missiles killed, he ran as if it were a hard rain, ducking beneath the safety of shields. The Romans formed up, attempting to escape the onslaught of slaves while knocking acorns thudded shields, whirling from everywhere. It was Manlius' job to know what to do. The centurion nearest dreaded what the fool might order, watching the man tremble with indecision. Manlius needed to look and see; he had to figure out something. The Roman administrator poked his head above the shields in time to catch a javelin with his eye.

### THE GOVERNOR'S MISFORTUNE

Cassius watched as his men were about to overrun the caravan; slaves magically poured out from covered wagons like dandelions blown in spring. The governor watched apoplectic as slaves built an impromptu fort of overturned carts. Gaius Cassius' best men, surprised by a sudden flurry of arrows, fell about below him. The outpost commander's candle-worth of hope was extinguished when slaves locked shields and charged, that hope blown cold by Spartacus' cavalry galloping hard upon the backs of his men.

Roman soldiers, freshly rotated from Gaul and well-versed in brutality, turned half their ranks and formed a second wall like true professionals. Soon, the five thousand war-hardened legionnaires drowned in a sea of forty thousand wine-crazed slaves bent on freedom. Cassius repeated, "Oh gods, oh gods, oh gods," the entire time it took to bridle the only horse in camp that could run. Ignoring a begging steward, Gaius Cassius Longinus flew south through the gate alone, leaving his men to die.

### PUBLIPOR LETS LOOSE

A Roman rode like wind over the rise while Spartacus busied himself killing the man's men in the valley below. The Roman had nearly fallen from his mount, ripping the red cape flapping at his neck, desperate to jettison the badge. For fun, I tightened my wrist guard to test the range on Marcos' expensive bow. My chest had swollen over the summer by then and it showed by how far I could pull the tight weapon. Watching the target run and leading ridiculously high, I released. The bolt arched until only the white of goose feathers could barely be seen. They waved at me from the distance in the dirt. It'd come close. I notched another. Three pygmies and Lelu's father, still and silent, waited as I led the target once more, groaning disappointment when it fell short as well. The mounted commander cleared my range, completely unaware he'd been loosed upon.

Lelu's dad and the three Pygmies shared in the disappointing miss by patting my back, speaking the universal language of encouragement, as if to say, "You'll get him next time." Thanking them, I gathered my things and left to retrieve my wife.

That night, Pila and I watched four hundred Roman soldiers fight each other to death. We ate beef with cheese and drank fresh milk as captured soldiers bumbled with demeaning weapons beneath ridiculous helmets. The Crixus Maximus, as Spartacus called it, went on for hours, illuminated by the camp's fire, literally setting the entire outpost of Mutina ablaze. Gaius Cassius' entire camp burned like a god's pyre, fed by brave men who withstood heat long enough to throw on more. The German was honored like a king in the unwalled frontier city outside Fort Mutina. I was amused when people who hadn't known Crixus spoke ignorantly and reverently about the incorrigible German. Most slaves couldn't get enough of the contests between their former owners. Quickly organized death became tedious; repulsed, we secreted away to our small tent when no one was looking. Pila experienced an eager husband until we fell asleep despite the clamor nearby.

In an obscure dream that night, I dreamt of my dead friends: Oenomaus, Crixus, Lelu, and Marcos. In it, we were all close, happily laughing as Crixus mocked me by standing on a long table, flapping arms like wings and bobbing his head like a chicken. We sat together drinking at the long table, laughing hysterically; I missed them terribly when I woke.

Spartacus and Helica spoke with the Thracian captives fresh from the front in their native tongue. "How old is this news, son?" Spartacus asked the black-haired men with dark eyes like his own in their common tongue.

"Last summer, lord," answered the countrymen. Spartacus gently grasped one of the man's shoulders, having just learned of devastation in the land of his birth. When Spartaks, Spartacus' father, had learned of Roman treachery perpetrated against his son, he aligned with Mithradates and went to war. The war had gone so badly that the tribe now ceased to exist.

### HELICA MOLDS THE FUTURE

Helica held the headless chicken upside down, draining its blood into a bowl while looking for answers. The dark red liquid told her to turn south and sack the city. "I'm still looking," she told her husband instead. Helica had known men all her life; she knew she'd have to make *this* man believe *her* idea was *his*, if they were to go.

"Keep trying," Spartacus requested. The smallness of Helica's prior vision made her blush; why would she go all the way to the other side of the world to kill Romans when they were all right here? Helica envisioned herself dressed in a fine toga with hair tied in the latest fashion, listening to the patter of tiny feet across marble—the Queen of Rome.

"Yes, husband," replied Helica.

The sun chariot dove into the horizon, dimming earth on mortals below as the army of slaves camped upon the Padus River's bank. Spartacus brushed Pegasus with straw, quietly asking the stallion for answers, knowing it too late in the day to begin an ascent; the slaves would wait and start fresh tomorrow. Spartacus was concerned with how to shed excess weight, hindering the climb, knowing full well greedy men would despise him for leaving behind their wealth. Spartacus watched an old woman outside weave a basket, then again in his mind, Spartacus saw her high in the pass the color of a blueberry, curled unnaturally and frozen. He looked away with the image of Crastus on a litter, dragged through the pain of recovery just to freeze. Spartacus looked toward the heavens and saw his father tormented by the loss of a son. Everywhere Spartacus turned, he saw death.

Spartacus had done it—the impossible idea cooked up in a cage by a woman between bouts birthed into reality. Now, the mountains beckoned; nothing would stop them. All Spartacus had to do was walk through the door. Promises kept, mission complete.

## PUBLIPOR FINDS HIS VOICE

"If it's all the same, commander," I spoke timidly, "my wife and I thought we had best stay behind."

"Why?" asked Spartacus, knowing full well the answer.

"We've heard," I said, "they kill just for having an accent."

"You doubt?"

"No, commander," I replied, frightened. My thoughts jumbled, trying to all get out at once.

"How small, can you scribe, in Greek?" Spartacus asked, confusingly changing the subject.

"Huh?" I replied, leaving my mouth ignorantly agape. Pegasus snorted and I felt his spray enter my mouth.

"The beast master, he still have bird?" asked Spartacus.

"I think so," I answered, spitting, knowing he'd meant Lelu's father.

"Go, find out."

I found the African mending a horse's split hoof upside down under the shade of a lean-to shed. I bent at the waist with him so we could see eye to eye. With a forelimb between us, I asked him in Latin, "Are the birds still alive?" The man smiled and stood upright, so I joined him. "You know, the rainbow-colored ones with the red eyes?" I asked foolishly, in Oscan this time. Lelu's dad laughed at my ignorance and I was grateful to have been alone with him as I pretended to be a homing pigeon. With my hands tucked beneath armpits, I flapped my elbows, making wings. Next, I stuck my neck in and out and walked in a stuttering figure eight. "Coo...coo..." I sounded, with the pursed lips of a bird's beak. It took a long time for Lelu's dad to get up from the ground after laughing so hard. Wiping tears from his face and holding his ribs, Lelu's father motioned for me to follow him while still giggling. While in his tent, birds eyed me, warily skittish in their wicker cages.

I left to inform the *bosa*, but Pila stopped me on my way, asking for help rolling our beds. Annoyed, I went to help and discovered her naked. Pila began desperately pulling at my leather girding to get it off. Spartacus eventually learned the fate of the birds: they were alive and in better health than when we'd gotten them.

### MARCUS CRASSUS WINS SPECIAL ELECTION

Marcus Licinius Crassus, the wealthiest man in the world, wanted the one thing his money couldn't buy: "real" political power. Constantly being one step behind the much younger Pompey irked him to no end. Youth and charisma eluded Marcus, even as a youngster. Strongarm tactics on opponents in the senate came much easier. Convincing plebeians who thought him disingenuous for support was impossible until he'd learned the secret. Many illustrious political careers were reduced to dust and stymied without help from the "great unwashed." Marcus Crassus decided to take his tremendous losses from the uprising and make them an opportunity. When the vote was finally tabulated, Marcus Crassus was nominated by a landslide. He'd been elected for six months to be Imperator, with help of votes bought from threats of eviction or outright bribes.

Imperator was the only title higher than both Proconsuls and was given to "great men" in periods of extreme peril and only for a specific amount of time—Sulla being the exception. It didn't hurt that Marcus Crassus could finance two legions from his own purse indefinitely, though he'd no intention of dipping into his own coffers. Marcus would raise the balance for the war from treasury loans first, long before he'd ever finance such an endeavor himself. He hadn't commanded an army since the civil war ten years prior, but he never cut ties with former officers, administrative advisors, and thugs. Marcus Crassus quickly appointed men the task of raising his six legions of thirty thousand men. Marcus only took advice from men he trusted, like his freed slave Merillius and the fire brigade marshal, Atticus Fabius Dominicus.

"Finally grabbing things with both hands, I see," Atticus said in soldiers' terms. "Kudos to you for coming up roses on this whole slave thing," he congratulated Marcus Crassus on the appointment, ignorant as a commoner of its expense. "Boy, that Glaber shit went tits-up quick, didn't it, Merl?" asked the soldier. Merillius smiled in agreement, privately detesting the way Marcus' centurion disrespectfully chopped his name, having given up trying to make the brute stop years ago.

"I thought I told you to keep Glaber out of trouble," Marcus reminded the vet.

"I thought you told me to recapture slaves; that jackass wouldn't know trouble if it stabbed him in his sleep." Atticus laughed at his own joke. Merillius bit his tongue. "How long are we going to keep this job, boss? Spartacus has got to be halfway through the pass by now," Atticus said, secretly rooting for his old compatriot's escape.

"Spartacus turns toward the city," Merillius spoke for his former owner. Atticus placed his hand over his nose and mouth to stop the spray of wine from hitting the other men. Grabbing Merillius' toga, Atticus wiped his dripping nose with the expensive garment while waiting for details. "Inexplicably, the slaves come at us," Merillius continued, wrenching his garment away. When Atticus settled, he gave his boss, Marcus Crassus, options.

"Wouldn't you?" asked Atticus. "I mean, they've kicked our ass all year and thrown a lot of your guys out of office—permanently. There's nothing in Gaul but cold, rain, mud, and ugly women; sometimes all together," quipped the old centurion. "Most slaves haven't set one foot in their own land in all their miserable lives. You'll need to draft 'wannabe' Romans if you want a chance to beat these guys. Lastly, you gotta make men more afraid of *you* than of *them*," he finished. Merillius made a face. Marcus understood the old soldier's meaning as the centurion drank Marcus' wine quickly—before he, or it, were run out. Marcus Crassus dipped the quill and let the excess drip before he carried it to the dried reed pulp to scratch a plan in Egyptian ink.

### THE LION PURRS

Pila was so startled to see me inside the hospital tent that she almost dropped her basin full of water. "You sneak!" she shouted, slapping my arm after setting it down on a table. "We can't do it here; Helica could walk in."

"That's not why I'm here," I said, and pointed to Crastus.

"Sheezin face," a frail voice cracked from the darkened corner. "*Vasser...*" it pleaded. Pila turned to the gaunt German lying in the corner to see his eyes cracked open. She ran from the tent screaming for Helica.

# CHAPTER TWENTY-TWO

**"And once when someone said, 'Pompeius Magnus is coming,' Crassus fell to laughing and asked: 'How big is he?'"**
**—Plutarch, *Life of the Caesars***

Marcus came from a nearly extinguished line of noble patricians. Publius Crassus, Marcus Crassus' father, had a Spartacus of his own in Spain, when Marcus was a very young man: Viriathus, a ruthless Spanish warlord bent on freedom. Just as Spartacus tormented Marcus, so Viriathus plagued Marcus' father long ago. So successful was Viriathus, he convinced the brilliant Roman general Sertorius to throw in with him, creating a true Roman senate in exile. Elder Crassus chased Viriathus across Spain with the entire might of Rome, dragging young Marcus in tow. Three years of chasing mist and one very close call with young Marcus caused his father to switch from a campaign of pursuing ghosts to one of local terror. Anyone so much as suspected of supporting the two outlaws with even one grain of wheat faced humiliating butchery. Young Marcus Crassus learned how not to fight, what Roman impatience should produce, and how to suppress a people by their own kinships. The biggest lesson young Marcus learned was great generalship isn't enough: you must kill the senate figuratively to have any success in the field literally. Hardship came for Marcus in those years when civil war first broke—especially after they'd impaled his father's head on a pike in the forum like a trophy ram from Carthage. His crime: backing the wrong political party.

Marcus Crassus fled to his father's supporters in Spain, where he lived in exile, hiding in caves until finally escaping east to join Sulla. Destitute and on his way out, Marcus clawed back to prominence with nothing but his own two hands and sheer Roman determination. By triangulating power with Sulla and Pompey, Marcus returned to end civil war and rule through law. Taking a page from his father's book in Spain, he whispered into Sulla's ear. Soon, public lists of condemned families appeared with laws to confiscate land, lives, and family with a writ from the senate. Marcus' cunning with the lists launched his fortune. He'd become a man with an innate ability to capitalize on the misery of others, finally making Marcus Crassus feared, wealthy, and powerful...everything he always wanted.

Marcus' time in exile and subsequent impoverishment taught him the virtues of frugality. The owner of palatial estates felt more comfortable in bricks from the old city, going so far as to refuse a resort villa in Campania that had recently become all the rage. "Just because everyone else has one doesn't mean I will," Marcus scoffed, choosing always instead to purchase real estate that made a return. Marcus bought vast hectares of farming tracts in southern Italy or blocks of stacked apartments inside the city's walls. He spent money only to buy influence or earn more. Early in his career and struggling for votes, he found the secret hiding on the lips of a Greek slave named Merillius. The slave had been purchased years before as an administrative assistant for a mere pittance after the sack of Athens. *Best money ever spent,* Marcus remembered thinking once the Greek Merillius revealed his many talents.

"Plebeians aren't interested in eloquent oratories or smart

reforms," Merillius opined. "They prefer silver coins to silver tongues when it comes to voting." Armed with this knowledge, Marcus implemented a strategy of making himself a "man of the people" overnight. Marcus Crassus was the epitome of what Rome offered to those willing to achieve: a man who could rise from irrelevance to Imperator in less than a decade.

Marcus should've been the beacon that lit future generations. His was the road map patrician children should strive to emulate—if it weren't for fucking Pompey. Just as the father had been outshined in his time, so too was younger Marcus relegated behind the brilliance and exceptionalism of his chief rival, "Pompey the Great," who'd appeared from nowhere. Whatever political accolades Marcus achieved, Pompey did it faster, better, and sooner. Before Pompey was even old enough to be eligible, the Butcher's Boy had a triumph through Rome, thanks to a smitten Sulla. What really stung Marcus Crassus—the thing most intolerable—was that Pompey was *novice homo*: a "new man." His family wasn't even truly patrician.

Now with this new appointment, Marcus, surpassed even young Pompey in title at last. Delightedly, Marcus had finally gotten the better of the youngster with unwitting help from Sulla's old cavalry sergeant, Spartacus of Thrace. Marcus enjoyed the fact that though Pompey had a slightly similar title, it was only valid in Spain, becoming void south of Rubicon Creek. Pompey, the Butcher's Boy, was forced to the world's edge just to be lauded, while Marcus Crassus could do the same thing right here in Italy. It gave Marcus a smirk of satisfaction knowing the two disgraced proconsuls, Gellius and Lentulus, were Pompey's supporters. The Roman smiled wickedly every time the irony of it crossed his mind.

"Why on earth, sir, would you ask Pompey for help with this?" Merillius asked, confounded. Marcus Crassus' freed slave stopped writing the letter to the senate long enough to question his former owner when the dictation's logic became confusing.

"Nothing is etched in stone...until it is," said Marcus. "In the unlikely event this gets out of our grasp, we'll need someone to hang the whole mess on." Merillius, seeing genius, nodded and re-dipped the quill to continue working. "Merillius?" asked Marcus Crassus.

"Yes, Imperator," answered the assistant.

"What of the lead pellets I requested?" asked the newly minted Imperator.

"The supplier says he's unable to fulfill the order in such copious amounts. All his lead has been earmarked for lining the aqueducts in the new quarter's waterworks," answered Merillius, the free Greek.

"What about the bread maker, Gavius, in Pompeii? Can we get clay acorns from him?" asked Marcus.

"Gavius has promised to supply all the baked clay acorns you desire, sir," Merillius answered.

"Order fifty barrels from that fat, bread-baking brickmaker," spoke Marcus, disdainful of any industrious plebeian who dirtied his hands in commerce.

### WINGED MESSAGES FLY EASTWARD

Spartacus repeated what he'd said a second time as I wrote right to left. Greek was hard enough; more so when written the size of bugs. Some ink ran, making the note illegible once again, so I crumpled it, tore more, cussed, and tried again.

*"Cockspur, Urium Bay, mid Dec."* I wrote, ending with the monetary symbol for sesterce—all that would fit on the tiny bit of papyrus. When the ink dried, I rolled the scroll tightly and stuffed it into the little container attached to the bird's leg with help from Lelu's dad. Two more were painfully written and packaged

the same way as the African held the bird gingerly upside down. Lelu's father released the pigeons with a gentle toss each time; they flew upward in tandem until the covey got their bearings and moved eastward, disappearing high in the sky.

Spartacus spoke after the birds' release, granting permission to anyone who wanted to escape over the mountain pass to do so. Those who accepted were mostly recent captives, non-Latin speakers who still had lives on the other side. Most slaves, like me, weren't old enough to remember a life before enslavement. We were slaves born of slaves in Italy; our lives and those of our children condemned to toil forever for the benefit of others. The recently liberated thanked Spartacus profusely before departing in a great procession full of supplication and prayers. I watched a vast swath of desperately needed sturdy steady hands exit the fight without a single puncture. When they'd gone, the void left behind without ever facing battle was perceptible.

"We come long way," Spartacus addressed the remaining masses. "Lost, many to get here. You think Rome beat?" he asked of everyone, "I promise, Rome not beat. I hear rumors, some wish, sack Roman city? Attack their lair? Do those speak such nonsense, ever been?" Spartacus asked, raising his chin. "Any you have you backs against twenty-foot wall, thirteen-inch stone?" Spartacus waited. "None, know porcupine, none, see stone thrower? I lead escape; now done, slave, not go?" questioned Spartacus, using theatrics learned in the ring. "Rome, not some village, no vacation villa, we hit thus far. Rome is teeth, that bite the world, and shits out, into Tibris. I tell slave army true—you have no hope, of take that city," he paused, deflating the crowd. "But...we kill, every Roman, caught outside their gates!" thundered the commander. The slave army's spirits lifted to the heavens instantly as everyone embraced, cheering Spartacus, whose reputation had by then surpassed that of Hercules.

Spartacus allowed only what could be carried. The carts were stripped for speed, and he ordered no more treasure hoarding, instead burning everything impractical and slaying the remaining captives. Spartacus fooled most into believing we marched southwest, but I'd written the note and knew we backtracked southeast, for the cock's spur, Mt. Garganos' little bay.

### THE ACCOUNTANT TALLIES A SUM

Merillius was right to fear that the ledger would upset his former owner once he showed the numbers tallied in red. Marcus Crassus raised his brows at the sight of the colossal losses. "Great Jupiter!" he exclaimed. Most large farms rented Marcus' slaves exclusively and the loss of manpower was exhausting. *I have to staunch the bleeding,* thought Marcus during his *consilium*—or war council—with the officers, all of whom served years prior, with the exception of Mummius. Mummius had been assigned from that old bastard, Gellius; Marcus eyed the senate's spy.

Lucius Mummius Achaius had a name older than the city and claimed blood lineage from Achaius of Troy, son of the goddess Venus. Marcus Crassus saw nothing of divinity in the man sitting across from him now.

"Lentulus was barely able to escape with his life," Officer Rufus said. "They took his horse right from under him! They've whipped everything we've thrown at them and they've even knocked over our backstop," Marcius Rufus exclaimed concerning the recent disastrous slave uprising, wondering how his fellow officers could make it stop.

"So, why didn't they escape?" asked Officer Caius Pomptinus.

"Who cares?" piped Atticus, the recent draftee promoted to officer by Marcus. "You ought to be asking why they turned south." He took a long drink.

"He's obviously waited too long and can't make the pass before winter," reasoned Officer Scrofa. "The slaves are trying to sail off our east coast."

"Gauls on the sea!" Atticus shouted the absurd out loud. "You're more likely to see the sun set in the east. They're hiding in the Apennines; I'd bet my dick on it," finished the old hand. Marcus Crassus knew his old fire marshal and former centurion was correct.

"So, what are we waiting for?" spoke a new voice. "Let's get after them," Mummius Achaius interjected. Everyone stopped to look.

"Ha!" exclaimed Atticus, the reliable old centurion stated aloud what was on everyone else's mind. "You first, asshole!" Atticus challenged. "Let's see you tackle them in their natural habitat!" A younger Marcus Crassus would've interceded, but experience taught one had to let subordinates work things out for themselves every now and then.

"Are you afraid of slaves?" Mummius retorted pompously.

"Only when they roll over six legions and are led by the undefeated heavyweight champ of Rome, son," Atticus said, staring the patrician with a legendary name in the eye.

"I'm not your son," Mummius retorted.

"Yeah, I know, *son*, otherwise, you'd be on my knee with a beet-red ass, boy," Atticus answered. Marcus interceded before he lost control.

"All right, thank you, Atticus," Marcus said coolly. Mummius, about to continue, was silenced with a wave of the new Imperator's hand.

"We all agree," reasoned Marcus Crassus, "they need to be found and kept from the city. What I need from the six of you is to tell me how."

"We blunt them," proposed the bright Lucius Quinctius. "Keep them from using the roads and herd them all the way to the Adriatic. We mitigate the damage until we trap and besiege them." Atticus raised his arms in frustration as if to say, "that's what I've been saying."

"Besiege them," Mummius scoffed, insulted. The new man with the famous name sneered at his peers, aghast at treating slaves like people. Marcus Crassus' suspicion that he had a rotten apple in his bunch became more apparent.

## MISERY BLANKETS NEWLYWEDS

It was miserably cold on the trek back south; I'd gone along with everything so far because it was better than being a slave, until the winter of 683 *auc*. The rain lashed and I was chilled to the bone on the trip, and I momentarily considered offering my wrists to a shackle if it would just make the cold stop. Pila and I looked at one another, trying to reassure the other that the cold couldn't last forever. Winter would soon close and warmth would be on its way, though it didn't feel like it at the time. We huddled beneath the blanket used to protect Crastus from the rain for weeks on the arduous journey that killed the sick and made some abandon hope. We trudged south for the cock's spur that seemed to be moving in the opposite direction. Somehow, Crastus survived.

I was ready to hail death gratefully by the time Mt. Garganos appeared in the distance. Features that would have been clear in spring became obscured by dark clouds and rain, making everything unfamiliar. I realized why men didn't fight in these conditions: it saps life, making you wish you could crawl back into your mother's womb. I'd led us to the huge cave Crixus used to store booty. Amazingly, everything was still there, either due to the location's remoteness or to the fear Crixus had dealt the region.

The next day, we loaded other untouched stashes of loot for

our ferry payment. We transported all of it to Urium Bay, where we'd meet the pirate Heracleo and his sailors, if the birds had survived.

MARCUS CRASSUS' EDICT

Spring arrived by the time Imperator Marcus Crassus pitched camp on the paved *Via Annia* in Eburum on the banks of the River Silaras. Between the borders of Campania and Lucania, he'd control the roads south and all the plains this side of the Apennines. The six new legions of thirty thousand men would grind Spartacus' forty thousand like a millstone, reducing the slave army to a manageable size before engaging them half-starved. Marcus shared his plan with the centurions and officers, ordering them not to engage in full-scale combat; not just yet. Instead, he explicitly ordered his men to nip at the heels of slaves, harrying them ever southward, where they'd be trapped. Though Marcus was outnumbered by the slave army, it hadn't concerned him. The scouts reported back, describing the fugitives as ragged and hungry. Almost half were women and children, with untold numbers burdened by sickness, they'd been told, by deserters of the calamitous hardship. Even with those reports, Marcus wouldn't make the mistakes his predecessors had by underestimating Spartacus. Nor would he allow himself to be paralyzed by the fear of failure. His movements would be cautious, measured, and calculated. Marcus and Merillius tabulated the numbers; if everything went as planned, the endeavor should work before Pompey returned. No one was aware that the new man with a famous name had already decided he knew better what to do about fugitive slaves than a wealthy old fool did.

HELICA

Helica helped Crastus drink a tonic she'd made by holding the back of his head, while Pila helped Helica's cult of Dionysus with the rest recovering from the winter's cough. Thankfully, spring was near, and all felt the warmth of its approach. The two women finished doing what they could for the infirmed and washed their hands in a basin before their usual forage for herbs. Pila wore a mask of apprehension and the attuned older woman sensed it as they walked together.

"You seem elsewhere this morning, my dear," pried Helica.

"Can a woman lose her seasons?" Pila asked. Helica lifted her head to look at the young woman knowingly.

# CHAPTER TWENTY-THREE

"Next, actually attacking generals of consular rank, he inflicted defeat on the army of Lentulus in the Apennines and destroyed the camp of Publius Cassius at Mutina. Elated by these victories, he entertained the project, in itself a sufficient disgrace to us, of attacking the city of Rome."

—Florus, *Epitome*

We quickly loaded heaps of treasure onto Heracleo's ship. Heracleo had brought four of the sleek vessels to carry our payment. Suddenly, Spartacus forbade any more offloading, upsetting the pirate. Our wagons remained mostly full, parked at the end of the pier. Heracleo took offense.

"We both-a de enemy of-a da Roma, lord, please; we have ah common-a cause. Surely you not believe, I sail off-a with de full payment and not-a fulfill-a da bargain as agree?" Heracleo asked, pretending to be shocked.

"Ensured so," Spartacus answered. The pirate flashed his black grin, genuflecting as his men scowled at the disrespect Spartacus implied. Heracleo attempted theft once more.

"The Messina a-Strait, she's guarded by Scylla," pleaded the captain, "the giant-a dog, who sits on-a da rock, devouring da passing a-sailor. Even if-a we make it through that-a pass, there's still de Charybdis, ah *mostro marino*; it must be-a contended wit." Heracleo spoke of the legendary beast that sucked water whirlpools in the narrow strait, swamping ships.

"Horseshit," answered the giant, unmoved; Heracleo changed tack.

"Ah, the Romani, she won't-a even attempt! Da strait, she's-a dangerous with swirling currents and-a da ships, some-a never make it out," he insisted, pointing at the sky with wrinkled tanned fingers.

"Less worry, then," challenged the barbarian. "Incentive for sailors, to meet slave army in Rhegium," Spartacus replied, pointing to mounds of treasure parked nearby for all the pirates to see. The scoundrel flashed his black teeth, thanking our commander and bowing, finally beaten.

### HERACLEO

Heracleo sailed away on a cloudless sunny day with a third of what he'd wanted, never having intended to sail for the tip of Italy and ferry Spartacus to Sicily for the remainder all along.

"Captain, why we not go to Rhegium," asked his first mate, "for rest of payment?"

"It better to have ah quarter, than a-none at all," commented Heracleo. The first mate cocked his head. "Would-a you prefer to be a-rich in life, or wealthy in a-death?" clarified Heracleo, concerning the double-cross. Heracleo grasped his first mate behind the neck, touching foreheads so that the man could hear. "Verres, a-promises to triple whatever a-Spartacus offers if-a we leave him a-stranded," the pirate with black teeth smiled. The four ships rowed away, three of them empty, leaving the former gladiator and a young scout standing on a pier watching them with Helios reflecting from the sea.

## SPARTACUS' AID

Spartacus stood silent in his thoughts, holding a scroll of papyrus with a fortune in goods parked nearby. I admired his fine blade's lead-weighted pommel, which was adorned with a screaming eagle's head made completely of ivory. The blade sat in a custom-made leather scabbard resting on Spartacus' left hip with "Lightning" stamped in Greek upon its hilt.

"Lord?" I asked.

"Speak," answered the commander.

"Why'd we lug all this stuff here, if we weren't going to load it?" I asked.

"Need ride, not promises," Spartacus explained. "Pirate take all, no more pirate. Pirate take some, pirate want more. That way, sailor take slave army, across the strait." Then Spartacus suddenly changed the subject. "Need you deliver message to Gavius in Pompeii," Spartacus ordered.

"How?" I asked, shocked. "The Romans are squeezing slaves like grapes everywhere now, commander."

"Easy—look not like slave," Spartacus answered, his mind made up; I knew by then there was no use in arguing with him when he was in this mood. I walked back to shore, leaving the commander to stand upon the pier alone, holding the document he couldn't read.

When I returned home, Pila seemed preoccupied as we ate supper. I dismissed it, believing her apprehension to be just worry about my upcoming trip. Trying to reassure her, I said, "Spartacus says, 'Just hold you head up, act like own place.'"

"What's that, love?" Pila asked, returning from the trip in her mind. Pila had hardly touched the wild conies and potatoes she'd cooked, and ended up throwing her share to the dogs following camp outside.

"He says I just have to think like a free man," I explained again.

"Oh, yes, you'll be fine," said Pila, a hundred miles away. That night before sleep, I rolled on top of her the way she normally preferred, but she pushed me away, rolling onto her side to sleep without a word. I felt sorry for worrying my new bride so much about my trip to Pompeii.

The next morning, Pila ran from our tent retching and vomiting. She cursed the dogs slinking nearby to get at it. She threw stones at them from her knees, holding her hair and trying not to cry. I felt terrible. *Pila has made herself sick with worry for me,* I thought.

I dressed in a clean new tunic and readied the horse early that morning. I'd made it a point to start my ruse on day one by sitting straight on the horse like a man who owned men. Spartacus told me what to tell Gavius when I found him, because nothing was written in case I was captured. I gave my young wife a kiss, wishing her farewell and promising to return soon—my attempt to soothe her fear.

"*Vala,*" said Pila, smiling. I handed down coins for her use in case she needed anything while I was gone. I turned the horse to the road and, on my way out of camp, I saw a small girl playing with Pila's old doll.

It was easier than I thought to fool people approaching the city limits. The first people I'd rode past made me nervous. *Act like you own the place,* said the voice in my head. I sat straight on the horse with my chin held high, the way I'd seen Romans do. I'd left my sword and breastplate with Pila; Gannicus said wearing captured armor would be a dead giveaway for a fugitive slave. I felt vulnerable without my breastplate, but the scratchy shirt of mail and dagger beneath my tunic helped.

A year ago, we'd ransacked Pompeii and put it to the sword. Today, it bustled with life like nothing had ever happened. The gate was wide open and the portcullis that nearly killed Crixus was drawn all the way up. I had to wait my turn to enter the busy city and was told by the soldiers guarding the gate that I'd have to leave my horse outside. One looked suspiciously at me, until I ordered a passing slave to hitch my horse to a post; they let me pass.

The streets were familiar yet strange, teeming with life. From my fat purse, I purchased a skewer of roasted chicken, asking the vendor to go easy on the *garum*. I had no need to ask where to find Gavius' bakery—I could smell it. I followed my nose up vaguely familiar streets, rinsing in the public fountain before entering Gavius' bakery. I found him chastising a slave who'd burned a batch of loaves. When I cleared my throat to interrupt them, Gavius saw me and said, "The scout!" with his pointer aimed in recognition. He turned whiter than Pila's wedding dress when I nodded in the affirmative. Gavius yelled for his slave to get back to work, grabbing my arm to whisk us to a dark and remote corner of the bakery for privacy.

"What in Hades are you doing here?" asked Gavius, whispering nervously with darting eyes and wiping flour from his apron.

"Spartacus sends a message."

"What are you doing in Italy?" asked the vexed entrepreneur. "I heard you'd turned back, but I didn't believe it." He spoke in low tones while craning his neck around both corners. I was about to convey the message when Gavius blurted, "Our transaction is concluded, the business finished. Can't you see the government is back in control here? No, I can't risk my neck again," resolved Gavius, exhaling. I stood silently staring at him, waiting. I watched greed overtake his eyes, just like Spartacus had said they would. "What's the message?" Gavius asked in a huge breath.

## MARCUS CRASSUS

Commander Marcus Crassus, newly appointed Imperator of

Rome, found the army of slaves. They'd been discovered moving in Lucania by scouts. Scrofa and Mummius were sent around while the rest of the army blocked movement west. Marcus had no wish to tangle in forested hills with a multitude of seasoned guerilla fighters. Scrofa and Mummius were sent to intimidate their flank, while he'd starve slaves into the open, where his army could properly form up and deploy. Marcus expressly ordered the two flanking officers not to engage; instead, he told them to hit targets of opportunity and keep the slaves from foraging. If Marcus couldn't starve them explicitly, then the next best thing was to make them nervous when they ventured out for food and fodder. The southern farms were sowing now; Marcus Crassus couldn't afford letting Italy's harvest feed the enemy. He knew from experience how challenging it was to feed so many mouths, and he knew starvation was the best course of action.

## VENUS' PROGENY RIDES FORTH IN THE ROMAN YEAR OF 683 AUC (72 BC)

Lucius Achaius Mummius knew what the commander ordered, but was sure the old man would get over it and thank him later when he brought back captives. The officer commanded what remained of Glaber, Gellius, and Lentulus' beleaguered legions. The shamed men begged for redemption. *What is the point of owning the element of surprise if I have to sit on my hands like a child?* thought the officer. By the time Mummius' couriers returned with permission, the moment would've passed. *Carpe diem,* he thought, ordering his men to form up and march toward the stupid slaves meandering in the field. Marcus' officer saw a few long shields, but not enough to stop his army, and there didn't seem to be a horse in the bunch. He couldn't see how the slave army could have made it any easier. The descendant of Venus wondered how the barbarians had made it this far, chalking it up to dumb luck. *So much for this cavalry everyone goes on about,* he thought, ordering trumpeters to blow the signal for attack.

Achaius Mummius' next thoughts escaped as terror for survival overcame him when Spartacus' cavalry bounded over the ridge. It appeared to the Roman that the entire barbarian horde had spilled out like ants toward his position, and he realized too late why the damn scout hadn't returned. Screaming banshees poured in on him from both sides. He caught a glimpse of dropping shields before kicking his horse to flight. The descendant of Venus was the first back to camp in Picentia. Mummius rode a lathered and foaming government-issued mare through the opened gate as stragglers wandered in, beaten and disheveled.

Marcus silently seethed, and his lean eyes squinted from his tent at defeated men as they staggered in shield-less, along with a despicable few who were scandalously unarmed.

### THE SCOUT RETURNS

When I'd finally made it back to camp, everyone was gone, leaving only tracks. Forty thousand people left a big enough impression upon the earth to follow at night, and as I began to set out, a horse nickered.

"I'd almost left without you," said Gannicus, walking his steed from the tree line.

"Where is everyone?" I asked.

"Driving south," Gannicus responded. "Spartacus knows the new Roman commander personally." He handed me my sheathed sword and turned to retrieve my breastplate from his horse's rump.

"New commander?" I asked, confused.

"They'd served in the east, then again during civil war."

"Pompey?" I proposed the most famous name I knew.

"Worse," corrected Gannicus. "Marcus Crassus, hero of

the Colline Gate." I'd heard of the man—everyone had. "Wish we'd made for the mountains now?" Gannicus asked. The most powerful and wealthy man in Rome was now prosecuting the war. He was a proven winner; the city was done experimenting with amateurs. Still naïve, I believed Spartacus was able to best anyone and spoke this hopeful nonsense aloud.

"We'll beat them, too," I said, like a man of fifteen years. Gannicus stared, waiting to see if I really believed what I'd just said.

"Maybe, Publipor, maybe," Gannicus concluded. "Want to find your wife?" he asked, changing the subject. I nodded, grateful.

# CHAPTER TWENTY-FOUR

**"...Crassus received also the two legions of the consuls, whom he decimated by lot for their bad conduct in several battles... demonstrated to them that he was more dangerous than the enemy."**

—**Appian**, *The Civil Wars*

Marcus Licinius Crassus, the new, legally sole-appointed Imperator of Rome, would not tolerate disrespect nor disobedience again. Commander Marcus Crassus planned to make examples of these straggling tremblers for the rest of his army. He'd revive *decimatio*—decimation, an archaic ritual of humiliation—with the last five hundred stumbling back to camp after their retreat. Marcus first had them accept new arms, replacing the ones they'd left for the enemy. One by one, they accepted new weapons and were forced to apologize aloud to all the legions present for arming their foe. Marcus had each man swear an oath publicly vowing to commit suicide if they ever did it again. He then had Mummius placed in stocks, parading the dishonored officer before the men with *"Non Audire"*—"I don't listen," painted in white across the beam for everyone to read. Atticus Fabius enjoyed shoving cow shit in the pompous little twit's ears in front of the men when

Marcus ordered him to do so.

Commander Marcus Crassus had the despicable five hundred pull lots from a clay pot with five hundred stones inside—fifty painted red. A man who pulled a red stone was marked, disarmed, and placed aside. With their new weapons confiscated and armor immediately removed, Marcus Crassus ordered the remainder to beat the condemned until death. A moment of shock stunned the entire legion as the ancient order sunk in. Men who'd grown up hearing war stories from their grandfathers about the outdated practice never considered they'd see such a thing in a modern army of professional soldiers. The lucky unchosen cried out for their comrades, tearing clothes and begging to trade places with the condemned in solidarity. All that stopped when Marcus obliged, having an entire legion face the cowards, ready to liquidate the whole lot with a nod. With that, men resolved to do their duty quickly, sparing brothers as much suffering as possible. A centurion took pity, throwing his cudgel into the mix to help things along. Imperator Marcus Lucinius Crassus had Merillius scribe the event for a litany to be entered into the official record back in Rome. Marcus had revived the ancient ceremony of decimation, reducing the number of cowards within the army by one-tenth. Setting a hard tone for the new order, Marcus' men would now stay in the fight till the end, by the gods.

Marcus finally ordered the survivors of decimation to camp outside, making them vulnerable to attack. The shamed were given only barley from the horses' rations at meals; Marcus forbade anyone from giving them bread.

Mummius Achaius, descendant of a god, was forced to sleep in the horses' paddock until finally committing suicide in an attempt to redeem lost honor. As an added jab to old man Gellius, Marcus sent a message ordering the Pompey supporter to finance a replacement. Marcus made his point with an exclamation; in the next fights he pursued, his men would obey and stand, or he'd kill them himself.

### THE LION LICKS HIS WOUNDS, A STORK ROOSTS IN THE EAST, 684 AUC (71 BC)

Crastus, the giant German, looked gaunt, and though the stretched appearance of his face remained, his eyes seemed sunken deeper somehow. "Pubes, *mina*, hero," Crastus said in his terrible Latin, smiling and limping toward me. I felt the frailness of his touch, and when he gathered me for an embrace, his ribs pressed against my newly muscled chest. Crastus had called me by my pet name and his feeble rendition of once-raucous laughter made me smile. "Getten zie vine, sheez face," pleaded Crastus, quickly returning to himself. I turned to leave, but Helica blocked my way, hands on her hips.

"Crastus isn't ready for wine yet; he may only have water for now," she instructed. Crastus' Adams apple vibrated in a baritone groan. "Come with me, young man," ordered Helica, slipping her arm over my shoulder. I glanced back at the shadow that was Crastus when he pointed at me, silently mouthing the word *wine*.

"Where's Pila?" I asked. Helica said nothing and terror struck. "Lady?" I pleaded.

"Pila's better than fine, Publipor. Come, I'll show you," Helica spoke. As we walked, she hit me with a bag full of Gavius' bricks.

### SPARTACUS REMEMBERS 677 (78 BC)

Spartacus stood at the pier's end, watching the four ships depart under power of long oars sweeping to and fro. Standing on boards alone over the sea with his thoughts, Spartacus remembered what had brought him here. He held the message Publipor had intercepted from a dead courier. It enraged him when Publipor read the senate's writ the first time, and it took all his control not to have an outburst. Written upon papyrus with Marcus Crassus' official seal, the document granted citizenship to all foreigners who volunteered to put down the slaves' rebellion. Spartacus had risked his life for years with Rome's army and an untold amount of time in the pits for amusement in search of something Romans now threw out like free loaves at the Circus. The injustice made him see red as his mind stretched back to the Roman year 677.

Dictator Sulla only allowed his loyal dog, Spartacus, in the room while recovering. Cornelius Felix Sulla the Lucky sat in his bed under a tent of cheesecloth that kept flies from the corruption afflicting his body. The windows were also draped with the material in an attempt to keep the pestilence at bay. It stifled the room in summer, but a priest assured Sulla the measures were necessary to kill parasites and stem the rot fouling his skin. Sulla had "retired" a year previous when his health began to decline. On paper, Sulla's reforms restored power to the dual proconsuls, but everyone knew real decisions were made from a sickbed in Rome's art colony. The cramped room with three men stank of decay as one begged for life. All three knew the accused was innocent as he confessed to a multitude of crimes in hope of mercy. Sulla the sadist smiled with glee from beneath the mesh, listening rapturously to the man's song of treason.

With a nod, Sulla's dog took the leather thong, wrapped it around the man's neck, and began tightening. Spartacus was strangling yet another enemy of the state for his commander. The young mercenary used to just snap their necks, but Sulla preferred dragging it out this way. Each time the condemned was about to lose consciousness, Sulla would order Spartacus to stop and let him recover. The man begged silently with hand gestures as his life slowly left the room while Sulla bounced on the bed in excitement. Sulla's loyal Thracian bodyguard's huge arms flexed, then released, and the traitor slumped to the floor dead without a trial. Spartacus put the worn strap of leather away in his girding and was about to remove the man's body when he noticed his commander's posture. Sulla's gleeful bouncing had stopped; his head leaned, the left shoulder slumped, and he made no movement. Spartacus pulled back the veil to find Sulla sitting motionless, half his face drooping unnaturally. The dictator stared glassy-eyed and moaned incoherently. Spartacus jumped and threw the curtain shut, spitting on the floor to keep Sulla's evil at bay. Felix Sulla's body tried to stand but collapsed from the bed and fell onto the floor beside his victim.

Spartacus panicked; he knew his land grant and citizenship papers were kept in the credenza. The huge, tattooed bodyguard raced to retrieve them before it was too late. Sulla had held them over Spartacus like a carrot, keeping him motivated and loyal, but Sulla also kept them in the room, knowing Spartacus was illiterate.

But young Spartacus could make out the characters of his name in Latin. He searched for it now, frantically, on a desk of jumbled documents. The bodyguard felt an hourglass running against him. Spartacus was about to give up searching and make a break for it when the physician entered. The doctor stepped through with tray in hand to see a tattooed, twenty-four-year-old foreign assassin standing over two dead Romans. Disheveled desks spilled official documents everywhere onto the floor. After locking eyes and becoming certain of foul play, the Roman dropped his tray and ran shouting for help. Spartacus took the cheesecloth meant to keep bugs at bay with him when he dove through the window and ran, knowing an avalanche was about to fall upon Rome.

Forty-four-year-old Spartacus dropped the insulting document he couldn't read into the bay and walked from the pier.

"A baby!" I exclaimed, disbelieving what I'd heard.

"Yes, if it doesn't kill her; the first is always the hardest and most dangerous," Helica repeated.

"How did this happen?" I asked. Helica stared at me like I was a crazy person.

I never thought I'd have a wife; now I was having a child on the sixteenth spring of my life. It was a tremendous burden, one I'd no idea if I could carry. I prayed to Helica's god for a boy and that Pila would live.

"Where are you going?" I thought I heard Helica ask over Pila's sobbing; I left to get Crastus wine, unable to handle the deluge of information drowning me into a state of overwhelmed indifference. I fled from it like the coward I was when Lelu needed me most.

I'd taken several pulls from the un-watered wine skin by the time I made it to the infirmary. Sitting with Crastus and trading drinks, I shared my fear of fatherhood. Crastus laughed meekly at my predicament between sips of advice, wincing in pain.

"Maybe, du sell enzie," recommended Crastus. I flashed him a look. "Yah, du right," he continued, "not get much for kinder-Pube-ein-poor." He pleaded not to make him laugh anymore. I tuned out the brute's prattling and drank instead; then I drank some more as life swirled.

Helica's kick to my head and shouting woke me; she yelled for me to find my wife. Helica cursed and threw rocks as I ran with a pounding head.

### SPARTACUS REVEALS HIS PLAN TO A TRUSTED CONFIDANT

That night, Spartacus shared with Helica the plan he'd had all along, disappointing her deeply. Helica asked for Lighting, and Spartacus pulled the enormous double-edged blade, offering it to her handle first. Helica knew immediately the blade had been forged by Vulcan himself—Vulcan, the ugly son of Hera, smith for the gods, who walked with a limp and forged the sacred arms for Mars. Vulcan's hand in the sword was evident, without a doubt. Helica placed a black rat snake on the blade's broadside, turning it to an angle. The serpent, unable to grab traction, slid from the fine blade, bleeding, but the incantation was still not enough to show the way forward. Helica already knew Spartacus was blessed by Dionysus with a great and terrible power, but she still could not discern if it was lucky. The snake told Helica that the sword was divine, but nothing of prophecy. Her eyes lifted within her head, searching for answers.

Rome was too vile, too contemptuous to start a new cult of Dionysus. *Of course*, thought Helica. How could she have been so shortsighted? Fighting as vassals for Mithradates had been too small, and the vision of ruling Rome as queen she recognized as selfishness; Helica saw clearly now. Blinded momentarily by a sunray gleaming from the sword, she caught a glimpse of fortune. Dionysus brought them here and spoke through her husband to be carried to Sicily. Helica knew the island had two slave rebellions already. *Why didn't I see it earlier?* she thought.

Helica envisioned Rome's children with distended bellies and flies plaguing their eyes. She saw them starving without grain in her mind, making her smile. Why would she want to be queen of a corrupt city when she could rule an entire country of her own? Sicily, the breadbasket of Italy with its vast fields of grain, was indeed key to destroying the vile people. "Of course," Helica said aloud, certain that events would prove her husband lucky. Helica returned the divine sword, forged for revenge, placing the power into hands that would deliver slaves from their Roman torment.

THURII, SEVEN MONTHS LATER, 684 AUC (71 BC)

We enjoyed a moment's respite in a *popina* by the bay, tucked within Italy's arch, before escaping north. I described the new Roman army coming south to Spartacus as a massive formation of soldiers with behemoth siegeworks and an endless support train, but worst of all, the soldiers showed discipline. When done, I looked all over for my pregnant bride until I found her in a bar with the German, Crastus. The *popina* was packed with slaves buying wine with stolen coins from a Greek refugee. Crastus had filled in a bit and was looking better. Likewise, Pila was looking bigger despite the lean times and depredations of winter. After a long trek back south, it felt good to enjoy the new days of summer with friends. Next to tranquil waters with warmth on the salted breeze, we almost forgot we were running for our lives. Pila eyed the dyes, pigments, and paints set up on a table next to a fresh stucco wall inside the establishment.

"What's it all for?" asked my pregnant wife to the innkeeper.

"Damn painter my woman hired wants a gold *aureus* just to paint a stupid fresco," answered the bar owner, exaggerating the price. "I kicked him out and kept his shit for the insult."

"I'll do one for free," Pila said, excited.

"Have at it, mom," said the owner about Pila's obvious condition. She set to work mixing powders with water, dabbing horsehair brushes into paint. Pila stood at the wall all day getting paint on the old linen frock that bulged at her middle. I marveled at Pila's creation and how absolutely drunk Crastus had gotten by evening's end.

"What...in Hades...*that?*" Crastus asked, hiccupping at the pregnant woman and pointing.

"*That* is my husband, riding with Spartacus," she answered proudly.

"No, woman...*that?*" Crastus hiccupped, pointing at the other image.

"*That* is the epic fight to a draw between the two fiercest competitors to ever face off in the arena," answered Pila. "The unbeatable Germans, Crixus and Crastus." Crastus stumbled out, grinning from ear to ear into the night air.

"How is anyone supposed to know who's in the painting?" I asked, upsetting her and throwing cold water on her enthusiasm by reminding my wife that she was illiterate.

"You know I can't spell," huffed Pila, disappointed. With candlelight I showed her how to write men's names in Oscan above their images. The inn's owner paid Pila a silver coin, commenting on how much he liked her masterpiece. Pila waddled out smiling bigger than Crastus when we left together that evening.

# CHAPTER TWENTY-FIVE

"...by summoning the slaves to their standard, they had quickly collected more than 10,000 adherents; these men, who had been originally content merely to have escaped, soon began to wish to take their revenge also."

—Florus, *Epitome*

Marcus Crassus owned holdings in Bruttium and had a cursory knowledge of the land, but he'd rely on Scrofa, who'd grown up in the area, to guide their way. They'd been able to herd the barbarians south easier than he thought; it was almost as if the army of slaves wanted to be bottled up on the peninsula's boot tip. It was hard work keeping up with the fast-moving brawlers in central Italy, so Marcus posted Quinctius and Pomptinus on the Pompitian Way to deny slaves any easier, faster route by road. In the unlikely event slaves slipped past, the two were supposed to stop them long enough for Marcus to return with his entire force. Marcus Crassus' plan forced slaves to take the rougher trails upon hills, hindering them and keeping them within reach, wearing them out in the process. The Imperator couldn't understand why the slaves wouldn't abandon their full wagons upon the rough terrain. He dismissed it as their natural greedy temperament. *Slaves steal firewood when you don't watch them*, he remembered.

Scrofa explained in the officer's meeting how local fishermen trapped migrating tuna through a system of nets, corralling an entire school, hauling them up all together. Marcus Crassus thought the "tuna trap" brilliant and worked its implementation upon the slave army that appeared to grow with every new estimate. He knew that forcing slaves into the mountains protected vulnerable coastal cities like Tempsa, Terina, and the large walled city of Hipponium, all of which were vulnerable Roman cities with vast amounts of slaves that Spartacus would recruit, if he could get his hands on them. Through his torturer, Marcus heard the slave leader had abandoned Copia, the city everyone seemed insistent on calling Thurii. Spartacus had taken his scum and run for the mountains like the fugitive he was. When Quinctius' light infantry captured several slaves foraging, Marcus grilled them for information. The dirty slaves quickly confessed their leader's plan to capture Rhegium and use its walls to repel Romans.

Marcus Crassus didn't buy that pile for a second; Spartacus was an old hand, a veteran of two wars and countless skirmishes. There was no way the old soldier Marcus knew would try something so futile. He knew if Sulla's old cavalryman didn't lose most of the men taking the city, they'd starve to death in a siege. Spartacus was well aware of the siege engines Marcus could bring to bear. No, the Imperator knew the slaves were lying. Sulla's crafty old dog had something else up his toga's sleeve; Marcus just needed to figure out what it was quick. Spartacus was a foreign cutthroat turned highwayman, who wound up a slave and was sold to a *ludis* for obvious reasons. Marcus knew the man well; Spartacus the barbarian was guilty on all those charges, but in Marcus' experience, never of foolishness.

### SPARTACUS SPECULATES

Spartacus knew he had to make for the sea before the weather got bad again and pirates wouldn't or couldn't sail. He would have to choose the perfect spot, close enough to Rhegium to come out of the mountains and juke past the Romans. He would make them believe he planned to sack the city, then cross into Caenys promontory and board ships for Sicily with payment. Spartacus knew if this was going to work, it would take perfect timing. The former gladiator looked at the sky, asking his father for help.

## THE CORRUPT GOVERNOR

Gaius Verres, the Roman governor appointed to run Sicily in the Roman year of 682, read the letter twice and smiled. Verres had become an unwitting beneficiary of the slave war; he'd been granted another two-year term of governorship after the old boxer, Quintus Arrius, was denied appointment. Gaius Verres was wrapping up the last of his term as governor and feared he'd not stolen everything from Sicily he'd wanted; now he could. The governor's thoughts were interrupted by a courier with some correspondence from Nauloclius. The centurion there sent word of a wealthy merchant in custody: Gavius had been caught using slaves to bury arms on the coast.

"Why in Hades would a plebian as wealthy as Gavius hoard weapons on my promontory?" Verres asked the courier. Gaius Verres, governor of Rome's Island province of Sicily, dismissed the man when he shrugged for an answer. It bothered Verres that he'd have to wait until the merchant was transported all twenty miles of the Valerian Way to Messana for interrogation.

Gaius Verres knew Gavius was a Roman upon arrival and didn't care. Gavius should've been offered another death as a citizen, but Governor Verres thought the display a fitting reminder for a multitude of slaves in attendance, especially since the condemned was a wealthy Roman. Verres feigned ignorance when Gavius protested the nails piercing through his hands, screaming citizenship with every hammer blow. Crucifixion of a

Roman was so hideous that it brought curses from the gods, so
Verres had slaves do it for him. Believing the display would keep
his island teeming with slaves in line, Verres had Gavius posted on
the beach facing the nearest part of the promontory—a warning
for those across the strait coming to depose him. One year later,
Verres would be prosecuted and convicted for the travesty by
Pompey's brilliant attorney, Cicero.

"Crastus," said Spartacus, "take cavalry, take women, stay on
mountain until ride comes." I saw Crastus the German twinge
with anxiety by grimacing before accepting the order with a nod.
I knew from our talks during his recovery that Crastus feared
losing his chance at paradise by letting Spartacus go without him.
And I could tell he resented being asked to protect women and
children, but I knew enough of the man by now to know Crastus
followed orders, always. Crastus had recovered well and was
strong enough by then but remained a shell of his former self.
Helica had cut Crastus' hair and shaved his beard, leaving only
a long mustache for the man, changing his appearance greatly.

Spartacus chose two thousand of his best men and me to sail
with pirates and acquire a beachhead on Sicily. When there,
we were to move up the northern coast to the unwalled city of
Nauloclius and recover hidden weapons. We'd planned to arm
slaves there and return in fishing boats to rescue our people.

"You speak language," said Spartacus to me. "We need many
slaves, many as can get." I nodded but feared leaving Pila alone.
I'd known that Sicily, Rome's first province, resented the yoke and
had tried throwing it off twice already. "Third time's the charm,"
went the Greek proverb. Spartacus explained that if we could just
make it to the island, he'd set the rebellion's embers ablaze once
more.

Pila kissed me in the mountain pass over her swelling midsection, making me promise to return. Helica handed Lightning to Spartacus and kissed the giant, wishing him every success. Spartacus sheathed the consecrated longsword, leaving the humongous black stallion for his wife. From there, we walked down the winding trail dotted with scrub brush to the beach.

We'd traveled the entire length of Italy by the summer of 683, killing every legion before us, until returning south to winter. I knew in my heart, once we crossed the strait, nothing could stop us. I fantasized about my life of husbandry in the bountiful new country with my wife and newborn son.

Fifty miles north of Rhegium, hidden in the wood, the Popitian Way lay in sight. We broke out for the Caenys promontory and its beach, leaving carts loaded with pirate's treasure stashed in the forested hills. We were spotted by a scout while crossing, who rode as hard as the wind blew to tattle. The land composed itself into natural ramparts with steep hills and deep crags all the way to the coast. We were forced to funnel through a narrow pass with sheer cliffs on both sides to get at it. I eyed the heights, fearing bolts would rain down on us at any moment. We were stopped by a churning gray sea foaming on shore. I squinted beneath whipping wind and dark clouds to keep sand from my eyes.

The prize was close enough to touch; across the strait stood the island, rising gradually all the way to Mount Etna, agonizingly close. The desire to walk across was palpable. My eyes scanned left and right, certain any moment to see sleek warships slice the windswept sea to beach and retrieve us. Instead, the only thing racing at us all that day and into the next was sand and stinging rain. Spartacus ordered driftwood set alight to signal the pirates, who were nowhere near and would never appear.

On the third day, Egus spoke the curse aloud: "We been had, boys," he spat, disgusted. Desperate men raided the fishing shed nearby and brought back huge clay *amphora*. They lashed them together with leather and vines to broad wooden beams, desperate to cross the narrow nine-mile strait. Spartacus allowed them the toil to keep men from despair. We watched as a few launched into the flowing currents. Those men must have been at the end of their ropes to brave freezing water and howling winds like that. The tide grabbed their makeshift rafts, launched them into the fast water, and quickly swept them out to sea. Poseidon smashed two of the vessels together, cracking the clay pots keeping them buoyant. My heart sank when rafts disintegrated into a tangled mess of hemp rope as men began swamping one another. Quickly they floated out of sight on raging currents. We watched helplessly as brave men drowned before our eyes. To our further dismay, we learned Marcus' army had arrived when one of our poor wretches was caught and crucified on the channel's beach. Pinned now between Romans and the sea, I thought of Pila and my unborn son being sold at auction with chalked feet.

## MARCUS CRASSUS

Marcus' officers had Sulla's old cavalryman pinned against the sea and hemmed in by cliffs; the men wanted to storm the beach and swamp the slaves trapped down there. "Nothing more dangerous than a cornered animal," reminded Atticus, recommending caution. Though the comment upset the other officers, Marcus knew his old centurion spoke rightly and though he felt like attacking himself, Marcus thought better, remembering all the careers Spartacus had buried recently. The newly minted Imperator followed his newly promoted officer's suggestion instead.

"Engineers!" he screamed.

# CHAPTER TWENTY-SIX

"...launch rafts of beams and casks bound together with withies on the swift waters of the straits. Failing in this attempt, they finally made the sally and met a death worthy of men, fighting to the death as became those who were commanded by a gladiator."

—Florus, *Epitome*

I woke in the miserable morning of that terrible time shaking interminable sand from my breastplate. The insipid, coarse grains found their way into every crease of my body and rinsing in the ocean only seemed to attract more. The horrible stuff seemed to stick as if applied with the glue made from horses' hooves. I beat the sand in frustration with my palm and lost the fight when a grain lodged in my eye.

"Don't cry, others will see it," Egus admonished, smiling when he saw me at my wit's end. Like Spartacus, all the former gladiators seemed to take every setback in stride. Personally, I wanted to join the drowned men—until I thought of my wife. I was sick of being cold, tired of chafing, and weary of hunger. I thanked Helica's god that Pila hadn't come. That evening and all night long, I listened to hammering and grunting with shouts in Latin to hurry.

In the morning, out of watering eyes, I saw what Spartacus

spoke of a year prior. Overnight, the Romans had dug a trench along the shoreline beyond the sandy beach and filled it with lily spikes. They'd thrown up an earthen wall and topped it with tall wooden planks across the expanse of tall crags at the beach's lone exit in no time. The bay's cul-de-sac was chosen as a means to defend a contested escape out to sea; now the features hemmed us in. The Romans were erecting towers when Spartacus met the men to discuss our plan for breakout. There we listened intently as Spartacus told us what to do, and soon, we did what was asked.

We gathered the driftwood and bundled it, tying it with vine cord into large cylinders. Spartacus ordered the attack; we began rolling bundles to the ditch at points along our front. While some pushed, others carried shields for cover, and within yards of the fortifications, our shields resembled porcupines at the tremendous volley of arrows stuck. When missiles found a gap, men fell, yet we continued. Once our bundles were rolled into the ditch, men with torches set them ablaze. I was in the far left, flying arrows at men above. One would duck while another slung from the ramparts. My quiver was running dry; I remembered Spartacus had said, "Make every shot count." I hit a man, and when he fell partially from the wall, his companions grabbed for him, trying desperately to pull him back. I hit both of them as well—they let their man go to take cover.

I caught an acorn with my helmet, and another rapped my breastplate. I accused the Romans of being homosexual girls in a fit of nonsensical rage before taking cover behind our shields. Quiet Vitelli grabbed the Roman who'd fallen and dragged him beneath our shields as we backed away to let the fire work. Our enemy poured buckets of water, dousing the palisades, until my fellow archers and I discouraged them. Clay, lead, and goose-fletched bolts of ash flew everywhere at once. The point we penetrated started to give; all others were screens. Here we threw the few hooks we had, attempting to pull down the planks and get out. When a man pulling a rope went down, others grasped it up, to replace those killed. Knocking of acorns on leather-wrapped birch *scutums*, along with vile language, filled the air up and down the line in raging, violent madness.

Death was everywhere and oddly, I'd no fear as I went about my business, walking in Crixus' "zone," a realm impervious to slings and arrows. Men stepped over the dead and pulled at the rope like mad before our enemy could dislodge the hooks. Vast numbers of men yanked with all their might, as others tried their best to shelter them with long shields. I emptied my quiver at the Romans trying to remove hooks—just then a stand of boards toppled in a burning heap. Smoke, sand, and dust billowed as they fell; the fallen planks bridged the ditch as men rushed the gap beneath an unrelenting rain of falling javelins. Never had I seen such an amount of the deadly bolts fall in one place, creating a grotesque burst of loud suffering everywhere. Iron sunk into men from above and our bodies seemed to catch every single one. For the rest of my life, I never got out of my mind the sight of one man, still alive, walking with a bolt through his helmet. How he was able to make it the few steps he did while staring at me was a marvel. I hated his death grimace as he walked past in the surreal moment. I waited for my turn through the horrible pass all the while, expecting to be struck down at any second. Slave and Roman clogged between the boards, stuffing the opening with stabbing shields. Before long, the gap rebuilt itself with bricks of bodies, mortised in blood. The ramp of fallen planks became viscous; men slid into the ditch from both sides of the impromptu bridge onto spikes below. Slaves clamored for traction to escape from impalement below while death rained from above.

"Damn, it!" roared Spartacus, exhausted with futility. The veteran commander could see that the enemy plugged his hole and knew at that moment, he was beaten. Spartacus signaled his bugler, who pulled the horn and blew retreat. We backed away behind our shields while the Romans continued to knock on them.

Absolute rage filled my soul like I'd never felt before and the urge to weep was overpowering. I hated backing from the fight and resented the commander for calling retreat. Spartacus had the ability to keep his eyes up in a fight; he could see where most saw only tunnel. Instinctually, Spartacus knew the moment to shoot our gap had expired, as the entirety of the Romans seemed to appear from every direction. My heart despaired after backing enough to really see the carnage of our dead littering a spot of wall we'd tried to break. Arrogant taunts in Latin from the battlefield made retreating intolerable.

Parched and voiceless, my insults ran as dry as the empty quiver dangling at my hip. I sat in the sea and cried as waves lapped my bruises. The clouds parted, letting the morning's sunshine through. Spartacus sat next to me with a grunt, handing me fresh water.

"Good job, son. Try again, when Roman face sun at day's end, before wall repair," he said, touching my shoulder and working our problem aloud. I would never see my son born or my pretty wife again—I was sure of it. And with battle rage gone, all thoughts of attempting another breakout like the last filled me with fear and despair.

"I'm out of arrows," I said, attempting to back out, feeling like a coward.

"Plenty in sand, straight enough," Spartacus replied. "You better with this anyway," he joked, jostling the sling in my belt. "No shortage of rocks," Spartacus said, placing a lead pellet in my hand. Holding it between my thumb and forefinger, I looked down and read, "You want me," etched across its surface. Not understanding the insult, I put it in the bag with the rest. Sitting there with the commander, my young eyes spied, across the sunlit narrow strait, a tiny outline of a crucifix staring back at me. A shiver ran through my spine. I vowed to commit suicide before I'd ever let them nail me to a post like that. Again, I thought of Pila.

### MARCUS CRASSUS

The Imperator watched a circling vulture before stepping into his tent, returning to the multitude of correspondences that needed a reply after taking a shit. There, Marcus Crassus spent five hours writing until his eyes hurt, then stepped outside for a break to clear his thoughts. He looked up and saw the sky filled with big, circling, ugly birds.

Just then, a courier leapt from his horse and ran to the command tent. "A verbal message from Marcius Rufus at his position in the ditch," the young Roman panted, trying to catch his breath, annoying the anxious Imperator. "Spartacus...attempts a breakout...at our section," spat the young soldier between breaths.

"And?" asked Marcus, angry and impatient for more information.

"That's all, sir. Commander Rufus is currently engaged," replied the young soldier.

### BESIEGED, 684 AUC (71 BC)

Helios wouldn't stop his track across the sky, filling me with dread the entire day. My hands shook when I thought of what was to come, and if I had anything to eat, I'd have surely vomited. A forlorn hope of fortune and the horizon held my gaze so long that a mirage of glorious Greek ships rounding the headway, heaving speedy oars, tormented me. Spartacus sent men to gather more driftwood and began binding them like before. We'd lost four hooks, leaving only two. My quiver was empty and I was reduced to finding stones that would fit my sling. As the sun set, we gathered where Spartacus had a plan, and there on the beach, he shared it with the army of slaves.

"Where's fucking Crastus, and the fucking cavalry?" someone spoke aloud in frustration.

"Crastus has hands full, watching women," Spartacus answered with a disapproving look before continuing. "We go right when Roman face Helios," explained the commander. "Skip trick, horn blow, everyone shift center, press there. Archer, snatch arrow from sand. Every man, pile bodies in ditch, pray for no clouds. But even so, we go anyway." He paused to let a man wretch. "Pirate cheat, double-cross, like pirate do, but surrender is suicide. Crucifix is Roman pity," explained Spartacus, pointing to the spit of the beach between the two armies. There stood a crucifix in the stretch of no man's land where Spartacus himself had nailed our captured Roman soldier to a beam. Spartacus hoisted the Roman as a reminder to slaves of what to expect from our enemy if we surrendered. The Roman had been dead for about an hour after his begging stopped; vultures perched themselves above him, bickering over the soft tissues.

My stomach churned and groaned so loudly that Egus smiled and said, "Empty them guts and pray to whichever god or gods, you think'll get us off this beach, little Pube-i-por, but do it before sunset." He smiled his perpetual smile through squinty hidden eyes. When a man complained of hunger, Spartacus explained that there was a feast just over the Roman wall and the slave could have his fill, once over.

### AN OFFICER'S LAMENT

Quintus Rufus had a feeling he'd be pressed again before day's end. Rufus' men were having a tough time repairing the damaged section that'd been pulled down as adjoining portions smoldered.

The slaves' commander placed archers to hamper its repair as Rufus' engineers worked with giant wicker baskets tied to their helmets, attempting to protect themselves from harassing bolts. The soldiers were most disturbed by one of their own hanging from a cross below. Rufus forbade several attempts from the man's fellows who threatened to go down and recover him. Only when Quintus Rufus promised the soldier a proper funeral were his comrades satisfied.

A Roman nailed to a cross was abhorrent and the men fumed with stories of slaves forcing soldiers to fight as gladiators in the north. Rufus was struck by how long the slave rebellion had been allowed to ravage his land, but was relieved it would be over soon. Scrofa's tuna trap had worked; they'd herded scum onto the beach easily enough, and there, they were trapped—Marcus Crassus' experience with sieges had paid off. Surely this couldn't last much longer, but Rufus couldn't comprehend why the slaves willingly ran into a dead-end spit of land. Quintus Rufus dismissed it as slave ignorance, wondering how they'd made it this far to begin with. The engineers gave endless excuses in technical talk as to why the wall hadn't been repaired. Rufus threatened to have them guard the opening themselves all night unless it was fixed.

## CRASTUS

Crastus the barbarian despaired upon sight of birds circling in the distance and his inability to fight his way to Spartacus' side. His greatest fear was that Spartacus was already dead and that Crastus missed his ride. Spending eternity with cowards inside the corpse ripper, tormented until Ragnarök, the end of time, made Crastus shudder. The barbarian did his duty: he'd gotten the women safely north as ordered. They were being stashed in a grotto somewhere on the Sabatus River, near *Ad Sabatum*, an unwalled ranching village near the *Via Popitian*. Crastus desperately wanted to take the road south to save time but had been ordered by Spartacus to stay off; it was being watched. Certain of ambush, Crastus cursed instead, turning the cavalry up the mountain trail, costing him hours.

### PUBLIPOR CONTEMPLATES SUICIDE

I relieved myself as Helios dove toward the sea, then walked to join the others as my hands trembled and my stomach fluttered while I tried desperately to gird myself for what was to come. I finally joined men at the appointed place upon the beach where Spartacus waited. The sun shone to our backs and everything within me said, *Jump in the ocean and swim away.* I focused on Pila instead and stood with the men to show them I wasn't shirking. All the tied cords of driftwood were lined up once more and torches were lit. No more feints; everything would be pushed into one point.

Spartacus spoke to the men while waiting for the sun chariot to drop. "Break through now, or die," was all he said, signaling men to ignite fires. Setting rays beat against the Roman wall. Our commander nodded to the trumpeter, who sounded the commencement. I thought my knees were going to collapse and I feared my hands were unable to hold the bow from tremors. My grasp held and my knees remained when the horn blew. I'd never stood in a phalanx before today—now I charged screaming into wolves' teeth twice since Helios' rise.

### RUFUS

Quintus Rufus squinted from the unfinished observation tower, shielding his eyes with his hand from the sun, when he heard a trumpet. "To arms! To arms!" yelled the officer to a centurion. Quickly, word passed down the row as men stood tightening straps and grabbing shields. Rufus couldn't see. Frustrated, he shielded his hand, covering the sun only to be blinded once more by the reflection in the sea. Rufus prayed to Jupiter that his engineers had repaired the wall sufficiently. The officer had no idea his engineers had been unable to secure new boards onto burned planks or repack the tilled earth they were set in. They'd merely laid the planks beside one another and nailed them with crossbeams to placate the officer and keep up appearances. The lead technician was sure slaves paid too high a price in lives to attack the same spot twice.

### PUBLIPOR

I ran behind shields, helping roll wrapped cylinders of wood on our line. Acorns and arrows thumped and knocked, looking for any way in. A vice-like grip seized my collar and my feet left the earth as I was confronted by an angry commander. "Men roll, you, grab arrow," ordered Spartacus. "Loose, damn you!" he demanded, setting me down.

I ran beneath the shields, this time plucking arrows from sand, quickly gathering handfuls and stuffing them into my quiver. The fear that had plagued me all day was suddenly gone; every movement was deliberate and without hesitation. Confusing noises faded as I worked in a bubble of silence, slipping around shields. I fixed a target. The Roman above moved slowly as if trudging through water. I released and had no need to watch, certain the bolt found its mark. Broken arrows avoided my grasp and I plucked only whole ones without fumbling, each time releasing and tucking back behind a *scutum* in the blink of an eye.

I couldn't make a mistake. The world slowed as my arrows flew true. It wasn't that I thought I was invincible—that wasn't even a passing thought at the time. The deadly spikes we once faced were broken or blunted from our morning's attempt. As we ran, some slaves held shields overhead, while others filled the ditch with bodies as we arrived beneath a hail of death. Our torches were thrown, reigniting embers from earlier. Flames licked upward. Spartacus himself threw the hook that grasped the top plank. The board toppled with a single mighty heave as slaves charged the breach with stabbing rage. I hadn't heard the Roman horn until my bolt struck the man blowing it. I grabbed for another to discover the quiver empty. I dropped Marcos' fine bow in the sand, pulled my sling, loaded an acorn, and wound it in a single motion. The man's face was ruined when I put the acorn between his cheek pieces at thirty paces. *They can't see us,* I realized. The sun chariot rode with us. The gap groaned, pressed by men behind their plywood birch *scutums*. Screams of pain and foul, angry curses arose as reckless slaves stormed the fallen planks, stabbing for blood.

## CRASTUS

Crastus the German saw smoke rise in the setting sun and leaned forward to kick his favorite bronze mare to a run. The slave cavalry followed in a storm of billowing dust as they chased pounding hooves. Crastus was desperate to join the fray before Spartacus fell; the German had a ride to catch.

## MARCUS CRASSUS

Imperator Marcus Crassus turned pale upon learning Scrofa faced the entire slave army alone. "Mummius' men were rolled into Pomptinus and Quinctius' legions," Merillius reiterated, "and they're guarding the crossroads. You instructed Atticus and Rufus not to abandon their positions in case it was another feint."

"Son of a *bitch!*" Crassus exclaimed, thinking of what to do next.

## PUBLIPOR

Mars himself seemed to direct my every movement. I think I was ten-for-ten when my bag of acorns finally ran dry; the little projectiles were everywhere beneath my sandals. All I had to do was bend to scoop and retrieve handfuls, but the thought of dropping my head to look around on the ground as the world unraveled seemed a bad idea. I pulled my sword instead, and shield-less, yanked the dagger as well, running after men up an earthen wall. I stood over smoldering, blood-stained planks on a rug of bodies, trying my best not to fall as thirty thousand slaves funneled through the six-foot gap.

### CRASTUS TAKES FLIGHT

Crastus the barbarian didn't bother dismounting before charging at the backs of the Romans. The German pulled his small shield, mounted at the horse's rump, and drew his sword at full gallop. The trained animal curbed itself once Crastus let go of the reins and stood on the creature's back. Leaping over the horse's neck, Crastus broke his fall upon the Roman rear, giving iron to a man before the Roman knew what happened. The rest of the cavalry followed Crastus' example and fell pell-mell into the melee. Crastus' only thought was to fight his way to Spartacus. He saw the cloaked vagabond watching from an unpatched eye off to the side as the world swallowed men. This was it: do or die—Crastus' ride to paradise.

### MARCUS CRASSUS

Marcus ordered three couriers to ride with all haste to his officers. One would race up the Pompitian to request Pomptinus and Quinctius move south to reinforce the line. The other two headed to Atticus and Rufus at their fortified positions on the ditch with orders to move north and reinforce Scrofa's beleaguered legion. The superstitious but unreligious Imperator, Marcus

Crassus, gave prayers to the gods that they'd make it in time.

# CHAPTER TWENTY-SEVEN

"Spartacus crucified a Roman prisoner in the gap between the armies to show his men what to expect without victory."
—Appian, *Civil Wars*

The sun chariot rode into the sea. Stars and fire lit our way as we fought beneath the embers of both, rushing up to heaven. Our men pressed the gap and bodies compressed as we began funneling faster in a line of men flowing quickly through the confinement. I felt the squeeze behind my breastplate, and lifting my head to gasp for air, I was carried through by momentum alone. My feet touched only to keep me upright and I knew if I fell, I'd never get up again. Both my blades were pulled so I kept them against my body to keep them from piercing anyone. I popped through to the other side miraculously without slicing my face. The press relented enough to feel earth beneath my feet and to see the backs of Roman soldiers fighting in both directions.

The sound of Crastus' awful laughter was music to my ears. I watched Romans fall like wheat to a scythe beneath his fury. A Roman soldier slashed at me; I crossed my blades to catch it, swinging them in a circle like Marcos had done to me that awful day. *"Stab, don't slash!"* Crixus screamed from death. My sword was stopped by a Roman breastplate, but my dagger continued to his neck, finding purchase just beneath the strap. The Roman grabbed at the wound, dropping his sword and falling to his knees. I moved on to make room for more slaves, stabbing with both hands at the nearest Roman. My luck held; I'd killed plenty with my own hands, and now, fatigue set in and muscles burned. Gone were the days when I doubted and fretted over killing. Whenever a shadow of doubt crossed my mind, I thought of my unborn son and became angry. A Roman would have no qualms about tossing my child on a rubbish heap. I kept stabbing inside the press, dodging blades, and bouncing off shields until I heard a trumpet, this time on their side of the wall, followed by Spartacus' war voice.

"To the hills, now, run!" yelled Spartacus. "More Romans appear; to mountain, everyone, go!" he bellowed over the din of war as we began a fighting retreat. Our uninjured covered the wounded as the Romans let us go, the fight beaten out of them, allowing escape. Battered and bruised, we crawled into the woods, knowing time was short before fresh troops arrived. Men with mounts raced up and down the line, discouraging any Roman who felt the need to press. Crastus was angry, having lost his favorite mare, grumbling at being alive. We limped, crawled, and staggered up Sila Mountain, escaping new soldiers who were certain to be after us any minute. One look at the mound of dead left behind showed we'd escaped the snare by chewing off our paw.

### MARCUS' FEARS MANIFEST

Even the senate couldn't undo a popular act of the people. Marcus Crassus' premonition had come to pass. The people wanted Pompey "the Great" to return with his Midas touch and handle this unseemly slave uprising once and for all. Many senators feared the second coming of Sulla as the young commander entered Italy and passed the Rubicon with his legions intact and armed.

With the rogue Sertorius finally defeated and his lieutenant executed, the Butcher's Boy could return in triumph from Spain after two years of ruthless pacification. Pompey, the young self-made commander who believed himself equal in excellence to Alexander the Great, ordered his legions to pack their things for the long journey home, promising citizenship for any foreigner who joined the cause.

### NEWLYWEDS REUNITE

It was an arduous journey, high on mountain trails, made slower by our wounded. Though afflicted with a few scrapes and cuts, I asked to watch our rear out of self-preservation anyway. While hiding in the woods, at a vantage with views of every approach, I watched them. Thankfully, the Romans wanted as much of us as we wanted of them. When Spartacus decided an attack wouldn't come, he sent me north to find Gannicus, who'd been ordered to stay with the women and protect our baggage. The barbarian Crastus described the lay of the land, explaining the landmarks to guide me to my wife. I pushed the pony harder than I should've, not wanting to wait another second to see Pila.

Gannicus found me banging stones in the creek and led me to a gully where freshwater fell from a brook high above, emptying into a small pond of a fern-filled grotto. The depression protected our women from a wind that still blew cold in this new year. Pila appeared from behind the fall and we hugged for a long time, both unwilling to release. She fretted over my bruises and insisted on dressing my cuts, asking if I'd eaten. My pregnant bride could tell I'd just come from Hades. Pila fed me palm roots and wild radishes, apologizing for the lack of food.

"It's the most delicious meal I've eaten since Pompeii," I said. Pila smiled, watching me eat ravenously.

## MARCUS' SETBACK

Marcus Crassus couldn't believe the slaves had escaped, and wouldn't tolerate the Sicilian words, *cosa nostra*, or "our thing," meaning the "tuna trap," within his hearing. The escape was equally demoralizing to men who'd toiled day and night, constructing embattlements and digging trenches, just to abandon everything for another chase. Marcus Crassus harshly rebuked the officers, admonishing them for not adapting to the situation's fluidity.

Atticus Fabius, recently promoted from centurion to officer and remembering decimation, thought to himself: *Well, which is it? Follow orders or take initiative?*

## HELICA DRINKS MUDDIED WATER

The slave army straggled into the grotto, beaten, bloody, and starving. Miraculously that night, a group of Vidovic's Celts killed a feral pig and roasted it inside our sanctuary. The meal, fresh water, and rest lifted everyone's spirits just enough to silence the grumbling, if only momentarily. The moon shone before dawn and many slaves held private rituals for dead friends.

Helica couldn't understand what happened and didn't have time for incantations to find out why the vision had failed. It nagged at her insides. Helica wondered if Dionysus was playing games or if one of the greater gods had tricked her god. She knew Jupiter and Hera were petty, jealous, and capable of treachery; surely, they'd played a trick on the God of Slaves at a cost in mortals for amusement. *Did I not sacrifice enough in Mutina?* thought Helica. *Did I forget something in Pompeii? Why do the gods need more blood, or were my husband's powers finally proven unlucky? If so, why were they allowed to escape?* The unanswered questions were as murky as the early morning fog she navigated now.

The slave army moved north, but for what? Surely the slaves

could see they were no match for Rome by now. The defiant captives taunted slaves. "The Butcher's Boy is coming," one said before his execution. In central southern Italy, Helica's women learned from locals that Lucullus had returned from the east, having destroyed the people of Thrace, and was moving inland with his legions.

Everything that was so clear just a month ago was in question now. Helica listened to grumblings from the Celts and Germans while they marched. Groups of people cursed her husband for not taking the ride with Heracleo when they had the chance. Helica spat when Heracleo entered her thoughts, remembering his treachery. That pirate and his sailors were the reason Helica and her husband were in the predicament they faced now. Heracleo was to blame for why Helica was without her new country. She prayed Antony would catch them, gouge out their eyes, and crucify them all. The darkness of Helica's vision was disturbing; she feared Dionysus had forsaken his people, the slaves, the wretches, the women.

## PUBLIPOR

Even defeat is better than chains, and the army of slaves was able to attract new men to our ranks, refilling them somewhat. The new people wouldn't get the training others had—theirs would be a trial by fire. I envied their ignorance. On and on we trudged through the difficult southern mountain passes. I wondered how I'd replace Marcos' fine bow, if I ever could. Our supplies were running low; Roman arrows and food were luxuries of which we had very little.

Spartacus turned the slaves east toward Thurii once again after reaching the Crathis River. The wide river paralleled *Via Popitian*, and Spartacus believed any time made by Romans taking the road would be lost trying to ford its swollen banks farther north later, after they'd realized we'd slipped them. We made all haste. Unaided stragglers were left behind as the weather warmed, which meant two things: I'd officially turned sixteen and the Romans would be spoiling for a fight. With every step, discontentment grew. Spartacus ordered our cavalry to forage ahead for food and horses, both in short supply.

## THE PLEBIAN OFFICER

"What do you mean, you lost them?" Atticus asked his two scouts.

"We thought they'd jump back on the road, once they were ahead of us," replied the older of the two.

"Well, there's your mistake," replied Atticus.

The two looked at each other warily, then back to their officer.

"You thought," Atticus finished. It heated the veteran to be outsmarted, especially by slaves. Now he'd either have to double back to use the bridge at Consentia or continue on to Caprasia's stone bridge. There was no way he could ford the river now that it was swollen with fresh snowmelt. Atticus decided he'd keep going north to Carpalia; it would set him back less and he had a diminished chance of running into Marcus, thus not having to explain why he'd turned south, outwitted by slaves.

## PILA PONDERS

"What if it's a girl?" asked Pila.

"Then we'll drown it and try again," I joked.

Pila slapped my arm.

I laughed and poked again, "We'll sell it!"

Pila looked horrified.

"Yeah, you're right; we wouldn't get much," I said, stealing Crastus' joke and laughing some more. Pila, knowing I had a huge bruise, punched me right where it was on my thigh and laughed when I winced, crying out. We soon began walking in good spirits again, once the pain subsided.

"What if it kills me?" she asked earnestly. I stopped and turned to face her.

"Then it kills me too," I said. We hugged and kissed, then set back on our way.

With the exception of Roman landowners, the people of Thurii had grown used to our slave army and stopped running when they saw us approaching. Thurii's gates remained open and we were welcomed or tolerated, for the most part. They knew we'd take what was needed and soon be on our way. We took horses and slaughtered some cattle; food was shared with settlers and slaves there in a celebratory way. That night, I listened to Celts speak to one another in their language and heard the tone they used when they spoke Spartacus' name. As for the Germans, I saw Crastus get furious, spitting rebukes at a man—I presumed the slave spoke ill of our commander. I felt their discontentment and could deduce that someone had cursed Spartacus from Crastus' reaction, because I had my own reservations about the retreat. We seemed to be driving north aimlessly; like everyone else, I desired to know the plan, if there was one.

I found Spartacus brushing Pegasus in a barn with straw. He spoke lovingly to the mammoth horse, stroking the beast. "Glad not to take horse on beach," said Spartacus when he saw me enter. He continued brushing.

"Me too, commander," I said, returning small talk.

"You want know, where slaves go next." Spartacus made the question a statement.

"Everyone does," I said, trying to help.

"Slave army go, to cock's spur, to Urium Bay."

"Commander?"

"We contract sailor there, take us to Illyricum, then on to

Thrace," said Spartacus, stabbing my heart.

"What about everyone else?" I asked, concerned really for just Pila and myself.

"You and woman, join us," Spartacus said. Unable to speak, I froze, dimwitted and speechless. Spartacus stopped brushing and turned to look at me. "Anything can happen, from here to there, everything can change in day, son," Spartacus spoke softly in his deep voice, returning to brush Pegasus. The horse snorted contentedly and I stood speechless until I thanked him. I left to find my wife, distraught. That night, Crastus and Spartacus argued until late in the evening. Crastus was loud, animated, and angry; Spartacus was firm, calm, and resolved.

The next day, Gannicus handed me a new bow, inferior to Marcos', but workable. I thanked him and saw in my mentor's face something amiss as he handed me a quiver full of arrows. We were mustering outside the gates of Thurii for the trip back into Lucania. I helped my pregnant wife climb up into the cart while Helica received quiet anger and discontentment from everywhere except in her hardest core of believers. Crastus wore a scowl while mounted, his horse bunched with the Celts. It reminded me that our slave army was still just the mash of humanity, a vast mosaic of tiny pieces that come together to make the bigger picture.

Years prior, when I was just a boy at slave auction, Romans called every foreigner "Gaul" when sold. Most slaves were indeed Gauls, but the next most-populous were Celts, followed by Spaniards, then Germans, and finally easterners like Thracians and Greeks. Least of all were Egyptians, Africans, and lastly, as Gannicus put it, "the pain-in-the-ass Hebrews with all their damned laws." These were the people Rome put to the yoke to provide a lifestyle Romans felt entitled to. While every slave but the native Italian was referred to simply as "Gaul" by the average Roman, slaves knew the difference—a source of contention between them at most times. Most groups preferred staying to their own kind, unless pressed by an outside force or brought together for common cause. Crixus and Crastus, both Germans, partnered with a Celt and a Thracian to escape the humiliation of dying for sport in the games. Now, with only the Thracian and a German left to lead, they should've partnered to escape Italy. Except the German with a death wish wanted to stay and defeat Rome, while the Thracian knew it was impossible and tried going home to a defeated land. The whole thing hurt my head; it threatened to break apart our rebellion along with them.

"Ve letten zie ride mit us to Lucania, maybe as en zie far as Grumentum," Crastus spoke resentfully with a thick accent that worsened as he raged. "Zie crossroad, you take vitch, go en zie hide mit Greek homosexual, cross sea," decried Crastus, looking Spartacus square in the eye, to snickers of those who wouldn't dare do it alone. Helica committed to memory the faces of those who'd scoffed. "If en zie du find balls, mit here and zier, maybe ve letten du come mit real men, du Campania," said Crastus, the only man who dared speak as such, as he adjusted himself on a new horse. "Vhen done setten zie fire due Campania, ve riden zie for Latium and city; maken zie slave of Roman!" shouted Crastus to his supporters, who hailed him. The German sat holding his reigns, satisfied and angry.

"In Grumentum," retorted Spartacus, "maybe find brain by then. You sound a fool, German." Spartacus' supporters laughed, infuriating the dark, ruddy-haired German with a long mustache. Crastus heeled his horse north, turning his back, and separately, we started off together...for the time being. My sixteenth spring was now in full bloom; I was to be a father soon, and my army was losing the war and beginning to tear itself apart.

## MARCUS CRASSUS IS INCENSED

Marcus Crassus' officers were ahead of him on the Popitian Way. Atticus waited in Concentia for the commander while Pomptinus and Quinctius continued on the road to Sybaris. The two of them were to block slaves from leaving Bruttium. Officers had scouts follow the fugitives closely. Marcus was shocked to hear the description of grotesque perversity. Slaves marched with *signum* and *fasces* in a mockery of Roman legions. The horror enraged Marcus to the point of drinking un-watered wine like a barbarian. He vowed to put a stop to the aberration now, before the Butcher's Boy came to steal Marcus' thunder. The injustice that afflicted his father would not be visited upon himself— Marcus Crassus swore it by Jupiter.

## CRASTUS THE BARBARIAN PONDERS THE HEREAFTER

The two camps walked on the unpaved cattle path northward together, yet separate. The barbarian Crastus, alone with his thoughts, began wondering if the deal with Crixus and Oden weren't just a fevered dream. Surely, such a superior warrior as himself wouldn't be barred from Asgard just for not dying with Spartacus. How could he? The thought defied imagination to the giant German; besides, he'd tried on the beach and they both survived. Why would Oden command something that hadn't and wouldn't come to pass? Did Thor know Commander Spartacus would curdle and run away? Was this the trickster Loki's work? It made his head hurt and he became angry for not having any wine. Crastus' mood soured and he slapped a young man riding nearest unprovoked on the back of the head. The younger man grabbed at his head, stunned by the sudden rebuke with a surprised look on his face. "Finden zie vine, now!" Crastus ordered. The young Celt curbed his horse and turned it to a run, looking for anyone in the back of the caravan who had wine for the chieftain.

PUBLIPOR WITNESSES FRUSTRATION

I walked my horse next to the cart with the women behind Crastus, when suddenly, he slapped a blond slave on the back of the head and shouted something.

"He's angry that Spartacus won't go to Rome with him," said Helica from the wagon's bench.

"Can Crastus take the city without Spartacus' help?" Pila asked from behind.

"No," Helica answered.

"Then why go?" I asked.

"Crastus wants to enter into his heaven with Crixus," answered Helica.

"Then why not just kill himself?" inquired Pila.

"To the Germans and people north of Germania," Helica answered, "that's the coward's death. They believe the faint of heart are eaten every day by a giant serpent with a mouth full of curved teeth beneath the world." The description caused Pila to shudder at the thought of such a creature.

"Why doesn't he come with us?" I asked the enchantress.

"Crastus is afraid of drowning," Helica explained, "or any death that results in him not dying in battle, blade in hand. He fears that Spartacus avoids battle, and that will keep him from Valhalla."

Pila and I had had many discussions lying together at night about the various religions practiced in camp. It was impossible to keep up with all the Celtic rituals; some nights they'd run naked, howling. They seemed to see gods in everything from bees and crickets to streams and trees. The women seemed to run their religious things and they were always looking to the moon's phases for answers to everything. The Gauls had a pantheon of gods all to themselves, while the Romans just copied Greek gods and changed the names. Egyptians had more rituals and gods than anyone, and their former slaves, the Hebrews, only had one.

"The most impoverished people in all the world are the Judeans, Pila," explained the older woman.

"Why?" asked my wife.

"They only have one god," answered Helica. Pila touched her chin, contemplating.

"Well, that would make things simple, I guess," Pila reasoned. Helica looked at her, mortified.

"One god is not enough for all the questions the world has in it," Helica scolded. The deep conversation was interrupted when the blond Celt sped past on a horse, kicking dust with a wine skin for Crastus. Crastus smiled, took the skin, and rubbed the younger man appreciatively where he'd slapped him earlier. Friends again, they drank while walking their horses together, gesturing with their hands to supplement their only shared language: unintelligible Latin.

"Publipor, go with Gannicus," ordered the commander from behind.

"Yes, lord," I said, halting my horse.

"*Vala,*" Pila said, waving from the wagon before I'd turned my mount.

THE BUTCHER'S BOY ENTERS ITALY, 684 AUC (71 BC)

Even in summer, the Alpine Pass was an arduous endeavor with no guarantees. Luckily, it was all downhill from here on out. Pompey made sure the men were properly provisioned, and he'd taken the route before. His men were hardened, seasoned warriors, accustomed to hardship and most of all, victory. He'd no doubt in his mind that he'd clear up this little slave bother in no time. Pompey rode, sure he'd celebrate his second triumph before his twenty-ninth birthday, thus deserving the title: "Pompey the Great." Soon, all of Italy would proclaim him Pompius Maximus as well.

## A YOUNG SCOUT HARDENS

I stood alone in the tree line, tucked within shadows, watching two mounted Roman scouts talk on the path. One turned south and left once they finished speaking; the other grabbed a bag and began rummaging through it. The Roman scout pulled out dried meat, tore off a piece with his teeth, and sat chewing with his focus still in the bag. I drew on his unprotected chest and released; the bolt struck and he fell from the spooked horse as it bolted. The young Roman scout writhed on the ground in pain while chewed meat fell from his mouth and he cried out for his mother on the trail. I stepped from the shadows, approaching carefully. The Roman pulled a dagger with his free hand as I closed—the other held my bolt in his chest. The young man let his blade fall, unable to keep it within his grasp. He spit curses at me between gasps, knowing he was dying. Standing over him, I stripped his arms at sword-point, taking his sword, dagger, bow, and quiver, along with his kit bag. I bent, lifting the strap of his bag from his neck, and walked away without a word. The young scout continued to spit curses at me in Latin with his last gasps. I thought of my unborn son chewing his ration of salted beef; I left him to die alone and rode away.

I'd ambushed a lot of scouts that way by the time our people reached Grumentum. We watched the Romans evacuate their farming village as soon as they caught sight of us. It became a familiar scene, performed countless times, played out once more as the massive slave army approached the town. Romans ran to the hills with their hands full of hastily grasped valuables, fleeing into the woods only to forget where they were buried. Every town did the same thing: they ran, burying coins, carrying keys to busted locks they'd never reopen.

"Crastus, you double back? Wrong way on road, swarming with

Roman?" Spartacus inquired, trying to convince the stubborn German to stay. "Stay with us, to Anaia, then to Potentia. From there, straight shot east to Campania, slave partway there," he reasoned, wanting to keep the extra manpower for long as possible. Crastus nodded wordless agreement. Spartacus held the army together a little longer, moving from various terrified farming villages while their slaves joined our cause. Once I'd returned, I gave the last stolen, pitted, rusting sword to a dirty slave in rags, who behaved as though I'd handed him a fortune. I told him to stab, not slash with it, before he ran off happier than what looked like he'd ever been in his entire life.

### ATTICUS LOSES TWO MEN

"What do you mean, 'they're on the wrong side of the road?'" Marcus Crassus asked, flabbergasted.

"We didn't think they'd leave the road so soon, and they put the swollen river between us before we realized it," Atticus answered, plainly unwilling to shift blame to his scouts, wanting to save the boys Marcus' wrath.

"Did you have scouts on them or not?" Marcus asked, working to the bottom of it.

"We did, sir; two," answered Atticus.

"Throttle them both in front of the others and let's get on with finding their trail again," Marcus ordered, angry and frustrated. Marcus Crassus sarcastically commented aloud to anyone nearby, "Maybe we should offer a pardon to *their* scouts. Maybe *then* we'd find them."

# CHAPTER TWENTY-EIGHT

"...disgracefully heedless of their fatherland, and most had a naturally slavish temperament that longed for nothing except plunder and bloodshed."

—Sallust, *Histories*

At Potentia, we took more slaves, food, coins, and plunder. The Mountain Vultur stood in the distance, indicating that the borders of Samnium, Campania, and Apulia were close. Very few words were spoken between the two former gladiators before setting off in opposite directions. The anger in Bruttium had been replaced with quiet respect; both men grasped forearms, wishing the other good fortune. Crastus the German rode west toward Mt. Balabo with fifteen thousand mostly Celtic slaves who deluded themselves into thinking Rome's slaves would open their gates.

We watched a quarter of our force march away. I was sad, until Spartacus ordered me to follow them.

"I don't wish to join them, lord," I pleaded, fearing his reaction to my insubordination.

"You, are not," replied Spartacus. "Need you watch German, just to Eburum. Not let Crastus see you. Sending Gannicus, north, scout Venusia. Publipor, you watch German. If Crastus, make Popitian Way, turn back. Most like, not make that far. If Roman attack, run to me," Spartacus clarified with a wink. I breathed a sigh of relief and returned his wink with a smile.

Vidovic, a sturdily built Celt who loved wine, women, and horses, went with his people. I could tell the Celt preferred to stay with Spartacus, but resigned to go with his kind out of a misplaced sense of duty. Vidovic, the closest thing to a Celtic leader since Oenomaus died, was a big loss to our force. Unfortunately, his leadership wasn't strong enough to hold the wayward bunch of breakaway fanatics to Spartacus. Vidovic had been swept up with the foolishness as well and was unable to find a way out. The Celts, a handful of Germans, and a few other ethnic mixes drove northward, foolheartedly believing their previous fortunes would continue all the way to victory over the massive city, recruiting and deluding ignorant slaves as they went.

It was harder to slip past Roman scouts than it was to remain unseen by an undisciplined German on my speedy colt. It astonished me that Crastus had no one ranging for him and I feared he'd make the same mistake Crixus had in Urium Bay. It seemed as if Crastus the barbarian had a wish for death as I followed them to a lake at the base of a mountain near the town of Volcei. Crastus' mostly Celtic army ransacked Volcei, setting slaves free and stealing, all while brazenly camped on the banks of the lake in stolen Roman tents.

I'd set up on the northern slope halfway up that mountain to keep an eye on them. It was comfortably warm enough at night and its chill was tolerable without a fire. I'd almost been discovered by Celtic women ascending to perform one of their many religious rituals. Before dawn, as the moon shone above brightly, they'd come to pray and look for food. Thankfully, my horse remained silent when I walked it around to get away from them. I'd watched them pass me on their way up and knew I'd have to be more careful not to be detected when they eventually descended. My biggest problem was the noises a horse makes at random. If the animal heard something startling, it'd whinny or nicker. Sometimes they just snort to communicate. So, my first job was keeping the beast contented. I was letting the colt graze liberally when I saw women suddenly running back down in a rush. They made such haste that it was easy to see they'd found Romans; the women ran, frightened, to warn their men. While investigating all this in the early cool before dawn, I stumbled upon a couple thousand light infantry wearing halos of vines wrapped around their helmets. The cover kept the sunrise from glinting and giving them away. Undetected, I backtracked, desperate for a way around. They were too close; I'd have to leave warning Crastus about the Romans to the fleeing women. My job was informing Spartacus, so that's what I did.

### TWO LIEUTENANTS FOLLOW THEIR DIRECTORATE

Marcus Crassus ordered Quintus Rufus to send light infantry up the mountain at night and gain high ground. Rufus took Pomptinus and prepared for a good old-fashioned, surprise downhill charge for his commander. Rufus had his best young men camouflage their helmets with foliage. The athletic young men ascended before dawn with a plan of crashing into the back of a breakaway slave army, once Marcus engaged them at the bottom.

### THE CELT

Vidovic sat before a campfire, sharpening iron with a stone in the early morning cool while most of the camp slept. His woman and some others had gone up the mountain before sunrise to attend to their womanly things and pray. Suddenly, Vidovic's wife appeared and ran at him with fright in her eyes, pointing up the mountain behind her and screaming, "Soldiers, soldiers!" Vidovic woke the men. The slaves grasped their arms and shields, starting up the slope for a fight within seconds.

## THE OFFICERS

Pomptinus and Rufus both heard the uproar in the early morning hours and knew Rufus' light infantry were had. Simultaneously, the two launched their men up at the wayward splinter group from different directions at the base of the little mountain. The officers had trumpets signal an attack upon the slaves' camp to relieve the outnumbered men now stuck upon the heights.

## THE GERMAN LAMENTS DAMNATION

Vidovic and Crastus heard trumpets behind them and knew they were both fucked. This new herald caused them to return down the slope and protect their women, leaving Romans approaching from the heights. The slaves returned just in time to set the shield wall in front of their wagons before it was too late. Two legions of ten thousand Roman soldiers attacked their front, shouting and banging shields. Bolts flew, sticking in shields, as acorns kept men ducking for cover while javelins fell, doing their terrible work. Slaves knew the crash of shields was coming and braced for impact. They thundered upon one another, evenly matched for the time being. Men weaved swords between and over shields, hoping to bite a man on the other side.

## CRASTUS DESCENDS

Crastus the German belted his fearsome laugh, figuring this was as good a time as any to join Crixus in Valhalla. Mightily, the German gripped his sword, preparing to join his brother in paradise. Crastus the barbarian yelled for the second of his two lines to turn, half facing the new threat now coming up the mountain at them.

An incline is of great benefit to the men who possess its heights. It turns a two-hundred-pound man into a four-hundred-pound boulder. It makes a five-foot man six-feet-tall with overreach. It makes foes lose heart and think of running away. Crastus couldn't die now, not as his army ran in terror with the women. Slaves, full of boastful talk just a day prior, now dropped shields and ran for their lives into the woods. Crastus looked at his Celtic brother, Vidovic, knowingly. There was no way Oden would excuse this. Crastus had to escape, and for only the second time in his life, Crastus the gladiator ran, fleeing from danger while vultures filled the sky.

### ROMAN SUCCESS

Pomptinus and Rufus were close enough to see each other when Rufus' young men charged down the mountain. They traded satisfied grins, knowing they'd wipe out the slaves before Crassus could even show up with reinforcements. Pomptinus ordered trumpeters to signal pursuit. Rufus sat disappointed, hearing Marcus Crassus' bugle return in the distance. It pissed off the officers that they couldn't mop up before Crassus' cavalry claimed credit.

### RALLY

Vidovic caught up to Crastus on the mountainside. Neither man could bear looking at the other, knowing they'd shamed themselves. Crastus was filled with despair, fearing eternity in the corpse ripper. He heard horses below and knew more Romans had arrived. Crastus the barbarian regretted not having Publipor scout for him. Believing this the end, he turned in a last-ditch effort at redemption, when he heard a familiar trumpet. Vidovic roared, *"Riyos!"*—Gallic for "freedom"—lifting the men's spirits sky high. Crastus joined the chant, rallying men from hiding.

### REVERSAL

The horsemen Rufus thought were his commander Marcus' cavalry turned out to be Spartacus' coming to aid the wayward Celts instead. Hidden slaves rejoiced from the woods at a chance to save their women. Pomptinus barely crouched in time to keep his head as the commander's sword swept past his neck. His red cape worked to attract Gauls like enraged bulls while mounted slaves flew trying to get at him. Rufus experienced the same at his end of the line and neither could believe the misfortune of what was happening. Jubilation soured as victory slipped away before their very eyes. Spartacus had appeared from nowhere as his entire force of fifty thousand angry slaves, bent on revenge, descended on the two Roman officers.

### REINFORCEMENTS ARRIVE

Imperator Marcus Crassus rode behind his marching men through the valley, following noises from a trumpet and the sound of war. Guided by circling birds, he prayed aloud to Jupiter, hoping Rufus' trick worked. The Imperator rounded the path's bend to make out what was happening.

### THE TIDE EBBS

Crastus the German and Vidovic the Celt were handed something that never happens in warfare: a reprieve and a second chance to pick up shields. Roman soldiers now showed the slaves their backs to deal with Spartacus. *"Riyos!"* they screamed, as more men came from the woods to form the line. Once Vidovic thought he'd mustered enough strength, he ordered them forward. Slaves pelted Romans with slings and pierced them with arrows before turning two lines back to back.

## POMPTINUS

Pomptinus was in despair; he'd given up the element of surprise, lost the high ground, and now his men were fighting for their lives. No doubt, if he survived, his friend Rufus would turn, as both men blamed each other for the fiasco. Pomptinus insanely thought he'd have the better argument, since it was Rufus' light infantry that failed. Mistaking the slave cavalry for Marcus' caused Rufus relief, followed by terror and the cursing of stars once he realized it was just more ruthless slaves.

## MARCUS LEANS ON AN OLD CENTURION

Marcus Crassus could tell his officers were in trouble once he rounded the bend. He shot Atticus a look, retaining a pretense of control to the men. The old hand knew exactly what to do without asking. Atticus Fabius shouted for his cohort to line up in the three-line standard formation and began marching them into the fray. Atticus ordered his centurions into the delicate maneuver of replacing Rufus and Pomptinus' spent men with his own fresh soldiers. Next, Marcus ordered Quinctius and Scrofa to deal with the new, larger army marching toward them in three rows. Marcus fumed inside when he saw the multitude of captured *signums* from Glaber, Servilius, Gellius, and Lentulus waving arrogantly from the opposite ranks. He vowed to Jupiter and Mars that he'd recapture the sacred symbols, hoping to get the *fasces* as well.

## SPARTACUS

Spartacus was balanced on a razor's edge. He didn't want to engage Crassus' entire army in this open, flat clearing where they could fully form up and engulf him. Spartacus planned to take pressure off Crastus and Vidovic just long enough for them to escape. He knew he could relieve the Celts from two legions but might not be able to save his own army from Crassus' entire strength. Spartacus lined up men, hoping the bluff would work, waiting to see who'd blink first.

### THE NEW OFFICER

Atticus had to keep the breakaway army's back against the mountain and separate from the former cavalryman with whom he'd once diced. "Hold!" yelled Atticus, stiffening his boys' backs as projectiles flew overhead, daring men to peek over and sneak a look.

### THE CONDUCTOR

Marcus Crassus saw the opportunity and seized it, ordering his signal corps to wave the flags and arranging his men in standard formation. The centurions' deftly drilled men perfectly arranged themselves in short order to repel the oncoming onslaught of raging slaves. The first row of veterans banged their shields, cursing and challenging slaves to bring it.

### REVELATION

Astride Pegasus, Spartacus saw from his vantage that the men facing him now weren't the boys of last summer. He ordered his bugler to blow the signal for withdrawal. The men folded in on each other, checking incoming cavalry by presenting a wall at all times in case the Romans decided to charge. *Old Marcus Crassus finally found men who are not intimidated,* Spartacus thought, realizing the game had finally changed. He nodded for the bugler to blow again.

Spartacus had caused enough diversion for Crastus and the men to escape, but he hoped privately they'd rejoin the fold. The former gladiator knew he had to own the high ground quickly before the Romans realized what he was doing. The nearest available refuge Spartacus could make in time was the little mountain of Cantenna. Sparing the new men confusion with bugle calls, Spartacus roared in his war voice, "Fall back to mountain! One row, don't turn until next moves! Cover infantry until they up to high ground. Horsemen, on me!" Pointing to his bugler for redundancy, Spartacus charged his cavalry at the methodically approaching Roman line. Veteran horsemen knew from experience how far to charge and turned once they'd reached bow range, sensing the perfect distance to wheel back around. This forced the Romans to stop and form their wall, buying time for the infantry to retreat. A garden of arrows sprouted just in front of the halted horsemen. Mounted slaves ran their powerful animals the entire length of the men's line upon the plain, drawing bow shots to buy even more time.

## REPRIEVE

Crastus, Vidovic, and the remaining Celts retrieved their shields, forming another wall in the confusing bedlam, and charged uphill at Pomptinus' light infantry posted above. Desperate for redemption, slaves charged upward into the unfavorable situation with renewed zeal. To the credit of Pomptinus' light infantry, they took the best advantage they could, considering the slaves numerical superiority in the back-and-forth momentum of the morning. The recently beaten slaves now fought like wild animals, threatening to overcome the high ground among sparse trees. Even with the height and weight of the incline, the Roman light infantry found it difficult to move newly determined slaves. Sharp iron jutted suddenly from beneath long shields while curses and insults were replaced by groans and cries of pain. Slaves fought like it was their last day on earth, each trying to outdo their nearest brother upon the slope. Crastus' terrible laugh traveled the entire length of the battlefield, heard all the way in the valley below. Crastus the barbarian gripped his sword, lest it slip from blood, sending Romans to Hades one after the other.

## REST

When Pomptinus and Rufus finally grasped the situation and realized Marcus Crassus' army had saved their bacon, they ordered their soldiers to return. The spent soldiers, exhausted from fighting earlier, had caught their breath enough to reenter the fray. They'd waited in reserve to be called up again to face the larger army that Marcus had just routed. Rested and rehydrated, the two officers sent their men uphill to aid the desperate light infantry in risk of being dislodged.

## REFUSAL

Vidovic was the first to notice soldiers approaching from behind. He nudged Crastus, who had just finished running a man through, and pointed down the hill. Iron lunging from their opponents above dipped in frequency, and the slaves took that as their cue to turn. Crastus, Vidovic, and the remaining uninjured all glanced knowingly at each other, and without a word spoken, a consensus was reached silently between the former slaves. Exchanging smiles, the line turned their backs on the whipped light infantry and ran headlong downhill to meet the new threat charging up at them. Crastus charged downhill, laughing with reckless abandon, sending fear down the spine of all below. Every slave blistered downhill full tilt, each grateful for the chance to redeem the shame from earlier and make the deeds of this day sing into eternity.

## RUFUS AND POMPTINUS

The two officers' newfound hope waned when wild men released their light infantry and turned. "Oh, my gods," commented Pomptinus when the slaves bowled over his first line from the heights. Light infantry gasped for air, pausing to rest instead of using their advantageous position to press down on the slaves. Both Roman officers glanced fearfully at each other when a tall, ruddy slave covered in tattoos actually laughed at his soldiers. *"Aw, aw, aw,"* bellowed the Gaul, while cutting men down mercilessly. Rufus prayed silently on his mount that the men could handle the barbarian, frightened witless by the prospect of having to face such a man himself.

## CRASTUS ASCENDS

Vidovic fell when a javelin pierced his side. Crastus took a second to look upon his friend's wound long enough to get bitten in the upper arm. Angered by gouts of blood, Crastus killed the man with a lunge to his neck. Crastus felt no pain, thankful his foe's edge was sharpened. He switched hands, grabbing tightly. Vidovic remained on a knee with the pilum stuck through him. He smiled at Crastus, satisfied with redemption and the damage they'd caused the enemy after all. Crastus watched Vidovic get bitten through the neck by a sword wielding arm thrust around a *scutum*. When Vidovic fell, a Northman with long blond hair replaced him, smashing Roman helmets with a hammer. Crastus recognized him as Thor, God of Thunder, and stepped inside the Roman's line with one good arm, laughing. The giant stabbed Romans as if they were helpless children, roaring until someone finally stopped Crastus with a javelin. Leaves and debris fluttered as giant wings from a Valkyrie spread above, completely blotting out the sun to descend upon the great warrior. Crastus the barbarian smiled as his vision darkened and, having never touched the ground, felt ascension. Crastus the German heartily laughed with joy at the sensation of weightlessness and flight, enjoying the cool breeze on a ride to see his brothers, gently clutched in the craw of an enormous bird soaring ever higher.

### POMPTINUS SIGHS

Pomptinus audibly breathed a sigh of relief when the giant, tattooed Gaul with the Roman haircut and long mustache fell. Certainly, the rabble would lay down arms and realize they were beaten now. Both officers were struck dumb with grudging respect at the bottom of the giant hill, watching barbarians fight to the last man. Pomptinus wished he had such men, while Rufus hoped they were the last of their kind, wanting to retire.

### OUR COMMANDER SAVES THE SLAVES

Spartacus' cavalry charged back to cover the retreating line.

"Go up!" Spartacus ordered the infantry. I rode to my lord's side, offering services of my bow. "Go, take women quick, before Roman! Go Brundisium, in Calabria," the commander ordered, then spoke to the mask of apprehension painted on my face. "Catch you before Bradanus River. If not, use coin, buy passage across sea." Before I could bog my lord down with questions, he thundered down at me from Pegasus, "Now!" I turned and ran my horse before his voice left my ears or a thought passed between them.

### MARCUS LOSES HIS GRIP

Marcus Crassus had to close the gap before the slaves could escape again up a mountain. He frantically waved his arms at a bugler to get the bastard's attention, trying to sound the order to charge. Marcus had led plenty of armies in lots of wars and could tell when men were spent. Like a mule that can't be beaten another inch, he saw the countenance of the soldiers. The slump in their shoulders when the bugle sounded told him the day was done. Desire made him want to kick them anyway; experience kept him from making a disastrous mistake.

"Scouts!" he shouted, frustrated.

It was hard to convince Helica to drive east; she insisted on joining her husband. "He's on our heels, thwarting them from hounding us. Your husband meets us in Potentia," I lied, doing my best to remind her of the need for wagons to get a head start. Helica fixed me in an icy gaze that set my stomach fluttering. Silence that would have sent me chattering a year ago was now answered with mere blank expression. Once I'd gotten her moving, I left Pila in the wagon and rode to the front, leading the yoked mules down the unpaved road with my horse into the night. Gannicus joined me and we spoke hushed beneath the stars. "Crastus, Vidovic, and the wayward Celts are dead," I told him, finally. I walked with the slow-moving train, hoping Gannicus was unable to see the tears running down my cheeks in the darkness. He made no comment and we rode in silence for miles.

### MARCUS CRASSUS OFFERS HIS BELLY

Marcus set camp uncomfortably close to the holed-up slaves, daring fugitives to attack, and thus demonstrating Roman power. Brazenly, the Imperator let his soldiers light fires and cook their meals, hoping the wind would carry smells of salted bacon and hard bread up to a starved enemy. Marcus meant for it to comfort his men, sending the unmistakable message: Marcus Crassus was in charge of southern Italy. Doctrine demanded Marcus build a camp and dig ditches for any charges the enemy may throw at night. The old commander had gotten a good feel for this enemy after chasing them the better part of a year, and knew he had no need to trench. Marcus had nipped at them, herded them, besieged them, and each time, they'd wriggled free—no more.

The Imperator indulged his men uncharacteristically with celebration; his soldiers had recovered three lost standards: the hallowed Roman *signum* and two of their sacred *fasces*. He allowed superfluidity, and they sang and danced around fires, worshiping the recovered holy symbols while lauding victory, dicing, and drinking. The Imperator knew it invited attack—exactly the message he intended.

## SPARTACUS BUYS TIME IN COUNTERFEIT CURRENCY

Spartacus may not have been hemmed in by cliffs with the sea at his back beneath ramparts, but he was besieged just the same. He had wanted to bring the fifteen thousand Celts and Germans back into the fold, but had managed to save so few. Spartacus knew how close disaster had neared in the last engagement, and how he flirted with losing everything today. It was going to be a long night, and from his vantage, with fires burning below, Spartacus watched Romans celebrate and feast within sight. Within his core, Spartacus knew the best move was to wager everything and charge down the mountain right now to surprise Romans in the dark. The smell of roasting meat and the sound of cheery Romans below made Spartacus do a cursory glance of his men's spirits; they were broken. Spartacus would let them sleep, after eating their meager rations; he'd try something new in the morning. As for now, his blood boiled. "Vitelli?" Spartacus asked the capable Italian bodyguard.

"Yes, commander?" the man responded.

"Find olive branch, yellow cloth...please," Spartacus ordered.

"Yes, lord," Vitelli responded, unquestioning, and went to retrieve those items.

# CHAPTER TWENTY-NINE

**"Accept his *fides*, a most beautiful dignity."**

**—Tacitus, *Annals***

The centurion, recently promoted to officer, knew better than to question his old commander, Rome's newly appointed Imperator. Atticus knew his old commander was taking a risk, but followed orders anyway. It was Crassus' neck ultimately on the line after all, and when Helios broke, Atticus fully expected to begin the chase once again. He was surprised instead to see two armored slaves, one waving a yellow rag and the other a bushy branch near the base of a hill. "What in Hades is that?" asked Atticus' centurion.

"Tell Marcus, the slaves wish to parley," ordered Atticus with the answer.

## SPARTACUS

Without any papyrus or his literate scout, Spartacus was forced to request *fides* verbally through a pair of lieutenants. He sent the Marius vet, who'd remained with the slaves after all, and an astute fieldhand to negotiate in his stead. The pair were trusted to convey a message from Spartacus. *Fides*, normally given to foreign armies in their homeland, required strict protocols and bestowed dignity on adversaries by giving them "protection" and forcing dependency. It would make Marcus Crassus Spartacus' patron, with all the protections therein. The Marius veteran held the yellow tunic tied to a stick. The field slave carried an olive branch; both walked their horses slowly to the midpoint between camps.

Two Romans did the same, walking horses out to meet a slave and an outlaw. "Spartacus wishes to end hostilities and negotiate a truce," said the Marian in perfect Latin. Atticus looked the man up and down from his mount.

"What's a Roman doing fighting for slaves?" Atticus asked.

"I don't fight for slaves; I fight for myself," said the Roman, indignant.

"Ah, a Marian Mule," Atticus surmised.

"A twist of fortunes and we'd be reversed," the man spoke. Atticus shrugged, acknowledging the truth of the outlaw's words.

"Does Sulla's dog really believe Marcus Crassus will accept such a bullshit treaty, especially since you're at the end of your road?" Atticus asked.

"I'm here on behalf of the commander to request terms. What I believe is irrelevant," said the plainspoken soldier. Atticus turned to the centurion mounted beside him.

"Leave us," Atticus told his companion. The other man balked. "Now!" Atticus snapped. When the Roman had gone, Atticus Fabius sat opposite the two men, outnumbered. The former slave looked confused and sat waiting, ready for whatever was next. "Before I tell you what I've been sent to say, let me tell you what I suggest," Atticus told the Roman outlaw. "Cornelius Sulla is dead. So are his grudges. Come with me right now, tell us what the slaves are planning, and I'll vouch for you." He tilted his head, waiting for the response. Vitelli sat mounted next to the outlawed Roman and looked uncomfortably at his companion, ready to kill everyone right then.

"There'll be no pardon, so let's not waste any more time," answered the Marian curtly. "Will he take our commander in *fides,* or not?" Two of the three men knew they engaged in formalities without resolution. Atticus raised his brows, resolved, and sighed.

"Pompey returns," revealed Atticus. "He's already on this side of the Alps with four legions of Iberians, Lusitanians, and Spaniards, all hungry for citizenship. As we speak," he continued, "Lucullus lands in Brundisium with his legions, fresh from destroying your gladiator's home." He paused, letting the news sink into the man and his companion. Atticus, a man of principle, turned his horse at the man's crestfallen expression. He rescinded the offer with his back without asking twice, refusing to convey any pointless messages from Marcus Crassus by walking his horse away.

### BITTER PEACE

The slave army, bitter and on the verge of mutiny, resented the commander for offering surrender terms. In reality, Spartacus sent the two volunteers to stall, frustrate, and confuse the enemy while the rest of the army of slaves slipped away even further to the other side of a mountain. Spartacus knew the offer of dignity from a slave would be repugnant to a Roman and would be refused—it worked. He had slipped an unwitting and unwilling slave army out of the noose once again. Spartacus had done it: a useless stunt had fooled the most powerful man in Rome to inaction.

### MARCUS CRASSUS REORGANIZES

The following day, Marcus sent Scrofa and Quinctius to pursue the giant army of slaves and nip at their heels until he could trap them once again. They were instructed to keep an eye on the slaves and keep them from foraging Lucania. The Imperator then sent Pomptinus and Rufus onto Aquitania. They were to block the slaves from using the Appian Way and keep them from threatening Rome. Marcus and Atticus would take the *Via Popitian* directly to the city of Nola, which was still recovering from last year's devastation. There they'd meet Merillius with a supply train to retrieve necessities for ending the war before his rivals Pompey or Lucullus could steal it. The Imperator had ordered fifty barrels of acorns and fifty thousand arrows to stop the slaves' cavalry. The weapons included five brand-new scorpions, along with the heavy iron shafts they threw. Food, shields, horses, and mules would supply new recruits. Pots of pitch, lamp oil to set arrows aflame, and fodder to keep the horses' strength would help the army crush this slave rebellion once and for all. No more chances. Marcus wouldn't be robbed like his father had by weasels from the capitol at the last hour. The spirit of his men rode a never-before high and Marcus Crassus the Imperator intended to capitalize on it before the sands ran out.

## PUBLIPOR

Our survivors embraced once reunited in Venusia, beneath the shadow of Mount Vultur. The Appian Way was within reach, and once on it, we'd make incredible speed south to Brundisium. Helica foretold my child's birth sometime in *Aprilis*, next month, if everything went right. Current events kept my focus elsewhere, but once in a while, I'd allow myself the luxury of dreaming about teaching my boy how to read, write, and ride.

"Hard time, for new mother," understated Spartacus. Helica stood behind him with a face full of sadness.

"They are, but Pila is made of tough stuff," I told him, reassuring myself.

"I have troubling news and there's no way to soften it, Publipor," Helica spoke.

"Is Pila all right?" I asked Helica fearfully.

"As far as I can tell, Pila and the child are healthy as horses," Helica answered. I looked at the commander, confused.

"Plan for Brundisium," explained Spartacus.

"What of it?" I asked.

"Roman General, Lucius Lucullus, land in Brundisium, he devastate our people," replied Spartacus. Helica spat on the ground, cursing in her native tongue at his name.

"Can we whip him?" I asked.

"Sure would like to," Spartacus softened, chuckling. "Can't shake Marcus Crassus, do so take too long."

"Can we try again for the Alps?" I asked, hopeful.

"No amount of swaddling would keep an infant from freezing in that pass by the time we got there," Helica answered for the commander.

"The Butcher Boy, ride south, as we speak," added the commander. Despair and dread filled my spirit from everything I'd heard of the man known to the world as Pompey the Great.

*Why are the two people I've given my life to crushing me?* I thought. "Pompey?" I spoke the dreaded name aloud.

"The same," Spartacus answered. Helica spat at the ground again. Stepping from behind Spartacus, she grasped my chin, forcing me to stare once more into her haunting blue eyes.

"You must be strong for the girl and the child," Helica instructed. "You'll be the one who has to tell her this news, young man." My mind remembered when the retired soldiers had me in their clutches and the feelings at that time. Every scenario ran to a dead end; all my ideas concluded with me on a cross, Pila in chains, and the baby boy on a rubbish heap, or worse.

"What are we to do?" I asked, desperate for answers.

"Every journey is one foot stepping after another," Helica spoke to me. "Soon, we'll know the answer to prophesy." For the first time—only for a moment—I hated the woman. *This is how she'll determine if Spartacus' power is lucky?* I thought, angry.

"We fall back, Urium Bay, on spur, beneath Mount Garganos, buy ride there," Spartacus said, attempting to reassure me. It didn't work. I was sixteen years old now and far too savvy to fall for lies anymore. I'd made the trip twice already; I knew how long it took. Pila would give birth before then and even I knew she wouldn't be able to survive all of that.

"Yes, lord," I answered, knowing then that Pila and I were on our own.

### SOMETHING COMPLETELY DIFFERENT

Scrofa and Quinctius divided their forces to cover more ground. Each had scouts scouring Magna Graecia in search of the slave army. Their scout could have told them if he weren't dead. My bolt broke off inside the Roman, rendering it useless. The scout's absence at muster later would tell them the vicinity of where he was harvested. I kept his food, money, and fine new bow, including the straight new arrows, stripping him of everything before leaving him for the birds without a moment's pause. I gave the arms and armor to a new young slave, who proceeded to not shut up or leave me alone, until I told him to get lost before I took it all back and gave it to someone more deserving.

"We have to escape," I said to my wife that night in our tent. Pila struggled to a knee, holding her swollen belly, trying to lie down.

"I thought that's what we were doing, husband," she said as if I were joking.

"This army's going to get us killed, Pila," I said earnestly, lying on my back and staring at the roof, waiting for her to get settled for sleep.

"No one can outride you, you're invisible, and no one's a better shot," she said, repeating the bullshit I'd sold her to keep her from worrying whenever I had to leave. I turned my head to look at her.

"I'm serious, Pila. I've got to get you to the grotto Crastus found, so you have somewhere safe to have the baby in *Aprilis.*" Pila's normally trusting, sweet face turned intent as we spoke by lamplight. I told her of Pompey crossing the Rubicon with his army intact and of Lucullus landing on the east coast. I described the machines I'd seen drawn by teams of mules and the size of Marcus' army. Pila grasped my hand to feel my son kick, trying to escape.

"Seems everyone," said Pila, "is trying to get out." She laughed desperately. I joined her out of absurdity, and we soon fell asleep. That night, I dreamt of three naked criminals hanging from crosses. At first, in the fog of dreams, my fear was that it was Pila, our child, and me. Closer inspection revealed it wasn't; the two men on the edges were dead, their legs broken at the shins. The man in the center labored for breath, unbroken. His face was an indistinguishable pulp. A cloaked woman wept before me beneath the beam. I couldn't make out the condemned man's face and moved closer to see a crown of thistle stuck upon his head. The shrouded woman grabbed my garment when I attempted to pass. I peered down to see a face of green with a two-pronged crown. Revulsion turned my gaze away to look once more at the criminal nailed to the post. His eyes opened, fixed upon me. The condemned opened his mouth. "It is done," he croaked, to a terrible tearing and wrenching of the air; the ground shook me awake.

The next morning, I slouched while mounted, watching the wide, stone Roman bridge of Aufidus spanning a swollen and raging river from the tree line's shadows. Apulia lay on the other side, along with a camped Roman legion.

"Is there another way across?" asked Gannicus. I shook my head, turning the horse to warn my commander. I halted the beast, giving the man my profile so that he could hear me.

"Even if there was, there would be nowhere to go." Gannicus peered earthward, mute as Va with sad understanding for a time.

"Everyone's time on Earth is borrowed," Gannicus attempted perspective.

"Why then, do they spend all theirs, trying to kill me and mine?" I gave him my back.

I knew the man who knew most things couldn't answer without taking most the day, so I heeled the pony forward to find Pila. *If time is on loan, then I'll be spending all mine with my sweet Samnite, lovely Pila, my little spear,* I resolved. Choosing the company of my bride over listening to the tired platitudes of old men.

### SPARTACUS CONTEMPLATES FATE

Spartacus scratched his chin, tired of the constant eye from Roman cavalry. They'd gotten too comfortable by approaching so close, and showed disrespect by flaunting a lack of fear. Spartacus wanted to remind them why his men still had five eagle standards, with Roman *fasces* currently in his possession. He wanted to show the new men he'd recruited why they'd made the right choice of throwing off chains to join the revolt. Spartacus needed to boost the defeated, demoralized men with a victory, so he decided to remind them why Rome trembled when his slave army approached.

### SCROFA SCRATCHES HIS HEAD

Scrofa scolded the young captain with curses, tired of excuses. The captain's scouts kept disappearing with unnerving frequency. Why young men would desert when things were finally going their way escaped his logic. "Pull some boys from the light infantry and give them mounts," Scrofa ordered the lead scout. "We need to know where this scum is hiding."

### QUINCTIUS COMMITS TO SNATCH AND GRAB

The Roman cavalry officer, Quinctius, caught a glimpse of a youthful horseman before he bolted out of sight down one of the rolling hills littering the area. "Let's grab him alive and squeeze him," Quinctius suggested. They kicked their horses after the scrawny little scout to capture him. Scrofa had his infantry give chase on foot at double time. Quinctius topped the hill with his horsemen and saw the rider stopped in the valley below, daring men to give chase. The fugitive kicked his mount again with Romans hot on his heels. "Does this slave really believe we can't catch him?" Quinctius called to men rhetorically.

Quinctius' mount tripped and rolled atop of him in full gallop. When the horse finally rolled off, five arrows were sunk in the animal's flesh. It bucked and kicked, neighing in pain to run off and bleed to death somewhere out of sight. Quinctius felt teeth-gnashing pain the moment he tried to rise. As the dust settled, horses and men lay about, dead and dying. Men groaned and horses whinnied, sprouting arrows in the narrow pass.

### SPARTACUS

Spartacus had men run down to dispatch them; Quinctius' throat was opened while crawling on elbows attempting escape.

"Back up!" yelled the Marian. "Let's show these suckers not to leap before looking, boys!"

### SCROFA STUMBLES

Scrofa kept his horse at a two-gate trot behind his men, who jogged his infantry in the valley trying to catch Quinctius' cavalry. Scrofa barely had enough time to reign the animal in when the line of men suddenly stopped. Roman dead littered the trail.

"Ambush!" yelled the *optio*, barely sheltering beneath shields in time before arrows rained upon him and his companions.

Scrofa caught one with his shoulder and another with his calf before the horse threw him.

"Wall!" screamed Scrofa's centurion when he saw slaves baring down on his men. Scrofa was dragged beneath the men's shields as they attempted to save their officer.

"Javelins!" screamed a man from habit, too late; the time to repel adversaries with missiles expired with sounds of cracking birch plywood *scutums*. Stabbing commenced with grunts and curses as men tried desperately to bite each other with iron.

## SPARTACUS IS LEERY

Spartacus watched from his vantage atop the hill, keeping most of his army in reserve. The men begged to go down and join the slaughter. The commander forbade them just in case there were more Romans nearby that he didn't know about. Spartacus nodded to his bugler, who sounded a retreat. The men waiting in the line below looked up at their commander with contempt, not understanding why they'd been called off.

"Why release them, sir?" I asked, confused and mounted beside my commander.

"Outnumbered here. You locate *other* legion?" asked Spartacus contentiously. Shaking my head, I answered, conceding that I hadn't. "Then how know slave not get ambush next?"

"I don't," I confessed.

"To camp!" Spartacus ordered. The surviving exhausted and beaten Romans thanked their stars to be released, remaining in formation as slaves backed away angrily. One slave spat a copious amount of phlegm at the enemy that landed on the huge, curved shield, showing his contempt. The army of slaves disappeared as quickly as it had appeared. Roman orderlies tended to the wounded once it was apparent that the slaves had gone, beginning first with the officer Scrofa, who winced and grimaced from forceps stanching wounds. Though Scrofa survived Quinctius, neither would return to war ever again.

A SLAVE CAMP GRUMBLES IN 684 AUC (71 BC).

At camp, I looked around and saw nothing but scowls and heard every sort of grumbling. We'd run nearly three years, declined escape, and been double-crossed by partners. We'd destroyed every army Rome had sent to kill us and narrowly avoided destruction on the beach. Spartacus had no more loyal soldier than I, but even I felt discouraged.

The bridge of Aufidus may as well have been the Strait of Messina for all intents and purposes. Marcus Crassus had Rufus and Pomptinus' legions blocking it, almost as if he knew we were desperate to get at the sea again. It was just a matter of time before Lucullus marched his men up the Appian Way and shut that door forever as well. Soon, Pompey's Spanish hammer would crush from the north, and everyone felt it looming over their heads. Spartacus had everyone muster to discuss our options. No one was forbidden from speaking and everyone was encouraged to throw options on the table. Quickly, it descended into chaos as threats were hurled and curses spat. Two fistfights erupted, and a man was stabbed. Spartacus brought the discussion to a halt.

"We go north, find route to bay," he ordered, pulling Lightning and daring anyone to challenge his authority in single combat. Men went to tents grumbling, finding courage alone and threatening reprisal once out of earshot.

It had to be fifty miles south to the little grotto beside the freshwater spring, a concealed alcove beneath a small fall that made enough noise to drown out a screaming girl and a squalling baby. It was the perfect place to hide Pila and the child from the elements and men, and it made me sick that we were headed in the opposite direction.

The men moved as if dragging a pirate's anchor. We didn't get far before Spartacus began shouting at his lieutenants to get lead out of the men's asses. Getting nowhere, Spartacus finally stopped the caravan.

"You! Want fight?" asked Spartacus, shouting at men on the left in his war voice. "You! Want fight?" he shouted to the column on the right; both sides roared. "We fight!" he ordered, pulling Lighting, the angriest I'd ever seen him. The calm, unflappable man had been replaced with something terrifying. His eyes burned with hate, his face a mask of rage.

"Scouts!" he snarled. I ran toward this stranger with Gannicus, frightened.

"Yes, lord?" I asked. Spartacus pointed to Gannicus.

"You, take men, go bridge, watch legions, report if Roman move," ordered the commander.

"Yes, commander," said Gannicus from his pony before riding off.

"You," Spartacus seethed, pointing at me. "Find Marcus Crassus, tell me where the Roman is," ordered the stranger in my lord's skin.

"Yes, lord," I said, and rode off. The mob that'd been the army of slaves was over the moon, cheering with satisfaction. I detoured quickly to the baggage area to find my pregnant wife.

"Gather the medicines and everything else Helica gave you for childbirth," I told her. "Wrap them in a blanket and be ready to take them with you when I return." Pila nodded. I told her that I loved her and rode away to find our enemy.

## MARCUS CRASSUS

Marcus could not believe his orders had been disobeyed again. The men, thankful they hadn't been completely wiped out by slaves, carried Scrofa back on a shield. When the soldiers brought him past, Marcus asked why they'd engaged against his orders. Scrofa was sweating and babbling incoherently but had enough wits to pass the blame to Quinctius. "The cavalry, they...we had to...support them..." mumbled Scrofa, fevered.

"Well, he's been punished," Atticus Fabius added smartly as orderlies carried Scrofa away. Marcus shot an unamused glare at his officer. "You heard him—it's the dead guy's fault," Atticus joked, unable to help himself. The Roman commander gave the man his back, while Merillius curled his lip at the impetuous plebian, following his former master into the command tent. Merillius reappeared moments later, sticking his head from the tent's flap with new orders for the pain-in-the-ass, recently promoted officer.

"Have mules hitched to the scorpions. Break camp, muster your men, and be ready to move east in an hour," ordered the Greek freedman for his former master.

"Yes, sir," Atticus snapped, pounding his chest, saluting sarcastically to the freed slave.

## PUBLIPOR

Forty thousand men are easy to find, especially when they're on the move. Birds circle when large forces assemble, plus that many men kick up huge clouds of dust. Once a force that size commits to a heading, it takes a lot to change it. Before returning to tell the commander our enemy's location, I took a short detour a few miles south, taking mental notes of the most prominent landmarks. The poor colt was ridden harder than he should've to make up time and I had to replace him when I arrived. "They drive north, at Potentia," I told the commander. I hadn't actually seen them take the road, but it was the only direction they could go. *They have eyes on us and wouldn't have gone south,* I thought, remembering that the road only turns north at the Casuentus

River. I'd been doing this long enough to know that armies don't swim across rivers or climb mountains if they don't have to. At the risk of my neck, I stuck it out now for my pregnant wife, telling the commander my hunch as fact.

Spartacus looked at me from the back of his huge black stallion for a moment. My stomach danced as he sat silent for a long time, and I feared he could read my lie. "Very well. Fear Roman, caught you, took long," he said, finally. "Glad you safe. Get food, check woman, fix horse, tell what you know when done."

"Yes, lord," I said, handing my reins to a boy. I found Pila showing a small girl holding a doll how to skin rabbits and prepare stew. I was apprehensive speaking in front of the girl until Pila spoke to me in Oscan.

"She doesn't speak our language, husband," said Pila, chopping carrots. "Tell me what you've found." I explained the distance, time, and landmarks to reach the grotto.

"You won't be able to ride there in your condition; we'll need to steal a cart," I said, trying to work out the particulars. Pila could walk a pony with me by its side, but at terrible risk. If the animal gave us any trouble, it could kill the baby. My mind spun with ideas and scenarios that would allow Pila to drive the hospital wagon off by herself. Pila had to get alone—groups brought attention and death.

"I remember the place and I'll find a way," said my clever, pregnant wife confidently in Oscan. "Go help the commander," Pila spoke, then switched to Latin, "figure out how to kill these Romans...and don't be late for supper." The little girl washing potatoes smiled, understanding the last part of our conversation.

### SPARTACUS CHOOSES THE PLACE

"Gannicus says, there is place west of here, advantage for slaves," said Spartacus to his lieutenants and scouts.

Twenty miles west of Mt. Vultur, just inside the southern border of Samnium, in the valley of Oliveto Citra, we prepared for Marcus Crassus' forces. Spartacus saw the valley as a place to keep the numerically superior Romans from outflanking his infantry, conceding it would constrict our cavalry to a head-on charge. Facing south, the plain dropped in gradual decline to our favor. On the right stood sheer cliffs where the Picentini Mountain range began, the Ogna Ridge blocking our left. The natural features would funnel both armies into the valley, keeping each from outflanking the other. Arriving first, Spartacus chose the spot for our clash after riding Pegasus up a small rise to survey.

### MARCUS CRASSUS ACCEPTS

Marcus' scouts informed him the slaves had stopped running and pitched camp in a valley just past the Fount of Bandusia, a natural hot spring that belched sulfur. Marcus brought a *flamen*, the priest of Mars, from Rome, for the men who assured the commander that the smell was a good omen. The priest explained the scent meant the underworld was near and it'd swallow the enemy whole. "Save that crap for the superstitious plebs," admonished Marcus, turning to Atticus. "Go with the scouts and see if this is a place we can win."

"Sir," Atticus responded, pounding his chest twice.

### HELICA SHOWS THE WAY

I rode alongside the baggage train with Helica. Pila reclined in the back with a wool blanket spread over straw while holding her swollen stomach.

"Publipor?" Helica asked from the driver's seat.

"Yes, lady?" I answered, my mind consumed on the problem at hand.

"Pila has no business going to war in her condition,"

commented Helica, halting the cart. I reined to a stop next to her.

"No, lady," I acknowledged.

"Do you know what day it is?" Helica asked.

"No, lady."

"It's the first day of Aprilis, and your wife will birth a child in spring beneath the goddess Venus any day now, and that is a very good thing," she said. Helica still thought of me as the boy she rescued three years ago, and not the man I'd become; I let her.

"Yes, lady," I answered.

"Let's trade rides," commented Helica. "The commander won't need the hospital litter any longer."

"Lady?" I asked, confused.

"Take the girl," Helica commanded. "Find a place to stash her. I don't want to know where you're going; just do it fast and return. The commander will need you soon." Relieved, feeling shame and gratitude at once, my eyes began watering. "No time for that, you'll need to hurry. Let me have your horse," Helica ordered, setting the brake to climb from the driver's seat. I dismounted and reached for Helica's burlap sack beneath the driver's bench. "No!" Helica exclaimed, quickly regaining her composure. "I'll handle that," she said, suddenly calm. We exchanged our things. Helica kissed me on the forehead as I helped her mount. "I'll tell the commander you went to hide the girl. Just be sure to return." She dropped her haunting gaze. "You never know; you might be the difference between victory or defeat." Turning to my wife, she said, "Pila, remember everything I told you, when the pains come quickly." Pila nodded.

"We will, lady," I reassured, and Helica rode off with the caravan.

"*Vala*," said a little girl who'd washed potatoes, waving and holding Pila's doll in a passing wagon. I turned our mules south, wondering how in Hades I'd get a dual-yoked wagon with a pregnant woman south past legions of men and scouts.

## SPARTACUS SURVEYS THE BATTLEFIELD, 684 AUC (71 BC)

"What do you think, commander?" Gannicus asked.

"We have slope, not steep enough to matter, though," commented Spartacus. "Publipor say Roman strength, fifty thousand. Outnumber us by ten thousand." The two sat mounted next to one another, old friends from the *ludis* surveying a prospective battlefield together as carrion birds circled in the distance, betraying both armies.

"Publipor says they have five scorpions," Gannicus added. Spartacus grunted acknowledgement.

"Cannot flank with horse. Both walls, make this fight, a slog," Spartacus reasoned. "Only chance against engine, is grab tight, keep close. Roman must kill both, soldier and slave, to use," he concluded. Gannicus nodded agreement. Spartacus turned his head to look Gannicus in the eye. "No more trick in bag. We win, or we lose, right here."

# CHAPTER THIRTY

"...They fought, *sine missone*: 'to the death.'"

—Plutarch, *The War Against Spartacus*

Using the Mountain Balabo as a reference, Pila and I rode south into Lucania. I stayed off the road and beat my poor wife with the rough cattle trail as she lay in the cart's rear, miserable. I prayed the wheels would stay on just a little longer. It was less difficult to avoid Marcus Crassus' men than I'd thought; I just gave the birds overhead and dust on the horizon a wide berth, but stayed ever vigilant for prying eyes as paranoia got the best of me a few times. I'd stop the wagon, grab my bow up in the seat, and notch an arrow, ready to pull on a moment's notice. It happened enough times that Pila stopped taking notice and just enjoyed the moment's respite. Thankfully, we made it to the grotto before nightfall. I helped my pregnant wife climb the steep trail down into our sanctuary to a path that allowed one to get beneath the falls without passing through it. It took many trips to unload the wagon and set her things out the way she asked. Fatigue began to set in on the last trip load of bundled straw as I spread it out for my woman to lay. I spread the giant woolen blanket over dry bedding, then helped my burdened wife lay upon it. Pila wriggled her fingers at a small blanket balled upon the grotto's floor nearby when she'd settled. The blanket contained Helica's surgical bag and I'd made the mistake of glancing at its contents while in transit. My stomach tingled at the sight of sharp scissors wrapped in so much raw cotton when I set it on my makeshift table near Pila's bed. I'd been responsible for animals my entire life; I knew what the scissors would be used for. I'd fought many battles, seen many injuries; I knew that raw cotton staunched bleeding best. Daring not a second look within the blanket's ghastliness, I crossed the cave to Pila. It wasn't the "what" of these things that disturbed me, it was the "who" they would be used on that caused me distress. After making Pila comfortable, I lay down next to her and slept the sleep of the dead. The next morning, on the last trip up to the wagon, terror gripped me when I heard a horse whinny. Mules didn't make that noise. I pulled my sword and peeked over the ridge. "I'll be damned," I said aloud in disbelief.

Dummy the black pony craned his neck from the back of the wagon, trying to rob my hanging kit bag. Dummy's head followed his ears and he snorted when he saw me. Holding up empty hands for the animal to see, I walked nonthreateningly toward him. "Hi, little Dummy. How have you been?" I sang. "Are you looking for a treat?" I spoke softly, getting ever closer. "You alone, Dummy?" I asked, walking almost close enough to touch him. The shaggy pony's body language said his stomach was fighting the urge to run. "Here, Dummy, look what I have," I spoke softly to him, reaching slowly for my bag atop the rope. With one hand moving carefully, I reached and pulled a bit of produce for him. Dummy nuzzled the turnip from my hand and began munching. I had a firm grip on the rope and quickly looped it around his neck, fully expecting to be pulled for a ride. Dummy took no notice, nudging my chest instead, demanding more food—just like Useless had. I tied him to the wagon, scratched his neck, and left him content before returning to my wife.

I built her a fire, stacked piles of wood nearby, and set the kettle, then filled two buckets with water and made her promise not to have the child until I returned.

*"Vala,"* she said instead, making no promises with just a kiss goodbye. The thought of abandoning the army crossed my mind, and with a heavy heart, I climbed from Pila's grotto. The mule team headed north once more, pulling a greedy little pony named Dummy. Lelu's words floated in my head, *"This pony go, where the horse can't...you'll see,"* and I knew then how I'd get back to my side of the lines.

## MARCUS CRASSUS

Marcus stood with Merillius and Atticus, considering his options. "They have the slope," said Merillius, pointing out the obvious.

"It's not steep enough to make any difference," Atticus remarked, pointing at the natural barriers on each side of the valley. "Sulla's hound won't be able to pull any tricks from those heights." Marcus Crassus' keen eye saw it as well: Spartacus' advantage had always been cavalry, and here in the valley with sheer cliffs on both sides, they'd be no use. "It'll be a slugfest," Atticus interrupted Marcus' thoughts, describing the coming battle in simple soldier's parlance.

"A real Thermopylae," the Greek commented nostalgically of his ancestors' plight.

Marcus looked at the scorpions unhitched behind him and patted the letter in his pocket, reminding him that Pompey was on his way to rob the Imperator of glory.

"Pitch camp under his nose. Start digging there, after Helios goes down," he ordered, pointing to his surviving officers Atticus, Rufus, and Pomptinus.

## SPARTACUS

Our commander had the last of the wine brought to a hill and decanted for the men. Spartacus let them drink while they performed their religious rituals. Women dressed men for war in stolen and dented armor as children played all about. Men slipped into mail or scale, tightening buckles and tying leather laces to the sounds of flint stones scraping iron and women's songs. It was too late to start the engagement; neither side wanted a fight this close in numbers to be a toss-up in the dark. Spartacus had chosen a spot where the sun would rise on the left and set on the right, without advantage for either army.

### PUBLIPOR SLIPS PAST MARCUS CRASSUS

Dusk settled and the smell of rotten eggs wafted through the breeze; I was very close. Birds descended to roost with the prospect of a feast on the morrow. I watched the back of a massive Roman army preparing for war. Up the gentle rise beyond them, my army began lighting fires, preparing for the night. I gathered my things, set the mules loose, and mounted Dummy for an evening climb.

### SLAVES PREP FOR THE WAR OF 684 (71 BC)

In the morning, men woke dressed in armor and started drinking for courage. The sun broke over the Ogna Ridges, lighting the battlefield in morning magic; a garden of rainbows glinted from dew beneath a carpet of wildflowers painting the field below. Spartacus mustered his infantry and roused the cavalry mounted behind them. "About time. Thought you, never show," joked Spartacus, winking at me when I came rushing through the throng. "Bring Peg," instructed Spartacus, using his loving pet name for the huge stallion, Pegasus. "Run, no more," Spartacus spoke, and silent men strained to hear every word from the famous former gladiator dressed for war. Helica had cut Spartacus' hair short and shaved him Roman fashion the night before. The scars on Spartacus' jaw jumped, grasping the eye as he spoke, and in the presence of such terrible damage, Spartacus seemed more godlike than ever. He held Lightning, the huge, polished double-edged blade, forged from the mysterious steel of Parthia, glinting in morning light. Gannicus walked Pegasus through the throng, handing Spartacus the bridle. The priceless black stallion's coat glistened in the morning light, muscles apparent with each step, and standing every bit of seventeen hands while dipping his massive head. The eight-year-old stallion smelled trouble, pawed the ground, and snorted. The animal checked his head up and down when war drums pounded from Romans in the valley below. Spartacus soothed the animal.

### ROMANS COMMENCE

"Begin," ordered Marcus Crassus once he'd mounted and gathered reins. Pomptinus nodded to his *optio*, the centurion then waved for a drummer to commence. Roman soldiers stood in a line, waiting one by one for orderlies to remove the leather covers from their *scutums*, the curved, oblong infantry shields. Roman breastplates gleamed from polish, along with shiny bronze helmets, in the morning light. Spit and polish, three rows thick and a mile long, lined the entire valley behind razor-sharp iron. Drums pounded and horns blew, signaling Romans to begin the methodical march to the enemy, left foot first.

### SLAVES RESPOND

Everyone's focus returned to the commander, treating the sound from Romans as an annoyance. Helica sidled beside me and began checking my armor while blessing me as her husband roused the troops.

"Polished tin, fool not," spoke Spartacus. "That shit show benefit only to Roman," Spartacus mused, pointing to new equipment marching toward the poor slaves. "Behind covering, is flesh, who know slave all too well," Spartacus continued with a clenched fist. "Promise, Roman fear slave, more than slave, fear Roman." He paused to let that sink in. "Roman, puffed bird, fly the moment, slave break Roman covey. Roman head, sit mounted, ready for flight," Spartacus mocked. Nervous men chuckled. Spartacus' speech built a coiling tension with his voice, like a professional showman of the arena.

Spartacus pointed to young men assigned to carry the captured *signums*; all the Roman standards with the silver eagles and disks were quickly raised on high to face the Romans in a gesture of the ultimate "Fuck you." My hair stood on end, electric, as I waited for lightning to erupt from the man. "Today, I fight, in infantry. If I ride, from this field," Spartacus pointed at the ground, "may it be over dead Roman!" Men screamed approval, instantly raucous, as the Romans advanced methodically below to drum and horn. Spartacus knew intimately the customs and traditions of all his men, and so, with a single thrust, he sank the enormous blade into his stallion's jugular furrow, all the way to Lightning's hilt. Blood jettisoned onto him and the men nearest.

"No one leave this valley, without victory!" roared Spartacus. Men went war-mad at the gesture, shouting fealty with their lives at the sacrifice of such wealth. The great stallion slumped in a mass of flesh, instantly dispatched with a single spasm. Infantrymen dipped their hands into the animal's dark red blood, marking their faces. Caught up, I did the same, unable to stop myself, lost in the moment. "Make engine useless!" ordered Spartacus. "Grab quick, grab tight, do not let go, until it is dead!" he shouted, pointing Lightning downfield, ordering his men to charge. Forty thousand men began jogging down the gentle slope, saving themselves like battle-hardened professionals for the bloody fifty-yard sprint to come. Men steeled themselves betting fortune would keep them from catching any of the bolts forecasted to fly soon. Experience taught men when falling shafts are imminent and quicken their pace to blunt the onslaught. That's when combatants trade harassing bolts for proximity. Our horses galloped full tilt toward our enemy, we chased after them when noise and shadow enveloped the sky. Everyone screamed for blood over drum and horn, and the noise was deafening.

### ROMANS BLINK

"Son of a bitch," said Pomptinus to himself when he heard the thunderclap and saw the behemoth loping toward them.

"Halt!" Atticus Fabius yelled from his point on the line at its center. Soldiers stopped to slam shields into earth. "Load!" Atticus shouted at the scorpion's operators and "Nock!" at his archers. "Wait, gods damn it, wait!" he ordered, shouting as the enemy cavalry closed, riding down hard on them.

On Atticus' left, Rufus struggled for courage; his eyes opened the size of serving dishes. Rufus froze, desperately waiting for Atticus to give the order to loose, wondering why in Jupiter's name the old centurion waited.

### THE IMPERATOR

Marcus Crassus sat mounted in the center of it all, watching the slaves close. He'd been here before, but it still wracked his nerves. Marcus had given operational control to his trusted old centurion—the man he had personally promoted to officer—Atticus Fabius Dominicus. On the right, Pomptinus was certain Marcus Crassus' pet would get them all killed, waiting so long. Pomptinus smiled when things changed before his very fearful eyes.

### THE OUTSET

We ran at the enemy, headlong after the cavalry, cursing, screaming, and swearing for a lifetime of revenge. Suddenly, our horses dipped, I watched men thrown into the air as our mounts fell upon the covered ditch, crashing violently and upending unsuspecting horsemen before me.

### PREPARATIONS UNLEASHED

"Loose!" Atticus shouted, and the deafening slap of cord hurling four iron bolts simultaneously skyward slammed the machine's mechanism with a bang. The five other siege engines, also slamming, wracked the battlefield. The sky darkened beneath a cloud of bolts flying to predetermined locations in the ditch. "Load!" Atticus screamed, unfazed by the momentary momentum shift, knowing from experience: not one volley does victory make.

### PUBLIPOR SINKS

The huge iron rods flew inhumanly at distressed cavalry. Like a spectator, I watched them descend. I saw Egus, a man beloved by everyone, as he was run through by one of the projectiles and pinned to his horse by the vicious bolt. Watching the horse crash with Egus attached was too terrible to witness. The shock of such a sight didn't seem earthly possible, yet there it was, and just when I thought I'd seen everything, a patch of goose-feather weeds sprouted over everyone. Men and horses crawled, hobbled, bucked, and kicked for safety, screaming in agony from bolts piercing them all over. The infantry slowed and quieted, registering the horror before them.

"Charge, don't stop!" shouted the God of War, as if from the heavens. Spartacus commanded my feet, and I began running before I realized it was him who ordered us onward. I heard a man scream in pain across the field as I put the shield over my head, instinctually copying my commander.

"Loose!" I'd heard their officer order. It was the same man who'd tried to trample me with his horse in Glaber's camp three years prior. Again, the thud of scorpions filled the valley, along with sinew slapping hundreds of arm guards.

My forearm was pierced slightly behind the shield's handle when a bolt barely penetrated my cover. I continued to carry my shield overhead, protecting myself from the deadly rain of arrows landing everywhere. I stumbled when my feet found the ditch uncovered by our cavalry, but somehow continued upright through the bramble of arrows. I ran, doing so because everyone else around me ran and not from any rational reasoning. An iron pole like the one Egus had caught with his horse landed very close, planting itself inches from me; I felt the percussion in my sandals in the madness of the moment. I thought it odd that someone would plant a *signum,* the legion's standard, there—it took a moment to realize how closely disaster visited. My feet continued.

### ATTICUS WADES INTO THE FRAY

"Charge!" ordered the only Roman officer still in command of his faculties. Atticus kicked a man in the ass to get everyone moving. "Get a hold of your shit!" Atticus Fabius yelled at his centurion. "CHARGE, you yellow bastards!" he screamed down the left at Pomptinus. "What are you waiting for?" Atticus hollered at Rufus, to his right. Marcus Crassus, watching from the rear, remembered why he'd promoted the man, while Merillius forgave all the man's crassness in that moment.

### THE COMMANDER

"Quick!" shouted Spartacus. "Charge hard, close gap!" he screamed, with both hands holding the shield, leaning into it with his shoulder as he ran. Everyone followed his example; I lowered my shield like the commander, trying to put every bit of my one-hundred-and-some-odd pounds behind it while cursing the Romans.

"Throw!" ordered officers when the slaves were within fifty feet. Practiced men hurled long javelins high at the onslaught. "Go!" centurions ordered, and legionaries lifted their shields and began running to blunt the crashing wave of Gauls about to break on them.

### THE WITNESS

The sound of colliding shields filled the valley below, heard all the way up to where Helica watched from a newly acquired wagon parked at the top's rise. The sorceress sat on the bench with a garden snake slithering behind her neck and a burlap bag writhing in her lap.

### PUBLIPOR SINKS FURTHER

Someone caught a pilum just a few men down from me; he fell from its force so quickly that he disappeared. One second the line was full, the next there was a gap, like the world opened and men fell into Hades. I kept running until I slammed into a wall—my face bounced from behind the shield, my helmet went askew. Ringing filled my ears and I thought my breath was gone. The terror of falling onto my back was averted when shields slammed from behind. Sandwiched between boards, I thought I'd suffocate until the men behind relented; I gasped for air. A blade slipped inches from my eyes. I studied it in the place where time stands still, then watched it disappear behind the shields before realizing it had tried to stab me. I pulled my sword and tried to stab him back; the otherworldly ringing in my ears began to be replaced by shouts and grunts of men laboring to kill one another. Losing track of time that felt like forever, my arms began to burn, and I became short of breath. I resolved myself with the distinct possibility that I'd never see my unborn son or newly wedded wife again when the man nearest screamed, "Relief!" A man stepped forward to replace him, fitting his shield into mine.

"Relief!" I screamed after I learned that was even a thing. The man behind jockeyed into my former place as I staggered behind the third line of men only to be spun around, facing a boy.

"Water or wine?" the boy asked.

"Water," I croaked without thinking. The boy lifted a bladder to my mouth; the refreshing liquid poured and I gulped it greedily. The boy moved down the row quickly before I'd had enough. I fell to a knee, exhausted. Behind me, the world buzzed like an angry wasp's nest as I lusted for more water. A hammer pounded my helmet—it was Spartacus' *Optio Primo*, Vitelli. He stood angrily before me.

"Get back in line, you lazy shit, and prepare to relieve your man!" shouted the normally quiet slave centurion, pointing his Spanish sword at my neck. With flagging strength, I shuffled to stand behind the third row with a shield hanging off me, hoping the two men ahead were vigorously fit and long on endurance.

### PILA FIGHTS FOR LIFE, 684 AUC (71 BC).

Hidden somewhere in the fern-covered recesses of a freshwater grotto, behind a waterfall curtain, the pregnant woman readied herself for the fight of her life—alone.

### PUBLIPOR PADDLES

I'd been relieved twice and was sure my luck was running out. The lines hadn't moved but inches and now we slipped back and forth through a swamp of blood, gore, and shit. I'd gotten used to the smell, waiting for the man in front to tire once again. I stepped over the same body once more and looked down the row of mud-splattered, shit-coated men, wondering if that was how I looked. We were down to two rows, keeping the valley full so Romans couldn't come around. This was it; I was sure. I looked up for the sun chariot, but it had moved. It was now falling on my right, and I wondered how many hours I'd passed in Hades. Any second, the man in front would call for his relief. My arms felt like they'd fallen off and my sword weighed more than ever.

The hand of Mars grasped my collar's breastplate, pulled me back, and spun me around. Inches from my face, Spartacus' blood-and mud-covered face yelled. His words only registered when Spartacus repeated himself a second time, close enough for me to smell his wine-soaked breath. "We punch, for command head! Get women, safe!" he yelled, waking me from my dream of death. Spartacus kicked me in my ass once he'd faced me toward the baggage train. I ran to it, wondering what had happened. My feet began to move in front of each other, then sped up when I let my shield fall.

Somehow, I made it up the incline all the way to Helica's cart where Dummy stood tied to its rear. She was seated on the wagon's bench, watching the battle dissolve below. "I'm to take you to safety, lady," I pleaded, attempting to catch my breath. Helica patted the seat next to her and asked me to sit instead. I did as Helica commanded, climbing, spent and weary, to sit beside her, looking for the reins that lay beneath her feet.

"I'm not going anywhere," said Helica, reading my thoughts and handing me water. "Not yet, anyway." She untied the cord of the sack resting in her lap. Watching the battle below, Spartacus wasn't hard to make out. He held an unusually long blade that gleamed where it wasn't coated with blood. His hardest men were arrayed around him; they balled close together in the line's center. The Roman, Marcus Crassus, sat mounted behind his line, directly across from them, distinguished by his purple cape. Suddenly, all at once, Spartacus and his retinue ran at the line; our side parted like birds to let the cadre of men punch a hole right in the center of Romans.

### THE OFFICER

Atticus Fabius continued to rally his men, encouraging and ordering them to rest when they could no longer tell they needed it themselves. This fight was the toughest of his life, and Atticus Fabius had been in some real scraps. He'd been pressed against the Roman wall with Marcus Crassus years ago at the Colline Gate; that all seemed a skirmish when faced with slaves fighting to the death now. Atticus knew none of these enemies planned to surrender—this was a fight to the last man. He prayed to Mars for strength to make it to the finish. The scorpions were useless at this range. Atticus turned, ordering archers to drop their bows and join the line.

When Atticus initially heard the commotion, he'd hoped the enemy had finally turned to run. He was horrified instead to see the man in the flesh, running straight at him. *Jupiter, bless the brave centurion,* thought Atticus of the man who mustered enough courage to step in front of the barbarian. Spartacus dispatched the soldier in moments and quickly stepped over the body. Atticus had no time to curse his fate before the massive former gladiator grabbed his shield, yanking him forward; he barely parried the gleaming sword threatening his neck.

### MARCUS CRASSUS IS SPOOKED

Marcus had to convince the horse to stay put as a band of warriors charged at him through the throng. They'd punched through the line, giving up any prospect of holding it to gamble at decapitating command. The slaves ran at him; Marcus was close enough to see Sulla's old cavalry sergeant's eyes as the huge Roman-looking barbarian made a determined dash to kill him. The Imperator yelled at the cadre of *lictors* and light infantry soldiers tasked as bodyguards, all standing motionless. "Attack, you sons of bitches! Attack now!" screamed Marcus, snapping them from their collective paralysis. Imperator of Rome, Marcus Crassus, pulled his sword in fear.

### THE DRIVE

Spartacus and his group drove through Romans like a hot knife through butter until hampered momentarily by a youthful centurion, whom he killed. Next, Spartacus was confronted by an old friend, an officer now but still a very skilled swordsman. Spartacus watched the lifer put up his shield like he'd been trained, expecting a crash.

### ATTICUS IS RELIEVED

Atticus had never faced a gladiator in battle before and was surprised when fingers grasped the top of his shield, pulling him forward. Reflexes alone brought up the sword to stop the oncoming blade, but Spartacus continued the lunge until his elbow shattered the officer's nose. Atticus fell on his back. Spartacus flipped Lightning in midair to shift his grasp. Straddling the Roman, Spartacus used his weight and both hands to drive Lightning through plate and mail, all the way to the man's pump. Spartacus used his foot, anchoring the body to quickly extract Lightning and continue pursuit until his leg was pierced by a *telum*, the short javelin carried by light infantry. Spartacus took a knee as Vitelli, the shepherd-turned-bodyguard, rushed to put up a shield in front of his chieftain. Spartacus pulled the vicious iron from his own leg and stood behind Vitelli's planted shield mere feet from Crassus with a wicked gash. The warlord reared the short missile to hurl it into the purple-caped Roman, whom he loathed.

Marcus Crassus' eyes widened upon a protesting mount, knowing full well the barbarian was fully capable of planting the removed bolt into him from here. Marcus grimaced, grasping the sword with all his might and looking as if he could feel its pierce already. The commander held the reins tight and dug his knees into the mount to keep it from bolting. Only the fear of humiliation kept Marcus from allowing the horse to read his shameful thought to flee. Marcus shut his eyes awaiting impact and didn't see Spartacus sprout an arrow when the barbarian's windup to throw was at its apex. "LORD!" barked Vitelli as bodyguards rushed to save Spartacus with their shields, planting them into the earth before their leader. The island of slaves was immediately engulfed by a sea of armed Romans. Relentless stabbing filled the confined space before the giant gladiator with impeccable aim could sink his deadly bolt upon its mark. Marcus opened his eyes to witness what looked like a hill of filth-covered, armored humanity made of lunging elbows all writhing to kill something big that he could not see. Marcus Crassus patted his body quickly for good measure, making sure he hadn't been pierced by the *pilum* after all. He sighed with relief, relaxing his knees and grip upon the reins, and scabbarding the sword before anyone noticed.

Vitelli planted his giant *scutum* before Spartacus to block the lunging blades. Old friends and new acquaintances all brought their shields in on each other to protect Spartacus, the greatest Thracian who ever lived. Blades bit within the confines as brave men screamed in pain with every new probe of the enemy. The noise was a cacophony of sadness and anger as death caved in on everyone. Vitelli looked back for his lord to see Spartacus sunk upon his knee, cradling an arrow in a vital place. The chieftain thanked his loyal protector with his eyes, exuding pride and gratitude to the bodyguard that they'd be together again soon. Without another word, the storm of blades fell upon them all.

# CHAPTER THIRTY-ONE

**"Spartacus was wounded in the thigh with a spear and sank upon his knee, holding his shield in front of him and contending in this way against his assailants until he and the great mass of those with him were surrounded and slain...his body was not recovered."**

**—Appian, *The Civil Wars***

Spartacus fell. The group of men surrounding our commander disappeared in a sea of stabbing humanity pouring in on top of them. Helica turned to me and smiled; we locked eyes. "Now we know," she said, her glacial blue eyes hypnotizing me as the world unraveled around us. "Spartacus' 'great and terrible power' is proven—unlucky," revealed Helica, releasing my chin to place her hand inside the burlap bag at her lap. Helica winced slightly when the fangs pierced her flesh. *"Vala,* sweet boy. Go find your wife," said the dying woman, as the fierce blue brightness of her eyes dulled, her beauty fouled by the absence of her soul and the froth upon her lips.

The sorceress slumped, lifeless, as I jumped to escape the terrible serpent with a triangular head that slithered from her bag. One look at the field below said we were finished. Our army had been cleaved; most poured into the spot where Spartacus had fallen, while a few ran at me, attempting escape. I untied Dummy and leapt on his back, kicking the shaggy pony toward sheer cliffs. Our women ran in all directions, screaming in terror as they gathered their children from the baggage carts. A small girl with dirty brown hair cried out in the open alone, shielding her eyes, holding a dingy doll. The little girl dropped Pila's old *pupae* when I grasped at her forearm galloping from my mount to swing her behind me, the way I'd seen Marcos grab Varinius long ago. Dummy hit his stride when the incline was at its greatest, clomping up the Ogna Ridges like a surefooted goat as I escaped defeat from the battlefield with a tiny, orphaned girl.

### A STRICT MASTER'S LESSON

Marcus Crassus spent half of *Aprilis* tracking down the remaining fugitive slaves hiding in the southern Italian hills. It cost him valuable time as "Pompey the Great," on his way south, happened upon the four thousand escaped survivors making for the Alps. Pompey fortuitously captured the exhausted miscreants without the loss of a single man. He promptly raced to Rome, arriving days before Marcus to claim credit for ending the entire affair.

Marcus had the dead Romans he could recover set ablaze while searching for Spartacus' body, but the barbarian had escaped Marcus even in death—apparently the body had been tilled into the dirt. The former Imperator, Marcus Crassus, took an eternity and spent a fortune teaching lessons to slaves at a cost of prestige in Rome. His poignant display of punished slaves, nailed upon the Appian outside the city, was too far out of sight to be on Roman minds. However, Pompey the Great's display of living slaves, dragged in chains—the ones who'd escaped Marcus' grasp—was appreciated much more in the arena by Rome's voting citizens.

### THE VULTURE SWOOPS AND IS LAUDED

By age thirty, Pompey, the "Butcher's Boy," Gnaeus Pompeius Magnus enjoyed his second triumph from an ornate chariot pulled by four unblemished white stallions down *Via Sacra*—the Sacred Way. Rose petals and garlands were thrown before him by grateful citizens. *"Io triumphe!"* the crowd cheered as Pompey went beneath the shade of palm branches, then cursed and spit, jeering when the fettered terrorists were finally paraded by.

### MARCUS GETS GOLD FEVER

Rome's former Imperator, Marcus Crassus, was given the privilege of walking behind Pompey's procession with a modest award—the laurel of civic duty—while dodging Pompey's horse-shit. The odium of that humiliating day would feed a bitterness into Marcus Licinius Crassus to resolve that, in at least wealth, the Butcher's Boy would never surpass him. The desire would drive Marcus to the ends of the world and feed a greed so great, only death by molten gold, melted in a Parthian crucible, would satiate it.

"Taxes!" yelled the Parthian translator. "Here, we pay your, taxes!" The warrior chief motioned for his men to tip the stone crucible. "Paid in full!" were the last Latin words heard by the defeated Roman commander who'd gone afield too far in search of Roman plunder.

"No! No! No!" were the last words from the former Imperator of Rome, Marcus Linicus Crassus, before his jaws were held agape forcefully by tongs, behind smashed teeth. Marcus Crassus' descendants would not receive the luxury of a death mask at his corpse-less funeral. His skull was bashed to pieces after the execution to retrieve all of the hardened precious metal. His body, left to rot.

71 BC; 684 *auc*; *anno urbis conditae* (year since founding).
Mile Marker XLIII; Appian Way.

"*EST ROMANUS!*" shouted the slave. "*Est Romanus!* He is Roman! He's Roman! You can't crucify him, or you'll be cursed," protested the condemned man vehemently from the cage, clutching and shaking bars to get the soldiers' attention. Once stopped, they'd pulled the huge man from another cage to nail him up at this new mile's marker, greatly upsetting another slave held caged nearby.

"Va!" cried the deaf man, incoherently fearful. The superstitious soldiers shot each other glances, then looked to their *optio* standing in the heat of the day for what to do. The indifferent centurion shrugged as the soldier holding the huge, bound deaf man repeating the word "Va" forced the big man to kneel. The soldier strangled Va until he was dead, returning to the cage with the hook to retrieve another slave and crucify them in Va's stead. The soldiers were ordered to nail up three slaves for every mile before reaching Rome; the rest would be thrown to the beasts at great personal expense to the former Imperator, Marcus Crassus.

"Why did you do that?" asked an angry slave from within the confine. "Now they'll kill another one of us."

"They're going to kill us all anyway," dismissed Gannicus, weeping and falling against the scalding-hot bars. "Va is my brother—he must not suffer," he begged, staring forlornly at nothing in the mob's direction, listening to them jeer. *Not because of me*, he thought. As his eyes began to glaze over, partially from tears, he noticed a shrouded, familiar face within the crowd. The serious young man holding a girl's hand stood out due to his markedly un-hostile demeanor, observing from among the unruly mob as slaves got what they deserved.

"We're all brothers," argued the angry captive to Gannicus' back. "I loved Va too; he was my brother as well."

"No! Va was *my* mother's son, elder to *me*. My sweet older brother, Lucius Varinius," explained Gannicus, staring intently at the young man who now stared back in similar fashion. "And he didn't deserve the disaster my choices brought him." Gannicus spoke as much to the young Roman-looking man in the crowd as to his co-captives, though he knew the cloaked figure was too far away to hear the words. In a moment of pitiful desperation, the captive grasped the bars with all his might and shouted to the sky so as not to betray his old partner.

"It was me, Publipor!" burst the captive from his cage as it began to roll for the Appian marker just a mile more down the road. "I did it—I told Flavius. I am the *hyacinthum et vulture!* He—he got me drunk—I'm sorry, by all the immortal gods, I'm sorry, Publipor!" Gannicus, his throat burning and hoarse from the need to be heard inside his rolling confine, confessed one last time to his best friend hiding within the crowd. "I betrayed Helica! I am the traitor, and I will pay for it, Publipor! I know I will pay!"

"Publipor!" shouted someone from within the mass of people milling about.

The young man in the crowd turned his head, recognizing the name intimately. But it was a stranger who'd spoke, a middle-aged Roman slapping a young brown-haired boy just a few paces away. "Go get me my wine and tell Claudia to start the stove before I smack you and tell these soldiers to nail you up next," ordered the Roman master to his boy.

The stern young man turned away, and rage settled in. *Nothing worse than a traitor, Publipor, nothing...*Oenomaus said from the hereafter. The young man, who now went by Publius, left the crowd to retrieve his horse. The steed was being watched by a small girl—too small to be left alone for long so near the road. She needed him, so *this* Publius went to her instead of following the slave boy's master to kill him like he wanted. Besides, newly named Publius had more pressing matters elsewhere to the south for a woman who would never betray him.

### A TRAITOR GETS HIS JUST DESSERTS

Gannicus Varinius rolled up the Appian with his head resting against sunburnt bars, adrift in contemplation and regret. If only Gannicus hadn't taken the wine from Flavius and gotten drunk that night those three long years ago, he would never have boasted of the plan with a traitor in his cups. If all two hundred gladiators, instead of just the seventy-five, had escaped, perhaps the breakout would have gone the way Helica had planned, and his brother would be alive now. Gannicus didn't bother protesting or declaring, *civis Romanus sum*—"I am Roman," when led into the arena during the day's great heat before the gladiator matches. He closed his eyes and lifted his neck when the lions were loosed. Gannicus felt the roar in the pit of his stomach and listened for their approach as he continued facing skyward, believing he deserved all of life's punishment. Over the cheers and jeers, Gannicus believed in the moment to have heard the chirping of frogs. In his mind, he saw the bright, sweet-tempered boy, Publipor, looking to him for help holding round river stones in a sunny ravine. But when his eyes were opened to a clear blue sky, all he saw was Flavius asking if he wanted another drink. He was pulverized and smothered by the largest male, mauled to death within seconds. The well-fed, muscular, trained beast sat upon the heap, licking his chops amongst the shrieks created by his cage mates in the arena, before resuming the spectacle's sport once more with an easy game of chase.

### THE COVER-UP

In the arch of Italy's boot, at a *popina* somewhere just outside Thurii, a bar owner yelled at a man to hurry and plaster over a mural of outlaws, one that had been painted by a young pregnant woman, before the Roman authorities found it.

"Plaster! Plaster, you fool," he belted at the contractor. There was no way the owner could open his bar with the image of Spartacus, complete with his name, painted upon the establishment's wall—not in this new climate.

"Sir, I have to prep the surface or the material won't adhere," explained the plasterer.

"I don't need it covered forever; I need it covered now!" yelled the barman. "Before someone tells a Roman what I have here." He pleaded frantically, waving his hands at the fresco as if he could vanish it from sight by flailing vigorously enough at its image.

"All right, all right, but I can't guarantee how long it'll stick," explained the contractor. The handyman had no idea his work would last eighteen hundred years, finally chipping away to reveal Pila's masterpiece to an unsuspecting new world.

REUNION

A young woman held a swaddled newborn to her breast in the ravine, following the sounds of chirping frogs. Once they'd spotted one another along the stream's bank, her husband dropped the river stones and ran to his young bride. After an emphatic embrace, the young groom peeled back swaddling, grateful to look upon the most beautiful baby girl he'd ever seen. In that moment, the man named Publius vowed to protect his beloved new daughter from any harm with every breath left of his life. A small girl interrupted the two, tugging at the woman's dress.

"What's her name?" asked the tiny girl, who considered them family ever since she'd been saved from a battlefield.

"Helica," Pila answered.

**THE END**

Forever grateful,
David P. Morris.

# ACKNOWLEDGEMENTS

I would like to thank the following people for whom none of this would have been possible. Foremost, the women of my life. To my beautiful bride Anna, thank you for allowing this indulgence. Mom, for encouraging creativity. Peg, my friend, mother-in-law, and first editor. Thank you, Hannah, my delightful daughter, for naming our heroine. To my sister Michele, our time together has not been forgotten. I've missed you. *Vala,* precious sister; see you soon.

Jeff, my brother, you know. Joe, my father and boyhood Spartacus. Thank you both for modeling proper manhood.

My gratitude to the scholars who devote their lives to anthropology scrutinizing antiquity. To Professor Barry Strauss, your novel *The Spartacus War* was truly inspirational.

Thank you, Sequoia, for building the platform on which this stands. I'm appreciative to everyone on the Di Angelo Publications team who honed this work. Thank you, Elizabeth. Thank you, Ashley. I'm especially indebted to my editor Mr. Cody Wootton, who saw me through the pile. Thank you all for dragging me back over plot holes and past simplicity. For expanding my universe and challenging me to make this good book great.

# ABOUT THE AUTHOR

David P. Morris, the debut author of "Revolting Slaves," brings an epic retelling of Spartacus' rebellion from the perspective of a young man thrust into the heart of the action. His own life's journey has been marked by trials, tragedy, and triumphs, facing poverty and prejudice while working multiple jobs. Through it all, he found solace in books and music, nurturing his passion for storytelling. Inspired by personal experiences and a desire to prove himself, Morris crafted this captivating tale, a testament to resilience and self-discovery. "Revolting Slaves" not only showcases Morris' literary talents but also stands as an inspiring story of determination and the transformative power of storytelling.